# *A Promise to Keep*

## ALEXANDRA MILLER

Dove Christian
Publishers

Dove Christian
Publishers

A Division of Kingdom Christian Enterprises
PO Box 611
Bladensburg, MD 20710-0611



Paperback ISBN 978-1-957497-55-6

Also by Alexandra Miller:
*A Debt to Pay,*
the first book in the Millcreek Series.

# *Chapter* One

*Ten Miles East of Lexington, Missouri*
*August 1876*

A sultry summer breeze drifted across the Missouri prairie and through the open windows of the McCoys' modest cabin. After wiping the beads of sweat from her forehead, Maegan McCoy tucked a stray curl behind her ear and continued preparing the meal. Glancing over her shoulder, she smiled at her younger brother, Cody, who sat at the kitchen table, bent over a book.

"I can't believe how quickly you're getting through that," she told him, admiration in her voice.

"I still don't see why I need to spend so much time readin'," twelve-year-old Cody replied with a sigh of exaggerated boredom. "Sawyer and Austin don't know how to read, and they don't need it."

"There will come a day when they will need it," Maegan said, referring to their older brothers. "And then guess who they'll go to for help?"

Cody looked up at her. "You?"

"No ... you," she said as she went to the cupboard and

began pulling out plates to set the table. "They won't come to me because they won't want to hear, 'I told you so.'"

Cody shrugged. "Maybe." He would still rather be out with his brothers working the farm and riding after outlaws like they did.

"After you're done that chapter, you can go see if they're back from town and call them in for supper."

Cody perked up at this and brought his book a little closer. Just a minute later, however, the door swung open, and Austin McCoy's tall, muscular frame filled the doorway. He was almost the spitting image of his father with the trademark black, curly hair and emerald-green eyes that all the McCoy children shared, save Cody, who had inherited his mother's blonde hair and blue eyes.

"You're back!" Cody exclaimed as he whirled around in his seat.

The spurs on his boots rattled as Austin walked across the wood-planked floor of the cabin. He tousled his little brother's hair and tossed a newspaper down in front of him. "Read this!" he said with excitement. "Folks all over town are talkin' 'bout it!"

Cody's blue eyes met his sister's "I told you so" glance for just a second before he opened the newspaper, entitled *Lexington Weekly Intelligencer*. Cody skimmed the paper until he found what Austin was referring to.

"'How the Train Robber Turned on His Pals and Exposed the Otterville Plot and its Outlaws'" was the heading. Cody read on. "'The names of the Otterville train robbers, as given in Hobbs Kerry's confession to Chief McDonough … were published about a week ago in the St. Louis Times. Kerry refused to "squeal" until he was shown a letter that the chief said had been intercepted by the officers. The letter in question was written by Hobbs Kerry to Richard Stapp, the Granby saloon keeper, who, after being taken into the confidence of the James and Youngers, betrayed them to the police.'"

"Sawyer was right!" Austin said, hitting the table for emphasis. "He was convinced that robbery was Jesse, Frank, and the Younger gang!" Austin ladled water from a nearby bucket and lifted it to his mouth.

"Where is Sawyer?" Maegan asked.

"He'll be along," Austin said, not mentioning that instead of going to town with him like his sister thought, Sawyer had instead ridden after a lead he had on the James gang's whereabouts.

"Best wash up and eat this while it's hot," Maegan told her brother. At twenty-two, he was only older by two years, but most of the time, she felt like the eldest. She had promised her mother that she would take care of her brothers, especially Cody, who had only been three when their ma died of the fever. The fatal illness had taken her just weeks after it claimed their father. The McCoys had always been a close bunch, but after their parents passed, that bond just grew stronger. Maegan felt more like a mother to Cody than his big sister and sometimes like a mother even to her older brothers as well.

After supper, Cody and Austin went outside to tend to the livestock and finish the chores while Maegan cleaned up the dishes and prepared for tomorrow's breakfast. Sawyer had slaughtered one of their pigs of late, and Maegan was looking forward to the sizzling sound of bacon that would be in the frying pan come morning. Carrying a bucket of dirty, sudsy water out the door, Maegan walked to the side of the cabin and dumped it into a pile of dirt. Then she went to the well that sat between their house and the barn and drew clean water for the morning.

A few minutes later, she carried the bucket of fresh water back to the house, trying not to spill the water on her trousers. Life on the farm with her brothers had made wearing a dress too impractical, and a pair of trousers, a vest, and a white cotton shirt had become her attire of choice … or rather, necessity.

The sound of an approaching rider turned her head to the road that led away from their home. She knew by the bay mare and tall man in the saddle that it was her eldest brother, Sawyer. A cloud of dust trailed behind him as his horse's hooves tore at the ground, making Maegan wonder at the urgency of his speed. Austin and Cody were coming out of the barn and met up with Maegan just as Sawyer reached the yard.

"Saddle up!" he called just before he reined in his horse and dismounted. "You too, Cody!"

Maegan's eyes shot toward her little brother, who looked as if he'd just been handed fifty dollars. "Wait, why? What's going on, Sawyer?" she asked.

"Spotted 'em just a few miles west."

"The James brothers?" Austin asked, excitement thick in his voice.

"Yep, and the Younger boys, too." Sawyer noticed the bucket of water on the ground by his sister's feet and lifted it up to his horse's mouth. "By the direction they were going, my best guess is they're headin' for their home in Kearney."

Maegan tried to reason with him. "But it's going to be dark soon."

"That's why we're going now. We'll catch them off guard while they're sleepin'."

Maegan cast a worried glance toward Austin and Cody, who had already taken off for the barn. "Surely, you didn't mean for Cody to go along," she said, now following Sawyer as he walked with fast strides toward the house.

"We'll need all the guns we have," he told her.

"No, Sawyer. He's too young for this. He's not ready!" Exasperated that her brother didn't seem to be listening to her, Maegan reached out and grabbed his arm. He finally stopped and turned to look at her.

"You weren't much older than him when you started ridin' with us, Mae. He's ready. He ain't a sharpshooter like you, but he's got better aim than some of the men I know."

Maegan felt a surge of panic at the thought of her younger brother in the line of gunfire. "Please, Sawyer. Make him stay. I'll go, but make him stay!"

Sawyer shook his head slightly, clearly dismissing her words. "Load your pistols, Mae," he said, letting her know he was making the final decision. The authority in his tone reminded her of her father's voice. Sawyer carried an air of leadership that seemed much older than his twenty-four years.

Only temporarily giving up her argument, Maegan moved into the house and to the chest she kept by her bed. She lifted the lid and took out a holster, buckling it around her waist before reaching back into the chest for two revolvers along with a tin can of bullets. She loaded the pistols, slid them into her holster, and then reached for a brown slouch hat that hung on a hook by the front door. For a moment, she just watched as her brother sat at the table, reloading his rifle and the pistols he kept in his holster. He had a smaller gun tucked in his boot, and Maegan knew there was a bowie knife in the other.

"Sawyer, I'm beggin' you to just hear me out. These aren't some amateur outlaws we're going after. This is Jesse and Frank James we're talking about! And the Youngers! They've murdered more people than all the criminals you've caught combined!"

"Which is why we need to catch 'em! Do you know the price of the bounty on their heads?"

"I know Cody's life is worth more than any bounty!"

"Listen, Mae, I say how it goes 'round here, and you coddling him isn't gonna help anybody! If I thought it was too dangerous, I wouldn't let him come, but he can take the higher ground and stay hidden for the most part. We need the extra gunfire!" He let out a short sigh. "Now, we're all going, and that's the end of it."

Maegan bit her lip to hold back an angry retort and spun away from her brother's stubborn gaze. She was still fuming when she got to the barn and began to saddle up her horse.

"You worried 'bout Cody?" Austin asked from nearby as he packed some things in his saddle bags.

"I swear, Austin, if something happens to Cody, I'll never forgive Sawyer!"

Austin's gaze swung past the barn doors and toward the house where he knew his brother was. "It ain't likely I can change his mind either," Austin told her apologetically. "But I'll see what I can do."

"Please try, Austin. Please try and convince him Cody's not ready for this!"

*****

Maegan guided her horse around the trees of the wooded acreage they were cutting through, deliberately staying close to Cody. Sawyer had just told them they were getting close and would soon dismount and go the rest of the way on foot. The twilight was giving way to night, and a full moon was making its appearance. As they came into the clearing, Sawyer dismounted, and Austin followed suit.

"You and Cody wait here," Sawyer told her.

Maegan watched as her older brothers walked ahead, disappearing temporarily around a bend of foliage and boulders.

"Do you think everything's alright?" Cody asked thirty minutes later when they hadn't returned.

"Yeah," Maegan replied. She'd been on enough of these pursuits to know how it worked. Seizing the moment, Megan looked at her little brother, who was sitting near her on his horse. Cody's eyes anxiously searched the darkness for a sign of his brothers.

"Cody, I want you to promise me something. If things get out of hand, swear to me you'll head back to the horses and ride to home as fast as you can."

Her words unnerved him, and he couldn't dismiss the fear that settled in his chest. Still, he sat up a little straighter in his saddle. "I ain't a coward, Mae."

"It ain't cowardly to use your brain, Cody. That's all I'm saying. You've got years to prove yourself, so I just don't want …"

"Shh, do you hear that?"

Maegan didn't hear anything besides crickets and the faint sound of the river that she knew was nearby. A twig snapped just before her brothers came into view, their figures like shadows beneath the moonlight.

"They're camped not far upstream. It's just two of 'em," Sawyer said as he lifted the rifle out of the scabbard attached to his saddle.

Maegan dismounted and tethered her horse to a nearby branch, making sure the animal had plenty of slack. She knew Cody was doing the same.

"Alright." Sawyer got his younger siblings' attention and then explained the plan. "We'll start together, but once they come into view, Mae, I want you and Cody to circle the gorge and set up behind the boulders at least thirty feet apart. If any shootin' starts, I want them to think they're surrounded. In that instance, take turns firing." Sawyer then glanced at Austin with a look that said, "You know what to do."

Maegan and Cody followed behind the older two as they returned to the path Austin and Sawyer had just come from. A few minutes later, Maegan felt her little brother step closer, his shoulder brushing hers. "You think I'm ready?" he whispered.

Maegan swallowed back her uncertainty and placed a reassuring hand on his shoulder. The worst thing would be for him to let insecurity override his better judgment in the event he needed to make a hasty decision. "You'll be just fine, Cody. Just take your lead from me. Don't shoot unless I start to."

The boy nodded, determination returning to him and re-solve to not let his older brothers down. He felt his courage wane once Sawyer motioned for them to be quiet and then gestured for him and Maegan to move away to their des-ignated spots. Cody instinctively touched the guns sticking up out of the holster that Austin had snugly secured around his waist. Cody kept close as Maegan led him through a thicket that eventually gave way to a ravine of boulders. After several minutes, his sister put out her hand for him to stop and then pointed downhill from where they stood.

"See their fire down there?" she whispered.

Cody nodded as he looked at the flicker of firelight below them in the distance.

"We've got to get a lot closer, so just watch where you're stepping."

As they walked, Cody could tell his sister was praying under her breath. It was something she did often, and on that night, he found himself silently joining her. He wouldn't admit to anyone that he was afraid, and if ever there was a time to pray, it was now.

It wasn't long before they were close enough to see the outline of two men sitting near the fire. "This is a good spot for you," Maegan whispered. "You just stay hunched down behind these rocks. I'm gonna head closer in just around those rocks over there." She pointed to their right so he could see where she would be. It was dark, but the full moon afforded just enough light for him to see where she gestured. "Everything's gonna be fine," she tried to assure him. "But remember what I said, Cody. You get back to the horses and head home if this goes south; do you understand?"

Cody nodded and tried not to let the seriousness of her tone frighten him. He watched as she moved away and then focused his gaze on the two men about fifty yards away. He didn't know where his brothers were but waited expectantly, his pistol poised and ready. The minutes seemed to drag on forever as he waited there, his eyes darting toward where he knew his sister was hiding and where the outlaws were bedding for the night.

Farther away and hidden behind brush, Sawyer's voice suddenly rang out in the gorge. "We've got you surrounded, boys! Put down your weapons, and you might live to see the morning!"

One of the James brothers fired a shot. Sawyer and Austin countered with a round of shots. Hearing the gunfire cease, Maegan followed with a well-aimed shot of her own.

Cody knew it was his turn next. His hands trembled as he pulled the trigger of his weapon, his bullet whizzing through the air seconds after Maegan's. He hoped their plan worked and that they created an illusion of having the James brothers surrounded.

Suddenly, the sound of a cocked gun just behind him froze Cody to his spot.

"Drop your weapon, kid."

The unfamiliar voice and feel of a rifle pressing into his back made his heart thunder in his chest. Slowly, Cody lowered his weapon.

At the bottom of the hill, Austin was carefully stepping out from behind a mound of rocks. "You're surrounded!" he yelled out. "Lower your weapons!"

Hearing his voice, Maegan moved closer and then glanced out from behind a boulder that protected her. With the moon's light and from her vantage point, she could make out two figures by the fire. They had stopped shooting and, to her surprise, had lowered their guns and were standing with arms raised to the sky. It had been too easy, making her feel apprehensive. She watched as Sawyer and Austin stepped out into the open and cautiously moved towards them, their pistols drawn and aimed to shoot.

"Down on the ground!" Austin shouted at them. The James brothers had last been seen with the Younger brothers, so where were they now? Austin's eyes darted around the surrounding hills and woods as if expecting one of the outlaws to emerge suddenly. It looked as if Jesse and Frank James were complying, but something didn't feel right.

Suddenly, a loud voice called out. "Don't shoot, or the boy dies!"

Sawyer and Austin swung their attention to a man walking in on the scene and were horrified at the sight of him firmly clutching Cody.

"Surrounded, huh?" Jesse James said, a sneer on his face as he looked at the kid. After a glance at Frank, Jesse whipped out a pistol and fired toward Sawyer.

Sawyer and Austin saw it coming and scrambled for cover.

"Now what?" Austin said, trying to peer out to see where his brother was being held hostage. Maegan's words echoed in his mind, and he found himself praying under his breath.

"Let the boy go!" Sawyer called out to them.

A gunshot fired toward them in response, and Sawyer ducked back behind the protection of a boulder. He wondered where Maegan was and if she was close enough to get a clean shot.

"Toss over your weapons!" Frank James called, "And come out with your hands up, else this boy's gonna die!"

Austin came out first, his hands raised as he threw his pistols to the ground. Sawyer followed suit and walked slowly with Austin toward the men. When they neared the fire, Frank came closer, his rifle roughly poking Sawyer's chest. "Unload all your weapons!" he ordered.

Sawyer reached inside his vest and pulled out a smaller gun that he soon dropped to the ground.

"What we gonna do with 'em, Jesse?"

Before Jesse could answer Frank's question, a shot rang out that grazed Frank's arm, causing him to drop his rifle.

"There's more of 'em!" Jesse shouted as he turned and fired in the direction the shot had come from.

Taking advantage of Jesse's back being turned, Sawyer ran toward him and wrestled him to the ground while Austin seized Frank's rifle. Frank surprised him by pulling out a pistol and firing it into his arm, causing Austin to hit the ground.

"Run, Cody!" Maegan screamed as she dodged between rocks and took a carefully aimed shot at the man who had apprehended Cody. The man fell to his knees but managed a shot toward her before firing another one in the direction Cody was running.

Sawyer scrambled to get to his feet, struggling because

of the knife that Jesse James had just thrust through his shoulder. Sawyer reached for the pistol he carried in his boot and fired a shot toward Jesse, but he had already made it to his horse and was starting to ride away. Frank wasn't far behind as he also mounted his horse and helped hoist the third man up in the saddle behind him.

As they rode off, Maegan ran to Austin, who lay on the ground clenching his arm.

"I'll be fine," Austin groaned as Maegan knelt beside him in the dirt. "Where's Cody?" he asked.

Megan shot back up to her feet, her eyes darting frantically around the darkness for her younger brother. "Cody!" She called as she ran in the direction she'd last seen him, but the light from the fire and the moon only illuminated so far. She slowed down, looking behind rocks and feeling around bushes. Maybe he had done as she told him and ran back to the horses. But then she tripped on something. She gasped at the realization that it was Cody's booted foot sticking out from behind some rocks. Calling his name, Megan dropped to her knees and leaned her ear against his chest. She suddenly realized her older brothers were standing by her side.

"I can't see what's wrong with him!" Maegan said through her tears. But then she felt something wet under her fingers. "He's been shot!"

"Let's carry him over to the fire!" Austin said, ignoring the pain shooting down his arm as he scooped the boy up.

Despite the pain from his own wound, Sawyer took off his shirt and handed it to Maegan. "Press this against the bleeding!" he told her.

Once Cody was laid by the fire, Maegan could see better where the bleeding was coming from. "He was hit in the back!" she said, rolling him carefully to his side and creating a makeshift tourniquet with Sawyer's shirt. "He's bleeding so much!" she said.

"I'll go for the doctor; you and Austin get him back to the house!" Sawyer said as he lifted Cody and led the way toward their horses.

"Sawyer, you're hurt, too; let me help you carry him," Austin offered.

Sawyer ignored him, the adrenaline to save his brother overriding the burning in his shoulder. Maegan came alongside him, trying to help by pushing back any branches or foliage that were in the way. When they finally reached their horses, Maegan helped Sawyer lift Cody up to Austin, where they situated him in front of him on his saddle.

Maegan tied Cody's horse to the back of hers and then mounted her horse quickly. Sawyer sped away toward the doctor's house while Maegan and Austin took off for home. Her heart raced as they rode, the fear of her brother dying overshadowing every thought. She forced herself not to think of what it would mean to lose him and prayed fervently under her breath that she wouldn't have to face that outcome.

*****

The sun was coming up when Sawyer arrived with the doctor. After a few minutes with the boy, the doctor asked who had taken the bullet out.

"I did," Maegan said from where she stood on the other side of Cody's bed. She had been holding a lamp for the doctor to see.

"You saved this boy's life then. Would have been too late by the time I got here."

Megan released a shaky breath. "So, he's gonna be alright then?"

The doctor let out a deep sigh. "Barely, but I think he should pull through. If a fever sets in or you see any other sign of infection, come for me right away." The doctor finished applying a clean bandage and then glanced toward the other McCoy boys. "I think I should check you two next."

"Nah, I'm fine, doc," Sawyer replied, but the doctor saw that his hand was still pressed firmly over the cloth he held to his shoulder. Austin had taken a seat nearby, and a makeshift bandage was around his arm as well.

"You boys are crazy goin' after the James gang like you did," the doctor said as he ignored their refusals and took time to tend to each of their wounds. It wasn't the first time the McCoy boys had gotten themselves shot up. He had been surprised to hear that young Cody had been pulled into it, though.

"A lot of good it did," Maegan said with a glance at Sawyer.

"Two of them are wounded, at least," Austin spoke up and then grimaced in pain as the doctor cleaned the gunshot wound in his arm.

"Should slow them down a little," Sawyer said. "We'll get 'em next time."

Maegan exchanged a concerned glance with Austin and forced herself not to respond. His words weighed on her the whole next day, though. As her brothers spent time mending, she kept herself busy taking care of them and tending to the farm. If Sawyer was serious about going after the James brothers again, she wanted nothing to do with it. What was more, she didn't want Cody anywhere near them, either. Would Sawyer be so obstinate as to make Cody go along again? Deep down, she knew the answer, and what was more, she knew what she had to do.

# *Chapter* Two



*Eight Weeks Later*
*Millcreek, Missouri*

Hearing a series of gunshots, Sheriff Bridger stepped out of the jailhouse and glanced down the main street of Millcreek's growing town. The ruckus was coming from the saloon, which was no surprise to him. While he had been the new sheriff in Millcreek for just a few months, it hadn't taken him long to identify who the usual troublemakers were. Mounting his brown and white Appaloosa, he rode toward the saloon, hoping the situation wouldn't take long to resolve.

The town of Millcreek was shaped like the letter T, with its main street branching off to the left and leading to the livery and church, while on the opposite end, there was a mill, restaurant, and saloon. Main Street was lined with a jailhouse, bank, shops, and homes, which were well-kept and sported small yards in the back. There was a large hotel that sat near the corner, and directly across from it was a post office and a falsely fronted building with a sign reading: *Bell's Newspaper Press.*

As soon as he entered the saloon, Bridger noticed a crowd of men gathered, looking at something on the floor. Joining them, he recognized it was Joe Spencer who had their attention.

"No worries here, Sheriff," one of the men said, a grin on his face. "He worked himself up and then passed out. No harm done."

"No harm done?" said another man from nearby, glancing at the roof. "Look at all them holes he put in my roof! He's gonna patch every last one!"

"I'll see that he does, Nick," Bridger assured the new saloon owner. He gave Joe Spencer's motionless body a little shove with his booted foot. "What was he going on about this time?" he asked the crowd.

"The usual," a man named Jack Dean replied. Because of Joe Spencer's tirades, almost everyone in town knew that he had lost his eldest son to the bullet of a Union soldier during the Civil War. Unfortunately, that Union soldier had been his brother-in-law, which had made his grief all the more shattering. Even though the war had been over ten years ago, Joe still ranted and raved about killing his brother-in-law and every other former Union soldier, for that matter.

Bridger motioned for Jack Dean to help him lift Joe off the ground. Together, they carried him outside and tossed him into a large horse trough full of water. The man immediately woke up, cursing loudly as he coughed up water.

"Sorry, Joe," Bridger said. "But you gotta stop your drunken outbursts. Someone's gonna get hurt, and then I'll be throwing you inside a jail cell rather than a trough."

Joe stumbled out of the water before hitting the ground on his hands and knees. "I ain't hurting nobody, Sheriff!" he bellowed.

"Just head home once you've sobered up," Bridger told

him. "And don't come back to town until you're prepared to patch those holes you put in Nick's roof."

Ignoring the round of curses Joe sent in his direction, Bridger headed to his horse and rode to the other end of town. He needed to stop by the General Store for a few things. Once there, he tethered his horse to the hitching post out front, stopping when he noticed Reverend Myles. He was sitting on the front steps of the store, looking worried.

"Afternoon, Sheriff," the young reverend greeted. Jacob Myles dressed as commonly as the cowboys of Millcreek, so most folks didn't realize right away that he was the town's minister. He had a disarming manner that went well with his attractive qualities, inside and out.

"Reverend." Bridger acknowledged him with a nod. He hadn't been to church yet, but Bridger had heard and seen enough of the reverend to know he was a good man. Bridger followed the other man's gaze down the street. "Stage is late, isn't it?"

"Nearly two hours," Reverend Myles replied, glancing at a watch he pulled from his vest pocket.

Bridger assumed he was expecting someone. "I can ride out a-ways and see if I can find it, if it'll make you feel better."

Reverend Myles thanked him. "My sister's on that coach, so that would be greatly appreciated."

Leaving the General Store for later, Bridger mounted his horse and directed her down the street, soon rounding the corner and following the dirt road as it coursed between tall prairie grass. It was warm that September afternoon, and he removed his wide-brimmed hat for a few minutes to let the breeze at his dark brown hair. Thirty minutes later, the stage still wasn't in view, making him hope it hadn't run into any trouble.

*****

"I still don't understand why we had to leave."

Maegan glanced at Cody, whose slouched posture matched the whine in his voice. "I've already told you," she said as patiently as she could. "Before he died, Pa made me promise that we'd know our relatives, and I've waited too long as it is. I'm sure they'll be excited to meet us."

"That's not the real reason, and you know it!" Cody retorted, a scowl on his boyish face. "I ain't a baby. You can just tell me the truth."

"And what do you think that is?"

"That you're scared Sawyer will take me with him again."

"Well, there can be more than one reason for doing something, Cody."

"If they'll be excited to meet us, why ain't Pa's brother or sister ever visited before?" When Maegan didn't answer, Cody realized she was distracted by something. He followed her gaze to where it rested in the distance.

"What do you think it is?" he asked, raising his hand to shield his eyes from the sun.

"I think it's a wagon or … a stagecoach. C'mon," Maegan said as she nudged her horse into a faster pace, Cody close beside her.

As they drew closer, she saw that it was indeed a stagecoach, its lopsided position conveying the loss of a wheel. The man who was on his hands and knees trying to dig the stage out of the ditch appeared to be the driver, while a lone passenger stood nearby watching with a distressed look on her face. Maegan thought she looked to be around her own age, but her comely blue dress was in stark contrast to the vested shirt and men's trousers Maegan wore.

"Looks like you need some help," Maegan said as she dismounted and walked toward the driver, whose shirt was wet from perspiration and dirty from the ground that he knelt on.

"Blasted wheel came loose and landed us in this ditch!" he explained.

Maegan saw Cody was already trying to help the man pry the carriage upright, and she joined them. A moment later, the woman came over to help as well, pushing her sleeves up and stepping near Maegan.

"You'll get your dress dirty," Maegan warned her.

"Never mind about that." The woman flickered a smile before pushing her blonde hair over her shoulder and finding a place of leverage for her fingers.

"On the count of three," the driver shouted. When he landed on three, the four of them managed to lift it out of the ditch enough for the driver to set a large rock underneath the rod where the wheel could be positioned again. Even with the wheel back on, however, it would be badly damaged.

"Why don't I ride to the next town for some help?" Maegan offered.

"I'd be mighty grateful. It's only 'bout an hour east," the driver told her.

Maegan mounted her horse and then glanced at the other woman, who was fanning her flushed face with her hand. "You can ride with me and my brother to town if you want," Maegan offered.

"Oh, really?" The girl's blue-green eyes widened, and she sounded relieved. "That would be wonderful!"

Just then, they heard an approaching rider and shifted their attention to a man on horseback who drew near. The silver star on his shirt and the pair of Colts in his holster said he was the sheriff before he introduced himself. He reined in his horse, taking in the situation.

"I suspected some such trouble," Sheriff Bridger said as

he dismounted and headed to help the driver. "You folks alright?" he asked, glancing at the group he assumed had all come from the carriage.

"We just came by a few minutes ago," Maegan told him, thinking he looked around Sawyer's age. His chiseled jawline had only a shadow of stubble, and while he sported a tall and muscular build, he wasn't overly burly. His blue eyes landed on her, and she thought them rather striking.

When Bridger glanced at her again, he realized with surprise that she was a woman. The trousers, vest, and wide-brimmed, slouch hat had thrown him off until he'd heard her voice. Suddenly, she ripped out a pistol from her holster and fired so quickly toward his feet that the sound and shock of it caused him to stumble backward onto his backside, narrowly missing a puddle of mud.

The other woman screamed at the sound of the shot, and the driver impulsively reached for his own gun.

"What the blazes are you trying to do?" Bridger hollered, still on the ground with his elbows now resting on his knees.

"Trying to keep you from gettin' bit," she replied calmly. That's when everyone noticed the large rattlesnake beside him, now lying lifeless on the ground, its head blown clean off.

"Well, I'll be darned," said the driver, admiration in his voice as he came close to inspect the snake. "You ain't Annie Oakley, are ya?"

"She's as good a shot as her," Cody said proudly, a little smile parting his lips.

"Sorry for startling you, mister," Maegan said to the sheriff as he stood and dusted off the back of his trousers. She noticed his hat had fallen to the ground when he did, and she went over to get it for him.

"It's Sheriff Bridger," he said, glancing suspiciously toward the holster on her waist that sported a pistol on either side. "And next time, just give me some fair warning," he added as she handed his hat to him. He was distracted for just a moment by her emerald-green eyes, accented by thick, dark lashes and softly curved eyebrows. A few long, dark curls escaped her hat, indicating the rest must have been hiding beneath it. There was a sturdiness to her demeanor, but it didn't detract from her pretty face, which he thought stood out against the rugged men's attire she wore.

"You need some help, Miss?" the driver asked his passenger as he saw her standing beside Cody's horse. She nodded, and he helped give her a boost. She gasped a little as the horse took a few steps before she settled on.

"Jest hold on to me," Cody told her.

"I'll be to Millcreek with your luggage as soon as we get this coach back on the road," the driver told his single passenger.

She thanked him absently, her concentration solely on not falling off the animal.

"Well, Sheriff, if you help me get this wheel back on, I think I can make it to Millcreek," the driver said.

Bridger replaced his hat and moved toward the wheel with the driver. He glanced over his shoulder at the group of three heading back to the road.

"Nearly jumped outta your skin, didn't ya?" the driver chuckled.

Bridger grinned in good humor but shook his head at the memory. "I hate surprises."

*****

"So, what's your name?" Maegan heard her brother ask the woman sitting behind him.

"Alison Myles," she replied. "But most folks call me Ali."

21

"I'm Cody, and my sister's name is Mae."

Alison smiled kindly in Maegan's direction, who was riding just to their right side. "Thanks for letting me ride to Millcreek with you both."

"Sure thing. You looked 'bout ready to wilt in the sun," Maegan said.

Alison laughed softly. "I'll be glad for some shade and a bath, that's for certain."

"Where you comin' from?" Cody asked.

"Kansas City."

"That's not too far from Lexington!" Cody exclaimed.

"Is that where you're from?" Alison asked.

"Well, we're a few hours from the city," Maegan clarified.

"I'm moving to Millcreek," Alison told them. "That's where my brother and his family live."

"The relatives we're visiting live there, too," Maegan said.

"What a perfect coincidence that you came when you did and that we're headed to the same place!" Alison smiled again, and Maegan thought she looked like one of the beautiful porcelain dolls she'd seen before in the mercantile window, right down to the soft blonde waves of hair that were secured with a ribbon and hanging down her back.

"So, you said you have family in Millcreek?" Alison asked.

"My father's brother and sister live somewhere near there," Maegan told her. "It'll be the first time we're meeting them, actually."

"Do you have other family?" Alison asked.

"Our folks died over nine years ago," Maegan replied.

"We have two older brothers," Cody told her proudly.

They conversed easily for the remainder of the ride, causing the time to go quickly. It wasn't long before the outline of a town came into view. They first passed a mill and restaurant at the edge of town, followed by a saloon on their left and then a livery which was across from it farther down the street. Rounding the corner brought them to the main street.

"If you wouldn't mind taking me just down this street," Alison said. "The stage usually arrives by the General Store, so that's where my brother will be if he hasn't given up waiting for me."

"So, you've been here before?" Cody asked.

"Mm-hm, two other times."

Maegan took in the shops and houses that lined either side of the street, thinking that Millcreek seemed a quiet, clean, and orderly town. She thought some of the buildings even looked newly constructed. The sizeable General Store at the end of the street couldn't be missed with its large hand-painted sign and towering false front. As they slowed their horses, Maegan noticed a man she could only guess was Alison's brother. He looked happy and relieved to see them and eagerly helped Alison off Cody's horse.

"I was really getting worried," he said, hugging her once her feet hit the ground. "What happened?"

"A wheel came loose, and we ended up going off the road in a ditch," she told him, her tone sounding not too put out. "Thanks to my new friends here, though, I got an early ride into town. My luggage will be coming when the stage eventually gets here."

"Did you happen to see a sheriff?"

Alison nodded. "He was helping the driver when we left."

"Good." His gaze shifted to Maegan and Cody, who still sat astride their horses. "Thanks for your help," he said, sincerity filling his brown eyes.

"Sure thing," Maegan replied, thinking the man had a kindness to his manner and was probably in his thirties.

"This is my brother, Jacob," Alison said. "And this is Mae and her brother Cody."

"Looks like you two are new to our town. Would you like to come for supper tonight? It would be my way of thanking you."

Maegan appreciated the generous offer, but she found herself shaking her head. "That's kind, but we should find our uncle before it gets dark." She hesitated, her eyes perusing the town for a moment. "Do you know where Ben McCoy lives?"

"Ben McCoy?" Reverend Myles echoed. "I haven't seen him for near a year. I can tell you where he lives, though. It's about a thirty-minute ride from town."

"We'd appreciate it," Maegan said.

"Follow us toward my place, and then I'll direct you from there."

Reverend Myles had a buckboard waiting and helped his sister in before jumping up himself and taking the reins. Maegan and Cody followed, and when they reached a fork in the road, Reverend Myles gave them directions to Ben McCoy's homestead.

"They were nice," Reverend Myles said as they rode off.

"I like them too. They lost their parents years ago, and they're here visiting relatives."

"Are you just visiting relatives like them, or do you think you're here to stay?" Reverend Myles asked with a smile.

"Here to stay, I hope," she answered with a soft laugh. "Although, I'm still fortunate enough to have my parents, even as meddlesome as they can be at times." While she loved her parents dearly, her mother's disposition lent itself to meddling. When Alison's brother Jacob married and left home, it made Alison something of an only child and something of a target for her well-meaning parents' attempts to run her life … specifically in her finding someone to marry.

Momentarily, they arrived at her brother's simple but

charming home. The rose bushes under the front windows were in full bloom, along with various flowers that stood out against the white house. It looked larger than the last time she'd seen it, and Alison realized they had built a small addition. She caught sight of her niece and nephew peering through the window, excitement all over their faces as they waved enthusiastically. Alison smiled and hastened her steps as they walked toward the front door, eager to see her niece and nephew and eager for this new chapter of her life to begin.

# Chapter Three

"Looks pretty rundown," Cody said as he and Maegan neared a cabin, its haphazard appearance neglected, to say the least. Ivy grew along both sides of the cabin, covering windows and pushing up shingles on the roof. The front door hung crooked on its hinges while weeds and overgrown grass grew in the place where flowerbeds had once been. The sight of some chickens roaming the yard and a bellow from a cow in the pasture was the only sign of life.

"It looks like no one lives here," Maegan said as she dismounted and walked hesitantly to the door.

"Can't we just go back to that reverend's house for supper? I'm starved!" Cody said.

Maegan ignored her brother and knocked on the front door, pausing to listen before knocking again.

"No one's home," Cody said. "Now, can we go?"

"Wait, I hear something," Maegan replied. She pushed softly on the door, which was already slightly ajar. "Hello? Is someone home?" She entered slowly, noting the mismatched furniture and unkempt appearance of everything from the unwashed dishes in the sink to the dust that lingered like a cloud. Next, she noticed a doorway to her left, where a blanket hung in place of a door. It was pushed to one side, allowing her to see into the room. Movement caught her eye, and she went toward the room.

From the doorway, Maegan saw that there was a man lying on the bed who looked barely alive. "Are you alright?" she asked, slowly moving towards him. She spotted a bucket on the floor by the bed at nearly the same time she smelled the horrible odor emanating from it. The man rolled to his side and leaned over enough to aim his vomit into the bucket.

Covering her mouth and nose, Maegan glanced at Cody, who had just entered the house behind her. "Better wait outside," she told him. She looked back at the man and saw that he seemed to notice her for the first time. He propped himself up on his elbow and tried to speak, but then his head fell back on the pillow as he groaned.

"Are you Ben McCoy?" Maegan asked, half hoping this pitiful-looking man wasn't her uncle. Maybe she'd come to the wrong house of an unwell neighbor.

"Who are you?" The man's voice was hoarse.

"I'm Maegan, Larson McCoy's daughter." Maegan watched as he tried to raise his head again only to drop it back down on the pillow and close his eyes. For a moment, she thought he'd slipped away, but a quick check of his pulse told her he'd only fallen asleep … or maybe unconscious. She noticed the dirty blankets around him and the mess of the living space that continued into the bedroom. She suddenly rolled up her sleeves and stepped into the situation. She first took the vomit bucket outside and dumped it far from the house. Then she brought in an empty one she found in the yard and set it by the bed. A hand on the man's forehead told her he was burning with a fever and no doubt dehydrated.

"Cody!" she called from the door. "Rinse this out and fill it with some water from the well." She handed him a bucket she'd found by the sink that looked decent. When he returned with it a few minutes later, she ladled the water into a cup and tried to help the man wake up to drink it. With one hand, she held the cup to his lips while her other propped up his head.

"Try and drink some," she coaxed as he came to and pursed his lips tight together.

"Drink some," she said again, but this time, he hit the cup out of her hand, sending it falling to the ground. Maegan saw that the simple action had drained him of strength, because he sank back down onto the bed.

"No," he mumbled, his brow furrowed in an expression of agony.

"You're dehydrated," Maegan tried to reason with him as she reached for the cup. "You got to try and …"

He suddenly grabbed her wrist, and his deep-set, green eyes glared at her with every ounce of energy he had left. "No! It's poison!"

Understanding dawned on her. In a flash, she jumped up and ran outside. "Cody! Don't drink the water!"

The boy looked up from where he stood by the well. He had just been pulling up another bucket full.

"It's poisoned!" Maegan told him as she neared the well and took his arm. "Can you look for a creek and get some fresh water?"

Cody nodded and went in search of one.

Releasing a heavy sigh, Maegan took off her hat and wiped at the sweat running down her forehead. She reentered the house and set to work, cleaning it and airing it out as best she could. When Cody returned with a bucket of fresh water, she told the sick man where it was from and convinced him to drink some. His hollow cheekbones suggested he'd been sick for quite some time, and Maegan did a search for some food, although she doubted that he could keep anything down yet. He hadn't thrown up the water she gave him, so that was a good sign.

"Are we just gonna stay here?" Cody asked, his tone conveying his hope she would say no.

"I'm afraid so," Maegan replied. "There's another room with a bed in it, and I noticed a cot in the loft one of us can take. I found some potatoes I can cook for supper. Why don't you go look for where those chickens lay their eggs, and I can hard-boil you some."

Cody nodded, the look on his face less than thrilled. "I wonder what Austin and Sawyer are doing right now," he mumbled as he left the house.

Maegan closed her eyes and mentally scolded herself for dragging Cody there. Maybe she should have just stayed with her brothers, regardless of the threat that Sawyer's obsession with bounty hunting posed. She missed the familiarity of home and the company of her older brothers just as much as Cody did. She heard the man begin coughing, breaking her out of her reverie. She couldn't think about their old life right now; she had to help this man, who was most likely her uncle, get well.

*****

Doctor Fletcher answered his front door to see a young woman he didn't recognize. In a faded white shirt, tan vest, and trousers, he almost mistook her for a young man. But then she turned around, and her pretty face clearly revealed her gender.

"Can I help you?" he asked.

"My uncle, Ben McCoy, is in a bad way. I've just come from his place. My brother and I arrived yesterday and found him barely conscious."

The doctor's thick, graying eyebrows nearly touched when he frowned. "Doesn't sound like Ben. He doesn't come to town but a few times a year, but I've never known him to be anything but healthy. I'll grab my bag."

When he returned, Maegan followed him to where his buckboard and horse were. "He said something about his well being poisoned," she told him.

"Poisoned?" The doctor repeated with alarm in his voice.

"I'm getting some things in town," Maegan told him. "I'll be back soon."

The doctor nodded, and soon, a small cloud of dust was trailing behind his buckboard as he drove down the street.

Maegan met Cody where he stood waiting for her, and he followed her to the General Store. When they got there, he said he would wait outside for her. As Cody sat there on the front steps, his eyes took in the wagons and men on horses passing by on the wide street. Someone walked around him to get into the store, and he moved away so as not to be in the path of other customers.

He noticed an establishment across the street. The elegantly painted sign on it read: *Lyddie's Room and Board.* Just outside the boarding house, a group of kids around his own age grabbed his attention, particularly a girl in the crowd who sounded upset.

"Give me back my bonnet!" she said, her voice clearly conveying her distress.

Cody took a few steps toward them, observing the way one of the three boys held a bonnet high above her head. He was obviously taunting her as she tried numerous times to take it from him. The boy reached over and tugged on one of her blonde braids, causing her to cry out in pain.

Cody didn't know if it was because he had watched his brothers go after criminals most of his life, but there was a determination in his young heart to see justice done, even in the smallest of situations. He strode across the street, planting his feet just behind the boy who appeared to be causing all the trouble.

"Leave her alone."

The boy spun around, indignation in his eyes. "Who in heck are you?"

"Just give her back her bonnet," Cody said.

"Or what?" The boy took a threatening step toward him, a smirk on his face as he widened his shoulders a bit and cocked his head up to appear even taller than his five-foot-four frame. His overgrown, ash-brown hair fell over his eyes, and he jerked his head slightly to get it out of his face.

"You must be pretty weak to be pickin' on a girl," Cody said. If he feared this bigger boy, he didn't give any indication. Far from it. His expression had the confidence of someone who had won a dozen such battles.

"Pretty weak, huh? I'll show you who's weak!" Then, in a split second, the boy's fist came hurling toward Cody's face, sending him backward.

The punch had come much faster than Cody had expected, and as he stood to his feet, he could taste the blood in his mouth. Tightening his fists, he quickly landed a punch back at the boy, who cursed and came at him even harder. Cody didn't know how long it went on for, but eventually, they were rolling on the ground; one minute, Cody was on top, and the next, the other boy had the advantage.

And then, suddenly, it was over. A man stepped in and pulled the other boy off Cody. "Stop it! Both of you!" His authoritative voice rang out.

As Cody stood up and blinked away some dust from his eyes, he saw it was the sheriff they had met at the stagecoach the previous day.

"He started it!" The boy from the fight said, realizing his friends must have taken off when they saw the sheriff.

"That's a lie!" The girl spoke up. "Jeb started it!"

The sheriff still had Jeb by the arm and looked from him to Cody. "You both look torn up! What's this about?"

Neither answered, so the girl explained. "Jeb was picking on me like he always does, and this boy here just stepped in, is all."

"You're a liar!" Jeb snapped at her.

The sheriff let go of his arm. "Go on, get outta here, Jeb, and tell your Pa to take a switch to ya for causing trouble!"

Jeb glared at Cody as he walked by. "I'll finish you later," he muttered under his breath.

"Cody! What on earth?" Maegan had just come on the scene after spotting her brother in a fight from across the street. She'd run as fast as she could, but the sheriff pulled them apart before she got there. "Who were you fightin' with?" She took him by the arm as she pulled out a hand-kerchief and gently pressed it to his bleeding nose.

"He was the one fightin' with me," Cody told her.

Maegan's eyes went to the sheriff, remembering him from the day before. "I'm sorry about this. Thanks for stepping in."

He nodded, thinking that Jeb was a little too much like his quick-tempered father, who was known for starting fights. He turned his attention to Reverend Myles' nine-year-old daughter. "Are you alright, Lilly?" he asked kindly.

She nodded, her eyes on Cody, who was still holding the handkerchief to his bloody nose.

"I'll make sure he stays out of trouble," Maegan told the sheriff with an apologetic expression before sending a dis-approving glance toward Cody.

"While I don't condone fighting, I'm sure it happened

as Lilly said it did," the sheriff told Maegan. "From what I've seen in my short time of being here, Jeb and his family aren't exactly peace-loving folk."

"We'll keep that in mind," Maegan said, absently thinking that the sheriff had the nicest deep blue eyes she'd ever seen.

"C'mon, Cody." She led the way to their horses, feeling frustrated that she'd left home to keep her brother out of trouble, and here he was, stepping into it the first chance he had.

When they returned to their uncle's, the doctor was still there. "I've given him something to ease his stomach. He looks like he's already thrown up everything in his system, so he should pull through."

"So, the well really was poisoned?" Maegan asked, confusion in her voice.

"I can't be sure, but his symptoms would say so. I can tell you've already done everything you can do," he said to Maegan. "Just keep after him with a lot of fluids and some good strong broth until he gets his strength back and can eat."

"I intend to do just that," she said, setting on the table the crate of food supplies that she'd been holding.

"Are you two planning to stay here, then?" the doctor asked, a fatherly concern in his eyes.

"For now," Maegan replied. "At least until he gets well. My brother and I are just here to visit."

"Well, you certainly picked an opportune time, young lady. I don't know if he would have made it another day had you not intervened when you did."

Maegan thanked him for coming and then held out a few coins toward him.

"No, no," he declined. "Ben's an old friend. This one's on me."

Maegan dropped the coins back in her pocket and thanked him with a smile.

"What happened to you?" The doctor asked, just now taking notice of Cody, who stood near Maegan, his left eye nearly swollen shut.

"He'll be fine," Maegan answered with a sigh. "He got into a fight with some boy in town."

"Well, guess you have two patients now," the doctor said, putting his hat on as he moved to the door. "I'll come by middle of the week to make sure he's doing better."

"Thanks, doctor."

"You two take care of yourselves, and make sure not to go near that well."

*****

"Come in," Alison called when she heard a light knocking on her bedroom door. The door opened, and her niece, Lilly, stepped in. "Ma said to tell you breakfast is ready."

Alison smiled kindly at her and then turned her attention back to the notebook on her desk. "I'm coming," she said as she jotted down a few more words and then stood.

"Were you writing another of your stories?" Lilly asked with curiosity in her big brown eyes. She knew her aunt loved to write and had even worked for some newspaper company in Kansas City.

"Yes," Alison told her as she followed her out to the main room of the house. "Maybe later I can read it to you, and you can help me put an ending on it."

Lilly looked thrilled as she nodded in agreement. "Pa always says I have a big imagination, so I'm sure I can help."

She followed the little girl to the table, where the rest of the family was already sitting.

"I still can't believe the little addition to the house you made for me …" Alison mentioned a few minutes later, and then, noticing Maggie's protruding belly, added, "… and the new addition to the family you're going to have in a few months!" Her brother Jacob had written to her parents to let them know Maggie was expecting, but it had still felt like a surprise when Alison arrived to see Maggie five months pregnant.

"We thought it would be nice for you to have a room to yourself," Jacob said, "but still be close enough to spend time with us. And … with our family growing, it doesn't hurt to have more space."

Alison didn't miss the look of affection Jacob and his wife exchanged. She loved seeing them together and remembered how it was just last year when she had visited for their wedding. Her brother's previous wife had passed away over three years ago, leaving him heartbroken and with two children to care for. Maggie had come to Millcreek looking for a new life, and Alison was glad the Lord had brought her and Jacob together. His children, Lilly and Lucas, adored her as well, and she loved them like they were her own.

"Well, I've got to be getting to the mill," Jacob said sometime later when he'd finished breakfast. He walked over to where his wife sat and leaned down to kiss her cheek before giving his daughter's braid a gentle tug. "Help your ma, and try to stay out of trouble today, young lady."

"I will, Pa," Lilly smiled, knowing her father was teasing. She had told him about Jeb's bothering her the day before and how Cody McCoy had stepped in to help her, making him sound like quite the hero.

"Can I ride with you?" Alison suddenly asked, standing to carry her plate to the sink. "Last time I was here, you mentioned that Harold Bell might need some help at his newspaper press. I was thinking about paying him a visit."

"I think he could use all the help he can get," Maggie said. "His eyesight seems to be getting worse."

"And his articles," Jacob added with a chuckle. "Sure, you can ride with me and then take the wagon back. I'll ask my friend Gideon to give me a lift home later this afternoon."

Twenty minutes later, they were riding into Millcreek, and Alison waved to Lyddie Hall, who was on the porch of her boarding house. She was an amiable and well-liked woman who had been widowed twenty years after she and her husband had settled in Millcreek. Her establishment was both elegant and sensible, just as she herself was.

"Not much has changed since I was here last year, has it?" Alison asked.

"Well, we got a new sheriff," her brother told her.

"I didn't officially meet him the other day. What's he like?"

"Quiet, but a dependable and good man from what I've seen so far."

"Who's that?" Alison asked as she noticed a poorly clad woman sitting on the steps outside the bakery, apparently waiting for the shop to open. The woman had lifted her eyes just as they passed, and Alison caught a quick glimpse of her face, which looked rather distressed.

"Lyn Hummel," Jacob told her. "She's only been here a few weeks. From what I've gathered on the times I've spoken with her, she passes from town to town looking for her son." Jacob sent a sympathetic glance in the woman's direction. "Unfortunately, it seems she can't accept the fact that he was killed during the war."

"That's heartbreaking," Alison said, turning around to get one more glance at the woman before passing traffic blocked her view.

"Lyddie is letting her stay in the extra building she has behind her boarding house."

"Well, at least she has a safe place to sleep at night."

"And food … for now, thanks to Lyddie's generosity."

A few minutes later, after her brother got off at the mill, Alison turned the wagon around and headed to Harold Bell's Newspaper Press.

The doorbell rang when she entered the newspaper office, and a man who looked to be getting on in years came out of an adjoining room. He was of average height, and his gray suit fit a little snugly around his midsection. "Can I help you?" he asked.

"Good morning, Mr. Bell," Alison greeted pleasantly. "I don't know if you remember me, but my name is Alison Myles. I'm Jacob Myles' sister."

"I think I remember you," he replied. "What brings you here this morning?"

"Well, I've just moved to Millcreek and will be here indefinitely. Back home, I wrote for a local newspaper, and I was curious if you might have room for a new column in your paper?"

"What sort of column?" he asked, but Alison couldn't tell if he was asking out of genuine interest or skepticism. He took off his spectacles and cleaned them with the sleeve of his pinstriped shirt.

"I often wrote advertisements for businesses, and I know about typesetting and even filled in as an assistant editor from time to time," she told him proudly. "The column I wrote lent itself to more of a source of entertainment, fictional stories and …"

"An assistant editor, you say?" He had replaced his spectacles and had a look of interest in his light blue eyes.

"Yes, sir."

"Humph." He tapped his index finger against his cheek as if contemplating something. "It just so happens, Miss Myles, that I've been in need of some editorial assistance."

Her eyebrows hiked in surprise at his admission, and she couldn't hide her smile. "Really?"

"I can't guarantee you a column at this point, but if you're looking for an editorial position and can work part-time, I'd pay two dollars a week."

"I'd be happy to take the position," Alison said as she took a few steps toward him. It was a little less than she'd made in Kansas City, but money wasn't her main motivation. "When would I start?" Her eyes glanced around the room, wondering if he would have space to set up an additional desk.

"As soon as you can," he said. He wouldn't admit it to anyone, but his vision had been waning for the last five years, and the eye strain was causing painful headaches.

"Thank you so much, Mr. Bell. I could start this week if that suits you."

"That would be fine. Could you work Mondays and Thursdays?"

"Yes, sir." Alison thanked him again before leaving, elated that she'd been hired so quickly. She couldn't help but take it as a sign that coming to Millcreek had been the right decision.

*****

"Alison, I'd like you to meet someone."

Alison had a stack of dishes in her hands as she was setting the table with Lilly when Jacob came home that evening. Another man, a few years younger than her brother, entered the house behind him.

"This is a friend of mine who works with me at the mill," Jacob said, looking back at the man. "This is Gideon Martin. Gideon, this is my younger sister, Alison."

"Pleased to meet you," Alison said as she met his eyes. They were a light shade of blue and went well with his

38

auburn hair. He smiled, displaying straight teeth. He was thin and tall, with his shirt a little too big and his trousers a little too short.

"Same to you," Gideon replied.

"Gideon's a reader, like you, Ali," Jacob said as he went to a bookshelf at the far end of the room. "Here's that book I was telling you about," Jacob said as he pulled a thick leather book off the shelf and then handed it to Gideon. "You can borrow it as long as you want," he told him.

"Thank you," Gideon replied, and then a moment later said, "Well, I should be going."

"Why don't you stay for supper?" Jacob offered.

"That's kind, but I need to get back and feed the stock. Maybe another time. Thanks again," he said to Jacob, and then, with a polite nod at Alison, he left.

"You'll never believe it!" Alison was excited to tell her brother. "Mr. Bell hired me on the spot ... as an assistant editor!"

"What? That's wonderful," Jacob said. "He's not one to ask for or accept help, so you must have made quite an impression on him."

"He couldn't guarantee a spot in the paper for a column I wanted to write, but at least it's a start!"

"It's a wonderful start," Maggie said as she pulled out a chair for Lucas to climb onto.

"Ma and Pa didn't like me working for the paper back home, so I'm sure they wouldn't approve of this either, but I'm thrilled!" Alison clasped her hands together and gave an airy sigh. "And I think it's just a matter of time until Mr. Bell lets me do some of my own writing for him."

*****

"I'm glad it worked out for Ali to meet Gideon," Jacob

39

said to his wife later that evening when they were alone in their room.

"What on earth for?" Maggie asked with a little laugh. Her sea-green eyes looked amused and suspicious all at once. She flipped her long, auburn braid over her shoulder. "You're not trying to marry her off so soon, are you?"

Jacob grinned. "He's just a good, steady fellow, is all."

"I don't think Alison's focus is on finding someone to marry right now."

"Well, there's no rush, of course, but eventually, she'll want to, and I figure it can't hurt to help her out."

Maggie was about to climb into bed but stopped and put her hands on her hips. "Jacob Myles, are you seriously trying to play matchmaker? She's only been here a few days!"

Jacob chuckled as his wife crawled into bed, and he pulled her close. "As happy as we are, I want that for Alison too."

"I'm sure she'll have it … eventually. She moved here to get some independence and to escape your mother trying to marry her off, remember?"

"I remember."

"I have a feeling," Maggie said before planting a kiss on her husband's lips, "that I may have to remind you of that from time to time."

# Chapter Four

"You're looking a little better today," Maegan said to her uncle a week later as she brought in a tray of food for him.

"I ain't throwin' up my guts, at least," he replied, looking at her as if for the first time. "You said you're my brother's daughter?" He saw she had the McCoy dark, curly hair and green eyes, but the rest of her look could be attributed to her mother.

"Yes. You've been only half-conscious since we got here, so we haven't been able to really introduce ourselves. I'm Maegan, and my brother Cody is outside."

"What about Larson's other boys?"

"Austin and Sawyer," Maegan supplied. "They're still back at our farm."

"So, what are you doing here?" he asked, not meaning to sound unwelcoming.

"Pa talked about you and Aunt Becky a lot. Before he died, he told me to make it a point to come meet you all." Maegan replied. "It's been a while in coming, but I figured it was time. Does Aunt Becky live far from here?" Maegan watched as a strange expression clouded his face. He didn't answer right away, but then said, "Just a few miles east of here, but she's as good as dead."

"What?" Maegan paused before setting the tray on his lap, confused by his answer.

"She's married to Joe Spencer." He said it like she should understand what that meant.

"You mean because she married someone you don't like, you disowned her?" Maegan tried to understand.

"No. I mean Joe would rather me dead than alive, and he don't let Becky come within a mile of here."

"But she's your sister."

Ben McCoy sighed and ran a hand through his unruly, salt-and-pepper hair. "It's complicated." He looked down at the tray she set on his lap. "You don't have to do this," he said, feeling uncomfortable at the thought of her serving him.

"The doctor said you needed to get your strength back as soon as you could keep food down. So, eat what you can."

Just then, the door opened, and Cody soon appeared in the doorway of their uncle's room, carrying a bucket of water. He noticed that Maegan was talking to their uncle and that he looked truly awake for the first time since they'd arrived. Setting the bucket down, Cody walked over to him and extended his hand. "Cody McCoy," he introduced himself.

Ben shook his offered hand, taking in the boy's appearance. "You don't look like a McCoy."

"Takes after our Ma," Maegan said. "At least in appearance," she added. "In all other respects, he's as McCoy as they come."

"Guess I'm beholdin' to ya for showing up when you did," Ben said, but his tone sounded akin to irritated that he had needed the help. "I ain't ever been that sick."

"How'd the well get poisoned?" Cody asked.

"Ha! I can only guess a Spencer done it."

"They would do something like that?" Maegan asked in disbelief.

"That and worse."

"Who are the Spencers?" Cody asked.

"A family that don't favor the likes of me or any other McCoy," Ben said. "Best to stay away from all of 'em."

*****

$\mathcal{M}$aegan shifted in her saddle as she pushed off her wide hat, letting it hang down her back. It was the following day, and there wasn't even a slight breeze to lessen the Indian summer heat. As her uncle wasn't keen on her idea of going to see her Aunt Becky, Maegan had asked Doc Fletcher for directions when he'd come by. Any quarrels her uncle had with the Spencers were his business. She wasn't going to let it keep her from keeping her word to her father. Besides, she was curious to meet her father's sister.

As she directed her horse over a mound of tall grass, she saw a log cabin just thirty yards away. Half a dozen cattle grazed in the field beside it, and more chickens than she could count wandered the yard. A dog began barking when it came around the corner of the house and spotted her dismounting. The front door opened, and a petite woman in her mid-forties stepped outside, wiping her hands on her apron.

"Can I help you?" she asked, lifting her hand to shield her eyes from the sun directly behind the stranger.

Maegan smiled softly as she took a step closer to her, thinking the woman's almost black hair, jade eyes, and freckles were very much like her own. "My name's Maegan. Are you Becky Spencer?"

"Yes."

"Then you're my Pa's sister."

The woman gasped, and her mouth hung open for a full five seconds. "You're Larson and Renae's little girl?"

Maegan nodded.

"Well, you ain't so little anymore. Look at you!" Becky stepped toward her and hugged her. "Land sakes, I never imagined you'd just show up on my doorstep." She stepped away, holding her at arm's length. "How are the rest of ya? There's three more, yes?"

"My brothers are fine. The oldest two are still living back home, but Cody and I came here to find you and Uncle Ben. We've been staying with him for about a week. Our Pa wanted us to know you both."

"I was so devastated to hear of his passing," she said quietly. Although it was nine years ago, the shock never quite wore off. "How's Ben?" she asked next.

Maegan thought it strange that she would ask when they lived less than thirty minutes away from each other, but she remembered her uncle's words the previous day. "He was sick as a dog when we found him. But he's doing better now."

"Sick, you say?"

"He thinks his well was poisoned," Maegan said and watched as all the color drained from her aunt's face.

Becky's eyes looked past Maegan before settling back on her. "You probably shouldn't stay too long. My husband, Joe, will be back soon, and he doesn't take kindly to anyone who is related to or friends with my brother."

Maegan didn't like the fear she saw in the woman's eyes. "Surely, he won't mind me just saying hello."

"Well, I suppose we could have a few more minutes. Why don't you come in, and I'll get you something cold to drink."

Maegan followed her inside and took a chair by the table. The house was small but tidy and efficiently set up. Maegan thought the light-yellow curtains hanging in the windows were a nice touch. "Do I have any cousins?" Maegan asked, glancing around for a sign of children.

"My youngest boy, Jeb, is thirteen, and my oldest, Thomas, was killed during the war."

"I'm so sorry," Maegan said sincerely, catching the sadness in her aunt's voice.

"How old is Cody now?" Becky changed the subject.

"Twelve, but he wishes he was an adult already. His dream is to be like his older brothers."

Becky smiled. "I'd love to meet him." They chatted for a few more minutes before the sound of approaching riders caused Becky to glance nervously toward the window. "You best go for now, Maegan. Things are a little tense between the Spencers and McCoys."

Maegan wanted to ask her why but sensed the same reluctance to talk about it that she had sensed from her uncle. Once outside, Maegan mounted her horse and said goodbye, riding away just as several men on horseback rode past her into the yard.

Fifteen minutes later, feeling almost dizzy from the heat, Maegan directed her horse toward a creek she had noticed on the ride in. It ran through a patch of woods that promised some shade. She followed the stream until it came to a portion nearly ten feet across. She dismounted and didn't have to lead her horse to the water. As he drank, she knelt on the bank and splashed her face with the cold water. She was debating taking off her shoes and wading in the water when she heard riders approaching through the woods. Branches snapped under the hooves, and one of the horses whinnied.

She looked over and saw three men on horseback. She wasn't positive, but it looked like the men who had just passed her while leaving Aunt Becky's. The older-looking of the three dismounted and walked toward her.

"What's a pretty girl like you dressed like that for?" he

snickered, taking in her boyish attire. He was Garret Spencer, the thirty-two-year-old son of Joe Spencer's brother, Robert. The other two were Bobby Spencer, Garret's nineteen-year-old brother, and their cousin Pete Keller.

Maegan didn't like the hint of mischief in his tone and moved cautiously toward her horse. By habit, she had slid a pistol into her saddle bag before she'd left and wanted to be near it if necessary.

"You must be new 'round here," he said, coming to stand just in front of her.

"Maybe," she replied, feeling slightly intimidated by his six-foot-two height and bulky frame. The look of trouble she detected in his bulgy eyes made her feel even more uneasy. He had a spotty, brownish-red beard, and the smell of alcohol and sweat surrounded him.

"Reason I know you're new is cuz you had the guts to trespass on our land. What's your name?"

"Maegan McCoy."

"McCoy?" Garret's jaw muscles jumped, and he swung a glance at his younger brother and cousin. "So, you're the one that's been stayin' with Ben. What are you doin' out here? Comin' to spy for him?"

"Of course not! I just came to see my Aunt Becky. How'd you know I was staying with my uncle, anyway?"

"Us Spencers know everything that goes on 'round here."

"Really? Then maybe you know who poisoned my uncle's well," Maegan heard herself say. She didn't want to get involved in the quarrel her uncle had with these people, but somehow, the words just spilled out.

"Maybe," he smirked. "But if you know what's good for you, you'll mind your own business."

"Is that a threat?" she asked, raising her chin a fraction and holding his gaze. She was not about to let him know he scared her. From the fear she had seen in her Aunt Becky's eyes to the look of trouble in this man's, she was starting to understand why her uncle had warned her about the Spencers.

"You can call it whatever you want." Garret stepped closer to her, flicking back the braid that hung over her shoulder.

"Keep your hands to yourself!" Maegan warned as she moved closer to her horse, using the animal as a barrier between her and Garret.

"I ain't done talkin' to you yet," he said as he reached over and firmly took the horse's reins and bridle.

"I'll leave when I want to," she said, suddenly reaching into her saddle bag and pulling out the small pistol.

"You gonna shoot me?" He laughed, looking unfazed by the weapon now aimed at him.

"I might … if you don't let go of my horse."

"Now, *that's* a threat," he said, an amused grin twisting his mouth. He hated to admit it to himself, but he liked her grit … even if she was a McCoy.

Hunting outlaws with her brothers, Maegan had dealt with her share of rough men and knew how quickly bad intentions could mount. She raised the pistol slightly. "Let go of my horse."

"You'll come to find out I do pretty much whatever I want," he replied, stepping around the front of the horse to get closer to her.

"Not another step," she warned as she edged backward. When he continued toward her, she aimed and fired, sending his hat flying off his head. Stepping backward, he immediately released his hold on the bridle and reached for his head as if to make sure it was still there. As soon as he moved, Maegan mounted her horse and regained control of the reins.

Bobby settled his horse, which had startled slightly at the sound of the gunshot. "C'mon, Garret! Let's get home," he called. Bobby had caused his share of tomfoolery over the years, usually because of his brother's influence, but he didn't go around looking for trouble like Garret did.

"I don't take kindly to trespassers!" Garret yelled after her. "Especially the likes of you!"

"I'll be sure to never trespass again!" Maegan called over her shoulder as she quickly directed her horse away.

"You better not, or I'll teach you a lesson you won't forget!" he hollered back angrily.

Maegan rode away without glancing back, hoping to never lay eyes on Garret Spencer again.

*****

"Where you been?" Cody asked Maegan when she rode into the yard. He was sitting on a tree stump near the door, whittling with his pocketknife.

"Just for a ride," Maegan told him. "Can you take Tuck to the barn for me so I can start supper?" she asked.

Cody nodded and stood to take the horse's reins.

Maegan paused at the door. "I actually went to visit our Aunt Becky," she admitted. She turned around to face him. "There's some kind of quarrel going on between the family she married into and our uncle. Try to stay clear of anyone with the name Spencer, alright?"

Cody shrugged. "Alright."

Maegan found her uncle at the stove when she came inside. "I think I got my appetite back," he said when he saw her. He picked up the pot that he'd just reheated leftover soup in and walked to the table.

"That's a good sign," Maegan replied, noting the way he favored his left leg and limped to the table.

"You bought all this food here?" he asked, gesturing toward the canned goods, coffee, sugar, flour, and other items on the shelves. He slumped into the chair and leaned over the table as if it had taken all his strength just to walk across the room.

Maegan nodded. "When we first arrived."

"So, you ain't hurtin' for money, then?"

"No, sir. We're not lookin' for any handouts," Maegan told him. She had a decent amount of money that she had been saving for years. Most of it was set aside to give to Cody one day, but the other portion would hold them over until she could get a job of some sort. "Like I said, we came just to meet our kin. Cody and I can support ourselves, and just as soon as you're well enough, we'll be finding our own place to stay."

"I thought you was just visiting."

"Well, I'm thinking about Cody and I staying in Millcreek a little longer than a visit."

Ben could hear something in her voice that made him wonder if there was another reason for their arrival. He wanted to ask but instead heard himself say, "I've lived alone for almost twenty years, so probably best if you do."

Maegan hung up her hat and then moved to sweep up a pile of dirt she'd brought in. "My Pa used to say you two were close growing up," she said a few minutes later.

Ben's hand paused on his utensil, his eyes on his bowl, but then he gave what Maegan thought was a faint smile. It was hard to tell behind his overgrown beard and mustache. "Weren't many like your Pa," Ben replied quietly. "Darn shame he left this earth."

"I thought Pa said you had a son," Maegan said.

"That's right," was all he said as he returned to eating.

"Does he live 'round here?" Megan was curious.

"Not too far."

Maegan thought it was obvious her uncle didn't want to talk about their cousin. "Maybe we could go see him," Maegan suggested.

"You can if you want. He won't come 'round here."

"You mean you're not on good terms?" Maegan asked carefully.

"I'd rather not talk about it." Ben stood from his chair and walked to the door. His intention was to step outside, but when he reached the door, he paused. "Reckon, I'll head back to bed."

Maegan saw his hand was resting on the door frame for support. She wanted to offer her arm, but he seemed intent on making it to his room on his own.

"I think Uncle Ben and his son had a falling out," Maegan told Cody that evening as they ate supper. Her uncle hadn't resurfaced the rest of the day.

"Doesn't seem to get along with anybody," Cody remarked, thinking of what she'd told him earlier.

Maegan thought just as much and wondered why not only the Spencers but also his own son had an issue with him. She glanced toward the door to his room, curious if she'd ever get some kind of explanation from him.

She and Cody went to bed a short time later, but around midnight, Maegan sat up suddenly, startled by a noise outside. Going into the main room of the house, she went to look outside the front window.

"You heard it too?"

Maegan glanced over her shoulder when she heard her uncle's voice and, in the darkness, could see him coming out of his bedroom, a rifle in his hands.

"Should I light a lamp?" she whispered. "Who is it?"

"I reckon it's just Robert's boys conjuring up some mischief."

"Who's Robert?"

"Joe Spencer's brother."

Maegan thought of the men she'd run into earlier that day and wondered if they were Robert's boys.

The sound of a window shattering suddenly caused her to jump back. A large rock had been thrown through the front window, barely missing her. Ben had jumped back too, but now he was moving hastily toward the front door. He flung it open and fired two shots up into the air. "Get off my property!" he yelled, firing another shot for emphasis.

Maegan could tell by the sound of horses' hooves that there were at least two riders, maybe three. She met her uncle outside. "What was that all about?" she asked, her heart beating fast.

"Best get inside," he told her, turning and following her into the house. Cody was awake and wide-eyed, buttoning his shirt frantically.

"What's goin' on?" he asked.

"Everything's alright," Maegan said with a glance toward her uncle, hoping her words were true.

As if being woken in the middle of the night wasn't bad enough, early that morning, there was a pounding on the door that awoke them for the second time. Ben got to it first, an angry scowl on his face. "Who is it?" he barked as he unlocked the door and opened it.

"I've had enough, Pa! You best make things right before I send one of those Spencer boys straight to …" Joshua McCoy stopped mid-sentence. He had barged through the door after Ben had opened it, but now he noticed Maegan and Cody standing in the room. "Who are you?" he asked, his eyes darting from them to his father.

"I ain't seen you for nearly a year, and this is your best hello?" Ben snapped at his son. He gestured toward Maegan and Cody. "These are my late brother's kids, your cousins."

In his mid-thirties, Maegan thought her cousin Joshua looked to be a younger version of his father with the trademark McCoy green eyes, six-foot height, and solid build. His thick eyebrows looked fitting with his dark mustache and beard, which was well-kept compared to his father's.

"I ain't seen you in over a year, Pa, because last time I was here, you told me not to come back. Or did you forget those parting words?"

Ben grunted and mumbled something before turning his attention back to the others. "This is Maegan and Cody."

"Nice to meet you," Joshua said with the tip of his black slouch hat. "I'm Joshua."

His attention swung back to his father. "The Spencer boys were at my place last night. They would have set my whole barn on fire if I hadn't stopped them when I did! This has gone on long enough, Pa. You need to do something!" He suddenly seemed to really notice his father for the first time, who was leaning against a chair for support. "You sick?" Joshua asked him.

Maegan signaled for Cody to follow her, and they thoughtfully left the cabin.

"I wanted to hear what else they say!" Cody said once they were outside.

"It's none of our business," Maegan told him. "If Joshua hasn't seen Uncle Ben in almost a year, they might want some privacy to talk."

Cody kicked at a rock in the dirt and stuffed his hands in his pockets. Some shattered glass from that night's broken window lay in the dirt, and he used his boot to sweep it into a pile.

Maegan moved to a makeshift seat, the trunk of a tree long ago cut down. She could hear the voices in the cabin and could tell the conversation was getting more heated.

Maybe this is why her father had moved away once he had married her ma. She'd never seen so much fighting within a family. After some time, the door opened, and Joshua stepped outside.

"Sorry, I ain't one for small talk," he told Maegan before mounting his horse that was tethered to a post near the house. "Good luck stayin' with my Pa. He's a stubborn mule!" With that, he clicked his tongue and tossed the reins to the side, which prompted his horse to lead him away from the cabin.

"Shouldn't we tell the sheriff about last night?" Maegan asked her Uncle Ben when he joined them outside.

"I don't like goin' to town, and I don't s'pose it'll do any good."

Maegen bit her bottom lip uncertainly as she considered his words. She wasn't a confrontational person unless she had to be, and she didn't want to go against her uncle. Still, the idea of the Spencer clan causing harm to her family was something that didn't settle well with her.

*****

Alison untied her ink-smudged apron and hung it on the back of the door before stepping out of Bell's Newspaper Press. Mr. Bell had asked her to post a letter for him, and she was glad for a brief break. On her way back, she spotted Maegan just across the street. With a friendly wave, Alison called to her and then maneuvered around some passing wagons to catch up to her.

"So good to see you," Alison said warmly. "Did you and Cody find your uncle?"

"Yes, thank you," Maegan said kindly. "Did you settle in alright?"

"Oh yes. My brother and his family are just wonderful.

You met him the other day. He's the minister of the church here in Millcreek. You should come Sunday and meet his whole family."

A thoughtful smile tugged on Maegan's lips at the mention of church. Her ma had often read to them from the Bible, and occasionally, when the weather permitted, they would take the two-hour trek to church. It was a distant but fond memory Maegan had stored in her heart.

"Maybe we will," she replied.

"Oh good! Well, I must get back to work, but it was nice seeing you again," Alison told her sincerely.

As Alison moved away, Maegan didn't miss the admiring looks several of the men on the street sent in her direction as she passed them. Alison didn't appear to notice, but Maegan couldn't help but note Alison's elegantly styled hair and stylish light-yellow dress that complemented her figure. Maegan glanced down at her own trousers and sighed. She couldn't even remember the last time she'd donned a dress. Over the years of keeping house, cooking, taking care of livestock, and riding after outlaws with her brothers, practicality had won out over femininity.

Looking up, she caught sight of the sheriff stepping out of the jail. He was walking that way, and after a moment of indecision, she decided to approach him.

"Afternoon, Sheriff," she greeted, flickering a smile.

"Afternoon," he returned with a courteous nod of his head.

"I didn't get to introduce myself the other day when you came by the stagecoach or when you were pulling my brother out of that fight. My name's Mae McCoy."

"Reckon I couldn't forget you, beings you nearly put a bullet through my foot."

"I didn't mean to startle you by shooting without warning at that snake," Maegan said apologetically. "I'm sorry about that."

Bridger smiled slightly, and Maegan thought it only added to his look. "I guess not as sorry as I'd have been had that rattler bit me," Bridger said. "Where'd you learn to shoot like that, anyway?" he asked.

"Having two older brothers rubbed off on me, I guess."

"And they didn't come with you to Millcreek?" he asked curiously.

She merely shook her head, but he detected a bit of sadness behind her eyes, which were rather beautiful, he thought.

"There was something I wanted to speak to you about," Maegan told him. "I wanted to report something on behalf of my Uncle Ben."

"Oh?" His expression became more attentive.

"Perhaps you know him? Ben McCoy?"

"I've heard of him but not personally met him."

"Well, my brother and I are staying with him, and last night, a large rock was thrown through his window. He's convinced it was Robert Spencer's sons, but we couldn't see their faces. My cousin Joshua also said that last night, someone was on his property and tried to set fire to his barn."

"I've only been in Millcreek a few months, but nearly all the trouble I've found so far has the Spencer name attached to it." He crossed his arms in front of his chest and sighed. "I'll pay the family a visit and find out if any of them are responsible for one or both incidents."

"Thank you." She paused a moment and then added, "My uncle thinks they were the ones who poisoned his well, too."

"Doctor Fletcher mentioned that to me. Reckon I'll look into that while I'm at it," he said, a thoughtful expression on his face.

Maegan tucked a stray curl behind her ear. "I don't understand why someone would go to such lengths to hurt my uncle. I'm afraid I don't know much about him, but even so, I can't believe he's deserving of this."

"From what I've gathered, the Spencer clan has some sort of vendetta against him."

"Him and anyone else with the name McCoy," Maegan said, thinking back to the other day when she had been confronted in the woods. "I haven't been able to get the cause out of my uncle, though," she added.

"Isn't Ben's sister married to Joe Spencer?" Bridger asked, still trying to put straight the folks he had met and heard about.

"She is. I guess whatever they're fighting over happened after the fact. I suppose I'll find out sooner or later."

"Well, I'll let you know what I find out."

Maegan thanked him again, thinking the sheriff's badge on his vest seemed very fitting. His even tone of voice and calm manner suited the position well. There was a decisiveness in the way he carried himself as well, which she knew was crucial in his line of work.

"Well, I should be getting back home," Maegan told him.

Bridger gave a nod and tipped his hat. "See you later, Miss McCoy."

"It's Mae," she reminded him before heading down the street. She had left her horse at the livery and headed there now.

A few minutes later, an odd feeling coursed through her, and she instinctively glanced over her shoulder. A young man who looked vaguely familiar wasn't far behind her, and his eyes met hers in a rather audacious way. Telling herself she was imagining being followed, Maegan crossed the street, only to glimpse him doing the same. Weaving around a parked wagon along the side of the street, she suddenly stopped and turned around.

"Are you following me?" she asked him point-blank. Looking into his face now, she realized he was one of the young men she'd seen in the woods after leaving her Aunt Becky's house.

"What were you runnin' to the sheriff about?" he asked, moving to stand just in front of her. He and his cousin Garret happened to be riding into town when they noticed her and Sheriff Bridger talking.

Maegan wasn't intimidated at all by his thin, lanky frame and boyish face. He was probably the same age as she was. "None of your business."

"Garret Spencer has a message for you," he said.

By habit, Maegan's eyes darted to his holster, where a pair of pistols hung at his hips. Her own hand was ready to draw if she needed to. After running into Garret the other day, she'd decided she'd carry her pistol with her, albeit hidden in her trouser pocket.

"And what's that?" she asked.

"Stay away from the sheriff."

"I don't like being told what to do," she countered, not about to be pushed around. She glimpsed down the street behind him, not liking the fact that he and Garret Spencer had been watching her. "You tell Garret Spencer I'll talk to whoever I please, and I don't want any trouble."

"Well, you're askin' for it if you get on Garret's bad side."

"He's askin' for it if he gets on mine," she replied.

Pete Keller clicked his tongue and wagged his head in a sympathetic fashion. "You can't say you wasn't warned, and I pity ya if you cause trouble."

Maegan released an irritated breath. "I wasn't the one throwing rocks through my uncle's window last night or trying to set Joshua McCoy's barn on fire."

"Just mind what you're told if you know what's good for you!"

"What's your name?" Maegan asked when he started to turn away. "So, I know to avoid you whenever I can."

He smirked. "Pete Keller."

Maegan watched him saunter off, his arrogant manner still provoking her frustration. Garret Spencer seemed like the type who had others do his dirty work, and Pete Keller seemed like the sort to do it.

# Chapter Five

Alison spent the remainder of the day reviewing the articles and advertisements Harold Bell had given her to proofread for the paper. Confident she had found and corrected all the errors, she stood from the desk that Harold Bell had set up for her and walked over to where he sat at his. He was closely bent over the newspaper he was reading, adjusting his spectacles every few seconds. She sent him an empathetic look, wishing there was something that could be done for his eyesight. He was a kind soul and passionate about his work, too. His eyes were just not keeping up.

"Mr. Bell, I've read and reread the newspaper proof and made the necessary edits."

He looked up. "Very good. Just sit it right here." He tapped the only blank spot on his oak desktop, which was mostly covered with papers and some leftover crumbs from his sandwich.

They both heard the door chime as someone entered. Alison stepped out of Mr. Bell's office and was surprised to see Lyn Hummel, the woman whom her brother had told her about the other day.

"Excuse me," she said. Her voice had an unexpected high-pitched ring of sweetness to it. "I'd like to speak with someone about putting an article in the paper."

Alison heard Mr. Bell coming from behind her and watched as he stepped around her and moved toward the woman. "Mrs. Hummel, remember we spoke last week?"

"Yes, but I didn't see anything in the paper yet," she explained.

Harold Bell sighed. "That's because I didn't have any room for it, remember?" He gently laid his hand on her hunched-over shoulders. "I'm sorry to say it, Mrs. Hummel, but if you haven't found your son by now, then you really should accept the fact that he's …"

"Missing … that he's missing," she said in a voice that kindly corrected what he was going to say before he said it. "That's why I'm looking for him. He wasn't at the hospital among the wounded. And they said that he'd gone."

Harold Bell let out another sigh, pitying the woman, even though he knew the person she was looking for must be dead. "Alison, why don't you take Mrs. Hummel with you to your desk and jot down what it is she wants in the paper?" He turned his attention to the older woman. "I'm not promising I'll put it in, but if I ever have space, I may."

"Oh, thank you," she said, moving to follow Alison. Once she saw Alison had a notepad and pencil in hand, she said, "William T. Hummel is my son's name."

"And you just want me to say for someone to contact you or the newspaper office if he is located?" Alison asked.

"That's perfect," Lyn Hummel said with a smile that, for a moment, made her look younger than her eighty years. Alison thought that even the wrinkles surrounding her light-blue eyes and the other marks of aging did not detract from a sort of youthful vigor in her demeanor. Her gray hair was loosely pulled back into a bun, with frizzy pieces escaping and settling around her temples. Alison asked her for a few more details, and after they had written it up, the woman thanked her and left.

"Poor woman." Mr. Bell shook his head and walked to the door. He watched through the window as the woman moved down the street. "She's gone off her rocker."

Alison had come to stand beside him and was also watching as Lyn Hummel disappeared into the crowd. "You don't think there's any chance her son's still alive?"

"It's hard to piece together her ramblings, but it seems he went off to war, and she never saw him again. It's been over ten years. Surely, if he were alive, she'd have found him by now."

Alison felt her heart break for the unfortunate woman and was still thinking about her when she left that day. Stepping outside the newspaper office, she was surprised to see Gideon Martin. He had been leaning on the porch rail of Bell's establishment and turned readily to face her when she exited.

"Hello," she said, wondering why he was apparently waiting there for her.

"Afternoon, Alison." He tipped his hat politely and flickered a nervous smile. "I thought you might like a ride home."

"Oh. Well, that's very thoughtful." She put her bonnet on and tied the ribbon under her chin. "I would appreciate that."

His smile broadened a little upon hearing her answer, and he led her to where his buggy was waiting. "Your brother said you'd be finishing up about now."

Alison sent a glance toward the mill where Gideon and her brother worked. "Did he?" she said, more to herself than to him. She had suspected her brother was fond of Gideon with as many times as she'd heard his name pop up in conversation, but she was starting to get an inkling that Jacob was up to some matchmaking.

"How was your day?" Gideon asked after he'd helped her into his wagon. He gave the reins a little flick and directed the horses down the street.

"Just fine," she answered. "Mr. Bell is neither too talkative nor too quiet, so working with him is very easy. How about yourself?"

"I think I'm more on the quiet side."

"I meant, how was your day?" Alison replied, hiding a smile.

"Oh, it … it was good," he stuttered, feeling a little embarrassed for misunderstanding her question.

"My brother says you live a few miles outside town."

"Yes, a small farm, but I plan to grow it."

"Gideon, you like to read, don't you?" she asked, remembering that the first time she'd met him, her brother had mentioned as much.

"When I have the time."

"And do you read Bell's newspaper often?" Alison asked.

He shrugged. "Sometimes."

"Do you think it's missing anything?"

"Like what?" He glanced at her, not knowing what he was supposed to say. He was glad she was talkative so he wouldn't have to work up a conversation.

"Well, like something more entertaining. Say, for instance, an exciting fictional story column full of mystery or even a column of poetry?"

He shrugged again. "I ain't one for poetry."

Alison crossed her arms as a reflective expression crossed her face. "I think folks would enjoy a good story. Especially a story that left you in suspense, so that you would look so forward to reading the next edition in the paper that you'd be guaranteed to buy weekly!"

"I suppose folks might like that, but hard to say."

"Only one way to find out," Alison replied, her imagination already taking her a hundred miles away. She couldn't wait to get back to her room and to her notebook.

*****

$\mathcal{M}$aegan and Cody stood back to survey their work. They had spent the entire morning and afternoon cutting and pulling off the vines that covered half their uncle's cabin, as well as fixing the lopsided front door and patching other areas of the house. Maegan had nailed up a small board to cover the shattered window for now and hoped to get the glass repaired before the week's end.

A few minutes later, Cody moved to the side of the house where a pile of wood lay. He stacked the chopped pieces and then set to work chopping down the larger ones and adding them to the wood pile. Maegan spotted a ladder and placed it against the house so she could climb onto the roof to cut away some vines she and Cody had missed. Sometime later, as she was kneeling on the shingles, the sound of an approaching rider caught her attention. As the rider neared, she saw it was Sheriff Bridger.

"Need some help?" he asked, surprised to find her up on the roof.

"I'm almost done," she replied, using the back of her hand to wipe beads of sweat from her brow. Edging carefully across the roof, she found her footing near the ladder and began to climb down. Sheriff Bridger had dismounted and was holding it steady as she did.

"Is your uncle still unwell?" Sheriff Bridger asked once she was standing on the ground.

"He's getting better every day. He's resting now," she said. "Cody and I thought we'd surprise him out here with some minor improvements," she smiled.

"Looks more like major improvements from the size of that heap," Sheriff Bridger said, his gaze swinging to the pile of vines and weeds at the corner of the yard. "Are you sure it's safe for you to be on that roof, though? I could finish up what you were trying to do."

"Thanks, but it's about done, and I can manage."

"I can see that," he replied, thinking she was probably the most independent woman he'd ever met. He took notice of the board over a portion of one of the front windows. "That where the rock came through?"

Maegan nodded as she glanced at it. "Unfortunately."

"I just came from Robert Spencer's," Sheriff Bridger told her. "It's why I came by. I wanted to tell you I spoke with him, his sons, and Joe. They all acted like they had no idea what I was talking about."

Maegan folded her arms across her chest and sighed. "Since we didn't see their faces, I can't be positive it was them, but Joshua seemed pretty certain."

"I talked with him as well," the sheriff said. "He didn't actually see them either, but I'm not doubting it was them; just don't have any proof to do anything, regrettably."

"Well, thanks for looking into it anyhow, Sheriff."

"How are you and Cody settling in?" he asked next, hearing someone chopping wood and assuming it was her younger brother.

"Alright," she replied with a smile. "We didn't really know what to expect coming here, but maybe it was the Lord's timing, since our uncle needed our help."

Bridger wasn't sure what to say to that, but he liked her optimism. "Well, I should be getting back to town, but if you need anything, or if the Spencers cause any trouble, be sure to let me know."

"Thanks," Maegan said, an appreciative expression on her face. For a moment, he seemed to linger, his blue eyes holding hers. Then, with a little tip of his hat, he headed back the way he'd come. After he left, she turned back to the ladder and was about to head back up to the roof when the front door opened, and her uncle came limping out, his eyes squinting against the sun.

"What are you two doing?" he asked, his tone a combination of annoyance and curiosity.

"Just thought the house and yard could use a little cleaning up."

"You don't have to do that," he grunted, noting the sizable pile of vines nearby. His son had been on him to keep the place up and had been more than willing to help, but an argument the last time he visited had interrupted any such plans.

"Place is fine. Don't need no more cleaning outside or inside," Ben said.

"It'll be the last thing we do," Maegan assured him. "Besides, I'm sure the weeds will return once we're gone," she smiled sheepishly.

"You plannin' on leavin' then?"

Maegan wasn't sure if she imagined the hint of disappointment in his tone. "Soon as I find a place to rent for Cody and me, we'll be leaving."

"Can I use your fishing pole, Uncle Ben?" The question came from Cody as he rounded the house. "Mae said she would cook trout for supper if I caught some."

"I guess I oughta go with you and show you the best spots," he grumbled.

"You sure you're up for it?" Maegan asked.

"The stream ain't far, and we can take the wagon. Can you handle a team?" he suddenly asked Cody.

"Sure can," Cody said proudly.

Once they'd left, Maegan finished the cleaning she'd set out to do and then began to prepare for supper. A few hours later, as they sat at the table eating the trout Cody and

Uncle Ben had caught, Maegan told them she planned to make inquiries in town the next day about a place to rent. Tired from the day of work, Cody went to bed early, but as Maegan finished tidying up, her uncle lingered at the table. In the lamplight, he was reading the newspaper.

"I guess I'll head to bed, too," Maegan said a few minutes later as she hung the wet dishcloth over the back of a chair.

Her uncle didn't glance up from his paper, but as she turned to go, he said, "Cody's a fine boy, what I see."

Maegan smiled softly. "I think so, too." She could tell he was working on saying something and waited for him to go on.

"Soon, I'll be leaving for a month or more."

Maegan looked at him questioningly, waiting for him to go on.

"Every fall, I take my furs to Jefferson City and a handful of other towns in Cole County. I'll be back before winter sets in, but it don't seem right for you to have to be worrying 'bout a place to rent when this house will be empty for a while."

"That's kind, Uncle Ben."

"It's practical," he shrugged. "I was thinking you and Cody could tend to the animals so I wouldn't have to hire help."

Maegan smiled, glad it would benefit them both. "We'd be happy to do that."

"You could even stay here the winter after I get back," he surprised her by going on. "Then come spring, if you decide to stay in Millcreek longer, look for somewhere else to stay."

"That's generous, but I wouldn't want to wear out our welcome," she said, remembering what he said about being used to living alone.

His lips pursed together, and he seemed to be thinking. "You and Cody don't run your mouth like some folks I've known. It ain't been bad having you both here," he added, turning a page in the paper and lifting it slightly to cover his face.

Maegan smiled to herself, thinking her uncle had a softer heart than he had initially let on. Maybe what he needed was companionship, and maybe what they needed was to be that for him.

*****

Maegan and Cody made it to church that Sunday, their uncle declining quite emphatically when they asked him if he was going. Maegan was surprised since she knew her own father to be a God-fearing man. Her parents' love and devotion to God had left an imprint on her heart, one that had caused her to want her own relationship with the Lord from an early age. She knew that without it, she could never have lived through the grief of losing her parents. Her father used to say God gave what you needed when you needed it. She found that truer than ever in the form of the comfort that came during those lonely nights as a young girl.

Now, as she listened to Reverend Myles teaching about the Lord's faithfulness, she felt a warmth settling in her heart. Off and on, she had doubted her decision to leave her older brothers, but she felt that morning an assurance that she was in God's will. Before concluding the service, Reverend Myles announced that a fall picnic would be taking place at the Carter Ranch in a few weeks. Maegan sensed an immediate rise of excitement in the room and gathered it was an anticipated event.

After the service, the Reverend's wife, Maggie, came up and greeted her warmly, along with a woman who seemed to be a close friend named Claire Carter. Maegan was told that Claire's husband, Will, owned a large ranch outside town and that they would be hosting the picnic. Another woman named Lyddie Hall was very kind, and Maegan learned that she owned the boarding house in town.

From across the church, Alison spotted Maegan and headed toward her to say hello. A few women she had met on previous visits to Millcreek noticed her and pulled her into conversation.

"Do you know anything about that woman talking to Lyddie Hall?" one of the ladies asked Alison.

"Oh yes, her name is Maegan McCoy," Alison replied. "She and her brother have just moved here."

"Did you ever see a woman wear trousers to church?" one of the ladies said, sending Maegan a look of disapproval.

"Disgraceful," said the first woman who had spoken.

"Irreverent is what I'd call it," another woman remarked.

"I think the Lord is more offended by gossip and hasty judgment than he is about what someone wears to church," Alison said. She paused long enough to see their mirrored expressions of shock and then said, "Excuse me, ladies," and moved away.

Maegan pretended to be listening to what Lyddie Hall was saying, but she could feel her cheeks redden a bit with embarrassment as she overheard what the ladies behind her were discussing.

Maegan recognized Alison's voice among them and was grateful for her backing. Upon meeting her and noting the fashionable way she dressed and learning that she was from the city, Maegan had first thought Alison might be stuck up. Maegan was glad her assessment had been wrong.

A few minutes later, as Maegan moved outside, she noticed the General Store owner talking with a young woman. Their conversation quickly sparked her interest.

"Hard to believe school has started up again already," Tom Maison was saying. "Seems the summer gets shorter every year."

"Isn't it the truth?" the woman replied. "But I don't mind. I was eager for school to start to see all the children again," she smiled.

Maegan waited until they had finished their conversation and then went over to Tom Maison.

"Was that Millcreek's school teacher?" Maegan asked him.

He nodded. "And a real fine one, too."

Maegan caught up with the woman before she met her husband at their wagon. "Excuse me." Maegan got her attention and waited for her to turn around. "You're the schoolteacher, right?"

The woman nodded. "My name's Sylvia Cooper. You are?"

"Maegan McCoy." Maegan noticed the way her stomach protruded under her skirt, divulging that she was a few months pregnant. "I just moved to Millcreek with my brother," Maegan told her. "He's twelve and hasn't had official schooling, but I've taught him how to read and write, and he knows how to figure."

"That's good," Sylvia Cooper said in an encouraging tone. "I'd be thrilled to have him join our class."

"Thank you. I ugh …" Maegan bit her lip uncertainly. "… don't know if he'll be on the right level for his age."

"Not to worry at all. It sounds like he's off to a good start. I'm sure if he's behind on anything, we can get him caught up."

Maegan released a sigh of relief, glad to know her brother would have such a devoted teacher. She knew Cody wouldn't take to the idea of going to school, but she hoped in time, he would come to appreciate the privilege of getting a good education.

*****

The following morning, Maegan was cooking hotcakes for breakfast and trying to convince Cody that going to school would be a positive experience. After some pushback, Cody finally agreed to go. Maegan drove him to school, and just as they reached the schoolyard, the bell finished ringing. Cody thought the sound somewhat intimidating and suddenly felt his stomach knot. He didn't want the younger kids to know more than he did. What if the teacher called on him to answer a question that he had no answer to?

His nerves only increased when he stepped inside the schoolhouse and saw everyone already in their seats. The teacher was facing the blackboard at the front of the room. Cody forced himself to walk up to her desk, and she turned around just as he reached it.

"Oh, good morning," Sylvia Cooper greeted, a smile in her eyes.

"My name's Cody McCoy," he said quietly. "My sister said she talked to you."

"Oh yes. I was expecting you." She turned her gaze to the classroom. "Class, this is Cody McCoy. Please make him feel welcome. Why don't you choose a seat?" she said to Cody. "We're just about to begin."

Cody thought the room seemed much larger as he looked at everyone from the front. Almost right away, he spotted the girl whom he'd stepped in to help the day after they'd arrived in Millcreek. She was sitting alone and had space beside her, but then he noticed an empty seat in the back and quickly chose that one. He felt better once he had reached his seat and tried to ignore the glances the other kids were sending in his direction.

"Okay, class, we're going to start with …"

The teacher's opening words were lost on him once he realized the boy from the fight was in the seat just a few feet away, glaring at him with a scowl that would frighten even the bravest of kids. Cody averted his gaze and pretended not to notice him, and finally, the kid turned back around. The teacher came by a few minutes later and laid a slate and a piece of chalk in front of him. "Cody, why don't you write out some of the words you know so I can get an idea of how much you've learned."

Cody appreciated that she said it quietly. He nodded his response and then did as she asked. There were some bigger words he remembered from the books his sister had taught him to read. He wrote them on the slate until he ran out of space and then waited for the teacher to come back around.

"My goodness," she smiled encouragingly. "You've got quite a vocabulary. Here, take this and start studying the words from lesson twenty."

Cody took the book she offered him, feeling a twinge of relief and pride at her words. In the next hour, Mrs. Cooper began an arithmetic lesson, writing various arithmetic problems on the board, separated in columns by grade. Cody was thankful his sister had also taught him how to multiply and divide, as every problem on the board seemed easy to him. He was looking forward to turning his slate in to the teacher at the end of the lesson.

Around noon, she announced it was recess and lunch, and Cody watched as the kids stood excitedly and headed past him toward the door. He stood slowly, reaching under the desk where he'd sat the lunch pail his sister had given him. He was the last one out and sat on the school steps to eat his lunch. He could hear the other children talking and laughing in the schoolyard, but he wasn't about to join any of their groups, at least not yet.

"Your name's Cody, right?"

Cody glanced up at the sound of the voice and saw the girl from the fight. He tried to remember her name but couldn't. "Yeah," he finally answered.

"You probably remember me from the other day. My name's Lilly." She twisted one of her blonde braids around her finger and smiled softly. "Sorry about gettin' you mixed up in that fight."

"It wasn't your fault," he said with a shrug, going back to his half-eaten apple.

"There's not many older kids," she told him, coming to take a seat on the step just below his. "I'll be ten next summer, but Mrs. Cooper has me doing some of the 5th grade work now," she told him proudly.

Cody thought she looked younger than nine, but it really didn't make any difference to him. She chattered on about this and that until the teacher appeared, calling everyone back in. The next few hours went quickly, and he was surprised that it was time to leave already when the teacher dismissed them. She called him forward as the others were leaving and handed him a few books. "These are for you to take home each day so you can study what we work on in class."

He thanked her before taking them and heading outside. As he reached the bottom step, he noticed Lilly was waiting there for him. "Which way are you headed?" she asked cheerfully.

"Down that way," he pointed toward a road that branched away from the school.

"Me too. We can walk together until I have to turn off for my place."

Cody fell into step beside her, not really in the mood to talk but not minding her company. She asked a lot of questions, but she seemed content with his short answers. They hadn't gone far when suddenly Jeb stepped out from behind a tree by the side of the dirt road. He crossed his hands in front of his chest and attempted to block their path.

"Now I know why I didn't like you," he said, looking at Cody. "You're a McCoy!"

Cody wasn't sure what he meant, but he took a steady breath and just kept walking. As he got closer, Jeb moved toward him and gave Cody's shoulder a hard shove. "I can lick you in a fight any day of the week!"

"I don't want trouble," Cody told him, purposely avoiding eye contact. Jeb was at least two inches taller and thicker, too. Although smaller, Cody knew he could hold his own, but he wasn't in a rush to get another black eye.

"What are you doing here, anyway?" Jeb asked, shoving him again. "Don't you know you ain't welcome 'round here?"

"Stop it, Jeb Spencer!" Lilly said when Jeb pulled Cody's hat off his head and threw it to the ground. The name Spencer made Cody remember what his sister Maegan had said about avoiding anyone with that name ... now he knew why.

"Or what?" Jeb snapped at Lilly. "You're so scrawny, a breeze could finish you off."

Lilly pursed her lips together in anger, her brown eyes indignant. She was about to say something back when the sound of an approaching wagon distracted them. Lilly sighed with relief as she waved to the man driving the wagon. "It's my pa!" she said.

"You jest stay away from me!" Jeb warned Cody, purposely knocking into him with his shoulder as he moved past him and disappeared into the woods.

"I was just coming from town and thought I might catch up to you," Reverend Myles said cheerfully to his daughter as he slowed his team of horses on the road. "Wanna jump in?"

"Oh, Pa, what perfect timing!" she exclaimed, and then, looking at Cody, she said. "C'mon, we'll give you a ride."

"I don't mind walkin'," Cody told her, but he found himself following her and climbing up into the back of the wagon.

"Good to see you again, Cody," Reverend Myles said as he glanced over his shoulder and sent Cody a smile. "How are you and your sister settling in?" Reverend Myles asked him as he guided his horses down the road.

"Just fine."

"Good. We'll have to have you two over for supper some-time soon. I know my sister Alison was grateful for your help the day you all arrived. Lilly said you were of assistance to her, too, the other day."

Cody nodded, not knowing what else to say. He decided he liked Reverend Myles and thought his friendly banter reminded him a lot of Lilly. When they reached a fork in the road, he slowed the wagon to let him off.

"Bye, Cody!" Lilly called as they pulled away. "See you in school tomorrow!"

# Chapter Six

"Well, Cody. How do you like school so far?" Maegan asked him as she drove him to school a week later in their uncle's wagon.

Cody shrugged. "It's not bad, I guess. Except for Jeb Spencer! He picks a fight with me every other day!" Cody didn't tell her that twice they'd gotten into a small brawl in the schoolyard, and an older kid had to break it up both times. "I can't believe that kid is my cousin!" he added.

"Just try and avoid him when you can," Maegan suggested with a little sigh. "I wish things were different."

After she had dropped him off, she went into town and ordered a new glass pane for her uncle's window. On the way back, before she reached her uncle's house, something caught her attention: a lone, saddled horse that seemed to be roaming aimlessly without a rider. Maegan led her wagon toward the horse and then shifted the brake and jumped off the seat. She clicked her tongue to get the horse's attention and then talked softly to her as she edged closer. The horse was calm and let Maegan lead her back to the wagon, where she secured her reins to it. Maegan returned to where she'd found the horse, looking around for a sign of a rider. She left the road and walked for a few minutes in the field.

Suddenly, she saw what appeared to be a man lying half-hidden in the tall prairie grass. Maegan quickly went to him and rolled the man over to his back. She gasped when she realized it was her cousin, Joshua. Blood oozed down his face, and he was groaning slightly as he appeared to be awakening from a previously unconscious state. There was a nasty gash to his head and bruises that were already causing his face to swell.

"Joshua," Maegan said, gently lifting his head off the ground. "Can you hear me?"

He continued to groan and then opened his eyes. A moment later, he very slowly attempted to push himself to a sitting position.

"I've got your pa's wagon," she told him. "I'll bring it closer and then help you get to it," she said. Minutes later, she had brought the wagon close to him and then proceeded to help him in.

She drove the wagon back to the road, amazed at her good fortune when she spotted Doc Fletcher's buggy coming down the road toward them. Once close enough, she told him about her cousin, who was lying motionless in the bed of the wagon. The doctor readily agreed to follow her back to her uncle's.

Ben McCoy was in the yard when they pulled up. "Joshua's been in some kind of accident," Maegan told him, noticing he rushed to the back of the wagon at her words.

"I'll help you get him inside," Doc Fletcher said. He and Ben moved the young man into the house and onto Ben's bed.

"I just found him like this, not far off the road," Maegan told them. She watched as her uncle sprang into action, grabbing a bucket of water and some clean rags from the cupboard. Even his limp couldn't deter his haste.

"Looks like someone ripped into him pretty good," the doctor said as he gently cleaned the blood with the wet rags Ben was handing him. A few minutes later, Joshua began to groan, and then he reached his left arm over to his ribs and winced. "I think my ribs are broken," he whispered.

"What happened, son?" Ben asked from where he stood just beside the doctor.

"Garret and Bobby Spencer," he mumbled before sucking in a breath of air against the pain of the doctor examining his ribs. "And Pete Keller," he added.

"They done this to you?" Ben asked.

"He really needs to rest," the doctor said. "We can find out the details later. Maegan, can you hand me my bag?"

Maegan brought it to the doctor and then watched as her uncle stepped back, a fiery look in his eyes. He paced the floor, coming over every few minutes to check on Joshua. After Joshua was cleaned up and his ribs wrapped securely with a bandage, the doctor headed to the door. "I'll be back tomorrow to check on him."

For the rest of the afternoon, Ben kept a close eye on his son, checking on him often, Maegan noticed. Maegan helped where she could and then went to get Cody from school. On the way home, she explained what had happened, but when Cody saw Joshua, he thought it looked a lot worse than she had described.

"The Spencers have gone too far!" Ben said. "I'm done with the lot of 'em!"

"Why would they hurt Joshua?" Maegan asked.

"They wanna hurt my son like I hurt Joe's!" Ben hollered, but Maegan knew his raised voice wasn't directed at her. He began pacing the cabin, a ferocious look on his face that frightened her a little. "This just ain't right, and I'm not gonna stand by another day and let it go on!"

On those words, Ben grabbed his rifle from over the mantle along with a box of bullets. A moment later, he was limping to the door and heading outside.

"Uncle Ben, wait!" Maegan followed him and tried to talk him down from his anger, but he headed to the barn and began saddling his horse.

"What are you going to do?" she asked.

"What I should have done years ago. End this!"

Maegan watched helplessly as he rode out of the yard. She ran back to the house. "Cody! I'm going with Uncle Ben. You stay here and look after Joshua."

About ten minutes after she left, Cody couldn't shake his uneasiness. He checked on Joshua, who seemed to be sleeping, and then headed outside to get his horse. He needed to get the sheriff before anything bad happened to Maegan or Uncle Ben.

*****

Ben McCoy reined in his horse just outside Joe Spencer's door, dust rising in a cloud around him. "Joe Spencer!" he yelled.

Not a minute later, the front door opened, and Joe Spencer came out, a fierce look on his face at the sight of Ben. "What do you want?" He walked out into the yard, stopping just feet away from Ben as he dismounted.

"I want you to let this go! None of this will bring back Thomas!"

Joe closed the space between them and pushed Ben hard against the chest. "Don't you dare say his name!"

"The war's been over for a long time, Joe! A lot of things happened that I'd take back if I could!"

"You're the one keepin' it going!" Joe hollered at him. "Look at my barn!"

For the first time, Ben noticed the front left corner of the barn bore the damage of a fire.

"Your boy was here yesterday tryin' to set fire to my barn!"

"That's bosh, and you know it!" Ben took an angry step toward him. "Joshua would never do that! But I can't say the same for your nephews! They're the ones startin' fires! And maybe the ones who poisoned my well! Or did you do that yourself?"

"Jeb saw Joshua here yesterday … setting fire to it!" Joe insisted. "Lucky for him, we put it out when we did, or your boy would've gotten more than a thrashin'!"

"You're a fool if you believe Joshua would do that!"

"You callin' my son a liar?" Joe swung a punch, which Ben sidestepped to avoid.

"Your nephews tore my son up, and I ain't gonna stand by for this any longer!" Ben said as he delivered a solid punch to Joe's gut, which sent the man into more of a rage. After doubling over for a moment, he regained his strength and came at Ben with his fists clenched.

"Joe! Stop it!" Becky screamed as she appeared in the doorway. Their son, Jeb, was just behind her and took off for his Uncle Robert's house.

This was the scene that Maegan rode up to. She jumped down and moved closer. There wasn't anything she or Becky could do. The men ended up on the ground, one man on top laying on punches and then the other gaining the upper hand. It seemed to go on forever. And then, Robert Spencer rode into the yard with his son Bobby and then Jeb also trailing behind.

Maegan was appalled when Robert stepped in, not to break up the fight but also to ram his fists into her uncle. He and his brother continued to land punches until Maegan raised her pistol and fired into the air.

"Stop it!" she screamed. Finally, the men quit, their eyes looking for where the gunfire had come from. "If you don't leave him be, I'll shoot both of ya!" she threatened Joe and his brother.

They clearly didn't look like they believed her, and when Joe kicked his boot into her uncle's side, she aimed at his hat and sent it flying off his head. Then she aimed at Robert's and did the same. The accuracy of her aim was enough for them to take her seriously. Becky rushed to her brother, kneeling beside him and pressing a cloth to his bleeding face. Her husband reached down and grabbed her arm, pulling her up to her feet in one swift, rough movement.

"Leave him be!" he ordered her.

Maegan fired at the fence post just behind him, the bullet grazing his shirt sleeve. "She'll do as she pleases!" Maegan told him. Startled, Joe let go of his wife, glaring at Maegan. "No one tells me what to do, especially not on my property!" But he knew he was at a disadvantage, at least for now.

Maegan slowly lowered her weapon but kept a tight grip on it. Just then, someone grabbed her from behind and ripped the weapon out of her hand. She kicked in resistance as she felt herself firmly being held against her will. She knew without seeing his face it was Robert's son, Garret. He must have sneaked around the back of the house.

"Let go of me!" she demanded, struggling against Garret's hold on her. She felt almost suffocated as his arm tightened around her waist.

"You're a real spitfire!" he said, his tone sounding amused. "Go ahead, Pa! She ain't a threat no more."

"Get back to the house!" Joe ordered his wife just before he grabbed one of Ben's arms and Robert grabbed the other. They started to drag him toward the barn when suddenly their attention was drawn to the rider who had just charged into the yard.

"Doesn't seem like a fair fight!" Sheriff Bridger called from his horse. "Two against one?"

"Weren't us who started it!" Joe spat back. "Ben McCoy come to my property lookin' for a fight, and he got one!"

"Well, the fight's over!" Sheriff Bridger told them. He dismounted and walked towards them, but not before stopping in front of Garret. "Let her go." He said, his command backed by his unwavering gaze and his hand resting on his holster.

Garret hesitated and then, very slowly, loosened his hands on her.

"And give her back her weapon," Bridger added.

Maegan shook free of his hold, hating the way his hands lingered on her waist. Garret reluctantly handed the gun back to her. Sliding the pistol back into her pocket, Maegan picked up her hat from where it had fallen during the struggle and then went quickly to her uncle. The sheriff was already trying to get him to his feet, and Maegan helped by supporting his other side. They helped him to his horse, which he struggled to mount even with their help.

"Next one of you I find in a fight is gonna end up in a cell," Bridger promised them.

"If you're taking sides with the McCoys, you're gonna find yourself in a heap of trouble, Sheriff."

The threat had come from Garret Spencer and didn't unnerve Sheriff Bridger in the slightest. "I don't want any more trouble from you boys!" he said firmly, his gaze moving from Garret to Robert and then ending on Joe.

"Get off my land!" Joe said through clenched teeth.

Maegan was glad to, although she hated to think of her aunt left with such a man. She rode close to her uncle, who was leaning over his horse's neck, while the sheriff held the reins to direct him. When they reached Ben's house, it was growing dark. Cody came running out, relieved to see them all.

Ben managed to walk to the house, with Maegan and the sheriff helping him. Once inside, he collapsed onto one of the chairs. Maegan began cleaning up his cuts and bandaging his wounds. "You best get into bed," she said when she'd finished.

"I think it's time I tell you what this is all about."

Maegan was surprised to hear him say it. Sheriff Bridger made a move toward the door, but Ben looked up at him, "I think you should hear this too, Sheriff."

Bridger took the seat opposite Ben, and Maegan and Cody also sat at the table. "You sure you're up to this?" Maegan asked him with concern.

"I was the first one out of all of us to enlist, but I joined the Union," Ben started right in, ignoring her question. "I knew the Spencers' sympathy lied with the Confederacy, but I knew which side I wanted to fight for. Every time I fired a shot, I prayed to God that Becky's husband and his family weren't on the receiving end. Toward the end of the war, I was made a guard at Myrtle Street Prison. We were ordered to shoot any rebel prisoners that tried to escape. Joe and his son, Thomas, were there at the time I was, and when Thomas tried to escape, my superior ordered me to shoot." Ben paused, his face clouding with the memory. "I didn't know it was Becky's boy." His voice caught on the words and trembled slightly. "I was just following orders."

Maegan felt her eyes fill with tears as she heard the emotion in her uncle's voice. "You must have felt horrible when you found out," she whispered empathetically.

"No words to describe it. Once I realized it was him, I went for the doctor, but … it was too late. Joe was with him when he breathed his last."

Bridger let out a heavy sigh at the new realization of what was at the core of Joe's rage. For a moment, the room was silent.

"Joe's got to know you didn't mean it," Bridger said quietly.

"He wouldn't believe me … that I didn't know it was Thomas."

"But Aunt Becky doesn't hate you for it," Maegan said.

"I don't know why she don't," Ben said, his eyes burning with tears.

"So, Joe and his family are still holding that against you," Bridger said.

"That and the fact that I fought with the North. There's more … my late wife was Joe and Robert's sister. It seemed a fine thing that Joe and Becky took up when Eliza and I got married. Believe it or not, there was a time when we were all friends." He paused, feeling like the memory of those days was another life.

"When Joshua was a boy, I …" Uncle Ben took in a steadying breath before continuing, "I flipped our wagon during a storm. Eliza was killed, and they still blame me for it. And rightly so," he added quietly.

Maegan felt like her heart was going to burst with anguish for her uncle and what he had endured. To feel the guilt of two lost lives was too much for anyone to bear.

"I was a terrible, neglectful father in my grief," Ben told them. "I drank for years after Eliza was gone and drank after the war, which eventually drove Joshua away. Poor kid needed me, and I failed him miserably." On these words, he lowered his head. "That's why they hate me and want to cause me grief. I don't know what foolishness Joe was saying today about Joshua setting fire to their barn … they make things up and just look for more reasons to justify a hatred that's already justified."

"But it's not justified," Maegan said in his defense. "I understand their right to feeling pain at losing their sister and Joe's son, but they have to see it pains you just as much. You didn't mean for any of this to happen. Not forgiving you is just bringing them more hurt." She hesitated a moment and then added, "And you not forgiving yourself is only bringing more hurt to you, too, Uncle Ben."

Ben McCoy didn't say anything for a moment, but his gaze flickered up to Maegan just long enough for her to see there were tears in his eyes. He struggled to stand up and began to limp toward the door. "I'm going to sleep in the barn tonight," he said.

"I'll help you get there," Cody offered as he met his uncle at the door.

Maegan watched as they went, her heart breaking for him. She looked over to Sheriff Bridger, who was also coming to his feet, a thoughtful expression on his face. "I guess you weren't expecting all this when you came to visit your uncle. That's a lot of past for him to work through."

"I pray he can work through it," Maegan said quietly, meaning it with all her heart. "Seems such a waste. Not only have they all lost Thomas and Eliza, but they've lost each other as well. I wish there was something I could do."

"I think you just being here with your uncle will do him good."

Maegan's eyes found his. "Do you really think so?"

The uncertainty in her expressive eyes suddenly made him want to reassure her. "Yes, I do."

Maegan appreciated the encouragement and smiled slightly. "Thanks for your help today," she said as she stood and followed him to the door.

Bridger turned to face her. "Are you okay?" The memory of Garret manhandling her still irked him.

Maegan was surprised that he asked. "Yes, I'm fine."

Bridger's eyes lingered on her face a moment longer as if to read if she was telling the truth. "You sure?" he asked again.

"Guess I'm no stranger to that kind of thing," she shrugged. She and her brothers had been in some dangerous scrapes before.

Her words made Bridger wonder just what sort of life she had lived until now. "Well, let me know if you need anything."

Maegan nodded, appreciating his friendship. After he had left, she checked on Joshua one more time, changing some of his dressings before heading to bed.

In his father's bed, Joshua lay wide awake, staring at the ceiling. Even though in the next room, he was in earshot of all his pa had shared. Joshua's body still ached from his run-in with Pete Keller and the Spencer boys, but it was the stirring in his heart for his father that kept him awake. He knew about the past, but he'd never heard his pa tell it in that way nor heard him so broken over it. For the first time, Joshua could feel the thick barrier of bitterness he kept intact begin to dissolve slowly.

*****

Joshua stayed with them for several days until his ribs had healed enough to travel home.

Fortunately, they were just badly bruised and not broken. Several days after he'd gone, Maegan rode out to see how he was doing. She was surprised when her Aunt Becky opened the door.

"Hello, Maegan," she greeted kindly as Maegan entered the house. A quick glance of the room told her Joshua was better at keeping house than his father.

"I wasn't expecting to see you here," Maegan told her as

she met her hug and followed her to the table where Joshua was sitting.

"I wanted to see how Joshua was getting on," Becky said, sending what Maegan thought was a motherly smile in Joshua's direction.

"I brought some supper for you," Maegan said. "So, I guess you're getting spoiled," she added when she noticed some baked goods that Becky had brought sitting on the table.

"Thank you," Joshua replied sincerely as he took the carefully wrapped tray of biscuits and fried chicken that Maegan handed him. "My pa must be grateful to have cookin' like this," he added with a smile.

"You're welcome to join us anytime," Maegan said, hoping she wasn't speaking out of turn. She noticed that Uncle Ben and Joshua seemed to be conversing more easily while he was staying with them.

"How is Ben?" Becky asked Maegan. "I'm still angry at Joe and Robert for what they did to him. If Robert's wife was still alive, she'd be so ashamed of him."

"He's mending," Maegan assured her.

"Can't believe he went to Uncle Joe's," Joshua said with a heavy sigh. His words to his father a few weeks ago, insisting that he do something about the Spencers, now returned to him as guilt. "He should have known better than to go alone."

"It's because he loves you," Becky said what Maegan was thinking. "It's hard for a father to stand by and see harm come to his son. That's why you and your pa need to work out anything between you while you both still have life on this earth to do so."

Her words hit hard, considering what had happened to her own son. Joshua nodded slightly. "I promise I'll try, Aunt Becky."

"Good." She smiled gently and then turned to Maegan.

"I should be going. Take care, Maegan." She hugged her and then slipped out the door.

"Shame Joe's the way he is," Joshua said after she'd gone. "Aunt Becky don't deserve it."

"Was Uncle Joe always this way?" Maegan asked.

"No. Losing Thomas and my ma changed him … and the war didn't help. I was around thirteen when my pa joined the Union. Aunt Becky took me in those four years he was gone."

Her aunt's motherly concern made sense now to Maegan. She reasoned Joshua must feel more like a son to her than a nephew after spending all that time together. Compassion for her cousin filled her heart when she thought about Joshua not having his father in his life for four years on top of losing his mother earlier in life.

"Losing my ma was hard enough for all of us, and it sure didn't help the family to be on divided sides during the war. I heard my pa tell you about what happened to Thomas. That was the final blow."

"It's so sad," Maegan said. "If only Uncle Joe would forgive your pa, they would both be able to heal from the past."

"Don't seem likely to happen," Joshua told her.

"Well, just as I'm sure Aunt Becky is … I'm praying every day for this feuding to end."

"I hate to be the one to break it to you, but even if there is a God up there, he ain't bothering himself with our mess. If he cared that much, he wouldn't have let all this happen in the first place."

"God grieves over our sorrow as much or even more than we do," she told him gently but with conviction.

"Then why does he allow it?"

Maegan saw a longing in her cousin's eyes and knew he really wanted an answer to that question. "From the beginning, he didn't want death to be a part of the equation, Joshua. It was disobedience that brought sin and death into this world. God's the one who made a way back to what life was really meant to be."

Joshua was rather stunned by her answer, mostly because it seemed to make sense to him. At a loss for what to say amid unfamiliar feelings, he was quiet a moment and then said, "Either way, praying ain't gonna change all this."

"I wouldn't be so sure about that," she told him.

Joshua chuckled slightly. "Tell you what, if Uncle Joe and my pa become friends again, then I'll believe prayin' is worth its time."

As Maegan headed home later, she couldn't help but hear Joshua's words echoing in her head. It was almost a challenge, she thought. She wanted him to know that God was real and that he cared exceedingly more than Joshua knew. "*Alright, Lord,*" she prayed. "*This is just one more reason to work a miracle in this family by putting this fighting to an end. Please, God … show Joshua just how real you are!*"

*****

Cody arrived at school the next morning, and as he tethered his horse, he spotted Jeb Spencer. The older kid was talking with a group of others but promptly left the group when he saw Cody.

"Hey! McCoy!"

Cody let out a sigh as he turned to face the boy. He wasn't in the mood for the older boy's teasing. "What do you want?" Cody asked.

"Some of us are headin' over to the gorge after school. You wanna come?"

Cody looked at him suspiciously.

"It's okay if you're too yella."

"Why would I be afraid of a gorge?"

"We're gonna stop by Billy Turner's house," he said as if Cody should know who that was.

"So, what?" Cody replied.

"You'll see," Jeb said, a smirk on his face.

After school, Cody found himself tagging along with Jeb and two other boys. The ride out to the gorge took nearly thirty minutes, but Cody noticed that instead of climbing down it, they rode around the steep ravine and reined in their horses in a patch of woods. Jeb dismounted first, followed by the others.

"His house is just through these woods," Jeb said.

"You said that last time," one of the boys said. "We never saw nobody."

"He wasn't home last time," Jeb said. "I'm sure we'll catch a glimpse of him this time. He looks like the devil himself!"

"Does he really not have a face?" the other boy asked, stepping over a log as he followed with the others.

"He doesn't have a face, and he's only got one arm!" Jeb said. "Ain't hardly anyone ever seen him. He never comes to town because he knows folks will holler at the sight of him!"

"Then how'd you know about him?" Cody asked skeptically.

"'Cuz my pa sold him this land when he moved here," Jeb said. "My cousin, Garret, told me all about him!"

"Have you ever seen him?" one of the boys asked Jeb.

Jeb suddenly held up his hand. "Shh, we'll have to be quiet from here." A house had just come into view, and Jeb ducked back behind a tree, the other boys following suit. "We can't let him see us. He's got a temper as ugly as his face, and I heard he'll kill anyone who steps foot on his property."

"What!" one of the boys whispered emphatically. "Then what are we doin' here!"

"He ain't gonna kill anyone," Cody assured him, knowing Jeb must be exaggerating. Deep down, though, he wasn't too sure.

"Go knock on the door," Jeb suddenly dared Cody.

"Why me?" Cody asked.

"'Cuz you're the most yellow-bellied. This'll prove you ain't a coward."

"This is your idea," Cody came back at him. "You go and knock on the door!"

"Alright, but you gotta come with me," Jeb said.

Cody reluctantly agreed as he stepped out from behind the tree and walked with Jeb into the yard. Suddenly, one of the boys pushed him to the ground, and the next thing he knew, Jeb was sitting on him, pulling his hands behind his back.

"What in heck are you doin'?" Cody screamed, struggling as the boys worked together to tie his hands behind his back.

"Get to your feet!" Jeb ordered him.

Awkwardly, Cody managed to stand up, wiggling his arms to try to break free from the rope. He saw the boys were laughing, and he chided himself for coming along. He winced in pain when Jeb grabbed the excess rope and began pulling him toward the house. "Knock it off, Jeb!" Cody hollered at him.

"Shh, you'll wake the devil!" Jeb told him, leading him to a tree that stood alone in the yard, just a few feet from the house.

To his horror, Cody realized Jeb was tying him to the tree. The other boys weren't too far off but remained hiding behind some brush. Laughing, Jeb stepped back. "Good luck gettin' out of that!" He said before jetting back toward the woods.

"Get back here!" Cody called, glancing nervously toward the house. But Jeb and the other boys ran off the way they'd come, leaving him alone. Cody felt like a fool for getting tricked. He knew they were having a good laugh at his expense and that he'd probably never hear the end of it … if he survived, that was. He sent another worried look toward the house, remembering what Jeb had said about the man who lived there. Surely, the man wouldn't really kill him for trespassing.

Cody tried to wiggle his hands free from the rope, but even after several minutes, the knots wouldn't loosen. He suddenly heard an approaching horse. Fighting panic, Cody waited and tried to talk himself down from the fear rising in his chest. A man who could have been no other than Billy Turner rode into the yard. Seeing Cody strapped to the tree, he glanced around, expecting to see others. Dismounting his horse, Billy Turner walked toward Cody.

Even before the man came close, Cody could see he was missing an arm and that his face was severely deformed. Scars ran in several directions, standing out over his discolored skin. One side of his face was notably worse, with one of his eyebrows appearing to have been singed clean off.

"What are you doing tied to my tree?"

Cody knew it looked ridiculous. "I was tricked," he told him.

"Obviously," the man replied, pulling out a sheath knife from his pocket and going to the ropes.

Cody could hear the knife cut through them and, a moment later, felt his wrists free. Rubbing them, he looked up at the man. "Thanks, mister."

"You and your friends comin' to spy on me?" Billy Turner asked next.

"They aren't my friends," Cody said, thinking immediately that Jeb had exaggerated this man's temper. Billy Turner didn't seem mean enough to hurt a fly. "Sorry for trespassing," Cody said next.

Just then, their attention shifted to the corner of the house where a large cow was making its way across the yard.

"Dagburnit!" Billy Turner said, moving toward the animal. "How'd you get loose again!"

Cody could have left, could have run off toward the woods to where he hoped his horse still was, but for some reason, he stayed. He watched as Billy tried to steer the cow toward a fenced-in pasture that was behind the house. Cody followed a few feet behind and noticed that a portion of the fence was down. He also noticed that Billy was having a difficult time, as the cow started running in the opposite direction.

"I'll head her off!" Cody said as he ran to the left and tried to block the opening between the house and the barn. Keeping his arms spread wide, Cody moved in whichever direction the cow tried to go. Finally, he succeeded in making the animal turn around and head through the opening in the fence that he'd come out of. Once the cow was in the pasture, Billy leaned over and picked up the broken fence railing. With only one arm, he was limited in what he could do and began trying to maneuver the board to block the opening.

"Here, I can help," Cody offered as he lifted the other end of the board and helped him rig up a temporary solution. "Looks like it'll need to be replaced," he said.

"I know," Billy Turner said in a tone that told Cody this wasn't the first time this had happened. "Thanks for your help, kid."

"I've worked on a farm and helped my brothers my whole life. I can repair this fence in no time if you want."

Billy opened his mouth to object, but knowing it would take this able-bodied boy half the time it would take him, he changed his mind. "I'll pay you to fix it," he said.

"Great! I'll do it now."

"Tools are in the barn. I'll be in the house. Just come by when you're done."

"Sure thing," Cody replied.

Billy Turner headed to his house but watched Cody from the window. Even from a distance, Billy could tell he was doing a good job. It was an hour later, and Billy had supper on the stove when Cody knocked on the door.

"I'm all finished, sir."

Billy opened the door wider for Cody to enter and then went toward a canister that sat on a nearby shelf. Lifting the lid, he reached in and pulled out some coins. He dropped them into Cody's hand. "Thanks, kid," was all he said. He then noticed Cody was eyeing one of the whittled creations he had lying on the table.

"Did you make that?" Cody asked curiously. He liked to whittle himself and couldn't help but admire the cross necklace that had small engravings skillfully etched. How the man did it with only one arm was even more admirable.

"I did," the man replied. "A long time ago."

"I do some whittling myself," Cody told him, "but nothing this good."

"Go ahead and take it," he surprised Cody by saying.

"Oh, I couldn't."

"Go on. I have hundreds. This is one of my better ones since it was made before …" He hesitated to finish his sentence. "Just take it."

Cody reached for the wooden cross that was attached to a thin strip of rawhide. "Thank you, sir," he said.

"You got a way home?" Billy Turner asked.

"My horse was tied up in the woods behind your house."

"Best get goin', then; it's gettin' late."

"Yes, sir."

Billy Turner watched from the window until Cody was

out of sight, and when he didn't return, he assumed he had found his horse. He chuckled to himself when he thought of the scene he had ridden up to. The kid had clearly been the target of mischief. Billy sighed as he sank into a chair at the table and picked up a wooden cross similar to the one that he had given Cody. Staring at it, he thought about his own childhood with fondness, and then his thoughts led him to more recent years, the latter bringing little joy. He glanced around his empty cabin, feeling a familiar ache in his heart. Then, as the lonely years had trained him to do, he pushed his despondent feelings aside and went back to existing.

*****

"Where have you been? It's supper time," Maegan said to Cody when he entered her uncle's cabin that evening.

"Some of the kids asked me to hang out after school."

"Next time, let me know. I was worried."

"Sorry," Cody apologized. "I ain't a baby, ya know," he added.

"I didn't say you were, but with what happened to Joshua the other day, I got nervous when you didn't come back."

Cody decided to leave out what had really happened since it would just cause his sister to worry even more, and he knew better than to trust Jeb ever again.

Later that night, Maegan had just fallen asleep when a noise awakened her. She sat up in bed, listening and realizing it sounded like someone was pacing; more specifically, it sounded like her uncle's distinct limp. Maegan went to her door and cracked it slightly, the glow of lamplight on the kitchen table illuminating her uncle as he moved about the room. She noticed he was holding a bottle and, after a moment, slumped into a chair by the table.

Maegan walked quietly toward him, unnoticed until she spoke. "Uncle Ben? Are you alright?"

He glanced up at her, and she saw his eyes were red and watery. He was looking right at her but didn't seem to really acknowledge she was there. Wordlessly, he took a drink from the bottle and then just stared into the lamplight.

"Uncle Ben?" she probed again, her voice even quieter than before. "Is something wrong?"

"I hate October eighteenth," he mumbled. "And it comes back every year." He let out a heavy sigh.

"What's wrong with October eighteenth?" Maegan asked as she sat in the chair opposite him.

"Worst day of my life."

Understanding dawned on Maegan. "Is that when … when your wife died?" she whispered.

"It's when I killed her," he answered, and Maegan could see that tears were starting to escape down his whiskered cheeks. "I should have had her walk down that hill," he said with a hazy look in his eyes as if remembering the very moment.

"Uncle Ben, it was an accident. Don't torture yourself like this."

"She was crying for near an hour, but I couldn't get to her," he said. "After the wagon flipped, my leg was pinned under it, and I couldn't get to her. I enlisted in the army hoping a Confederate bullet would end all this," his voice trembled as a small sob shook his shoulders.

Maegan's heart broke for him, imagining the scene he described and feeling his despair at being trapped under his wagon while he desperately wanted to get to his wife. Maegan stood and went to her uncle, gently placing her arm around his shoulder as he cried. "I'm so sorry, Uncle Ben."

"I made things worse by enlisting," he went on. "It would have been better for Becky and Joe if I'd never joined." He shook his head, now thinking of Thomas. "He was a beautiful boy."

Maegan felt a rush of her own tears as she stood there listening to her uncle's sobs for the next few minutes. The grief of his heart felt as tangible as any sorrow of her own. She remembered well the pain of losing her parents … but that sting of death had been bearable knowing they were with the Lord and she would see them again.

"Joshua would have been better off if I would have died in that accident or in the war," he said, wiping his nose with his sleeve. "Everyone would have been better off."

"Uncle Ben, your grief may have kept you from being the father you wanted to be, but … Joshua's still alive and so are you. Time was lost, but … you can still make your time with him now worth something. He loves you, Uncle Ben. Despite everything, he still loves you."

"I don't see how," Ben sniffed, shaking his head as regret materialized into a shaky sigh. He could feel his head getting heavy, and the room was beginning to be a blur.

Maegan could see he was exhausted and clearly waning from drinking so much. "Let me help you get to bed, Uncle Ben."

He nodded, knowing he might not make it without her. Once he was lying on his bed, she removed his boots and laid a blanket over him. She returned to the kitchen table and took the whiskey bottle he'd nearly finished to the sink. There wasn't much left, but she poured it out and set the bottle in a waste basket, not wanting Cody to have any questions in the morning. As she returned to her room, her heart was heavy for her uncle and for her cousin Joshua as she remembered their conversation the previous day. It wasn't until she had prayed for them both that she could finally fall back asleep.

# Chapter Seven

The next morning, while Maegan was making breakfast, she heard movement behind her and realized her uncle was awake. He moved toward the pot of coffee she had brewing on the stove and wordlessly poured himself a cup.

"Morning, Uncle Ben," she said quietly.

"Mornin'," he replied. "Gonna go feed the stock."

"This is almost done, if you want to wait," Maegan replied.

"I'll eat later," he said as he moved toward the door.

Even with her back toward him, Maegan could sense he had paused at the door.

"I'm sorry about last night."

Maegan turned. She couldn't see his face since he had his back to her, but she could hear the sincerity in his voice. "You don't need to apologize."

He lingered a moment longer, as if thinking, and then left. Maegan sighed as she turned back to the stove, wishing there was something she could do to ease his pain and his guilt.

A little later, while looking for Cody, Maegan found him in the barn. Her brother was admiring all the pelts that her uncle had hanging in his barn.

"I wish I could go with ya," Maegan overheard him say to their uncle, who she heard chuckle slightly and reply, "You like adventure, don't ya?"

"Sure do! I'd be with my brothers right now, if my sister'd let me."

"Well, travelin' ain't all it's cracked up to be," Ben told him.

"Breakfast is ready," Maegan said as she stood there in the doorway. They turned and noticed her for the first time.

"Come look at all these pelts!" Cody said to her. Maegan walked over and carefully ran her hand down the soft fox fur.

"They're beautiful," she said.

"Do you usually sell all of 'em?" Cody asked their uncle.

"Most. What I don't sell, I trade."

"When will you be leaving?" Maegan asked.

"Day after tomorrow," Uncle Ben replied.

"When will you be back?" Cody wanted to know.

"'Bout a month, maybe longer."

"We'll take care of everything while you're gone," Cody assured him with a glance at his sister. "Right, Mae?"

"We sure will," Maegan promised with a kind smile in her uncle's direction. After breakfast, she and Cody drove into town to get some supplies at the General Store.

"Good morning," Tom Maison greeted in his normal friendly fashion. His dark hair was combed neatly, matching his trim mustache. "What can I help you with today?"

Maegan walked to the counter and laid a list on it. It was mostly items for baking. "It'll just take me a minute," he smiled as he took the list and moved down a nearby aisle.

Maegan's eyes were drawn to a bolt of light-yellow cotton fabric near the sewing section of the store. She gingerly touched it, admiring its softness. There were other fabrics, too—a pale blue that she thought would make a nice new shirt for Cody. She glanced over her shoulder toward him, noticing the shirt he wore had seen better days. "I'll also take three yards worth of this blue cotton," she told the store owner a few minutes later. He measured it out for her, and then Maegan paid for the items before heading toward the door. She passed Cody and noticed he was admiring one of the rifles displayed in a glass case.

"Look at that Winchester!" he exclaimed, pointing to one of the company's latest models.

"We gotta get going," was all Maegan said, hoping he would show even a glimmer of that same excitement over a new shirt. He didn't follow her right away, but she headed outside and began to pack her purchased items into her saddle bags. She was securing the buckle when she felt someone tapping her shoulder. Turning around, she gasped in surprise.

"Austin!"

Laughing, he met her hug and then stepped back, a grin widening on his sun-tanned face.

"What in the world are you doing here?" Maegan asked. Before he could answer her question, Cody spotted him as he came out of the store.

"Austin!" Cody exclaimed, jumping over the steps and running to his brother, who met him in a hug.

"I missed you, buddy!" Austin said, tousling his brother's blonde hair.

"What are you doing here?" Maegan asked again.

"Came to see you two, of course," Austin replied.

"How's Sawyer?" Cody asked him, an eager look in his eyes.

"He's fine," Austin replied.

Maegan thought she saw a hint of something in Austin's eyes but decided to press him later when Cody wasn't around.

"This is a nice town," Austin said next. "Least what I've seen of it."

"Most folks are nice, too," Maegan said. "We found Uncle Ben and have been staying with him."

"Glad to hear it," Austin said. He had confidence in his sister's ability to look after herself and Cody, but he had also been worried about them.

They mounted their horses and headed down the street, weaving through the traffic of wagons, riders on horseback, and people. Maegan began to fill Austin in on their uncle and how they'd found him nearly dead when they'd arrived.

"Uncle Ben's back on his feet now, though, and about to leave for …"

"Who's that?" Austin interrupted her, his gaze resting on someone to Maegan's right.

She turned her head and spotted Alison Myles leaving Bell's Newspaper Press. "Oh, that's Ali Myles," Maegan told him. Then, looking back at him, she saw his eyes hadn't moved from her.

"Introduce me," Austin said, suddenly jumping down from his horse.

Rolling her eyes, Maegan dismounted as well. Alison had spotted her and was already heading toward her, waving. "Afternoon, Mae," she greeted with a warm smile. She glanced from her to Cody, who was still astride his horse, and then her eyes met with Austin's as he came to stand beside his sister.

"Afternoon, Ali," Maegan returned the greeting and then nudged her head slightly toward her brother. "This is my older brother, Austin. He's just arrived."

"Howdy, Miss," Austin flashed a smile as he briefly lifted his hat.

"Nice to meet you, Austin," she replied with a courteous nod and smile of her own. She thought he looked quite like his sister with the same thickly lashed emerald-green eyes and almost black, curly hair. His teeth looked bright white against his suntanned face, and there was a trail of freckles across his cheeks and nose. "Will you be in Millcreek long?" she asked, a little taken aback by how good-looking he was.

"'Till I wear out my welcome," he replied with a wink at her.

Alison held his gaze, feeling an unfamiliar rush of something in her heart. Was it just his handsome face that made her want to keep staring into his eyes? She certainly wasn't as shallow as that; then again, she couldn't remember ever meeting any man as attractive as Austin McCoy.

"Well, nice meeting you, Ali," Austin said. "Hope to run into you again." He moved to mount his horse, and Alison switched her attention back to Maegan.

"Maybe we'll see you in church this Sunday," Alison said.

"We plan on it," Maegan told her.

Alison was glad to hear it and told herself it wasn't just because she wanted another chance to see Austin McCoy.

"I think she's the prettiest girl I've ever seen," Austin stated as they rode away. He glanced over his shoulder for the second time, even though Alison was long out of sight.

"You certainly are shy about your feelings," Maegan jested, smiling slightly. But then her expression turned more serious. "You better not lead her on. Ali's been a good friend to me." She remembered how Alison stood up for her when the other women had been gossiping about her.

"You say that as if I'm some kind of flirt," Austin replied, an innocent expression on his face.

"That's because you are a flirt."

"Well, I guess I've been accused of worse," he grinned.

"I'm serious, Austin. Besides, she's Reverend Myles' sister."

"Don't worry, Mae. I won't go makin' any declarations of love yet."

*****

"So, why are you really here?" Maegan asked her brother a few hours later. Everyone had gone to bed, but she and Austin stayed up to finish a card game. Austin had offered to get a room at the hotel, but their uncle insisted he stay the night. Maegan thought Uncle Ben seemed interested in learning more about Austin, and while her Uncle Ben wasn't easy to read, Maegan got the feeling he took a genuine liking to him. He'd mentioned more than once how much he resembled their father.

Austin sighed, adjusting the lamp light to better see his cards. "Sawyer sent me to bring you guys back." He didn't divulge that Sawyer had become consumed with finding the James brothers again, and Austin and Sawyer had split up to cover more territory, hoping to get a lead on their whereabouts.

"I thought as much," Maegan replied, laying down her cards. "We're not going back, Austin."

He leaned back in his chair. "I know. I just had to tell Sawyer I tried." He paused and then added, "He's sorry, ya know."

"I'm sure he is, but not sorry enough to not pull something like that again."

Austin knew she was right. While he outwardly appeared to side with Sawyer on most things, it was rare that he didn't inwardly agree with Maegan. She had the tenderness of their mother and the gumption of their father; a flawless mix, he thought. There weren't many he admired as much as he did his sister. She'd kept them together and practically raised Cody. He knew his parents would be proud.

"How's the farm?" Maegan asked, interrupting his reverie.

"Fine. We hired Tony Sprig to look after the animals when we're not there."

"Another reason I'm sure Sawyer wants me back," Maegan laughed slightly, shaking her head.

"Nah. You know he's not one to show emotions, but he misses you and Cody a lot."

It was good to know, but still not enough to convince Maegan. "I miss you both tremendously, but until Cody's older, I just don't think I can trust Sawyer won't get him killed."

Austin knew Sawyer would never intentionally put their brother in harm's way, but he also knew that bounty hunting had become an obsession for their brother. Again, he knew Maegan was right. "Uncle Ben's nothin' like Pa, is he?" Austin changed the subject, thinking how different from their father their uncle's personality seemed.

"He's a bit of a lone wolf and appears rough, but he's softer than he lets on," Maegan told him.

"You meet any other kin?"

"Pa's sister, Becky, is real nice, but she's married to a man named Joe Spencer, who has a long-standing grudge with Uncle Ben, so they're not on good terms. We've met Uncle Ben's son, Joshua, a few times too, but he and Uncle Ben aren't on the best terms either, so he doesn't come around much."

"Geez, don't sound like the man's very good at making friends."

"There's a lot to it," Maegan told him, thinking of all she had recently learned about their uncle's past. "From what I saw tonight, he seemed to like you." She paused and then said, "How long do you think you'll stay?"

"Well, if I can't persuade you to come back with me, 'least I can visit for a week or two."

"Long as you don't wear out your welcome," Maegan reminded him with a playful smile.

*****

"There's no way you're gonna hit that!" Austin said with confidence, grinning at Maegan as he walked back from the fence post that he'd just set several small cans on. Their uncle had left that morning, and they had been target-shooting, with Austin making the target objects smaller after each round. With their uncle's departure and Austin in town, Maegan had given in and let Cody miss school that day.

"Let me try!" Cody said, raising the pistol in his hand and closing one eye to gain focus.

"Go ahead, little brother," Austin encouraged.

He fired, missing, but the bullet ricocheted off the fence.

"Close!" Austin said. "Go ahead, Mae. Your turn."

Maegan sighed, used to this, as Austin had always enjoyed challenging her shot. "I do have laundry to do, you know," she said as she aimed the gun in her hand. She pulled the trigger and fired, hitting the target dead on. She was about to shoot the next target Austin had set up when the nicker of a horse caught her attention. She looked over to see Sheriff Bridger riding up.

"Sorry to interrupt," he apologized. "Just heard the shots as I was passing by and wanted to check it out."

Maegan lowered the gun and smiled. "This is my brother, Austin. Austin, this is Sheriff Bridger."

Bridger dismounted and stepped toward Austin to shake his hand. "Nice to meet you." He stepped back, his gaze traveling toward the fence post twenty yards away. "Target practice, huh?"

"Yep. Wanna take a shot?" Austin asked.

"From what I just saw, I don't know if I want to embarrass myself in front of your sister," he grinned. "She's a sharpshooter, alright."

"Trained her myself," Austin proudly took credit, sending a wink in his sister's direction. "She ain't gonna make this shot, though," Austin added.

"I really should get back to my chores," Maegan said, handing her pistol to Austin.

"Just try and take this shot first," Austin said over his shoulder as he ran toward the fence and placed an even smaller object on the fence. "Go on," he encouraged when he returned.

Maegan let out a little sigh. "Oh, alright." She calmly lifted her pistol, paused, and then pulled the trigger. The small object flew off the fence, causing Austin to erupt in a shout. "I'll be switched, Mae! You hit it!"

She handed the gun back to Cody and then met the sheriff's look of admiration for a moment before looking away.

"Now I'm definitely not gonna try," Bridger said.

"C'mon, Sheriff," Austin prodded. "A man in your line of work needs all the practice he can get. 'Sides, you don't wanna be shown up by a woman, do ya?"

Bridger chuckled slightly, not missing the look Maegan sent to her brother. "Leave him be, Austin," she said.

Bridger tilted his hat back a tad and then surprised them by pulling out both of his revolvers, firing once with his right hand and then his left. The remaining target objects went flying into the air as a bullet from each gun hit them head-on.

"Now you're just showing off!" Austin said with a grin. "I thought I sensed some skill behind your modesty," he added.

Bridger replaced his guns in their holster, a smile on his face. "Had a good teacher of my own," he said.

"We're about to eat lunch," Cody spoke up with a new admiration for the sheriff. "You can join us if you want."

"Oh, I wouldn't want to impose."

"Bosh," Austin added. "We've got plenty, right, Mae?"

Maegan nodded. "You're welcome to stay," she assured him.

"If you're sure you don't mind," he said, realizing he hadn't eaten breakfast and was indeed hungry, with it being nearly noon.

"Mae's cookin' is as good as her shot," Austin told him as he gave him a sound pat on the shoulder and led the way into the house.

Bridger enjoyed the banter of the two brothers and sister. Having grown up as an only child himself, he hadn't experienced the camaraderie of having siblings. He found himself lingering after the meal as they exchanged stories and asked him questions about himself. Being new to Millcreek, he hadn't gotten to know too many people yet. He knew it was for his own lack of trying, as he didn't possess an outgoing personality that attracted friends easily. As the sheriff, he was also careful to maintain a proper boundary with most of the folks.

"Your family live around here?" Austin asked after some minutes into their conversation.

"Nope. They live 'bout a day's ride north of Jefferson City."

"You have any siblings?" Cody asked.

"I was adopted by a couple who didn't have any other children," he said. "But I was told I had a sister."

"Had?" Maegan asked curiously. "What happened to her?"

"My parents died when I was around four. A neighbor dropped me and my older sister at a local orphanage. She was adopted soon after, and I was there till age ten before I was adopted."

Cody couldn't help but think that it might be his situation if he not had older siblings to take care of him. He cast a glance at his sister, feeling grateful that she had been there after they lost their parents.

"Were they good folks?" Cody asked.

"They put a roof over my head and kept me fed, but it didn't take long for me to see they wanted more of a hired hand than a son." He smiled slightly, but Maegan detected a sadness behind it. Bridger didn't elaborate on his childhood, having accepted the lot life gave him a long time ago. His adoptive parents hadn't been loving, but they hadn't been cruel, either.

"Whatever happened to your sister?" Maegan asked.

"I don't even know." A regretful expression clouded his face.

"Did you ever try to find her?" Maegan said. She couldn't imagine having a sibling and not knowing where they were.

"I returned to the orphanage once I was old enough to leave home, but they didn't have much in their records of her." He shrugged. "Wasn't anything I could do."

"What made you choose your profession?" Austin asked next.

Bridger shrugged. "Didn't seem like a bad idea to try and keep justice in whatever tiny corner of the earth I lived in." He set his cup of coffee down, realizing the conversation had been centered on him too long. "What is it you do?"

"My brother and I run a farm outside Lexington City and, much like yourself, fight for justice in our small corner." He paused and added, "My brother Sawyer and I hunt down outlaws in our spare time."

"Bounty hunting can be risky business," Bridger said, understanding the meaning of his words.

"That's why we got good at it," he smiled.

Maegan held her tongue from commenting on what had happened the last time they'd gone after outlaws.

"More coffee?" she offered instead.

"Actually, I should be getting back to town," Bridger said as he came to his feet.

"See ya 'round, Sheriff," Austin said.

Bridger stopped when he reached the door. "The Spencers giving you folks trouble lately?" he asked.

"No, thank goodness. Probably with my Uncle Ben gone for a while, they eased up," Maegan replied.

"Well, I hope things stay that way."

"Thanks," Maegan said, a look of sincerity in her eyes. Bridger realized it was the first time he'd seen her without her hat. A few dark curls loitered around her face as if refusing to stay in the thick braid that hung over her shoulder. Even in a baggy, flannel shirt and men's trousers, there was a comeliness to her, he thought.

"Well, I'll be going then. Thanks for the meal," he tipped his hat at Maegan. "… and for the target practice," he added with a smile.

"Nice fellow," Austin said when he'd gone. He carried his dish to the sink and began pumping water into it. He turned around, wiping his hands on a dish towel, and Maegan moved to take his place at the sink. She had to agree, and the more she got to know Sheriff Bridger, the more she liked him.

# *Chapter* Eight

"*C*'mon, Mae, can I please miss school another day while Austin is here?"

Maegan was scrambling eggs in the cast iron pan and shook her head as she turned around. It was the following morning, and Cody was giving her a hard time. "For the third time, the answer is no, Cody. You're doing so well, and I don't want you falling behind in your schoolwork."

"We'll hang out when you get back," Austin promised from where he sat at the kitchen table. After they had eaten breakfast, Cody left for school, albeit unhappily, and Maegan thanked Austin for his support.

"Sure thing," Austin replied. He stood from the table and reached for his hat on the hook by the door. "I think I'll head into town for a bit."

"By town, you wouldn't mean the saloon, would you?"

Austin met her disapproving gaze. "Don't worry. I only gamble when I'm feeling lucky."

He only said that because it was fun getting a reaction out of his sister. In truth, he didn't like to gamble at all but did so only when he had to blend in to acquire necessary information. He needed to get to know some of the locals and keep his ears open in case there were any leads concerning the James brothers. Austin had been telling Maegan the truth when he said Sawyer had sent him to persuade her to come home, but he purposely failed to mention his other reason for being there.

In September, the James brothers, along with the Younger brothers and a few others in their gang, had attempted a bank robbery in Northfield, Minnesota. After the failed raid, the James brothers were said to have headed southwest. With several of their gang shot and killed and the Younger brothers captured, Jesse and Frank were on their own, making their capture more possible. Sawyer had headed west of Lexington to search for them, and since Austin's destination was Millcreek, he was supposed to scout out surrounding areas.

When he entered the Millcreek Saloon, he thought it was brighter and cleaner than most he had seen. Light blue wallpaper with gold-flecked designs covered the walls, the pattern broken up by wood panels every ten feet. On the wall opposite the door was a piano and, near that, a staircase wound upward to a landing with a wood railing continuing from one end to the other.

"This town don't need any more McCoys."

Austin turned at the voice, and the man who had spoken stood from the chair he'd been reclining in, finishing his drink. Austin had never seen the tall, bulky man before and was confused by the glint of disdain that flashed from his dark eyes.

"I don't think I've had the pleasure of meeting you," Austin replied sarcastically, extending his hand.

"The name's Robert Spencer, and I'd spit on your hand before I'd shake it."

"Not sure what I've done to offend you, but …"

"You're Ben's kin, and that's offense enough. If you've come to Millcreek to side with that murderer, then you should leave town now before you get hurt."

Austin remembered that Maegan had filled him in on who the Spencers were, along with the backstory of their hatred for Ben McCoy. "Listen, I don't have any hard feelings for any of you Spencers, especially since my aunt is married to your brother. But I don't like being threatened. I'll stay in Millcreek until I'm good and ready to leave."

Robert Spencer's eyes narrowed, and then he leaned in closer. "When he gets back, you tell your Uncle Ben I said there's comin' a day when he's gonna get what he deserves."

"When he gets back, you can tell him yourself," Austin replied, cocking his head slightly. "He ain't scared of you," he added in his uncle's defense, even though he had never spoken to him about anything related to the Spencers.

Robert Spencer clenched his teeth, balled his fists, and looked like he was about to explode into a fight when suddenly another man appeared beside them. It was Joshua McCoy, and he knew all too well how fast Robert's temper could escalate. He had been watching the exchange from across the room.

"He don't know nothin' 'bout all this," Joshua told Robert. "You and my pa can work out your troubles. You don't need us to get involved." He paused, his expression cautioning him. "Do you?"

Seeing he would be outnumbered by two to one, Robert took a step back. "Your pa will stay gone if he knows what's good for him."

After he watched Robert Spencer move toward the swinging saloon doors, Austin turned his attention to Joshua. "Thanks," he said.

"Before he left, my pa came by and told me you were in town. I'm Joshua, your cousin," he introduced himself. "I'm guessing that was your first run-in with Robert."

"Yep. It's good to meet you," he added, shaking his extended hand.

"Robert's sons, Bobby and Garret and their cousin Pete are even worse," Joshua told him with a roll of his eyes. "Even though the war's over, Garret's still got fight in his blood, and he's an addle-headed influence to his brother and cousin. You'd be best to avoid the whole lot of 'em if you can."

"I'll do that," Austin replied. He and Joshua conversed for a few minutes, and after Joshua left, Austin stuck around for a little longer. His time there didn't earn him any information about the James brothers, but by the time he left the saloon, he was stuffing some easy cash he'd won into his pocket. Stepping onto the street, he spotted Alison Myles coming from the mill. For a moment, he just watched her, and then once she was near enough, he waved and moved to meet her.

"Afternoon," he greeted, sliding his hands in his pockets as he came to walk alongside her.

She looked past him for a second, noting the direction he had just come from.

"I just saw you coming from the mill and thought I'd say hello," he said.

She looked up at him and raised an eyebrow. "And where were you just coming from? The saloon?"

His lips pursed together slightly, and he gave a sheepish shrug. "Just wanted to meet some of the locals, with being new to town and all." It wasn't a lie. Getting acquainted with the men who frequented the saloon could lead to gaining information about the James brothers and other outlaws on his and Sawyer's list.

"I see." She didn't approve, but something about him made her smile nonetheless.

"Where you headed?" He changed the subject.

"Oh, just back to work. I was stopping by the mill to tell my brother something."

"Isn't your brother the preacher?"

"Yes, but he also works at the mill."

"Where do you work at?" Austin asked next, glancing down the street at the shops ahead of them. As fashionable as she dressed, his guess was maybe the dress shop.

"Bell's Newspaper. I'm an editor for his paper."

"Really? That's swell! You don't look like you'd be …" he paused, swallowing down the word he was going to use.

"Smart?" she finished.

"No, no, that's not what I was going to say," he tried to convince her but found himself tripping over words. "I just meant I didn't think you would … well, I was just surprised, is all."

"I'm not just editing either," she told him, hoping to shock him further. "I'm writing a column for the paper as well."

"Well, I'll certainly look forward to reading it."

She found her eyes locked with his again, and she dragged her gaze away as a little smile tugged on her lips. She paused a moment and then said, "Are you and your siblings going to the fall picnic this Saturday?" she asked.

"I didn't know about it, but I'm sure we'll be there," he smiled. "Are you going?"

"Yes."

"Then we'll definitely be there."

She tried to hide her smile. "What is it you do?" she asked curiously.

Austin shrugged. "A little this and that, but mostly, I bring criminals to justice."

She looked confused and slowed her steps as she looked up at him. "What do you mean by that?"

"My older brother and I are bounty hunters. You'd be mighty relieved to know of all the outlaws we got behind bars."

"I see."

Austin didn't think her tone sounded relieved—more disappointed, if he had to describe it. He knew not all folks thought well of bounty hunters, and some downright hated them. He hoped she wasn't the latter.

"Well, this is my stop," she said as they came to the newspaper press. She knew she needed to go in but, for some reason, found herself dawdling outside with him to talk. After a few more minutes, she reached for the door.

"You sure you gotta go back to work already?" he asked.

"I'm afraid so," she replied, feeling reluctant.

"Guess I'll see you at the picnic then."

Alison nodded. "Have a good day, Austin."

*****

The Saturday of the picnic came. Being more introverted, Cody and Maegan were a little apprehensive about attending, but Austin was all about it. "With being new to town, it would be a good opportunity for you both to get better acquainted with your neighbors," he said to them.

"And for you to get better acquainted with Alison Myles." Maegan returned, knowing his underlying reason for wanting to go.

With their uncle gone, they no longer had his wagon to borrow. Austin had bought a used one from Eli Greene, who owned the livery in town, and replaced the wheels so they'd have one of their own. Now, on that pristine October afternoon, they rode in their wagon to the picnic at the Carters'. The sky was a dome of sapphire blue with white wispy clouds, and the early autumn breeze carried a sense of future change along with the loose leaves it snatched from obliging trees.

Austin, Maegan, and Cody arrived along with a dozen

other wagons and buggies. The Carter Ranch was vast and something akin to a paradise, Maegan thought. The immense barn easily drew attention, as did Will and Claire Carter's two-story brick house with its double porch. Horses and cattle roamed the surrounding pastures, beautifully speckled with towering trees and colorful wildflowers.

"I wouldn't mind living in a place like this," Austin remarked as his gaze tracked the acreage.

"Afternoon, Mae and Cody," Claire Carter greeted a few minutes later as they walked into the yard. A friendly smile accentuated her pretty face, which was framed with chestnut-colored hair that matched the shade of her eyes. She was around the same age as Maegan and had just married Will Carter the previous year. Maegan introduced her to Austin.

"Your husband owns all this property?" Austin asked, a bit of awe in his voice.

"It was his father's before him, but yes, he does. Have you met him?"

As if on cue, Will Carter exited the house and came down the front steps. Claire called him over and introduced him. Maegan thought him a handsome and respectable-looking man whose friendliness and kind demeanor seemed a good match beside Claire. Will and Austin fell easily into conversation and were soon walking off to see some purebred horses Austin had expressed interest in seeing, Cody trailing close behind.

"You've been here for a few weeks now," Claire said to Maegan. "How are you feeling about Millcreek?"

"I like it," Maegan answered honestly.

"I'm somewhat new to Millcreek myself," Claire admitted. "I moved here after living in the city most of my life, so this was a complete change of pace for me, but I love it!"

Maegan saw the sincerity in her eyes and thought her manner very disarming.

They talked a few more minutes, and then some other woman approached them and began conversing with Claire. Maegan spotted Cody in a small group of other kids and was about to head toward them when she heard a familiar voice.

"Afternoon, Mae," Bridger said with the tip of his hat.

"Hello," Maegan replied, feeling a sudden wave of self-consciousness around the handsome sheriff. "Did you just get here?" she asked, unrolling the sleeves she realized were still hiked up from when she'd washed dishes earlier that day.

"Yeah. Looks like most the town's here!"

Maegan looked out to the yard and noticed more people were arriving and filling the yard.

"I heard there's a shooting contest after lunch," Bridger said. "I was curious if you'd be entering, just so I can gauge what my chances of winning are."

Maegan laughed softly. "Don't worry. I'm not planning on it."

"Oh, I wasn't worried," he lied, rubbing the back of his neck and trying not to smile.

"Austin's the one you should watch out for," Maegan told him. "You might luck out, though," she added. "He might be so distracted with Alison Myles, he may forget about the contest."

Bridger had seen Austin and Alison walking in town together the other day. "Your brother doesn't waste any time, does he?"

"I'm afraid he's famous for throwing caution to the wind," Maegan said not unkindly.

"And are you the more levelheaded one of the bunch?" Bridger asked.

"I suppose," Maegan shrugged.

"You seem like it," he said, meaning it as a compliment.

She wasn't sure what he meant by that but hoped it wasn't the same as saying she was boring.

"Mae! Guess what?" Cody had just run over, his cheeks rosy and excitement flashing in his blue eyes. "There's gonna be a target shooting contest after lunch, and you're gonna win! The prize money is fifty dollars!"

Maegan rolled her eyes. "I'm not going to do any such thing, Cody."

"Please, Mae! You know we could use the money!"

That was true, but Maegan sent him a look that reminded him not to say such things in front of others. "I'll think about it," she finally said after a few minutes of protesting while he tried to persuade her.

"As the new sheriff in town, I can't lose respect by being shown up," Sheriff Bridger told her teasingly.

A playful smile suddenly tugged on Maegan's lips. "Are you saying you want me to be sure to lose if I decide to compete?"

He chuckled. "Guess if I can't hold my own, it's my own fault."

Maegan smiled. "Well, I don't have any intention of competing, even with Cody's persuading."

Maegan and Cody walked with the sheriff toward the tables of food, as it seemed lunchtime had officially begun. Bridger ended up in a conversation with a few other men while Maegan and Cody found a spot at one of the tables. As they were finishing, Garret Spencer walked up to the end of their table. His younger brother Bobby was trailing behind him like a puppy. He resembled him in the face but was shorter and much thinner than Garret's bulky frame. When Maegan saw them, she half expected to see Pete Keller as well, since the three of them seemed thick as thieves.

"Did I hear right?" Garret said. "That you're gonna be shootin' in the contest?"

Maegan cast a glance at Cody, who shrugged sheepishly. "I bragged to Jeb that you might."

Maegan released a sigh. "I'm not shooting in any contest," she told Garret.

"Good. 'Cuz you'd make a real fool out of yourself if you did."

"She's got better aim than you," Cody said. "She could shoot the wings off a fly."

Maegan sent Cody a warning glance to keep his mouth shut.

"Wings off a fly, huh?" he chuckled. He put his hands on the edge of the table and leaned toward her. "I'm curious now. What else are you good at, Mae McCoy?"

She didn't like the underlying tone in his voice nor the look in his shifty eyes. "I'm good at ignoring ten-cent men like you. But this once, I might make an exception and put you in your place."

An amused grin split his face, and he laughed. "You might look like a fellow in those trousers, but I doubt you shoot like one."

"I thought I proved that on the first day we met," she reminded him. "You still got that hole in your hat?"

"That was just a lucky shot," he said. "Or maybe, you were aiming for my heart and missed."

"I never miss," she countered, surprised even at her own grit.

"You've got enough nerve to spur a dead horse!" he sneered. He was about to say something else but then caught Sheriff Bridger's eye and realized the man was watching him from his place at the next table. "I'll see you two later," Garret said, a smirk on his face as he walked away.

Maegan let out a sigh. "Ugh! Me and my big mouth."

"More like Garret and his," Cody corrected.

"I don't even want to shoot," Maegan said. "I didn't even bring my pistols."

"You can use Austin's," Cody said. "Don't let that tin horn unnerve you, Mae," he encouraged. "You're gonna win those fifty dollars!"

Maegan let out a little groan, wishing she hadn't let Garret Spencer get to her.

*****

Austin liked Will Carter instantly, finding the man was down to earth and easy to talk with. They walked around the barn and corral as Austin asked him about various horses and the process of running the ranch.

"Oh, no, Robert Spencer and his boys are here," Will said, noticing them for the first time.

Austin glanced in the direction Will was looking. "I met Robert the other day."

"Whether it's Joe or Robert, they just seem to bring trouble wherever they go. Rob has two sons, but his oldest, Garret, is probably the worst of the whole crew." He let out a sigh. "I'll just keep an eye. Glad Sheriff Bridger is here in case anything gets out of hand."

"My aunt is married to Joe," Austin told him. "From what Maegan has told me, the Spencers don't like my uncle … or any McCoy for that matter."

"That's a shame, especially with the connection your family has. But yeah, you might just want to stay clear if you can," Will told him. "Will I see you at the shooting contest?" He suddenly changed the subject.

"You might," Austin replied.

"You any good?" Will asked, a smile on his face.

Austin shrugged, downplaying his skill. "Some days." The sight of Alison Myles just a few yards away suddenly caught his eye, and as a few men by the corral approached Will Carter, Austin moved toward her.

"Afternoon," he greeted, tilting his hat slightly.

Alison had been scanning the crowds for his face and was glad to finally find him.

"Afternoon, Austin," she replied, looking up into his warm green eyes.

"Are you enjoying yourself?" he asked.

"Yes, thank you."

"Is this your first time at the Carter ranch?" he asked, remembering that Maegan had told him she had recently moved to Millcreek.

"My brother and sister-in-law are good friends with the Carters, so I've been here several times."

"Then how 'bout giving me the tour?"

"Alright," she replied, glad for a chance to spend more time with him.

"If I had to settle down somewhere, I wouldn't mind if it were in a place like this," Austin said as they walked across the yard.

"I guess with bounty hunting, you find yourself moving around often," Alison replied.

"I practically live in a saddle some months."

"Must get tiresome, but I think I can understand the thrill of seeing new places."

Austin shrugged. "I never gave it much thought, honestly. My older brother and I fell into it, and it's just become a way of life."

"Do you enjoy it?"

Austin was a little taken aback by the question. He'd never really stopped to consider if what he did for a living was something he enjoyed. Like he had told her, it had just become a way of life. Now, however, as the question hung in the air, it seemed to open a new door to reflection.

"I don't know," he heard himself answer quietly, and then he saw her looking at him with such genuine interest in her expression, it almost made him feel she could see into his soul. He rarely let down his guard of confidence, and the fact that she'd made him answer honestly was refreshing somehow.

"Well, I suppose if you miss something, that's a good indicator if it's something you enjoy," Alison said.

"I guess that's true," Austin agreed, and for the first time, he found himself wondering if bounty hunting was something he would miss.

*****

"Looks like the shooting contest is starting up," Cody said to Maegan sometime later. "Look, Austin's already over there!"

Maegan reluctantly followed her younger brother to the crowd of gathering men. Austin met them and asked Cody if he wanted to have a go. "Nope, but Maegan's gonna shoot in the contest!" he added.

"There go my chances," Austin winked at his sister.

Maegan released a sigh and shook her head slightly. "I was kind of provoked into entering," she told him.

"Garret Spencer's gonna eat some humble pie," Cody said with a smile.

"That's the second time I've heard that name today," Austin said.

Their conversation was cut short when they heard Doctor Fletcher's voice getting everyone's attention and explaining the rules.

"This is how it's going to work, folks. We'll start at twenty meters, and each man—"

"Or woman!" someone yelled from the group, causing an eruption of laughter.

"Or woman"—Doc Fletcher corrected with a wink in Maegan's direction—"will get one shot at the target per each of the three rounds."

"If I don't win it, you will," Austin whispered to Maegan as the doc continued to explain the rules.

"Not so sure it'll be as easy as it looks," Maegan said. "That second target is small and pretty far."

"Nah, we got this."

Maegan suddenly felt nervous and wished she had a dose of his confidence. She normally felt no need to prove herself, but Garret's taunting had sparked something in her that wanted to set the record straight.

Nearly a dozen men, including Sheriff Bridger, took their turn. As it went on, the crowd of contestants thinned until only Garret Spencer, Sheriff Bridger, Austin, and Maegan remained. The crowd was in an amused uproar seeing a woman make it so far. After the second round, Garret was the farthest off the mark. His face was red with anger as he joined the others to watch who was the last man or *woman* standing.

Austin was disappointed but not begrudging as he watched Sheriff Bridger and Maegan make it to the final round. "C'mon, Mae!" he encouraged.

Maegan could feel her nerves coming to the surface with so many eyes on her.

"You're not nervous, are you?" Bridger asked Maegan while the new targets were being set up.

She sent him a look that made him smile.

"I guess that answers my question," he said. "You made it

this far. Win or lose, you're already a better shot than most the town."

"Alright!" Doc Fletcher shouted, bringing everyone's attention to the final round.

Bridger lifted his pistol and fired. Then Maegan was next. They waited while the men who were judging checked the target.

"Looks like we have a winner, folks!" A hush fell over the otherwise noisy crowd.

"The winner of this year's target shooting contest is … Maegan McCoy!"

There was a loud sea of applause, with whoops and hollering.

"There's a first time for everything, I guess," Doc Fletcher said, looking at Maegan with admiration.

She was glad when the crowd began to disperse, some folks heading to another contest while others loitered around the food.

"Congratulations," Sheriff Bridger said to her. "You won that fair and square."

"Just remember, I was the one who taught her how to shoot," Austin said.

"I think some of that credit goes to Sawyer, too," Maegan smiled.

"And some of that credit to you," Bridger reminded her. "I wouldn't want to be at the receiving end of your Colt."

"Well, you don't ever have to worry about that, Sheriff," she said.

"Garret looks mad enough to swallow a bonnet!" Austin chuckled as he gestured toward the man who was very obviously a sore loser.

"Guess he won't say nothin' now that you put him in his place," Cody alleged.

"Every fellow here's been put in his place," Austin said.

"I wish I had your courage to go up against all those men!" Alison said to Maegan. She shook her head in amazement. "Just to see the look on some of their faces was worth you entering that contest!" She noted Sheriff Bridger still standing there. "And congratulations to you, too, Sheriff, for coming in second!"

"Now, don't forget who came in third," Austin joked.

"Maybe you could teach me how to shoot like that," Alison said to Austin.

"Nah, you're too pretty to be holdin' a gun," he winked at her. He realized his mistake too late and sent his sister an apologetic smile. "Don't take that the wrong way, Mae."

Maegan knew he had not meant to insult her in his effort to compliment Alison, but she couldn't ignore the twinge of insecurity that coursed through her. She smiled and laughed it off as if it hadn't fazed her. "I'm gonna get a drink," she said, missing the way Sheriff Bridger noticed the whole exchange.

Maegan walked off toward a table where several pitchers of water sat.

"That was some fine shootin'."

Maegan lowered the glass she had just raised to her lips as a middle-aged, friendly man began talking to her.

"I'm Jack Dean." He extended his hand, and Maegan met his handshake.

"Sorry," he chuckled. "Guess it ain't proper to shake a lady's hand."

"No offense taken," she said kindly.

"I never saw a girl shoot like that. I reckon you're just as good a shot as Annie Oakley … maybe better!"

"Do you live around here?" She tried to change the subject.

"I live on the other side of town, past the mill about a mile."

"You live in Millcreek all your life?" she asked, although she really had no interest in knowing.

"Jest about." He poured himself some water. "You jest moved here, right?"

Maegan nodded. "We're visiting relatives and possibly staying on for some time."

"Well, you're a real fine addition to our town, Mae Mc-Coy."

She saw he was genuinely being kind and thanked him. She didn't mind when he walked away to talk to someone else, though. She was tired of talking about shooting and regretted competing in the contest. She regretted it even more when she overheard a group of women nearby gossiping about her.

"You'd think she'd be embarrassed to traipse around in men's clothing," one woman said.

"It's vulgar, if you ask me," another replied. "Dressing like a man and shooting like a man!"

Feeling painfully aware of how out of place she was, Maegan slipped away quickly, spying out a large weeping willow tree that promised some solitude. Once behind its dangling branches, she sat on the grass and leaned against its thick trunk. She took off her wide-brimmed hat and laid it on the grass, letting the breeze pull at her hair. Plucking a small, purple wildflower out of the ground, she absently pulled at its petals.

Not wearing a dress or being considered "ladylike" had never bothered her before, but now it felt like she stood out like a sore thumb. *You're too pretty to be holdin' a gun.* Austin's comment to Alison had stung, too, especially in front of the sheriff.

"Are you hiding back there?"

Maegan glanced up, a little startled as Sheriff Bridger

pushed the branches to one side and stepped into the tree's covering.

"No," she smiled slightly, coming to her feet.

"Doc Fletcher asked me to give you this." Bridger extended an envelope toward her. "Your prize money."

"Oh." Maegan looked down at the envelope, took it, and slid it into her pocket. She'd forgotten about the fifty-dollar award.

"You don't look too thrilled."

"I just wish I hadn't entered the contest. Folks'll just think I was trying to show off."

"If anyone has a right to show off, it's you. I've never seen anyone shoot like that … except maybe myself," he added with a little twinkle in his eyes. "… on a better day, of course."

"I didn't expect to beat you," she told him.

"I did," he admitted with a slight smile. "This is a nice spot you found," he changed the subject. "I think you have the right idea."

"Oh?"

"There's a lot of people out there," he glanced over his shoulder. "It's a little overwhelming for an introvert like myself."

Maegan smiled softly. "For me, too," she agreed. "I'm not sure I fit in."

"Nothin' wrong with standing out," he said, meaning it as a compliment.

"Not for the wrong reasons," she said with a soft laugh, turning to reach for her hat that still sat on the grass.

Bridger didn't think she stood out for the wrong reasons, and he didn't think having good aim with a firearm made her any less attractive than someone like Alison Myles. "I should be getting back," he said, a little surprised at the direction of his thoughts.

"Me, too. I haven't seen Cody for a while and should make sure he hasn't gotten himself into any trouble."

*****

*G*arret leaned up against the corral fence and reached inside his vest pocket for his whiskey flask, promptly taking a long swig. His eyes scanned through the crowds, not taking long to pick out Mae McCoy. He hated that she'd shown him up in the contest. A moment later, his eyes rested on the reverend's sister. She was walking toward the back of the barn, and Garret decided to follow her.

Maegan was looking for Cody and thought she remembered seeing him, Lilly, and a group of other kids heading behind the barn. As she reached the back side of it, however, she found Garret talking to Alison. She recognized right away that Alison seemed uncomfortable and decided to come to her rescue.

"There you are," Maegan said, pretending like she'd been looking for her. She noticed an immediate look of relief cross Alison's face. "I need your help with something," Maegan said, gently taking Alison's arm.

"Now, wait a minute!" Garret said, his voice slurring slightly. He reached out and grabbed Maegan's arm as she and Alison nearly passed him. "We weren't done talkin'!"

"Get your hand off my sister!" Austin had just arrived on the scene in time to see Garret roughly grab Maegan's arm.

Garret did so, but the look of trouble in his eyes now turned to Austin. "Don't boss me around!"

"Then keep your hands to yourself," Austin told him in a tone that Garret didn't like.

"Or what? You think I'm gonna listen to you?"

Maegan and Alison edged away, both women feeling concerned as they could sense the tension mounting between

Austin and Garret. Garret suddenly covered the distance between himself and Austin, taking a fast swing toward his face. Austin saw it coming and swiftly moved out of the way. Garret was a little taller, a lot thicker, too, but he wasn't quick on his feet like Austin.

"I don't wanna fight you," Austin told him.

"Course you don't! You're too yella!"

Irritated at this man, first for grabbing Maegan and then for acting like a hotshot, Austin felt he had no choice but to counter his next punch with one of his own. Garret stumbled backward, cursing and bending over as blood began to drip from his nose. He straightened, and for a moment, it seemed he was going to walk away. Austin had also turned around and was walking to meet Alison and Maegan where they stood several feet away at the corner of the barn.

"Austin, watch out!" Alison called to him as she saw Garret charging towards him. The man delivered a series of well-placed punches that landed Austin on his knees. Alison screamed and ran toward him. "Stop it!" she yelled out to Garret, who attempted to pull her away from him.

That's when Reverend Myles came around the corner. "What's going on?" he said, noticing his sister on her knees by Austin McCoy, who was slowly starting to come to his feet. Maegan had gone to her brother as well, and Garret was just standing there, a pleased expression on his face.

"Everything's alright now, Reverend," Garret said as he gave one last look at Austin before walking away.

Reverend Myles looked with concern from Austin to Alison.

"Let's get you inside," Alison said to Austin. "We can get you cleaned up."

"Nah," Austin replied, wiggling his jaw slightly and wiping at some blood by his lip. "I'm fine. I think I'll head home."

"You go on to the wagon," Maegan told him kindly as she picked up his hat from the ground and handed it to him. "I'll find Cody and be right along."

"That Garret Spencer is a bully and a brute!" Alison exclaimed as she watched Maegan and Austin walk away.

"I'm glad you weren't hurt," Reverend Myles said to her, wondering if Austin McCoy was the kind of man he wanted her hanging around. He'd noticed them stealing away or talking most of the afternoon, which made him curious about what sort of man Austin was and, more importantly, what sort of intentions he had toward Alison.

# *Chapter* Nine

After church the next day, Alison was pleased when Austin invited her to have lunch with him and his siblings. Alison told Maggie about her plans for lunch and then headed toward the McCoys' wagon.

"Thanks for having me," Alison said to Maegan, who was climbing into the back of the wagon with Cody. Maegan didn't want Alison to get her dress dirty, so she offered her the seat next to Austin.

"Glad to," Maegan replied sincerely, hoping Austin's invitation didn't seem too forward. She had been meaning to invite Alison over for some time and was glad she had accepted Austin's invitation.

"What's that scowl for?" Maggie asked her husband as he came to stand next to her outside in the churchyard, his gaze on his sister, who was taking Austin McCoy's extended hand as he helped her up into the wagon seat.

"It seems like Alison is spending a lot of time with Maegan and Cody's older brother."

"Austin seems like a nice young man."

"A nice young man who seems to spend a lot of time near the saloon."

"Well, he's just visiting. I'm sure there's nothing to worry about where Alison is concerned." She was a little amused at how protective her husband was being over his sister. She rose on tiptoe and kissed his cheek. "C'mon, we've got our own lunch to get to, and I'd rather not stand around watching you glaring at Austin McCoy."

*****

"Do you mean to tell me you went after *the* James brothers?"

"Sure did," Austin said, enjoying the astonishment in Alison's voice and expression. "And it was as dangerous as it sounds."

Maegan wished he were exaggerating the events of that night, but it was all as he said. They had finished lunch an hour ago and were sitting around the table as Austin recounted tales from their past.

"Oh, Cody. Weren't you scared?" Alison asked.

"Not really," Cody lied. "The James brothers were the ones that ran off."

Maegan sighed, remembering the horrible night all too vividly. "I'm sure Ali's getting tired of all these stories," she said, hoping to change the subject.

"No, not at all," Alison replied, looking at Austin. "I think they're exciting."

"Nah, Mae's right," Austin said. "You've heard enough about us. Tell us 'bout yourself, Ali."

"Me?" Alison said, thinking she liked the way her name sounded when Austin said it. "I don't have anything as thrilling as all that. The closest I've ever come to those sorts of adventures are the stories that I write."

"Real stories?" Cody asked.

"No," Alison laughed softly. "Fictional ones that I make up."

"Well, feel free to use anything we shared for inspiration,"

Austin winked at her.

"I just might have to," she said with a playful smile back. She enjoyed the next few hours so much that she didn't realize how late it had gotten until she noticed Maegan was starting to make dinner preparations. Hoping she hadn't overstayed her welcome, she told them she should be getting back.

"I'll hitch up the wagon," Austin said, coming to his feet and heading to the door.

"Oh, I'd hate for you to go through all that trouble," Alison told him. "I don't mind just riding horseback if it's easier." The last and only time she had ridden was with Cody on their way into Millcreek, and she told herself she wouldn't be as jumpy this time.

Surprised, Austin looked at her and then shrugged. "Alright, I'll just saddle up my horse then."

"He looks even larger than Cody's horse," Alison remarked a short time later, just before Austin reached down from his place on the saddle and helped her climb up behind him.

"You ain't scared, are you?" Austin asked, amused when he felt her arms hastily wrap around his waist when the horse had only taken a few steps in place.

"Scared or not, just don't let me fall off," she replied, trying not to squeeze Austin too tight.

"Don't worry, I'll go slow," he assured her.

"It's a good thing my mother isn't here to see me," Alison commented a little later. "She wouldn't even let me learn to ride side-saddle."

"Well, what she doesn't know can't hurt her," he chuckled. He liked the feeling of her arms around him and was tempted to pick up the pace just so she'd hold on a little tighter. Alison told him which way to go, and they reached her brother's homestead just as he was coming out of the front door.

Jacob Myles paused at the door as Austin rode up with his sister seated behind him. Moving to be of assistance, Jacob reached up and helped his sister slide down.

"Howdy, Reverend," Austin greeted.

"Thanks for bringing her back," Jacob replied, surprised that the man hadn't taken the time to hitch up the wagon for his sister's benefit.

"It was a fun afternoon. Tell your sister thank you again," Alison said to Austin as she stepped away from the horse.

"Sure thing." Austin tipped his hat, flashed a smile in her direction, and then rode off.

"What's wrong?" Alison asked when she noticed her brother's tense expression.

"Don't they have a wagon?"

"Oh, riding horseback was my idea. Seemed a lot easier," she smiled as she led the way into the house.

"Seems more dangerous to me," he mumbled under his breath, although he wasn't referring to her physical safety.

*****

On an errand for Mr. Bell on Monday, Alison stopped briefly to admire a dress hanging in the window of Mrs. Murry's shop.

"Get off my steps!"

Hearing the angry shout just across the street, Alison turned and watched as a man shooed away Lyn Hummel.

"If I see you sitting outside my house again, I'll get the sheriff!"

The old woman staggered a bit as she tried to regain her balance after being forced to move quickly. Alison took in the scene and hastily crossed over to where she was.

"Can I help you get somewhere?" Alison asked her, glad the man who had yelled at the woman had returned inside his house.

"Who are you?" the woman asked in the sweet voice Alison remembered from the other day.

"We met a few days ago, remember … at Bell's Newspaper Press? My name is Alison."

"Oh, that's right. I do remember you now."

"Your name is Lyn, right?"

"Yes, dear."

"Where are you headed?" Alison asked.

"I'm looking for someone," she replied.

"Your son?" Alison asked, although she already knew the answer.

"Yes. He's missing."

Alison smiled sympathetically at her, realizing the woman must not remember she had already explained that to her when they had met. "Why don't you walk with me for a bit? I'm heading back to work, but I can walk with you to Mrs. Lyddie's first. It's almost the lunch hour."

"Alright," she replied simply.

Alison looped her arm inside the woman's, noting the threadbare black shawl that hung over her slumped shoulders. The cool air of late October reminded everyone that it would be winter before long. "Where are you from?" Alison asked as they walked.

"St. Louis."

"Do you have family there?"

"Not anymore. My husband's been dead thirty years, and my house is sitting empty, I'm afraid."

"When is the last time you were there?"

"'Bout seven years ago, I 'spect."

"You've been away from home that long?" Alison couldn't keep the surprise from her voice.

"My home is wherever he is," she answered as she reached

into the collar of her blouse and pulled out a necklace with a wooden cross. "I waited for over five years for him to come home after the war, and then one day, I decided I'm not going to wait any longer. I've been searching for him ever since." Her hands trembled slightly as she tried to angle it so Alison could read the name etched on it.

"Here, let me," Alison offered, turning the cross over. "William," she read the name whittled into the cross. "Did your son make that for you?" she asked.

"Yes. Just before he left for war. I've never taken it off." A reminiscent smile touched her lips. "I thought I'd never have a child. I had given up hope, and then on my fortieth birthday, I realized I was pregnant." She shook her head fondly at the memory. "My husband was so shocked … and happy."

"A better gift, I'm sure you never had," Alison said thoughtfully.

"That's the truth. He was a gift from God, and I would know if God had taken him back." She said the words with such conviction that Alison believed her.

"I'm sorry it's taken you so long to find him," Alison said.

"Me too," the woman sighed. "But I know I will."

"How can you be so certain?" Alison asked hesitantly, hoping the question wouldn't upset her.

"Because if he wasn't on this earth anymore, I would feel it … deep down, I would feel it. That's the way a mother's love is, you know."

Alison smiled kindly at her. "I'll pray you find him soon."

Once they reached the boarding house, the older woman took Alison's hands as she faced her. "You will tell me if you find anything out about William, won't you?"

Alison nodded, her heart in her eyes. "Of course, Mrs. Hummel, of course, I will."

Thinking about the woman all the way back to work, Alison hurried since she'd been gone longer than she should have. She'd just entered the building when Mr. Bell's voice thundered from his office.

"Alison Myles!"

Alison had never heard him raise his voice before, and it froze her in place. Still, she had been preparing for this since the paper came out that morning, just waiting for him to finish reading the finished copy as he always did.

"Yes, Mr. Bell?" She closed the door behind her and watched as he walked out of his office toward her.

"What is the meaning of this?" He held up the paper in his hands and shook it for emphasis. "Can you tell me how *The Mystery of Brooks Hill* made its way into *my* paper?"

"Yes, sir, I can." Alison took a deep breath, hoping she wasn't about to lose her job. "Remember a few weeks ago when I mentioned about possibly writing a column for the paper?"

"You went ahead and did it." He finished for her. "And without my approval, I'd like to add!"

"Mr. Bell, I'm sorry. I know it wasn't right, but I didn't think you would give me a chance until you saw how much it will increase sales."

"People don't buy the newspaper to read imaginary stories, Miss Myles! They want relevant news, information, political and social issues, and … well, facts!"

"Yes, sir, you're right. But I just thought this would spice it up a bit."

"Spice it up? This isn't a bakery! I hired you to edit this paper, not underhandedly run it as you see fit."

Alison nodded, feeling the compunction of her actions. "I am sorry, sir. I won't do it again."

"Yes, well, I hope you don't." He tossed the paper onto her desk and returned to his office, shutting the door with a little more force than usual.

Even though she felt bad for going behind his back, she couldn't suppress the smile that was tugging at her lips as she picked up the paper he'd thrown to her desk. She released a little breath of pleasure at seeing her story in print. She hoped Mr. Bell would get over being angry at her, and when he saw how much people liked her column, maybe he'd ask her to write it every week. She only hoped her intuition was correct and had not misled her.

As she left work later that day, she was surprised to see Austin pulling up in his wagon. "Afternoon!" he called to her.

She moved toward his wagon, which he had parked parallel to Bell's Newspaper Press. "Well, this is a coincidence," she said with a smile.

"Not really," he grinned. "I asked Maegan what time you finish. I thought I could give you a ride home."

"Could we go by the mill first so I can tell my brother he doesn't have to get me?"

"Of course," Austin said. "Here, climb in." He shifted over and extended his hand.

After she was seated beside him, Austin turned his rig around and headed toward the mill. "How was your day?" he asked.

"Not so good, actually." She let out a sigh and stared at her hands in her lap. "I'm afraid I got myself into some trouble."

"Oh?"

"Without getting Mr. Bell's permission, I slipped in a column of my own into the paper ... a short story I wrote."

"You won't get fired, will you?"

"I don't think so," she said, but she didn't sound too certain.

"Well, you must have felt like your story was worth the risk." He shrugged. "Sometimes you just gotta go with your gut."

"That's exactly what I was thinking when I did it," she

told him, glad he could understand.

"Sometimes, to reach your goal, a risk is the only option," Austin went on to say. "I've sure taken a heap of 'em."

"I haven't taken many," Alison admitted. "But sometimes, when I get an idea into my head, I can't seem to stop until I act on it!"

"I think that's called impulsive … or maybe determined," Austin said.

Alison smiled. "Well, whatever it's called … it may have cost me my job." She paused and then said, "Was it an impulse that caused you to come to Millcreek? Maegan and Cody seemed surprised when you arrived."

"I just wanted to make sure they were alright … and see if they would be willing to come back. My brother Sawyer was sort of the reason they had to leave, and he wanted me to try and smooth things over."

"I see," Alison said. "So, do you think they will leave when you do?"

"Nah. I think they'll stay, for a while anyway, 'specially now that Cody's in school. I know that's real important to Mae."

"Well, it was good of you to make sure they were alright. How long do you think you'll stay in Millcreek?" she couldn't help but ask.

"I keep finding reasons to extend my visit," he told her. "My uncle's roof needs some fixin', the barn loft needs repaired … one thing after another."

"I guess you can't always foresee these things," she said, tucking a wisp of blonde hair behind her ear. "Who knows what other reasons you may find to stay longer," she added with a coy smile.

Austin glanced at her, his cheeks rosy and his eyes twinkling. "I was just thinking that very thing."

After they went by the mill so Alison could tell Jacob she

had a ride home, Austin drove slowly through the town and down the road that led to the Myles' house. He liked being with Alison Myles and was in no rush to get her home. They conversed easily, and he loved the sound of her laugh and the vibrancy and pureness in her eyes when their gaze met. When they eventually stopped the wagon in the yard, Alison didn't move to climb down right away. Instead, she turned to face Austin.

"Maybe you can tell me if you think my story was worth the risk." She pulled out a folded section of the newspaper from her handbag and handed it to him.

"Not sure I'm the best judge, but I'd be honored to read it," Austin said, taking the paper she handed him. He knew now wasn't the time to tell her that he couldn't read.

*****

"I'm just about done, Mr. Bell," Alison said when she heard the main door open and close. It was a few days later, and she was in a large closet, stacking paper and reorganizing some supplies that had been formerly a mess. Since procuring his censure for her "presumptuous" behavior, as he had reminded her several times that week, she was eager to regain his good approval and had been working extra hard. When she came out of the room, she was surprised to see Austin standing there instead of Harold Bell.

"Howdy," he said with a little tip of his hat and an inviting smile she was becoming familiar with.

"Hi, Austin; what are you doing here?"

"Lookin' for you," he replied. "I was wondering if you'd help me with something when you're through with work."

"Oh, of course. I'm actually done for the day. What do you need help with?"

"Picking out a gift for Mae. It's her birthday tomorrow. I

was wondering if you'd come to the General Store with me."

Alison smiled. "I'd love to." She untied the apron around her waist and took a few steps to hang it over a hook on the wall.

"So, how does it all work?"

Alison turned to see Austin standing beside one of the machines in the room, looking at it curiously. "That's a galley proof press," she told him. "You arrange the type in a composing stick," she reached around him to a case that contained various boxes of metal letters. "After the type is in this tray, you ink the type with one of these rollers," she held one up and then mimicked the motion of rolling ink over them.

He looked genuinely interested, so she went on. "Next, you position a piece of paper over the inked type and then that heavy cylinder," she gestured toward the large metal roll that spanned the width of the galley table, "rolls over it, and the pressure transfers the ink from the type to the paper, creating a proof. After Mr. Bell or I make sure there aren't any mistakes, we can print off hundreds!"

"Sounds complicated," Austin said, looking at her with a bit of awe.

"Not really. Once you learn how, anyone can do it."

"Not sure I could," he admitted, wondering what she'd think of him if she knew he couldn't read. He gently reached down and took her hand, turning it upside down. "Guess this is why you always have ink stains on your fingers."

Alison looked down and smiled, a little self-conscious about the black smears all over her fingers. "Comes with the job, I guess," she said, her eyes meeting his.

"I think it's right impressive you can do all this."

"Thanks," she replied softly, unable to think about anything except the pair of inducing eyes staring back at her. She slowly withdrew her hand. "We should probably go," she said.

"Yep," Austin replied, finding it somewhat difficult to drag his eyes away from hers. He moved to hold the door open for her, and then they stepped out onto the platform that ran along the street in front of the other buildings and shops. Side by side, they walked toward the store.

"Have anything in mind?" she asked him.

"Not a thing."

She laughed at his reply. "Not a good start."

"Well, that's what you're for," he nudged her slightly with his elbow.

"What sort of things does your sister like? Books, jewelry?"

"I'm not sure, but I think books more than jewelry. Maybe that's just because she ain't ever had the chance to wear jewelry, though."

They arrived at the store in short order. Mr. Maison was helping another customer, so they began browsing. "Winter's coming. Would she want a new scarf?" Alison asked as she lifted one off a shelf.

"She makes that sort of stuff herself."

"Oh, I know!" Alison moved past him in the aisle. "Look at that dress in the window! That dark green would look so good with her eyes! And it looks her size!"

"A dress?" Austin's expression was doubtful. "I can't see her wearing a dress."

"Has she always dressed in boys' clothes?" Alison asked.

"Far back as I can recall. She's just too practical for all that lace and flounce."

Alison laughed softly. "You can be practical and still dress like a woman, you know."

"I know that, but I don't think Mae does."

"Well, maybe she just needs someone to help her along." A moment later, Alison was gesturing for Mr. Maison to come over. "Austin would like to buy the dress in the window for his sister."

"Sure thing," Tom Maison said as he moved to take the mannequin out of the window. "I'll just be a minute," he said as he carried it to the backroom.

"I don't know, Ali. There might be something else she'd like better." He strolled down the aisle, stopping at the front counter where several pieces of jewelry caught his eye. "What about that bracelet? That's real pretty."

"Oh, I like that, too," Alison agreed.

"Those rings are real nice," Austin said.

"Would you like to see one?" Tom Maison asked as he came to the counter, the dress draped over his arm. He reached into the back of the counter and set two different rings on the counter.

"This looks like a sapphire," Alison said with admiration, gently sliding it onto her finger.

"An imitation sapphire," Tom Maison remarked with a chuckle.

"What do you think?" Alison asked as she extended her hand out slightly.

Austin gently took her wrist and tilted her hand slightly so that the light caught the jewel. "I think it's real pretty on you."

"Good afternoon, Reverend. I didn't hear you come in."

The greeting had come from Tom Maison, and Alison and Austin turned to see Reverend Myles standing just behind them.

"Oh, hi Jacob," Alison said cheerfully.

"What's going on here?" he asked, trying to sound calm as his eyes went from the ring on his sister's finger to Austin, who had quickly dropped his hand from Alison's wrist.

"We're looking at rings," Alison said as if it were an everyday occurrence. She missed the concern in her brother's eyes and added, "Austin's trying to find a birthday gift for Mae."

Austin didn't miss the look of relief that crossed the reverend's face. It almost made him laugh outright. He knew Alison hadn't picked up on it, but he could sense what was going through the reverend's mind when he saw his sister looking at rings with him.

"I think I'll stick with the dress," Austin said. "And maybe I'll take that vase on the shelf behind you, too," he told Tom Maison.

Tom Maison carefully picked up the vase. "A good choice, Mr. McCoy. I'll wrap it for you."

"Are you about finished here?" Jacob asked his sister. He'd gone by the press as he usually did when he finished work to give her a ride home, but someone had said they had seen her heading to the General Store.

"Yes, I think we're done." She smiled at Austin.

"Thanks for your help, Ali." Austin nodded his head in Jacob's direction. "See you Sunday, Reverend."

Jacob nodded and then headed outside with Alison close in tow.

"You don't like Austin McCoy very much, do you?"

Jacob climbed up into the wagon, a surprised expression on his face. "I never said I didn't like him."

Alison grinned slightly. "You say it with your eyes every time you see him."

Jacob cleared his throat, unaware that his distrust of the young man was so obvious. "I'm sorry if I seem unfriendly to the man. I really don't mean to come across that way."

"He's very nice," she said, glancing over her shoulder and glimpsing him leaving the store.

"Just because he's nice doesn't mean he's trustworthy, Ali. You told me yourself he's a bounty hunter. They aren't always an honest bunch. Everyone deserves a fair trial, and bounty hunters are just out for the reward money."

"I know that's true with some, but Austin cares about justice and getting lawless men behind bars."

Jacob didn't want to burst her bubble and sighed as he contemplated what to say. "You haven't seen as much of the world as I have, Ali. Trust me, men like Austin don't always have good intentions. If I were you, I'd keep your distance."

"You don't know him at all. How can you say that?"

"You barely know him either, Ali. A picnic, lunch, a few conversations …"

"His sister is kind and honest. That ought to say something."

Jacob shrugged. "I don't want to argue about it. I'm just warning you to be careful, is all."

"I have every intention of being *careful*," Alison repeated and emphasized his choice of words. It bothered her that her brother would disapprove of her friendship with Austin McCoy, partly because it suggested she didn't have good discernment and partly because Jacob's approval had always meant so much to her.

*****

*M*aegan was surprised and delighted when she awoke the next morning to a vase of flowers and a box tied with ribbons sitting on the kitchen table. There was a note written in Cody's handwriting but signed with Austin's name.

*Happy Birthday Mae!*
*Cody and I left early to do some hunting so we can have a real feast tonight for your special day. Enjoy some time to yourself, Austin.*

Maegan smelled the bouquet of flowers, and then her eyes rested on the parcel. It was wrapped so nicely that she hesitated to open it. She slowly untied the ribbon and, a moment later, gasped when she lifted the lid and saw the beautiful dress inside. Pulling it out, she stepped back and held it up to her body, amazed at how perfectly it matched her height and frame. She bit her bottom lip, wondering if she should try it on. She glanced toward the window and then went to it and moved the curtains to the side as if making sure no one was around.

She sighed as she went back to the table and just stared at the dress. She hadn't worn one since she was a young girl. Life with her brothers just became too inconvenient for a dress. She moved to the stove and began to make coffee. As she waited, she turned and looked at the dress again.

"I might as well," she said aloud to herself, finally lifting it from the table and going to her room. A few minutes later, she was smiling as she ran her hands along the soft fabric that hugged her slim waist and flattered the other curves in her body. She rocked back and forth as the material swished around her legs, marveling that it fit as if it was made for her.

Maegan reached up to her hair, smoothing it down so the wavy curls rested around her face, lying over her shoulders. She only had a small mirror, but it was enough to show her that the dress was beautiful. She almost felt pretty in it, and for some reason, the dress made her think of her mother.

Maegan sat on the edge of her bed as tears filled her eyes. For the first time in a long time, she missed, really missed her mother. She was surprised at the sudden rise of emotion in her heart and had to force herself not to cry.

She nearly dropped the mirror still in her hand when she heard knocking on the front door. She glanced at her trousers that lay over a chair and wondered if she ought to try to change first before answering it. The knock came again, and she found herself going to the door. She hesitantly reached for the handle and opened it, surprised to see Sheriff Bridger on the other side.

"Morning, Sheriff. Can I help you?"

He opened his mouth, but no words came out right away. "Oh, I'm sorry," he apologized for his hesitancy. "I thought I was at the wrong house for a minute." He smiled slightly. "I didn't recognize you right away."

"Oh, that's because I'm … well …" She didn't know what to say and fiddled nervously with her sleeve.

"I was riding nearby and saw one of your horses got out of the pasture," he explained his reason for stopping by. "Must have a broken fence somewhere."

Maegan opened the door wider and started to step outside.

"I put her in the barn already," Bridger said, breaking through her thoughts.

"Oh, thank you." Maegan suddenly remembered her manners. "I just put some coffee on; would you like some?"

"Thanks, that would actually be great," Bridger replied as he followed her inside. He immediately noticed the vase of wildflowers and the ribbon lying around an opened box on the table.

Maegan had moved to the stove and was reaching for a tin cup from a shelf overhead. It fell to the floor the moment she reached for it, and, with an apology for the sudden noise, she bent down and picked it up. Why did being seen in a dress make her all jitters and nerves? She carefully poured the coffee into a new cup and then forced herself not to drop it as she carried it over to him. He'd already taken a seat at the table, so she set it in front of him.

"Smells good, thanks." He noticed she looked nervous, almost jumpy. He also couldn't help but notice how different she looked. "I saw the other horses were gone," he said. "Your brothers aren't here?"

"No, they went hunting this morning. Here, let me clean

this up." She collected the box and then balled up the ribbon, but as she turned with it, her elbow met the vase, which was sitting a little too close to the edge of the table.

"Oh, no!" Maegan gasped as the vase fell to the ground, spilling out the water and flowers over the shattered glass. Tears filled her eyes as she knelt and tried to save the flowers from the wreckage.

Realizing she was crying, Bridger came to his feet, but for a moment, he just stood there, feeling helpless. He could handle an angry mob, a shoot-out, a brawl, but a woman crying? For the first time in his life, he had no clue what to do. He went with his gut, knelt beside her, and began helping her pull out the flowers.

"It's okay," he said, the first thing that came to his mind. "I can get more flowers out in the field."

"It's not that," Maegan sniffed. "They were a gift for my birthday."

The box and ribbons, the dress, and the vase of flowers all made sense now.

"I just feel so bad; Austin bought this vase, and I broke it."

"I'm sure he won't be upset about it," Bridger encouraged. He saw she was still distraught and, as he stood, found himself reaching gently for her arms. "Here, why don't you sit down and let me clean up this glass." He helped her to her feet and then, with his hand still on her arm, moved her to the nearest chair. She sat there with her hands in her lap, holding the flowers she'd managed to save.

Bridger spotted a broom and dustpan near the door and promptly used it to clean up the mess. Most of the water had already been absorbed into the wood-planked floor. For the moment, he set the dustpan full of glass outside and then returned to the house. His eyes rested on Maegan, who still had some leftover tears on her cheeks. She was wiping them with her sleeve and then looked up at him with a watery smile that did something unexpected to his heart. Every other time he'd ever seen her, she was calm, collected, and strong. This vulnerable side to her was something new and … attractive somehow.

"I'm sorry for being such a baby," she said, suddenly coming to her feet and shaking her head slightly as if to dispel what had just happened. "It's just a vase." She laid the flowers on the table and then looked at him again, her brows raised slightly. "More coffee?"

He smiled softly but shook his head. "I better be going."

"Well, thank you for returning the horse. We'll fix the fence."

He nodded. "Thanks for the coffee."

Maegan followed him to the door, standing in the doorway as she watched him walk to his horse. She was about to shut the door when he turned around in his saddle. "Happy Birthday, Mae," he said before riding off.

Maegan watched him head down the road, and then she returned to the house. She glanced down at her dress, which was partially wet from where she'd knelt on the floor. Before she did anything else, she went to her room, took off the dress, and carefully put it back in the box. It had been a mistake to try it on, and she'd made a fool of herself in front of the sheriff because of it. She put the box out of sight and donned her normal apparel. The blouse and trousers brought a familiar feeling of resolve. Maybe one day she would get that dress out again, but not for a very long time.

# *Chapter* Ten

Austin shuffled the deck of cards in his hands before dealing to the fellow across from him. "You said your brother knew Charlie Pitts?" Austin returned to his conversation with a man he had met at the saloon that Thursday afternoon.

"He sure did," the man named Harvey replied as he picked up his cards.

"How close were they? Would Charlie have shared any information with him?" Austin wanted to know. Charlie Pitts was one of the men who raided the bank in North-field, Minnesota, with the James and Younger gang. He had ended up with a bullet through his heart two weeks later, but maybe he had relayed something to Harvey's brother before the fact.

"Deal me in."

Austin and Harvey glanced up at Garret Spencer, who had just entered the saloon and approached their table.

"This is a private conversation," Austin told him, returning his gaze to the cards in his hands.

"You movin' in to your uncle's house too, now?" Garret pressed him as he put his bottle of whiskey on their table and slouched into a chair.

Austin sighed with irritation. "We'll continue this later,"

Austin said to Harvey. He wasn't about to let Garret in on their conversation.

Austin pushed off the table and slid his chair out. As soon as he came to his feet, however, Garret also came to his and suddenly pushed Austin back in his chair. "I wanna talk to you!"

"Keep your hands off me!" Austin said, rising back to his feet. It took everything in him not to wallop Garret there on the spot. The man was obviously drunk and stumbled back into a chair as Austin moved past him. Having had enough of the saloon for one afternoon, Austin headed outside. He had just been moving toward the street when Garret's voice called to him.

"You as weak as that uncle of yours? My pa and Uncle Joe gave him a good thrashin'! It's what we'll do to all of you McCoys if you don't watch out. Even that sister of yours has it coming to her!"

Austin stopped in his tracks, turned, and headed back to the edge of the saloon where Garret stood. "You better not come anywhere close to my sister!" he told him, his muscles tense and his fists balled.

"Or what?" Garret taunted him, a smirk on his face. He was trying to start a fight, and he was about to get one.

*****

Alison had finished work early and was heading toward the mill to get a ride home with her brother. As she passed Mrs. Murry's Dress Shop, someone called her name. Turning, Alison saw Claire Carter exiting the shop and walking towards her.

"Oh, Alison!" she exclaimed. "I just read your story in the paper! I was supposed to be helping Mrs. Murry with an order she is working on, but I couldn't put it down until I'd read the whole thing!"

Alison smiled. "I'm so glad you liked it."

"Mrs. Murry did, too. We can't wait for the rest! You are going to continue it in next week's paper, right?"

"I was hoping to," Alison replied carefully, not sure Mr. Bell would warm to the idea.

"I think that's brilliant. Just what Bell's paper needs. An exciting column that will keep readers wanting to buy the next issue."

Alison appreciated the encouragement, especially coming from Claire Carter, who was a good friend of her brother and sister-in-law. By the time she reached the end of Main Street, she was surprised that several more people stopped her and commented that they had enjoyed the work of fiction. She could only hope their good opinions would get back to Harold Bell.

As she turned the corner to reach the mill, a loud commotion caught her attention. Half a dozen men were gathered in something akin to a circle, whooping and hollering. Normally, Alison would have walked the other way, but she had to pass the ruckus to reach the mill. As she neared, the sight of Austin at the center of the action caused her to gasp and edge closer. His dirt-covered clothing and bloody nose told her the fight had been going on for some time. She pushed her way to the circle of men just as Austin delivered a hard left hook into Garret's jaw. Garret swung several punches that kept Austin on his toes, and as he moved away from Garret, the crowd shifted as well. One of the men knocked into her, and Alison found herself tripping backward and landing on the ground.

That's when Austin caught sight of her and was momentarily distracted. He only turned his head for a moment, but it was enough for Garret to get the upper hand.

"Stop!" Alison screamed as she got back to her feet and

watched Garret lay into Austin. Unable to stand it another second, Alison rushed toward him, hoping the presence of a woman would at least give Garret pause.

"Get outta the way!" Garret ordered her when she put herself between him and Austin, who was trying to get back on his feet. When she didn't move, Garret took her by the arm and pushed her away.

"Stop!" a voice rang out, and everyone turned to see Reverend Myles entering the circle. He walked swiftly up to Garret and stared the man down. "How dare you touch her!"

"She butted in, Reverend!" he defended himself, wiping his bloody face with the back of his hand.

"Get out of here! All of you!" Reverend Myles said to the crowd.

Slowly, they began to move away, Garret along with them. "I'll finish you off later!" he called to Austin before leaving the scene.

Alison was helping Austin to his feet when the reverend turned his attention back to them. "Are you alright?" he asked his sister, gently taking her arm.

"I'm fine," she assured him, her concern more for Austin than herself.

The scene reminded him of a similar one during the fall picnic. It seemed this kind of trouble and Austin McCoy weren't strangers, and both times, he'd found Alison's safety compromised.

"Are you alright?" Reverend Myles asked Austin, who was attempting to wipe off the dirt and blood from his face.

"I'll be fine," Austin replied.

"My wagon's just this way," Reverend Myles told him, not wanting Alison to think he was heartless. "We can give you a ride home."

"Thanks, Reverend, but I'll be alright."

Alison placed a hand on Austin's arm, getting him to look at her. "Are you sure you don't want us to give you a ride home?"

"Nah, I'm fine. Go on with your brother," Austin tried to reassure her with a smile, but the blood pouring from his busted lip hindered the attempt.

As she reluctantly followed her brother, Alison glanced over her shoulder at Austin, who looked to be making his way toward his horse.

"I think you should stay away from that young man," Reverend Myles told his sister on the ride home. "I'm telling you, he's trouble."

"Garret Spencer's trouble," she corrected him.

"Austin McCoy is not the kind of man you want to get involved with. Trust me, I've seen his kind before."

"You keep saying that, but you don't know him at all," Alison disagreed. Her brother may be ten years older than her, but even his life experience couldn't change her mind that he was wrong about Austin.

"I've seen enough of him to know he's a magnet for trouble, and I don't want to see you hurt, like you could have been today!"

"I shouldn't have stepped in," she said. "That was my fault."

"You didn't leave home and come all the way out here to get tangled up with some hooligan."

"Austin McCoy is not a hooligan," Alison told him. "I know he's ended up in a fight or two, but neither were his fault."

"It's not just that," Reverend Myles said. "He's a bounty hunter, and that's not the kind of lifestyle you want to marry into."

Alison sighed, not sure what to say to convince her brother. "I'm not a bad judge of character, Jacob. I think I'll know if he's not someone I should be friends with."

"Just be careful," Reverend Myles advised her, still not convinced.

*****

When Alison arrived at work on Monday, Mr. Bell was at his desk and mumbled a hello when he heard her footsteps.

"I've put some work on your desk," he told her.

She went there directly and began reading through the articles that would go into the paper.

"I've had at least a dozen people mention your column," he said a few minutes later.

Alison paused, her pencil poised above the paper as she waited for him to go on.

"Seems it's caused quite a stir. In fact …" the chair scraped against the floor as he stood. "I haven't had readers this excited for the next edition of my paper in a long time. Looks like I owe you an apology."

Alison turned around to face him. "No, sir. I should have gotten your permission before I put that in there."

"I may have been too set in my ways to ever say yes, so I guess you did what you had to."

"Oh, Mr. Bell, are you really okay with it?" Alison had come to her feet now, excitement in her eyes.

"I'm going to have to be; otherwise, I'm going to have a lot of disappointed customers."

Alison beamed. "Oh, thank you, Mr. Bell."

"Just as long as it doesn't interfere with your work."

"Oh, it won't, I promise." She turned back to the desk, her smile growing.

"I have to admit," Mr. Bell said a moment later, "I'm wondering myself what's going to happen to that Brooks fellow."

Alison was feeling elated as she left work later that day,

and her head was a bit in the clouds as she walked down the street and nearly collided with Gideon Martin. He was coming out of the tack shop and had a crate in his hands.

"I'm so sorry, Gideon," Alison apologized.

"No harm done," he smiled kindly at her.

"How have you been?" she asked politely.

He shrugged. "Workin' a lot. How 'bout you?"

"I'm very well, actually." She could not keep the enthusiasm from her voice. "Did you happen to read my column in the paper the other week?" she asked.

"Nah," he admitted. "Ain't got much time lately to read, and when I do, it usually puts me to sleep."

"Oh." She didn't know what to say to that. "Well, I should be getting to the mill before Jacob leaves without me."

"I could give you a ride home?" he offered.

"Thank you, but my brother's expecting me. Good day, Gideon."

Alison crossed the street once she'd reached the end of the shops. Just as she passed the livery, a familiar voice called out to her. She turned and saw Austin leaving the livery.

"Afternoon, Ali."

She smiled, feeling that familiar rush of warmth when she saw him. "Afternoon. What are you up to?"

"Just gettin' some new shoes for the horse," he gestured behind him toward the livery. "How 'bout yourself? You look like you just got handed the moon."

Alison laughed. "Well, I am excited. Folks liked my column so much that Mr. Bell wants me to continue it every week!"

"That's tremendous! I guess your risk paid off," he smiled, remembering their conversation.

Alison smiled, too. "Thanks. I'm so thankful it did!" She bit her bottom lip, a little uncertain. "What did you think when you read it? Your honest opinion?"

"My honest opinion?" Austin stalled, mentally chiding himself for not having asked Cody to read it to him. As well-educated as Alison was, he couldn't let her know he couldn't even read. "I thought it was real exciting! You're a great writer, Ali."

She couldn't have been more pleased. "I may have fantasized the gun-slinging part a little," she laughed softly.

"I thought it was perfect," he reassured her. He smiled, and then his expression grew more serious. "I'm sorry about the other day. I hope you weren't hurt."

"That was my fault for stepping in like I did," she said, noticing the marks and bruises that lingered on his face from the fight. "I hope you weren't hurt too badly."

"Nah, Garret roughed me up a bit, but nothing I ain't had before. Sorry you had to see that, though."

"I'm sorry for distracting you from the fight," she apologized.

"You can't help it if you're a distraction," he said, complimenting her.

She smiled softly, catching his meaning.

Austin suddenly looked past her, noticing Jacob approaching his wagon. "Your brother's coming."

Alison didn't even glance back. "Would you want to come for supper tomorrow night?" she asked suddenly, blurting it out before she had time to think if it was proper to do the inviting.

"Not sure your brother's taken a shine to me, Ali."

"Oh, he'll be fine," Alison said with a little roll of her eyes. "He just needs to get to know you, and you'll just love Maggie and my niece and nephew."

He shrugged, not able to resist the chance to spend time with her. "What time?"

*****

Alison was right. Lilly and Lucas warmed to Austin like butter on a hot pan. Lucas climbed up on his lap to show him his toy train and didn't leave until his mother picked him up so Austin could eat without the boy in his way. Lilly was talkative and pleasant, asking him a hundred and one questions until her father gave her a gentle but reminding look to let others have a chance in the conversation. After supper, Maggie directed the kids across the room to play while the adults continued in conversation.

"This was delicious, Mrs. Myles; thank you," Austin said as Alison began to clear the table with her sister-in-law.

"I'm glad you liked it, and please call me Maggie. I hope you're not too full; we still have dessert coming."

"No, ma'am, never too full for dessert." He smiled at her. "When's the baby due?"

"January," Maggie replied, instinctively placing a hand on her growing belly.

"Alison tells us you're a bounty hunter," Jacob said a few minutes later, leaning back in his chair as his wife handed him a cup of coffee.

"Yes, sir."

"Seems a rather dangerous profession."

"Not if you know what you're doing," Austin replied, hoping he didn't sound too cocky.

"What made you get into that, if you don't mind me asking?"

"Not at all. I think my older brother and I stumbled upon it by accident, really. If I recall correctly, a friend of ours was robbed at gunpoint and then …" He glanced toward Lilly and Lucas to make sure they were out of earshot. "… and then killed. We went and apprehended the fellow, not knowing he was a wanted man in most territories. After that first payday, it just seemed to stick."

"And you can see yourself doing that for a while yet?" Jacob probed.

"Until something better comes along," Austin replied, his eyes subconsciously swinging to Alison.

"Not a real steady or safe way to make income, unfortunately," Jacob said, ignoring the look his wife was trying to send in his direction.

"It is if you know how to handle yourself and your cash," Austin returned.

"Still, it would be hard for a man to have a family and stay in that line of work."

"True. Which is why I don't intend on doing it forever," Austin said, holding the other man's gaze. He knew what he was trying to do.

"I hope you like peach pie," Maggie said as she suddenly swept up to the table and placed the dessert between the two men. Alison was just beside her, setting down small plates.

"How did Mae like her gift?" Alison asked Austin, hoping to break some of the tension.

"She said she loved it, but I ain't seen the vase or the dress since I gave it to her."

"Well, I'm sure she'll wear it at the right time."

"Your sister is such a nice girl," Maggie added as she cut a slice of pie and set it on the plate in front of Austin.

"That she is. Not many I admire and respect as much as her. After our parents died, she took care of the lot of us, practically raising my little brother."

Alison loved the affection she could hear in his voice when he talked about his sister. "I haven't known her that long, but I think Mae is something special, too, and Cody. Lilly told me the first day she met him, he came to her rescue when Jeb Spencer was picking on her."

"Glad to hear it," Austin said before taking another bite of pie. "Sometimes a bully needs taught a lesson."

"Sometimes fighting isn't always the best way," Reverend Myles added, thinking it seemed second nature to Austin McCoy.

"Unfortunately, sometimes it's the only way," Austin replied. "Not to disagree with you, Reverend," he quickly added.

Alison and Maggie again jumped into the conversation and successfully steered it in another direction, managing to keep it lighter for the remainder of the evening.

"Guess I oughta be going before it gets too late," Austin said a while later.

"Thank you for coming," Maggie said with a kind smile.

"You're not weaving yet, are you?" Lucas suddenly appeared at his side.

"'Fraid so, little buddy, but thanks for showing me your train." Austin smiled at the boy before coming to his feet. He extended his hand to Jacob Myles, who was also standing. The man shook it wordlessly and seemed to force a smile.

"I'll walk you out," Alison said.

"Me, too," Lilly said as she reached for her sweater.

"Actually, I could use your help with the dishes," Maggie told her daughter.

Alison smiled at the little girl and then followed Austin outside. "Sorry my brother was drilling you a bit," she said as he untethered his horse's reins.

"I don't mind," Austin grinned as he turned to face her. He felt a little taken aback by how striking she was. He wasn't sure if it was just his perception, but in the moonlight, her beauty looked akin to magical. "He just wants to make sure you don't end up with some scoundrel."

Alison took a few steps closer to him. "Well, then, it's a good thing I don't know anyone like that."

He wasn't sure if she realized what her nearness was doing to him. Almost as if they had a life of their own, his hands reached out and took hers. "Will your brother kill me if I kiss you … and can I kiss you?"

"No, he won't … and yes, you can." She relished the moment his lips met hers. It was brief and sweet and perfect.

"I've never met anyone like you, Ali," he whispered as he lifted his head but kept his eyes on hers.

Her heart was pounding, yet she felt so at home standing there with Austin. She knew things were moving fast, but she didn't know how to slow down the feelings that were welling in her heart for this man she barely knew. She wanted to tell him how much she was coming to care for him, but she just couldn't find the words. She decided she would have to write him a letter to explain it.

"I should go," he said, reluctantly breaking the moment. He slowly released his hold on her hands. "It's getting cold out here; you best get inside."

She reluctantly stepped back as he stuck his foot in the stirrup and swung his other leg over the saddle.

"Good night, Austin," was all she could say before he rode off into the night, taking her heart right along with him.

*****

The next day, Austin pulled Cody aside and asked him to meet him in the barn. "I need your help with something," he told him.

Cody was expecting to help him lift something or muck out a stable, so he was surprised when Austin pressed a newspaper into his hands. "I need you to read me that last bit on the back. There's two different ones, so read the one from last week first and then the more recent."

"Why? What's it about?" Cody asked curiously as he flipped one of the papers over.

"It's a column or something that Ali writes for the newspaper. She's gonna ask me if I read it, and I have to know what it's about."

Cody smiled to himself, thinking Maegan had been right all along about reading. He was glad he could help his brother out. "Alright, let's sit down. It's a little wordy, so it might take a few minutes."

# *Chapter* Eleven

"Ilike Millcreek," Austin said to Maegan a few nights later after supper.

She was sitting across from him at the table and glanced up from the book she was reading. "Millcreek or Alison Myles?"

"Both."

"It's a shame you'll be leaving, then." It had been three weeks since he had arrived, and she knew he had already stayed longer than he planned. She heard him sigh and saw the regret in his eyes.

"You don't think Sawyer would ever want to sell the farm, do you?" Austin surprised her by asking.

"You're really serious about Alison, aren't you?" Maegan lowered her book, knowing her brother wouldn't have any reason to leave their farm except to settle permanently somewhere else.

"I've only known her a few weeks, but … when you know, you know."

"Does she feel the same way about you?" Maegan asked.

"I think so."

"So … what are you saying?"

Austin leaned back in his chair. "I don't rightly know. I

mean, if you and Cody are planning to stay here and Alison wants to live here …" he shrugged. "Maybe I should look for land and make it my home, too. I know Sawyer would be none too thrilled about my leaving the farm though … and bounty huntin'."

"He'll understand if you want to leave a life of bounty hunting and settle somewhere else."

"But that's the problem," Austin said. "I don't know what else I'd do to earn a livin'."

"Just pray about it, Austin. The Lord will lead you."

A thoughtful smile touched his lips. His sister had been saying that to him for as many years as he could recount, and usually, she was right. He came to his feet. "Well, I'm gonna turn in. 'Night, Mae."

Once alone, Maegan found herself deep in thought. Leaving their home had been somewhat of a hasty decision, a desperate move to keep Cody safe. More than ever, it seemed the hand of providence had led her to leave when she did. Now, with the friends they had made, she was missing home less and less, and it almost made her heart ache more at the thought of leaving Millcreek than at the prospect of not going back to their farm. It appeared Austin had found a reason for staying as well. Maybe that was a sure sign that they had been meant to come to Millcreek all along.

*****

Knowing Alison worked on Mondays, Austin made it a point to head into town, hoping to catch her as she was leaving work. He was passing the livery when Toby Jackson, an older man he had played poker with occasionally, caught sight of him as he was crossing the street. He was a talker and knew a little about everyone who had passed through Millcreek or lived there.

"Austin! Glad to catch you," Toby said. "You still lookin' for information 'bout them James boys?"

The man had Austin's attention. Maybe his visits to the saloon were about to pay off. "Go on," Austin said.

"Fellow I was talking to yesterday said a week ago he was on a stage that was robbed by two fellows fitting the James brothers' description, 'bout twenty miles north of here."

"Who told you that?"

"His name was Davis, I think." Toby scratched his heavily bearded cheek. "He's staying a few more days in Millcreek and is at the saloon most nights if you wanna catch him."

"Thanks," Austin said, making a mental note to talk to the man himself. If he did find out specific information on Jesse's' and Frank's whereabouts, he knew he really should meet back up with Sawyer. He hated the thought of leaving Maegan and Cody, though ... and Alison.

His steps were heavy as he walked toward the newspaper press, but he couldn't hold back a smile when Alison stepped out and ran up to him. "I told my brother not to worry about giving me a ride home," Alison told him as she finished pulling on and buttoning up her coat. "Thought I'd just catch a ride with you if it's ok."

"How'd you know I'd be coming by?" he asked with a curious expression.

"I just figured you would."

"I don't know if I like being that predictable," he joked. "Oh, I read your most recent column," he suddenly remembered to tell her. "It was good ... really good." He was glad he could honestly say it. He was surprised at how much he had enjoyed the story and how vividly he could imagine what Cody read to him.

"Honest? You didn't think it was too farfetched?"

"Nah, not at all." He grinned. "I mean, that Brooks fellow

single-handedly fighting off those four ruffians was a little bit of a stretch, but he kind of reminded me of myself."

Alison laughed. "I'm sure he did." She glanced past him at his horse, no longer afraid of riding. "C'mon, let's ride out of here."

Without a moment's hesitation, he helped her up and then mounted behind her, enjoying her nearness. He nudged his horse down the dirt street, the rhythmic clip-clop of the horse's hooves blending in with the other riders passing. Once at the edge of town, Austin propelled him into a gallop, loving the feeling of Alison resting against him. A sudden sting pricked his heart at the thought of having to say goodbye.

The November air was icy, making Austin's nearness even more welcome. Alison had never felt so happy and was beginning to feel sort of homesick whenever she wasn't with him. Eventually, they reached a place folks of Millcreek called Pond Point. After riding across the covered bridge that spanned the narrowest point of the pond, Austin slowed his horse and dismounted before helping Alison down. Holding her hand, he walked with her along the bank of a nearby stream, his other hand on the reins of his horse that followed a few feet behind. They talked easily, and before too long, he found himself kissing her for the second time. She stood on tiptoe and wrapped her arms around his neck. "I could stay out here with you forever," she said quietly.

Her words reminded him that he needed to tell her he would have to leave soon. But he also wanted her to know he'd be back. "It's getting cold. I should get you home" was all he heard himself say.

When they reached her brother's house, Austin helped her down from the saddle and, for a moment, just stared into her eyes, wishing he could say all that was in his heart.

He would have been surprised to know just how much Alison's thoughts mirrored his own. She reached into her pocket and handed him an envelope.

"I express myself much better in writing." She smiled sweetly and then placed a quick kiss on his cheek before heading toward the door, turning briefly to wave.

Austin waved back at her and then looked down at the envelope she had given him. He resolved that even if he couldn't read what was inside, he could still keep it tucked safely in his pocket, close to his heart where Alison already was.

*****

After supper that night, Austin told Maegan not to wait up. He was heading to town, hoping to meet up with the Davis fellow that Toby Jackson had told him about. When Austin walked into the saloon, he thought it seemed busier than usual, with scarcely an empty seat available. The clinking of glasses and the clunking of the out-of-tune piano filled the room, which smelled of tobacco and spilled whiskey. Austin went to the bar, ordered a drink, and then let his eyes wander the room in search of Toby. He spotted him near a smoky table where a heated game of poker was taking place.

"Evenin', Toby." Austin came alongside him. "Is that fellow, Davis, here?"

"Sure is," Toby Jackson replied without breaking his gaze off his cards. "He's over there." He gestured toward a nearby table.

Austin moved toward the man and opened the conversation. "Mind if I sit a spell? I'm looking for information on the James brothers and heard you might know a thing or two."

The man nudged his head toward the chair opposite him, which had just been vacated.

Austin sat down. "What do you know about the stage robbery north of here?"

"I was on that stage less than a week ago."

"You have any idea who was behind it?" Austin asked.

"It was the James brothers."

"You saw their faces?"

"I saw Frank's cuz his bandanna slipped."

Austin conversed a few more minutes until he'd gotten all the information the man had to offer and then moved toward the door. Less than a week ago was a good indication that the James brothers were still in the territory. Austin knew he needed to meet up with Sawyer right away. As he exited through the double swinging doors, a saloon girl who had momentarily stepped outside turned and greeted him with a broad smile.

"You're not leaving already, are you?" she asked sweetly as she stepped closer to him and flirtatiously laid her hand on his arm.

Even in the dim streetlight, he could see she was wearing an excessive amount of makeup and appeared to be a little drunk. He gently lifted her hand off his arm and stepped past her.

"I wanted to buy you a drink, handsome," she said, her tone feigning sadness. She stumbled as she tried to catch up to him, and he reached out to save her from hitting the ground. "I'm sorry, I'm so clumsy," she apologized as she tightly wrapped her arms around his neck and pushed herself against him.

Trying to pry her fingers loose, Austin moved toward a bench that sat under the saloon window. Once she was seated, he managed to pull away from her embrace.

"Good night, handsome!" she called as he turned and walked away.

“Reverend Myles didn't get too many late-night calls, but that night, someone rode to his house to tell him Widow Grayson was asking for him. He went right away, knowing the woman was pushing ninety-three and that her health had been declining steadily for the last year. He had half expected to see her breathe her last that night but was thankful when the doctor arrived and said she still had some fight in her. When he left her home, which was located just off Main Street, he directed his horse toward home. He'd have to pass back through the town and soon heard the unmistakable ruckus of drunken laughter and shouts of commotion coming from the saloon. Thankfully for residents who lived in Millcreek, the saloon was located at the edge of town.

Something caught Reverend Myles' eye as he passed the saloon … or *someone,* rather. He was appalled to see Austin McCoy in close contact with a woman who seemed to be all over him. Anger rose up in him when he thought of Alison falling for a man like him. He didn't deserve to have someone like Alison care for him. Afraid he wouldn't be able to restrain his ire if he confronted the man that instant, Jacob Myles rode a little faster to get home. Sleep evaded him most of the night, and by early morning, he had made a decision about Austin McCoy.

*****

Even though he had gotten to bed late, Austin was up before the sun, his thoughts keeping him from sleeping. He knew he had to leave, but he also knew he wanted to talk with Alison before he did. He needed her to know he was serious about a future with her and that he would be back. It surprised even him how quickly he had fallen for her.

He had been content with his life until this point, but after meeting Alison, he couldn't imagine a future without her.

It was confusing, to say the least. If he married her, where would they live? How could he provide for her if he left his life of bounty hunting? If they married, he didn't want to chase down outlaws anymore, a job that could take him away for weeks or months at a time. The dangers his profession posed had never bothered him before, but now there was so much more to consider.

Austin stepped outside into the cold, still-dark morning and buttoned his jacket. There was a tree in the yard with a stump near it that caught his attention. Sitting on it, he let his head rest in his hands and, for the first time in a while, heard his own whispers of prayer. He had been raised to believe in God and had always accepted the fact that God was all-powerful. He could attribute many good outcomes to his sister's prayers, but even so, he had never made it too personal. It had always seemed like Maegan's faith and prayers were enough for all of them ... until now.

He found himself asking God for guidance ... and did some soul-searching and repenting while he was at it. He knew he needed to make more time for the Lord in his life and more space for him in his heart. It was a realization that brought a new peace that swept over him, as tangible as the cold morning breeze. He didn't know how long he sat there praying, but when he lifted his head, the sun was beginning to climb the eastern horizon.

He stood and headed toward the house, only to pause and turn at the sound of an approaching rider. As the rider neared, Austin realized it was Reverend Myles. He watched as he dismounted and then met him in the yard. "Everything okay?" Austin asked with concern. He thought it odd that Jacob Myles would come by at such an hour.

"I'm sorry to come by so early, but I wanted to catch you right away." He dismounted and stood in front of Austin.

"Go on," Austin said.

"I'll come right to the point. I don't usually interfere, but in this instance, I feel I have no other option. Whatever is going on between you and my sister, I want it to stop."

"Sir?"

"I think you understand me. She deserves someone who will be faithful to her and take care of her."

"I'm capable of both of those things," Austin held his ground.

"Not as I see it." Jacob didn't want to bring up what he'd seen the night before, as it was probably just one of many similar incidents. "If you can't keep your distance, then it might be better for you to leave."

Austin was genuinely taken aback by the man's boldness. He suspected he didn't particularly like him, but this seemed a little extreme.

"Alison's an enthusiastic person," Reverend Myles went on. "She tends to throw herself headlong into whatever she's excited about, sometimes prematurely. I'm sure after further reflection, she'll come to see what I have where you're concerned."

"I appreciate your candidness," Austin said, his tone saying the opposite.

"I don't care if you appreciate it or not; just mind what I say." On those words, he mounted his horse and rode off, leaving Austin standing there feeling a sense of deep loss. He had just spent the better part of an hour praying for an answer. Maybe this was it, and it cut him to the heart. Maybe desiring a life with Alison was a foolish dream. What did he even have to offer her, anyway? His insecurities mounted and overshadowed any sense of hope he had previously had.

When he returned to the house, Maegan and Cody were starting to wake up. The smell of freshly brewing coffee filled the small cabin. "I've got to be going," he told them after breakfast. "The James brothers aren't far, and I need to reach Sawyer."

"Can't you just stay in Millcreek?" Cody pleaded, his eyes saying more than his words.

"'Fraid not, little brother. My short visit turned into almost a month, as it is."

"But you'll be back, won't you?" Cody asked.

"I don't know" was all Austin could offer. He glanced at Maegan, and she saw something in his eyes that concerned her. Once Cody had gone to his room to get his things for school, she asked him privately. "Does Alison know you're going?"

His silence was all the answer she needed.

"Austin, you have to tell her. I think she's come to care for you."

"It's better if I just go," he said. "Uncle Ben will be back soon anyway, so at least I know you two will be safe." He stood from the table and went to the window. Absently, he pushed the curtains to one side and sighed. "Would you tell her something for me, though?"

Maegan nodded. "Of course I will."

"Tell her I'm sorry."

*****

Later that same day, Alison rode to town with Maggie. They stopped by the General Store and then headed toward school to pick up Lilly before going home. Children were pouring out of the front doors of the church turned schoolhouse, and Alison spotted Cody walking alongside Lilly.

"Hi, Ma!" Lilly greeted cheerily. "Can we give Cody a ride, too?"

"Of course," she smiled. "Hello, Cody."

"Hello, Mrs. Myles." He climbed in the back and sat across from Lilly, who chatted about their school day until Maggie slowed the wagon for Cody to get off.

"Tell Maegan and your brother I might be by later," Alison said to him as he hopped down.

"I'll tell Mae, but Austin left this mornin'."

"What?"

"He left this mornin'," Cody repeated.

Alison climbed down from her seat and met Cody before he walked any farther. "What do you mean?"

"He said he needed to get to Sawyer soon as possible."

Alison's mouth dropped a little at the shock of such news. "He's coming back though, right?"

Cody shrugged. "It didn't sound like he was anytime soon."

Alison suddenly felt weak all over, as if someone had just knocked the wind out of her. Quietly, she climbed back into the wagon, ignoring Maggie's empathetic glances. "I'm sure there's a good explanation," Maggie tried to reassure her, all the while worrying her husband had been right all along about Austin McCoy.

Alison helped Maggie with some chores around the house and the meal preparations, but once that was completed, she took the buckboard and headed to see Maegan. Maegan answered the door and kindly invited her in.

"Cody mentioned earlier that Austin had left. Is that true?" Alison jumped right to the point of her visit.

Maegan closed the door behind her and sighed. "I'm afraid so."

"But without even a goodbye?" Alison shook her head in astonishment. "Was it that urgent that he couldn't even say goodbye?"

"He did ask me to tell you that he's sorry."

*What is that supposed to mean?* Alison wondered. *Sorry that he had to leave, or sorry that he had taken an interest in her?*

"I know it's not enough, and I urged him to wait until he could tell you."

"But he wouldn't?" Alison sat down in a chair at the table, her eyes starting to fill with tears. "How long do you think he'll be gone?"

"Well, he didn't exactly say. I know he was anxious to get back to Sawyer with some information he'd discovered about the outlaws they're tracking."

Alison was crushed. Even if that were true, he could have spared a few minutes to say goodbye. Maybe bounty hunting had a higher claim to his heart than she did. She suddenly remembered the letter she had written him and wished she could take back what she'd said. Maybe she'd made a fool of herself, and he had only been leading her on the whole time. Her brother's warnings about Austin suddenly echoed through her mind.

"I need to get back to help Maggie," Alison lied politely. Maegan apologized for her brother's sudden departure, although she knew it did little to ease Alison's heart.

Once on her way home, Alison returned to her thoughts. Maybe Austin had read the letter and had a good laugh at her expense. No, she argued with herself. He had to have felt the same way for her as she did for him. Their last few times together had been so … wonderful. What had happened to change all of that?

When Alison reached her brother's home, she went right to her room. She wanted to be alone, if for no other reason than to have a good cry.

# *Chapter* Twelve



Alison climbed down from her brother's wagon and knocked on the door of the little house behind Lyddie Hall's boarding house. It was Friday, and a few days ago, she'd invited Lyn Hummel for the second time to dine with her and her brother's family. Having company and conversation was the last thing she wanted right now, but Alison felt like she had to keep her word to the elderly woman. She told herself that, at the least, maybe it would take her mind off Austin for a short time. The last two weeks had been more difficult than any she had ever had, her heart feeling tangled in confusion, hurt, and vexation regarding Austin McCoy.

There was no answer after several tries, so Alison turned the knob and opened the door. The room wasn't large enough for anything more than a bed, a small table, and a rocking chair, which Alison spotted Lyn Hummel rocking in. Stepping inside the clean but dim room, Alison smiled at the woman. "Lyn? Can I come in?"

The woman didn't answer, but Alison wasn't deterred. "Did you remember about coming with me for dinner tonight?"

When she didn't answer again, Alison went to stand

beside her, eventually kneeling to better see her face. "Lyn? Are you alright?"

"I just don't feel like company tonight," the woman said quietly.

For the first time, Alison noticed there was something in her hands. It looked like a letter of some sort. "I can understand that," Alison said, "but maybe you'll feel differently by the time we get to my brother's house."

"I don't think so, dear."

The letter grabbed Alison's attention again. "Do you mind if I … read this?" she asked, carefully taking the paper from the woman's fingers. Her hands didn't even move as Alison took it. She had to walk to the window for more light to see the faded ink. The address in the upper corner caught her eye first. It was a letter from the hospital at Jefferson Barracks, the date reading July 7, 1863.

*We regret to inform you …* it began, and it didn't take Alison long to read the rest. Lyn's son had been severely wounded in battle with very little chance of recovery. It advised any family members to come quickly. Alison folded the letter on its very worn indents and handed it back to Lyn Hummel. "If you're not up for dinner with us, what if you and I just spend dinner together here?"

There was no expression or response to her words, but empathy in Alison's heart told her not to give up. There was suddenly a knock on the door, and it opened as Mrs. Lyddie stepped inside, a smile on her face and a tray in her hands. "Oh, Alison. I didn't know you were here."

"I was coming to take Mrs. Hummel for dinner, but she isn't feeling up to it."

"Well, I'll just leave this tray here then," Lyddie said as she set the tray on the table and then turned to Alison.

"I'll stay with her while she eats it," Alison told the woman.

"That's kind. There's extra bowls and cutlery on that shelf over there and more than enough for two on that tray, so please help yourself."

"I will, thank you."

After she had gone, Alison went back to Lyn and reached gently for her arm. "Can I help you to the table?" Alison was glad when she rose to her feet. Once she was seated, Alison set the bowl of soup and some of the bread Lyddie had brought in front of her.

"There's lemonade here, too," Alison said as she tipped the pitcher to pour lemonade into a glass.

"As soon as I got the letter, I left for the hospital," Lyn told her. "But by the time I got there, they said William was gone … not dead, gone. There were so many wounded and killed that they couldn't locate where his body was. Some said he'd probably died, but others just said he had left."

Alison sat slowly in the chair beside the woman. "You think he's still alive?"

"Yes. I don't know why he wouldn't come home unless he had a good reason, but I know he's alive somewhere." She picked up her spoon but then set it back down as her deep-set, light blue eyes lifted to meet Alison's. "Why wouldn't he come home?"

The woman's voice broke as soft sobs began to shake her frail shoulders. Alison immediately stood from her chair and hugged the woman, who seemed too fragile to be on her own. Kneeling beside her, Alison gently smoothed some straying gray hair out of the woman's face.

"I have an idea," Alison said softly, a light in her eyes. "Let's pray right now and ask God to either help you find your son very soon or give you peace to live without him if … if he can't be found—on this earth, anyway."

Slowly, Lyn nodded in agreement, but she whispered, "I don't want to live on this earth without him."

Alison reached out and lovingly squeezed her hand. "Let's pray," she said.

Together, they closed their eyes and bowed their heads, and although probability told Alison that William Hummel was dead, she prayed with every ounce of faith she possessed that if he were alive, he would be found … and soon.

*****

"Hey Cody, wait up!"

Cody turned around to see Lilly running towards him. It was the following day, and school had let out earlier than usual since Mrs. Cooper said she wasn't feeling well. Cody had been one of the first ones out the door. He couldn't help the smile that tugged on his lips as he watched Lilly trying to catch up. She wasn't all that much shorter than him, but she was a skinny thing and reminded him of what it might be like to have a little sister.

"Thanks for waiting," she said, trying to catch her breath. "I was wondering if you wanted to go by the gorge." She smiled, hoping he would agree. "I don't live that far from it, so we could go by there and then go to my place. Mrs. Cooper let us out early, so I doubt anyone would miss us."

Cody shrugged; it was an interesting spot to walk around, and that day in November wasn't too cold. The last time he'd been near there was when he had been stupid enough to go with Jeb. "I guess," he said. He'd ridden his horse to school and, after mounting, reached down to help Lilly climb up behind him in the saddle. Cody directed his horse across the road to the field adjacent to it. After some time, they came upon a creek that they followed for half an hour until it led into a forest, where the ground eventually began to slope into a gorge. After tying the horse to a tree, they went on foot, venturing toward the ravine.

"Be careful," Cody warned as she neared the edge of the flat area.

"What do you want for Christmas?" Lilly suddenly asked as she held onto the trunk of a tree for balance.

"Christmas?"

"Yeah, what do you want?"

"I don't know."

"There's got to be something."

Cody sighed, shoving his bare hands in his pockets. What he really wanted was to see his brothers again. Living in Millcreek wasn't bad, and although he would scarcely admit it to himself, he liked school. "The only thing I want is to see my brothers again … and maybe that new Winchester in Mr. Maison's store window," he added with a grin.

"Your brother Austin was nice. What's your other brother like?"

"He's kind of like the opposite of Austin, but not in a bad way. What do you want for Christmas?" he said and thought she looked glad he'd asked.

"What I really want is my own horse, but Pa said he'll probably make me wait until I'm twelve. Hey, look at that!"

Cody followed the direction that her hand pointed and noticed some wildflowers growing at the corner of a large boulder.

"I can't believe they're still in bloom," Lilly said as she removed her red mitten to pick them.

"It gets pretty steep right about there," Cody warned. "Better let me get them for you."

"I can do it," she argued, but then, at her next step, some loose dirt under her foot gave way, and she felt herself sliding downwards. She screamed as she lost her balance and started tumbling down the ravine.

"Lilly!" Cody moved as quickly as he could to keep up with her, reaching out and grabbing her hand to help steady her.

"Thanks," she said, dusting the dirt off her dress. "I'm fine." Something caught her eye, and she realized Cody saw it, too. "What do you think that is?"

They were both looking at what appeared to be a cave of sorts, just fifteen yards farther down the slope. They edged closer and saw the outline of an entrance, half hidden with vines and brush.

"Looks like an old mine," Cody said.

"That's exciting!" Lilly exclaimed. "We should get a lantern and come back to explore it!"

They agreed to come back the next day but with a lantern. During school, Cody hid the lantern so no one would ask questions, and then afterward, they hurried to the same spot, this time being more careful not to slip down the ravine. Once back at the cave, Cody lit the lantern and led the way inside.

"It's so dark … and cold," Lilly said. As Cody lifted the lantern to see, it was clear it was an old mine shaft. It was wide until they got about twenty feet in, and then it narrowed considerably.

"We should probably go back," Cody said. And then they heard what sounded like shuffled footsteps. Turning around, Cody raised the lantern.

"Jeb Spencer! What are you doing here?" Lilly said in a tone that told him he was not welcome.

"Just wanted to see what you halfwits were up to," he replied. "'Sides, I've known about this mine for years."

"You're lying," Lilly said. "Why'd you have to follow us? Now all the kids are gonna find out about this place."

Jeb ignored her and came closer. "If you give me that lantern, I'll show you something I found back here." Jeb grabbed it out of Cody's hands before he could answer.

"Follow me," Jeb said, and he sounded so sure of himself that Cody and Lilly did follow, at least for a minute.

"I don't want to go any further," Lilly whispered as she glanced over her shoulder and realized she couldn't see the opening anymore.

"I ain't surprised that she's yella, but don't tell me you're a coward, too," he said to Cody.

"I ain't no coward, but I'm not a fool either."

"Fine, then I'll go alone."

"Not with my lantern, you're not," Cody said. He reached for it, but Jeb stepped away and kept walking. The shaft broke into two tunnels, and he took the one on the right. He'd barely taken a few steps when he tripped on something and fell into the wall.

"What's that noise?" Lilly whimpered.

"We gotta get out of here!" Cody said as he felt the walls shaking around them. He grabbed her hand and started running with her toward the entrance. Just then, they could hear the sound of rock falling between them and Jeb.

"Don't leave me!" he screamed.

Cody and Lilly stopped to run back to him, lifting their hands to shield their heads from some rocks and dirt that were falling in. The light from the lantern Jeb held was visible behind the mound of rock that had fallen between them. Immediately, Cody and Lilly began helping him move rocks so he could get through to where they were. They managed to create an opening for him to pass through, and then the three of them started back to the exit. Suddenly, just a few feet in front of them, rocks and dirt tumbled from the ceiling and settled into a wall.

Lilly screamed and clutched Cody's arm. The three kids ducked down until the rumbling stopped.

"We're trapped!" Lilly exclaimed, fear making her voice

tremble. She turned toward Jeb. "It's your fault for leading us back here!"

With a shaky sigh, Cody took the lantern from Jeb's hand. "Maybe there's another way out of here … down that shaft," he added, lifting the lantern toward the wall they had broken down to get to Jeb. They could go back that way and see if the tunnel took them to another exit.

Cody led the way, walking carefully through the darkness with the lantern poised high. Soon, they were crawling through the opening they had made only minutes earlier to get to Jeb and moving down the tunnel that led from it.

"Dead end," Jeb said as they reached a wall of rock several minutes later. "There's no way out," he said, his voice thick with dread.

"What are we gonna do?" Lilly asked.

Cody wished he had an answer, but inwardly, he felt as panicked as her voice sounded.

"Someone will come for us," Jeb said.

"But no one knows where we are." Lilly began to cry.

"We'll figure something out," Cody said, trying to sound more confident than he felt. "Let's start trying to move these rocks."

*****

For the third time in the last hour, Maegan went to the door and called Cody's name. She hadn't seen him since that morning when he'd left for school, and it wasn't like him not to come home before dark. The twilight would give way to night soon. Maegan paced the length of the house for a few more minutes before grabbing a lantern and rechecking the barn, but he wasn't there.

A sick feeling settled in Maegan's gut, and she quickly saddled her horse. Where could he possibly be? At a friend's house, maybe? Maegan thought of Lilly and started to ride toward her house.

It was completely dark when Maegan reached the reverend's house. Maggie opened the door when she knocked, and instantly, Maegan saw anxiety in the other woman's eyes.

"I'm looking for Cody. Is he here?"

Maggie gasped. "We can't find Lilly either! Jacob is out looking for her right now."

"Did they come back here after school at all?"

Maggie shook her head. "I don't know where they could be, but it does give me a little comfort knowing perhaps she is with Cody."

"We'll find them," Maegan promised as she swung up into her saddle and rode off into the night.

She didn't have the first idea where to look next, and with it being so dark, there was very little chance of finding them if they were lost somewhere. A gust of wind crept into her coat and sent a shiver through her. It was cold and windy, making her worry even more for Cody and now Lilly. The little bit of light from her lantern made it difficult to ride fast, but she kept to the main roads, yelling out Cody's and Lilly's names and then listening for any response. She knew there were a few spots Cody liked to ride to, so she searched those areas the best she could before heading into town. Not knowing what else to do, she ended up at the jailhouse, banging on the door.

Sheriff Bridger opened it, a mixture of surprise and concern on his face at the sight of Maegan. "What's wrong?" he asked as he stepped back to let her inside. He saw she wasn't wearing any gloves and encouraged her to warm up beside the small iron stove that kept the jailhouse warm.

"I've been out searching for Cody. He and Lilly are missing."

"What?"

"He never came home after school. I went over to Reverend Myles thinking he might have gone home with Lilly, and Maggie told me the reverend was out looking for Lilly as well."

"That's strange."

"It's not like Cody at all, which is why I'm so worried."

Sheriff Bridger jumped into action and began gathering lanterns from the jailhouse. "Let's call folks to the church and get other men out searching." Maegan was already following him outside and then toward the church. He rang the bell, which the townspeople knew was a call to alarm. Eli Greene from the Livery, Tom Maison, and other men who lived in the town were soon spilling into the church.

"I need all of your help," Sheriff Bridger told them. "Lilly Myles and Cody McCoy have gone missing. They were last seen leaving here after school. Break into groups and head in every direction!"

Maegan was grateful for the dozen men who joined the search, but she couldn't shake the awful heaviness that something was terribly wrong.

"Come with me," she heard the sheriff say. They took the main road that led out of town and away from the school, the one Lilly and Cody would have taken to walk home. An hour later, Maegan was fighting complete panic. "You don't think the Spencers could have something to do with this?" she asked.

"I admit, the thought did cross my mind. Let's head over there."

It was a cold ride to Joe and Becky Spencer's, the darkness broken only by the moonlight and limited light from the lanterns Maegan and Bridger held. When they arrived at Joe's, Maegan stayed on her horse and watched as the sheriff went to the door and knocked. Becky opened it, and in the dim light coming from inside the house, Maegan could see the alarm on her face at the sight of the sheriff.

"Have you seen Cody McCoy or Lilly Myles?" the sheriff asked.

"No. I haven't seen Jeb either! Joe's been out searching for hours! Jeb never came home from school!"

Bridger glanced over at Maegan and back at Becky. "We have half the town out lookin'. We'll find them."

"I pray to God you do," she said, her voice trembling.

"Jeb's missing too?" Maegan said with confusion as she and the sheriff rode out. "Why would all three not come home? It doesn't make any sense."

"Is there anywhere Cody likes to ride or walk to?"

Maegan shook her head. "I looked in the places I could think of."

"I hate to say it, but it's so dark that we could be missing clues. Best thing would be to set out at first light."

Maegan knew he was right, but her heart ached at the thought of her little brother and the others out in the night.

"You're right," she said, thinking she wouldn't sleep a wink that night.

*****

"Did you really know about this mine already?"

Jeb shifted slightly, blowing his breath into his bare hands to warm them. "No," he answered Cody's question.

Cody figured as much but didn't say anything. They'd given up trying to move the rocks after several hours of hardly getting anywhere. Every time they moved too many, it threatened to bring more down. The fear of the entire place caving in kept them hesitant to keep trying. Lilly had fallen asleep, her head resting on Cody's shoulder as they all three sat huddled together in the darkness. The lamp had burned out, and they had no way of knowing what time it was or how many hours they had spent in the mine, even though it was beginning to feel like an eternity.

"Does anyone else in Millcreek know about this mine?" Cody asked.

"Not that I know of," Jeb answered quietly. "I wish I'd never followed you guys."

"I wish we'd never come in here," Cody added.

"Do you think anyone'll find us?"

Cody could hear the other boy's voice quiver. "My sister won't stop looking."

"My pa neither." Jeb tried to sound confident, but Cody thought he sensed doubt in the boy's tone.

"Your pa sure does hate my uncle," Cody said.

"That's cuz he killed my brother."

"I know," Cody replied quietly. "My uncle told us about it. He's real sorry, but I know that's something most folks can't forgive."

Jeb was quiet. "I don't even remember Thomas," he said. "But Pa sure does. Sometimes I wish …"

"What?" Cody asked when he didn't go on.

"That he loved me half as much as he must have loved Thomas. Ma said he hurt so bad over it that it changed him."

"I lost my parents, but I don't remember them, either. My sister Mae's been closest to a ma I've ever had."

Jeb was thoughtful, imagining his life for a moment without his mother, or his father, for that matter. Joe Spencer could be a hard man, but Jeb remembered good moments, too. "My ma's probably sick with worryin'."

Cody shifted his position slightly, careful not to wake Lilly. His arm was starting to fall asleep. "I wonder what time it is."

"Feels like we've been in here forever," Jeb said.

"Must be hours past supper," Cody said as his stomach growled. "If my sister were here, she'd be prayin' for a way out."

"Well, she ain't, so maybe you should," Jeb said. "I don't wanna die in here," he added quietly.

Cody had never felt such fear in his life, not even that night he'd gone looking for the James brothers with Austin, Sawyer, and Maegan. In that instance, he'd had his older siblings, but now, the uncertainty of ever being found was real enough to shake his soul to the core. He'd heard Maegan pray enough times to know how to do it, and for the next half hour, he prayed like he had never prayed before.

# *Chapter* Thirteen

As the first light of the morning broke the dark Missouri sky, Maegan and Sheriff Bridger were already astride their horses. A fog blanketed the ground, rising and dispersing ever so slowly as the sun began to climb in the sky. Now that they had light, they headed toward the schoolhouse to retrace the kids' usual path home. When no trace of them turned up, they veered off the path and decided to follow the creek that ran through some woods and fields that they hadn't searched the night before.

From his place on his horse, Bridger glanced at Maegan, who rode just beside him. Her gaze was locked on the fields ahead, her eyes anxiously searching the surroundings. He watched as she removed her wide-brimmed hat, letting it hang down over the dark, curly hair that lay loose to the middle of her back. He noticed her lips were moving ever so slightly, as if talking, and realized she must be praying.

"Your brother's got a good head on his shoulders," Bridger tried to encourage her. "I'm sure we'll find him."

Maegan nodded slightly, her eyes still fixed ahead of her. She couldn't dispel the fear that seemed to be rising with each hour they didn't find them. She knew the sheriff was just trying to keep her hope alive, but right now, all she could feel was the prospect that something truly horrible had happened.

The forest they had reached became dense as they neared a steep ravine. The stream they had been following began to run down the gorge at an angle that made continuing to follow it impossible on horseback. Sheriff Bridger suggested they go the rest of the way on foot, and soon, they were moving closer to the edge of the level area.

"I can't imagine they'd be out here," Maegan said, scanning the landscape that was more of a wilderness. She sighed heavily and then slumped down onto a nearby boulder. "This was a mistake," she suddenly said. "I should have never come here with Cody. And to think, I left home to keep him safe!"

"What do you mean?" Bridger asked curiously.

"He was shot and almost killed when my older brother forced him to join us pursuing the James brothers. That's why I left, to keep Cody from getting placed in that kind of situation again."

"You and your brothers went after the James gang?" Bridger couldn't keep the astonishment from his voice.

Maegan nodded. "I promised myself I wouldn't let him be put in harm's way like that again. And I promised my ma I would take care of Cody!"

"This isn't your fault. Some things are just out of our control," he said, thinking back to some of his own life's circumstances. "We'll find him, Mae."

There was a determination in his voice that snapped her out of her fear. And then they heard something. "What's that?" Maegan said, standing as she heard the snapping of twigs and the rustling of leaves. They waited, listening, and then Maegan spotted a familiar animal. "It's Cody's horse!" she exclaimed, moving toward her brother's horse that was tethered to a tree.

"Then we know they came this way," Bridger said.

Maegan raised her voice to call out Cody's name several times. The song of birds and the babble of the stream seemed even louder while they listened for a response, but there was no answer.

Maegan eagerly began to move down the slope, holding onto trees and bulging roots to keep from slipping. She noticed the smeared path of dirt and dead leaves just below them that looked as if they had been pushed downward by another set of feet. "Maybe they slipped down the ravine!" she said, moving faster down the slope. A loose pile of rocks gave way under her foot, and she reached out to grab something before she slid further.

Sheriff Bridger saw it coming and was there to grab her arm to keep her from falling.

"Thanks," she said, as he slowly let go of her once he saw she was steady again.

"Let me go first," he offered. "This is steeper than it looks." He carefully moved past her and then proceeded to lead the way. When they neared the bottom, they both noticed the same thing Cody and Lilly had.

"Do you think they could have ventured inside?" Sheriff Bridger asked as they moved toward the mine. He and Maegan pushed back some of the brush to get a look inside.

"Maybe."

"Wait here. I'm gonna go back to the horses and get a lantern."

As she waited for him to return, Maegan called Cody's name into the mine, venturing a few steps inside. When Bridger returned, they went in further, and it wasn't long before Maegan noticed something on the ground. She gasped. "Cody's hat!" She leaned over to pick it up, and then she and Bridger noticed a newly settled wall of rock just a few yards away.

"Cody!" Maegan called, eagerly springing into action as she began moving the rocks that lay as a barrier in front of them.

"Mae, wait," Bridger warned, glancing at the sketchy beams overhead. She was undeterred, pulling at the rocks anxiously and calling Cody's name.

"Mae," Bridger reached out and took her arm. "Wait a second. We've got to think this through, or the whole place will fall in."

Maegan stopped digging. "Alright. What do you think we should do?"

"Well, we know they came this way, so they are on the other side of this wall. They may have even found another way out. I think we should check around outside first and see if there is another entrance in."

Maegan nodded in agreement, but just as they moved in the direction they had come, there was a loud rumbling. Maegan screamed as an avalanche of rock began to fill the opening they had come through. Bridger grabbed her and pulled her down, shielding her body with his until the sound abated. When they straightened up, it was to find a cloud of dirt and dust enveloping them, with the darkness only slightly broken by the lantern they had.

Coughing against the rush of dust to his lungs, Bridger went to the wall of rock that had just fallen. Feeling a sense of panic, he ran his hands along the rocks and began trying to pull them out. As he did, dirt from the ceiling spilled down on them.

"We're stuck," Maegan said, her own fear rising. "What are we going to do?"

Bridger turned to face her, barely able to see her in the lantern's dim glow. "I don't know."

Maegan took a steadying breath, telling herself not to

panic, but she couldn't help the foreboding that overshadowed her thoughts. The wall in front of them barred the way they had entered, while the wall just behind them blocked their path to find any other exit.

"Alright …" Maegan said suddenly, as if she had an idea. "We need to pray."

"Pray? I don't mean to sound doubtful, but unless God can come move this rock himself, you're wasting your time."

"The Lord's gotten me through more scrapes than I can count," she told him. "There's no reason He won't get me through this one."

"Go ahead, if it makes you feel better," Bridger said, not knowing what else to say in the face of such confidence in the unseen. One thing he did know, however, was that his own conviction was nowhere near hers, and the size of the shaft they found themselves in was growing smaller by the minute.

*****

After an uncomfortable night, Cody was the first to wake up that morning, his eyes widening with excitement when he realized there were small bits of sunlight peeking through the rock wall in front of them.

"Hey guys, wake up!" Cody said. "This wall isn't as thick as we thought!"

Jeb and Lilly were soon awake and noticed what he had.

"There's more light in this area," Cody said as he ran his hands along the upper right side of the wall. "If we're careful, maybe we can make an opening at the top and climb out."

Carefully, they pulled out rocks in the upper right corner until they made a space small enough for Lilly to get through. The sudden rush of air and the burst of bright sun as the rocks fell away was a welcome relief. Working together, Jeb and Cody helped boost her up, but just as they were about to push her through the opening, a pile of dirt and rocks from overhead began to fall into the area.

"The dirt's in my mouth!" Lilly said as she coughed.

"Now what!" Jeb groaned, sounding very close to tears.

"Let's try the same thing at the other corner. Maybe the roof is more secure over there," Cody said.

He found himself praying again and trying to trust that God would make a way for them to be found.

*****

Billy Turner rarely left his cabin, and when he did, it was usually to go hunting. That day, he had shot one of the largest bucks he'd ever seen. Tracking the wounded animal's blood had led him to the gorge, where the deer had breathed its last breath, just a few feet away from an old mine shaft. Billy Turner had seen it before, but today, it looked different. There were rocks blocking the opening, and a cloud of dust lingered in the surrounding air.

Curiously, he went closer and could hear movement from the other side, almost as if someone was moving rocks or digging. "Hello!" he called.

"Hello!" a muffled woman's voice shouted back. "We're trapped!"

"Get help!" A male voice then hollered.

Billy Turner glanced up at the top of the opening and the sides, which seemed precarious, to say the least. He knew if he started moving rock, the whole thing could cave in. And then there was his impediment. With only one arm to use, he certainly wouldn't be able to get them out himself. "I'll get help!" he yelled back to them. Even as he said the words, he felt an anxious and uncomfortable feeling rising in his heart. He'd spent years trying to avoid people at all costs.

For the sake of the people who needed his help, however, he forced himself to make an exception this once.

*****

"Thank God," Maegan breathed a sigh of relief. Everything was going to be okay. She had been holding the lantern while Bridger worked on prying various rocks loose, having to stop and move to another each time it seemed to jeopardize the stability of the roof overhead. She raised it now in her hands to see Bridger's face. "We're gonna be alright," she said. "And once that man gets help, we'll be able to find Cody and the others."

She suddenly noticed Sheriff Bridger's breathing was a little shallow. "Are you alright?" she asked.

He didn't answer right away, and then she heard him exhaling slowly. "I'm, ugh, not very good in tight spaces."

She could hear the tightness in his voice as he said it. He suddenly began pacing the enclosed area, feeling along the wall anxiously. Maegan gently touched his arm. "Sheriff Bridger, why don't you sit down and try to relax for a minute?" She instinctively reached out and took his hand and then sat next to him in the dirt. "We're gonna be okay," she assured him.

"I feel like I … can't breathe," he admitted, using his left hand to loosen the top button of his shirt.

"You just need to think about something else. Tell me more about … about your life in the orphanage," she said as she remembered that he had briefly mentioned that before.

"The orphanage?" he echoed.

"Yes. You said you had a sister, didn't you?"

"I barely remember her. I can't even recall her name; I was so young."

"There's got to be something you remember about her,"

Maegan probed, hoping to keep his mind off their current situation.

He was quiet for a moment and then said, "I remember her singing to me."

"What song did she sing?"

He was thoughtful for a moment, as if trying to find the memory. Maegan was getting a little worried when he was quiet for so long, and then he said, "She always sang this one about an oak tree, but I can't remember the exact words. The tune always stuck with me, though," he added. He suddenly realized that she was still holding his hand. It surprised him how calming her nearness was.

"But she was adopted almost as soon as you got to the orphanage?" Maegan asked, trying to remember what he'd already shared with her and her brothers before.

"Yeah. I remember her crying when she hugged me good-bye that day. I was so young, I didn't fully understand that I would never see her again."

"I can't imagine how hard that must have been," she said quietly. "I'm sure she missed you as much as you did her. What else do you remember about being at the orphanage?" Maegan asked when she worried that he'd been quiet for too long and might be getting anxious.

"They used to lock me in a tiny closet if I acted out," he told her. "Maybe that's what started this," he said, referring to his anxiety in small spaces.

"Oh, that's horrible," Maegan said, sorry her question had produced the memory. "I guess asking you about the orphanage was not the right diversion."

"It's alright," he laughed softly. "Life there made life with my adoptive parents seem a whole lot better."

"Can I ask you something?"

"Sure."

"Is Bridger your first or last name?"

"Last. It's not the last name I was born with, but my adoptive parents changed it when they took me in. I became more used to Bridger than even my first name. It's all I remember them calling me."

"They didn't call you by your first name?"

"I was more like hired help," he told her. "I think just calling me Bridger kept the relationship detached and impersonal … like they wanted."

Maegan felt her heart ache for him. He had lost his parents and then his sister at such a young age. Losing her own parents had been devastating, but she had taken comfort in the closeness she had with her brothers and the closeness she had with the Lord.

Bridger shifted slightly but didn't let go of her hand. It brought a comfort he wasn't used to. Aside from his sister, in the brief time he was with her, he couldn't remember anyone even hugging him as a child or ever holding his hand. His childhood had left him feeling lonely and forgotten for the most part, but at some point, he'd just decided to accept it and no longer look for the love he had craved as a kid. Even now, it seemed his title as sheriff kept him from really being able to get close to anyone.

"In the Bible, there's a passage in the book of John where Jesus is talking to his disciples, and although He would physically have to leave them, He promises them that He would not abandon them as orphans," Maegan said. "He was referring to the Holy Spirit that He would send. I often think of that when I'm feeling alone—that Jesus promised He would not leave or forsake those who love Him. There's even a place in the book of Acts where the Holy Spirit is called the promise of the Father."

Bridger had never heard anything like that in his life

and felt like she had just glimpsed into his thoughts. Some things changed with age, but he had never stopped feeling like an orphan.

"In reality, we're all orphans until God adopts us as His children," she went on.

"And how does He do that?" Bridger asked, hoping he didn't sound too skeptical.

"'To anyone who believed, He gave the right to become children of God,'" Maegan quoted the verse to answer his question. "That's also from the Bible," she explained. "Jesus is the only one who made a way for us to come back to the Father after sin separated us from Him. When you repent of your sin and put your faith in Him for salvation, God gives you His Spirit and adopts you as His child. His Spirit helps you, teaches you, and leads you … and you're no longer an orphan."

"You sure you didn't miss your calling to be a minister?"

Maegan laughed softly. "You don't have to be a minister to know how it works. God reveals who He is through His word. You just have to want the truth to understand it."

"You make it sound very believable. I mean, I guess I believe there's a God, but I always thought of Him as just existing and not being that involved or concerned."

"God didn't create humans and everything around us to then not want interaction. If you're going to believe in God, then you got to know what He's like." She paused a moment and then added, "There's a difference between believing something with your head and believing it with your heart."

Her words made him realize more than ever that he had never known a loving relationship in his entire life. His adoptive parents had been the closest form of family he'd known, and they had been content to not have a relationship with him. He had unintentionally assumed God was the same way.

"I remember one time," Maegan said quietly. "My older brothers were gone, and I was home with Cody for the night. He was only seven at the time, and I remember feeling such an overwhelming sense of loneliness and fear. It almost seemed to have walked into the house; it was so tangible. I'll never forget how I prayed out loud for God to take away those feelings, and then … he actually did. It was like he came into the room, and every bit of darkness left. It's … it's hard to explain."

"I think you're doing a pretty good job," Bridger said.

"We all have fears and things we struggle with. The biggest mistake we can make, though, is going through life thinking the Lord doesn't want to be involved."

"What's your biggest fear?" Bridger asked, interested in knowing more about her.

"Something bad happening to Cody," she answered without hesitation. "What's yours?"

"You mean besides getting trapped inside a tiny, dark space like a caved-in mine shaft?" he chuckled slightly.

"Yes, besides that," she laughed with him, glad he was beginning to relax enough to joke about it.

"Probably …" Bridger paused. He'd never shared this much about himself or his past with anyone before. While he would hardly admit it to himself, his biggest fear was going through life alone. He should be used to it by now, but there was still a shred of hope that remained that maybe he'd have a family to make up for what he lacked as a child. "… probably living alone the rest of my life," he finally answered.

"Maybe you'll find your sister one day," she offered optimistically. "And I'm sure you'll have a family of your own eventually."

"I don't know. I'm not very good at making friends," he said.

"I don't think that's true," Maegan told him. "You're just on the quiet side … unless you get stuck in a mine and are forced to talk," she added, giving him a playful nudge with her elbow. She could tell he was smiling, even in the dark. "I'm not outgoing like Austin, but I've found most folks are friendly if you strike up a conversation," she said.

"Are you saying I ought to make more of an effort?" Bridger asked with a little laugh.

"It couldn't hurt," Maegan replied. "When you grew up and left your adoptive parents, what did you do after that?" she asked curiously.

"I traveled for a little while and then worked as a wrangler on a few cattle drives. My adoptive father had a friend who was a marshal in Jefferson City. The man's profession had always interested me, so I sought him out, and it wasn't long before he made me a deputy. After Millcreek lost their sheriff, the marshal sent me here."

"Do you like Millcreek so far?"

"Everything but the abandoned mine."

Maegan smiled and then released a sigh. "I am sorry for this. If you hadn't been helping me find Cody, you wouldn't be in this mess."

"It's not your fault."

"Honestly, I had no idea coming here would land us in the middle of a family feud. If one more bad thing happens, I may take that as a sign to take Cody and head home."

Bridger hoped she wasn't serious. He hadn't known her long, but more and more, she was making an impression. It was quiet for a few minutes. "Is it just me, or is it getting harder to breathe in here?"

"It's not just you," Maegan admitted quietly. She knew their oxygen supply wouldn't last long and prayed silently that the stranger who had found them would bring help in time.

"Maybe we should conserve the oxygen and not talk anymore," Bridger whispered.

"Alright," Maegan whispered back. She started to pull her hand away from his but felt him gently squeeze it. She smiled to herself, liking the warmth and comfort of his hand around hers.

*****

Alison had just finished giving Lucas breakfast when there was a knock on the door. That morning, Maggie had joined her husband in the search for Lilly and the other children, and Alison had stayed back to watch Lucas. Curious, she went to the door, hoping it was some good news. She had to stifle a gasp when she opened the door and saw a disfigured man standing there. His face bore the deep scars and defacement of being severely burned, and only a shoulder nub stood in the place where his left arm used to be.

"Can I help you?" she asked.

"There's some people trapped in the mine." Billy Turner had stopped at the closest house he came upon, not knowing who even lived there. He thought it would be quicker than riding to town and would spare him seeing more people than he needed to.

"My niece and her friends are missing!" Alison exclaimed. "Is it children who are trapped?"

"It sounded like a man and a woman, but maybe the kids are in there too," he said as he turned to leave.

"Wait!" Alison said. "I don't know where the mine is! Can you show me?"

He nodded, and as Alison was preparing to get Lucas and follow him, Maggie came driving into the yard.

"Maggie! Thank goodness!" Alison exclaimed, running

outside to tell her what she'd just found out.

*****

  It seemed like forever, but finally, Maegan and Bridger heard noises coming from the other side of the wall. They could hear more than one man's voice as they seemed to be talking to each other and planning the rescue.

"Hold tight!" They recognized Reverend Myles' voice calling to them. "We're gonna get you two out of there!"

From the other side of where they were trapped, the men were rigging up supports to strengthen the structure of the roof and sides of the shaft so they could slowly and cautiously dismantle the wall of rock that separated them. It took almost two hours, and by the time they'd cleared enough rock for Maegan and Bridger to crawl through, they were both getting desperate for oxygen.

The cold air had never felt so welcome, and Maegan's lungs gasped for breath as the opening the men had created allowed her and Bridger to escape from the mine. Almost immediately, she spotted Cody. He ran up and threw his arms around her, feeling like a thousand pounds of guilt were falling off his shoulders. He would have never forgiven himself if Maegan had died because of him.

"Cody! Thank God! Are you okay?" She was so relieved to see him.

"We were trapped in the mine, too," he told her. "But we ended up at the other end. They found us and dug us out."

Maegan hugged him and then spotted Lilly and Jeb not too far away. She looked around for Sheriff Bridger and saw he was drinking from a canteen someone had put in his hands. She did the same as she realized Alison was there handing her water.

"Oh, Maegan!" she exclaimed, hugging the girl. "Thank the

Lord you're alright! I think he sent an angel to rescue you!"

"What?" Maegan asked.

"A man came to my brother's house and showed us where you and Sheriff Bridger were!"

Maegan knew it had to be the same man who had promised to get help. "Who was he?" she asked.

Alison shook her head. "I've never seen him before in my life, but my brother said his name is Billy Turner."

The name caught Cody's attention, and he glanced at the faces of the crowd that still remained, curious if the man was there.

Maegan, too, glanced around. "I have to thank him!"

"He's not here," Alison said. "He left rather quickly the moment he showed Maggie and me where you were. After we got help, one of the men who came to dig you two out knew about the mine and suggested trying to get you out from the other entrance. That's when they found Cody and the others!"

"I'm so glad they're alright," Maegan said, hugging her brother again before hugging Lilly, who was now standing nearby.

"Well, your prayers worked, just like you said they would."

Maegan turned toward Sheriff Bridger, who had come over to stand beside her. "I may have panicked if you hadn't been there," she told him.

"I think it's quite the other way around," he replied.

Maegan met his smile, thinking that as dangerous as the situation had been, she was thankful to have spent it with him.

# *Chapter* Fourteen

Alison leaned against a post on the porch outside the General Store and smiled at her nephew. Maggie and Lilly were inside making some purchases, and Alison had agreed to watch Lucas outside until they were done. He tended to touch everything and spilled a bag of flour the last time they were inside. Maggie had also been feeling more tired as she grew closer to her delivery date, and Alison was trying to be helpful.

With the recent event at the mine, Alison was keeping an extra close eye on Lucas. She had never seen Maggie so distraught, and the only other time she'd seen her brother in such turmoil had been at the funeral of his first wife. Having Lilly missing had shaken them all up, but now, a few days after the incident, everyone was starting to recover from the emotional strain.

"Afternoon, Alison."

She turned her attention to the voice and saw Gideon Martin approaching from the next shop over. "Afternoon, Gideon."

"I heard about your niece gettin' stuck in that mine. Glad everything worked out okay."

"Thanks," she replied sincerely. Her attention swung back

to Lucas, who was hopping up and down the store's front steps, his slightly too-big knit cap flopping as he did.

"It sure is gettin' cold," he said. "I've been hearing folks say we're gonna have a hard winter."

"I don't mind the snow," Alison said with a smile.

"Did you hear 'bout the Christmas dance they're having at the restaurant next month?"

"Mm-hm."

"You reckon you'll go?"

At the thought of going to a dance, Austin's face popped into Alison's thoughts. She imagined herself dancing in his arms for just a moment, and then the notion dissipated. She had checked the post office nearly every day since he'd left, each time leaving her more disappointed than the last. "I doubt it. I'll probably stay back to watch Lucas and Lilly so my brother and his wife can go." She missed the regret that crossed Gideon's clean-shaven face.

"What were you and Gideon talking about?" Maggie asked her on the ride home.

"Not much. He mentioned the Christmas dance. Are you and Jacob going?"

"That might be nice, although I'm not sure I can fit into a fancy dress at this point," Maggie said with a smile as she glanced down at her growing belly. "Did Gideon ask you to go?"

"No. But I think he was trying to get around to it." She let out a little sigh and looked off into the distance.

"Thinking about Austin?" Maggie asked knowingly.

"I still can't believe he just … left."

Maggie felt for the girl's broken heart, and she was also a little surprised at how things had turned out. There was something very likable about Austin McCoy, and despite some of his apparent immaturities, she had genuinely thought he might be a good match for Alison. Jacob had been right, though, and with what he'd told her he had witnessed at the saloon between Austin and another woman, she realized Austin wasn't the trustworthy young man she had hoped he was. She still wrestled with the thought of telling Alison what Jacob had seen, but he had thought her knowing would only hurt her further.

"If you and Jacob want to go to that Christmas dance next month, I'd be happy to stay back with Lucas and Lilly."

"That's kind," Maggie replied, knowing that if Austin was in town, Alison might not have made such a ready offer.

"I know he was just visiting, but to leave without a good-bye?" Alison climbed down from the wagon once they reached home, still in deep thought about it. "It's almost as if … as if something happened."

Maggie helped Lilly and Lucas out of the back of the wagon while listening to Alison. Biting her lower lip in indecision, she wished there was something she could say. The poor girl was clearly depressed about the whole thing.

"What's that look?"

Maggie glanced up, surprised to find Alison staring at her questioningly.

"What look?"

"That look on your face just now," Alison pressed. "I said it was as if something happened, and you … you looked rather distressed. Do you know something I don't know?"

"Well, I … it's not for me to say."

"You do know something!" Alison came around to the back of the wagon, her blue-green eyes pleading with Maggie. "Maggie, what is it?"

Maggie was hesitant but finally admitted, "Jacob confronted Austin about something, and I think Austin felt guilty about it, and that's why he left so suddenly."

"What! Jacob had no right to interfere!"

"He was just concerned because ..."

"Because he doesn't know a thing about Austin! Jacob's just like my mother ... trying to match me up with the person *he* thinks is best suited for me! I can't believe I came here to escape that, and here I am in the same predicament!"

"No, Ali. It's not what you think. He didn't want to interfere. He had to, for your sake."

Alison saw such tenderness and empathy in her sister-in-law's face; it scared her a little. What could she be referring to?

"Why don't you ask your brother what he saw?" Maggie said softly, hating that Alison's heart was about to be even more devastated.

*****

Alison felt like the hours were crawling by. When her brother finally arrived home from the mill, she slipped out to the barn to speak with him before he came into the house. He was unsaddling his horse when she entered the barn.

"Jacob, do you know anything about why Austin left so suddenly?"

Jacob turned to see his sister standing nearby, and he was quiet for a moment, not expecting the question.

"Maggie said you confronted Austin about something."

Jacob had wanted to spare her this but knew he had no way around it now. "The night I went to see Widow Grayson, I was passing the saloon on my way home and saw him with another woman. It looked like one of the women who work there, and they were embracing rather intimately."

"Are you sure it was him?" Alison's mind was reeling at the idea.

Jacob nodded, his expression apologetic. "I wish I could have been wrong about him, Ali."

"That was the night before he left, wasn't it?"

Jacob nodded. Since that night, he had wrestled with the idea of telling Alison what he had seen, but when Austin responded so quickly to his advice to leave Millcreek, Jacob thought it best to spare his sister the details.

"You should have told me sooner," Alison said quietly as she began to turn away.

"I thought I was doing right in sparing you knowing."

"Maybe it will be easier to let him go now that I know what sort of man he really is." Alison walked toward the house and then to the road, hoping a walk would somehow help. It just didn't make sense! Austin had seemed so genuine … so in love with her.

She let out a frustrated sigh, feeling on the verge of tears. The fact that her brother had seen Austin in the arms of another woman, a saloon girl to boot, made her feel humiliated and betrayed. His tender glances, his loving words, and fervent kisses … what a joke they must have all been to him.

She had never felt like such a fool in all her life. No wonder he could just leave without so much as a goodbye. She'd been nothing but another flirtatious relationship for him. She wanted to scream when she thought of all the other women that he must have behaved that way towards, and she wanted to cry when she thought of how much she still cared for him.

"Well, no more of that!" she said aloud to herself. Starting at that moment, she decided she would not allow herself to care for or even think of Austin McCoy ever again.

For several more minutes, she walked briskly, almost as if each step was setting in stone her decision to forget about Austin. She had almost reached a fork in the road when she spotted Lyn Hummel just ahead. Surprised to see the woman so far from town, Alison approached her.

"Why, Lyn, what are you doing all the way out here?" She slipped out of her jacket when she noticed the woman wasn't dressed warm enough to be out in the cold. Alison quickly laid it over her shoulders.

"I'm just on my way back to town," Lyn told her.

"I think you got turned around, because town is the other direction."

"Oh?" The woman glanced around and then shook her head. "I get confused sometimes."

"It's alright," Alison told her, giving her a little hug. "My brother's house isn't too far. What if you wait here, and I'll go and get his buggy? Then I can give you a ride to town."

The woman nodded and promised to wait until Alison returned. Alison moved quickly to get back to her brother's, and it wasn't long before she returned to where Lyn stood waiting by the road.

"Thank you, dear," Lyn said as Alison helped her up to the seat and then directed the horse toward town.

"Have you been out walking most of the day?" Alison asked her, more than a little concerned.

"It wasn't this cold earlier in the day, and there were a few houses outside town I wanted to inquire at about William."

"I see," Alison replied quietly.

"I'm sorry to put you out like this," Lyn apologized. "I'm sure you have better things to do with your time than drive an old lady home."

"Not really," Alison said with a soft laugh.

"I'm sure a pretty, young girl like you has a beau filling her time."

"I thought I did," Alison admitted, "But I was wrong about him. I thought he cared about me, but he left town without even saying goodbye."

"Maybe he does still care. Maybe there's a good reason he had to leave suddenly," Lyn tried to console her.

Alison wasn't about to go into the details she had just learned. Instead, she said, "I just thought he was someone he isn't. It's probably best to forget about him."

"Forgetting can be a hard thing to do," Lyn said, a thoughtful expression clouding her light blue eyes. "I think it's the hardest thing to do," she added.

Alison gave the woman a tender smile, knowing how she clung to the memory of her son. "It can be hard to move on when someone has such a large part of your heart," Alison said.

Lyn let out a sigh. "That's the truth. I've let go many a time … sometimes, you got to just leave folks in the Lord's hands and move on. But then there are the times when deep, deep down, you know you're supposed to be patient … to keep hoping and never give up on them."

"But how do you know when to let go and when to hang on?"

"Only the good Lord can answer that, hunnie. And once he tells you, you don't let anyone tell you any different."

Alison blinked away some tears that were filling her eyes, the cold wind drying them as they trickled down her cheeks. She marveled a little at how this woman could seem so lost one moment and then so sharp-minded the next. She reached over and gave her hand a little squeeze. "Thanks for the advice, Lyn. I think I'll spend some time asking the Lord what to do."

*****

"Are you going to the Christmas dance?" Maegan asked Alison after the church service the following week.

"No. Are you?" Alison asked.

"Sounds like fun, but I'm not one to get all dressed up and such."

Alison's face suddenly lit up. "Oh, Mae, what if you let me help you? It would be great fun. You could borrow one of my dresses, and I could even do your hair!"

Maegan's first reaction was a firm no, but as she listened to Alison talking, she felt a little nudge of excitement. "Don't you have to go with someone?" she asked.

"Not necessarily. My brother and Maggie are going, and they could pick you up. You should go, Mae!"

"Well, I'll think on it."

Alison suddenly smiled, a look of anticipation on her face. "I've got the perfect idea. You and Cody come over that night so I can help you get ready, then you could go with Jacob and Maggie while Cody stays with me, Lilly, and Lucas!"

Maegan opened her mouth to say that it seemed like an inconvenience, but Alison seemed so excited about the idea. The notion of going to a formal Christmas dance—to any dance, for that matter—scared her to death, but there was still an inkling of elation at the idea. She wondered suddenly if Sheriff Bridger would be there but then quickly dismissed the thought.

Cody had not been feeling well that morning and had asked to stay home from church. He also asked her to relay a message to Sheriff Bridger, so after the service, Maegan headed toward the jailhouse. Maegan knocked on the door of the jailhouse as she turned the knob and opened it but found no one was there. She took a step inside and almost immediately noticed a Bible lying open on the sheriff's desk. Walking toward it, she saw notes scribbled in it and several of the verses underlined.

"Lookin' for me?"

Maegan turned around, a little surprised at the sound of Sheriff Bridger's voice. "Oh, hello. Yes, I was."

"What can I help you with?" he asked as he walked to where she stood by the desk and leaned against its edge.

"Cody asked me to see if you had any free time next week. He was hoping you'd be able to come by for some target practice."

Bridger grinned. "Missing Austin, is he?"

"Yes."

"I'd be happy to," Bridger said.

"He'll be glad to hear it," Maegan replied, realizing the sheriff's nearness was reminding her of their time together in the mine. She hadn't seen him since the incident but had thought of it often. Her gaze wandered back to the Bible on his desk. "You've been reading?" she asked.

Bridger nodded. "Are you surprised?"

Maegan smiled softly. "A little," she answered honestly. "But I'm glad you are."

He let out a sigh and shrugged. "What you said kind of stuck with me."

"What do you mean?" she asked.

"In the mine. You said if a person's gonna believe in God, they should know what he's like. I figured this was a good place to start."

Maegan was encouraged to hear he had taken their conversation to heart. The memory of how her hand felt in his flashed through her mind, and she found herself wondering if he had thought back to it as much as she had. "Well, I guess I should be going," Maegan said as she moved toward the door. "Any time after school works for Cody."

"Mae?"

She turned around as she reached for the handle. "Yes?"

"Would you …" he paused, suddenly questioning himself. Since their incident in the mine, he hadn't been able to stop thinking about her. Her nearness during that dark hour and their conversation had made him aware of how lonely his life had been. "… want to have dinner with me sometime?"

"Dinner with you?" Mae replied, her tone revealing her surprise.

He shrugged. "I still don't have many friends yet in Millcreek, and you told me to make an effort."

She smiled, flattered he would ask. "I'd like that."

He seemed to relax a bit. "Great. Is Friday okay? I'll pick you up at five?"

Maegan nodded. "Sure."

As she left the jailhouse and headed home, she couldn't keep herself from smiling. Sheriff Bridger had just asked her to dinner!

*****

To carry out his plan, Cody told his sister he wasn't feeling well enough to attend church that morning. Once Maegan had left for church, however, Cody saddled his horse and headed toward the gorge, riding around it and taking the same path he had on that day he had followed Jeb and his friends. Cody felt compunction for telling his sister a fib, but since the mine incident, she had been watching him like a mother hen, and he didn't want to risk her telling him he couldn't ride off alone.

Once in Billy Turner's yard, he dismounted and then walked up to the door. He knocked and waited. He could hear some noise from inside, and then the door opened slightly, Billy's face shadowed under the large hat he usually wore.

"What do you want?" Billy Turner asked when he saw Cody standing there.

"Just wanted to come by and thank you."

Billy looked at him curiously but then opened the door wider for him to come inside. A cold wind followed Cody in, and Billy shut the door. "What are you talkin' about?"

"A few weeks ago, me and my sister and a few others were trapped in the mine near here. We'd probably still be there if it hadn't been for you."

Understanding filled the man's eyes, and he nodded. Until that moment, he hadn't realized Cody was one of the kids who was missing.

"The others would have thanked you, too, but this place is hard to find, and rumor has it you don't like company."

"Rumors aren't often true, but that one is."

"Well, I just wanted to thank you on behalf of all of us," Cody said again. He started to leave but then hesitated, turning back before he opened the door. "I'm not big for my age, but I'm strong. If you ever need any help 'round here, I wouldn't mind giving you a hand."

"Seeing I'm short one?"

Cody hadn't meant to offend him and felt bad for his choice of words. He opened his mouth to apologize but then heard Billy Turner chuckle. "It's alright, kid, I'm only teasing."

Cody relaxed noticeably and smiled slightly. "Just let me know if you need anything."

"Actually … there is something. As you can see why, I hate going into town. If I paid you, would you pick up some things for me from town from time to time?"

"Sure!" Cody was genuinely glad to help, feeling empathy for this man who had obviously suffered some sort of tragedy.

"I'll make a list now, if you don't mind waitin'. I just need some things from the store … and a newspaper would be nice."

Cody nodded. "Glad to help, sir."

"You can call me Billy."

"My name's Cody, Cody McCoy."

*****

Friday couldn't come soon enough, and when it did, Maegan found herself nervously donning the dress Austin had given her. The last time she had worn it, she'd made a spectacle of herself in front of the sheriff. She just hoped it wouldn't happen a second time. Her long curls were surprisingly cooperative, and she decided to just pull the sides back rather than lump it all into a braid like she often did.

As Maegan stepped out of her bedroom, she was glad she'd made arrangements ahead of time for Cody to have supper with Lilly Myles and her family. She didn't want him thinking anything of her having dinner with the sheriff. She tried not to think anything of it herself but was having a hard time convincing herself she only had feelings of friendship toward the handsome sheriff. She looked at the clock on the mantle before her glance rested on the stove. She was surprised that the pot of sauce from lunch still sat there and realized she'd never put it away. She had a few minutes until five, so she quickly went to grab a jar to pour the sauce into it. To her absolute horror, the pot slipped out of her hand, sending red sauce down the front of her skirt!

"Oh no!" Maegan cried aloud, anxiously searching for a dish towel. Wiping at the mess only smeared the sauce more on her dress and sent her into tears. There was no chance of wearing the dress now, especially since it was now past five, and Sheriff Bridger would be arriving at any moment.

Rushing to her bedroom, Maegan undressed and put on her trousers, white blouse, and vest, grateful that at least her clothes were clean, if nothing else. She had just finished buttoning her vest when a knock sounded on the door. Trying to calm her heart, which was beating fast from the last-minute dilemma, Maegan hurried to the door.

"Sorry I'm late," Bridger apologized when he arrived.

"Oh, that's okay." She stepped outside and followed him, telling herself to stop feeling so nervous.

"I'm sorry about … my clothes. I spilled sauce down my dress just a few minutes ago."

"You look fine to me," Bridger replied, not seeing anything out of the norm.

Once they started toward town in his buggy, their easy conversation put her more at ease.

They went to the Millcreek Restaurant, its interior decorated more lavishly than she had expected. Self-consciously, she fiddled with one of the curls that hung over her shoulder, wishing she had been able to wear her dress. She could feel some of the looks various people were giving her attire and was glad when Sheriff Bridger's voice broke into her musings.

"Have you ever been here before?" he asked as he sat across from her at a table nicely secluded in the corner.

"I don't think I've ever been out to eat at any restaurant," she confessed.

"Then I'm glad you'll get to have someone cook for you for a change."

She smiled at him, appreciating his thoughtfulness.

"This is much better than the mine," he joked a few minutes later.

"I don't know," Maegan teased back. "I kind of miss that soot and dirt settling in my throat."

Bridger smiled, and then his expression became more serious. "Thanks again, Mae."

"For what?"

"It was your level head and ability to create a diversion that helped me not panic when we were in that mine."

"I'm not sure the conversation evoked the best memories for you," she said apologetically.

"It was actually good for me to talk about it. I've never shared any of that with anyone," he added a little quieter.

Maegan was touched by the vulnerability she heard in his voice and saw in his eyes. Their conversation continued to flow easily throughout the meal and even as they left the restaurant. Bridger had just climbed up into the buggy seat beside her when someone shouting his name altered his attention.

"Sheriff Bridger!" The fellow's voice grew louder as he neared them, obviously out of breath from running.

Bridger recognized him right away. "What is it, Toby?"

"A fight in the saloon's gettin' out of hand! Nick sent me to find ya!"

Bridger glanced over at Maegan, an apologetic expression on his face.

"It's alright," Maegan assured him. "I understand."

"I'll be back," he promised before leaving her to follow Toby, both men running down the street toward the saloon.

Maegan waited in the buggy for a little while and then climbed out and leaned against the hitching post. A few minutes later, feeling antsy and a little cold in the November evening, she began to pace. There was still some daylight left, but she knew it wouldn't last much longer. A not-so-distant gunshot halted her steps for just a moment before she followed her instinct and took off toward the saloon where the gunfire had come from. As she neared, she saw several men stumbling out of the swinging doors as if evading the danger from inside.

Cautiously, Maegan edged along the wall and peered through the window. She could see a man was being held at gunpoint, and the man holding him hostage was yelling at Sheriff Bridger to slowly lower his weapons.

"Is there a back way in?" Maegan suddenly asked a man who had slipped out of the saloon and was moving past her.

"What?" he asked, a little drunk, confused, and eager to get out of the danger zone.

"Is there a back way in?" she asked again.

"From the alley there is," he slurred.

"I'll just need to borrow this," Maegan said as she hastily reached for the pistol tucked in his holster.

"Wait a minute!" he called after her, but he was too slow on his feet to catch up.

Maegan ran down the alley the man had told her about and almost immediately spotted a back door. She slowly opened it and then stepped inside. The saloon was eerily quiet, a stark contrast to the usual noise that filled the place. Maegan stepped around the corner, moving down the narrow hall with her back against the wall. As she neared the main room, she could see it had all but cleared out. The man who held the gun had his back toward her, and as she stepped out behind him, she hoped Bridger's seeing her wouldn't give her away.

"Lower your weapon! Slow!" Maegan ordered the man.

Hearing the words behind him, accompanied by the cock of a pistol, caused the man to realize he was outnumbered.

Maegan saw a flicker of shock in Bridger's eyes at the sight of her, but he quickly returned his attention to the man. "Do it!" she added in a fiercer tone when the man seemed to hesitate.

She kept her weapon poised and was standing just two feet behind the man. He slowly lowered his weapon and released his hold on the fellow in front of him.

"Drop it!" Maegan said, her eyes intent on the weapon in his hand.

Suddenly, the man dove behind the bar, firing a shot in her direction. Maegan dodged behind a table just as Sheriff Bridger grabbed the weapon he had been forced to surrender just a moment earlier. As the man who had been freed ran out the door, Bridger took shelter behind a table that had been flipped at the onset of the fight. Bridger fired back as the man shot at them from behind the protection of the bar.

"Get out of here!" Bridger yelled toward Maegan.

But from where Maegan was positioned, she could see into the bar and that the man was frantically trying to reload his pistol. She signaled to the sheriff to close in from the other side just as she swiftly moved to the bar counter and stood in the opening. "Drop it, or I'm pulling this trigger!"

Sheriff Bridger had reached the other side of the bar and stepped in to grab the man, who was now at a complete disadvantage. Sheriff Bridger pulled him to his feet and pushed him against the bar counter, promptly handcuffing him. Maegan followed as he led the man outside the saloon and saw that a crowd lingered, waiting for the outcome. Maegan could feel several pairs of eyes on her as she walked through the swinging doors. They were obviously shocked that it had been a woman helping the sheriff.

Maegan spotted the man she'd lifted the gun from and approached him in the crowd. "Thanks," was all she said as she slipped it into his hand. She glimpsed down the road and saw the sheriff moving toward the jailhouse. For a moment, she didn't know if she should follow him or just go back to the buggy and wait for him. She chose the latter.

She didn't have a long wait before she spotted the sheriff rounding the corner of the buildings.

"What were you thinking!" were the first words out of his mouth when he was close to her.

It didn't sound like a question the way he said it—more like a reprimand, Maegan thought. "I just saw you needed some help," she answered evenly. She hadn't gotten into the buggy yet but stood there, feeling almost like a small child when he came to stand in front of her.

"You could have gotten yourself killed in there!" He knew he sounded angry, but he couldn't help it.

"I knew what I was doing," she tried to assure him.

Bridger released a short breath, shaking his head in disbelief. "I had the situation under control. You should have never risked your life like that!"

"It didn't look like you had the situation under control," Maegan said not unkindly. She just wanted him to understand why she had done what she did. How could she explain that she had merely acted upon instinct? She and her brothers had always looked out for each other in that way, and she had been in more dangerous scenarios than this.

"Maybe it didn't appear that way, but I had a plan." He pulled his hat off and ran a hand through his hair. "Where did you get that gun, anyway?"

"I took it from one of the men in the street. But I gave it back to him," she added.

"Target practice is one thing, Mae, but bursting into a gunfight is another. What if that shot he took at you hadn't missed? What then? When I think of how close you came to …" Sheriff Bridger glanced away, trying to gain some composure. "Think of Cody. What would he have done if you had gotten killed in there?"

Maegan looked back at him, feeling the weight of his words. "I … I didn't think through all that," she admitted quietly. "I just did the first thing that came to my mind." She let out a soft sigh. "I'm sorry."

Bridger searched her face, wondering how someone could be so thoughtful and reckless all at once. She was tough enough to burst into a gunfight yet tender enough to apologize and stand there in front of him with tears pooling in her eyes.

"I'm used to jumping in to help when my brothers are

in similar situations," she tried to explain. "It's like second nature to me, but … you're right. I shouldn't have been so hasty." On those words, Maegan turned to climb into the buggy, trying to hide a sudden rise of emotion that was eliciting some unwanted tears. She was surprised when she felt the sheriff's hand on her arm, gently turning her to face him again.

"I'm glad you're alright," he told her around a sudden lump in his throat.

"I'm glad you are, too," she said.

Her heart was in her eyes, and Bridger saw it. Knowing she cared about him stirred his heart unexpectedly. She had even put his safety above her own in coming into the saloon. He let his eyes wander over her face again, thinking how beautiful she was. A few curls had become dislodged and hung over her emerald-green eyes. He couldn't help himself from tucking one behind her ear, his fingers brushing her cheek every so softly.

"Maybe you could try to get used to someone protecting you for a change," he said.

Maegan wondered if she imagined the attentiveness in his eyes as he reached out to smooth away a tress of her hair. She suddenly felt very aware of his nearness and hoped he couldn't hear how loudly her heart was beating.

"I should get you home," he said quietly, offering his hand to help her into the wagon.

The dusk was fading into night as they drove away from town. Maegan wasn't sure what to say, and Sheriff Bridger was quiet as well.

"So, what happened before I got there?" she asked a few minutes later.

"Just the result of too much liquor and not enough sense. From what I gathered, the fellow with the gun had been cheating all night. When someone called him out, the fight escalated."

"Do you ever get tired of it?" Maegan asked him. "I mean, having to break up fights and being the sheriff."

Sheriff Bridger shrugged. "I'm used to it by now, but like you saw tonight, it can be inconvenient at times."

"Maybe in the future, you'll have a deputy, so you won't have to be on call all the time."

"Don't even *think* about applying for the job."

Maegan laughed softly, knowing he didn't seriously think she would, and relieved that he was no longer angry with her.

"I can't believe your brothers were okay with you going after outlaws with them."

It was Maegan's turn to shrug. "I ended up being a good enough shot to quell their worries, I guess. And it wasn't all the time. Sawyer and Austin didn't like to get me involved unless they really needed me."

"And I reckon they *really needed* you the night you all went after the James gang?"

Maegan nodded, forgetting she had told him about that. "I've never prayed as much as I did that night," she said quietly, thinking of the fear she had at losing Cody, both before and after he was shot. "We almost lost him."

"Well, you shouldn't have to worry about that here in Millcreek," he wanted to reassure her.

Maegan glanced over at him, not able to fully see his face in the dark, but she could hear the kindness in his voice. She was almost disappointed when they reached her uncle's house and the sheriff left. Reverend Myles brought Cody home shortly after, and Maegan was temporarily distracted from her thoughts while she and Cody talked and readied for bed. It wasn't until she was alone in her room trying to fall asleep that she let herself remember the way it had felt having Sheriff Bridger looking into her eyes and making her heart flutter.

*****

"Bobby said you wanted to talk to me," Pete Keller said when Garret Spencer answered his knock on the door. Garret opened the door of his small cabin wider so that Pete could come in. "Help yourself," he said with a nudge of his head toward a bottle of whiskey on the table. Garret waited until his cousin had a few drinks before opening the conversation.

"I'm thinkin' Mae McCoy didn't take you seriously when you warned her to stay away from the sheriff. I just saw 'em in town together."

"What's the big deal?" Pete asked, wiping his mouth with his sleeve.

"Ben McCoy's got it comin' to him, and the last thing we need is for that sheriff to be on their side!" Garret had slammed his fist on the table, irritated that Pete didn't seem to understand the gravity of the situation. "I've got a bad feelin' where Mae McCoy's concerned. The sheriff never stuck his nose in until she showed up. And then he started comin' round all the time asking us questions. I always feel like he's got his eye on me!"

Pete let out a sigh of frustration. He was getting tired of being Garret's henchman. "What do you want me to do?"

"I want you to make sure Mae knows you ain't just talk."

"Got something specific in mind?"

"Yeah, I do."

*****

"When do you think Uncle Ben will be home?" Maegan gave her brother an understanding smile from across the table, knowing that even with their uncle's rough exterior, they had both come to care about him. It was after dinner, and Cody was in and out of studying for a spelling test.

"He said sometime end of this month or early December," Maegan reminded him. "You want me to quiz you on your words?"

"Nah, I'm gonna turn in." His chair scraped the floor as he slid it out from the table and stood. "I know them all anyhow." He paused at the ladder leading to the loft. "Is it okay if I go fishing tomorrow after school?"

Maegan felt uncertain. Since the incident in the mine, she hadn't let Cody go anywhere alone but to school. He looked so hopeful, she heard herself tell him it was fine. "Just don't be too long. It gets dark early now."

The following evening, Maegan questioned her decision as dusk began to settle and Cody hadn't returned. She was just about to really worry when she heard the nicker of his horse and saw him moving across the yard to the barn.

"You almost had me worried," she told him when he entered the house. Her back was to him as she faced the stove, so she missed how he pulled his hat low over his face and moved to the ladder. "How many did you catch?" she asked.

"They weren't biting at all," he said quietly. "I'm, ugh, not hungry. I think I'll just go to bed early."

Maegan turned around. "You? Not hungry?" She noticed how quickly he was scrambling up the ladder. "Cody?"

He paused but then climbed the rest of the way up, disappearing into the loft. "Cody, are you alright?" Maegan asked, her hands on her hips as she looked up toward the loft.

"I'm fine. I'm just tired."

Maegan thought he didn't sound like himself, but she didn't want to press him. He had been missing his brothers and Uncle Ben lately. She thought maybe he just needed a good night's sleep. When he tried to sneak out the front door the following morning, however, she knew something was up. She had just come out of her bedroom when she spotted him trying to quietly open the door.

"You're up early," she said.

"Just thought I'd get an early start to school," he said, keeping his back to her.

"Without breakfast? And you had no dinner. Cody, what's going on?"

She gasped when he turned around and then rushed over to him. "What on earth happened?"

His left eye was swollen shut, and a painful-looking bruise covered his upper cheek. "We've got to get something cold on that right away!" she said.

"It's not too bad," he said.

"Did Jeb do this?" Maegan suddenly asked, her anger rising. "If that boy …"

"No, it wasn't Jeb," Cody interrupted her. "We're friends since the mine."

"Then what happened?" Maegan had her hands on his shoulders. "I want the truth, Cody."

"That one fella who hangs with Garret and Bobby Spencer."

"Pete Keller?"

"Yeah, he's their cousin or something. He met me on my way back from fishin' and said he had a message for you. I thought he meant a telegram or something." Cody released a sigh, his gaze falling. "Wasn't long before I realized the black eye was the message." Cody looked up to see tears pouring down his sister's face. "Don't cry, Mae! It doesn't hurt, honest!"

The idea of such a thing happening to Cody made her

heart hurt, and then it burned with anger. The last time she'd felt that way had been toward Sawyer after Cody had gotten shot. She gently hugged her brother. "I won't let anything like this happen to you again."

*****

Maegan let Cody stay home from school, but later that day, she rode to the school when she knew it was letting out. She wanted to explain to Mrs. Cooper why Cody hadn't been there and get any homework assignments for him. Her heart was still distraught when she left the schoolhouse and headed toward the store to get a few things. In the early weeks of arriving in Millcreek, Pete Keller had warned her to stay away from Sheriff Bridger. It had seemed an arrogant, idle threat that Maegan had dismissed as ridiculous. Now, it was making her rethink moving to Millcreek. All she wanted was to keep her promise to her mother and protect Cody, but once again, she found his life in danger.

Maegan's destination was the General Store, but as she rounded the corner of the hotel, she noticed Pete Keller striding across the street and slipping into the saloon. She immediately nudged her horse in that direction, dismounting when she reached the saloon. She tethered her horse to the hitching post out front and, without a moment's hesitation, walked through the saloon's double swinging doors.

Pete Keller was leaning against the bar counter, his back to her, and had he any intuition, he might have felt her hot gaze burning into him. When he heard his name, he turned around, and the look of surprise on his face mirrored the expressions of the other men in the room upon seeing a woman walk in.

"What are you doing in here?"

"Looking for you," Maegan replied, ignoring the smirk on his face. "How could you do that? He's just a kid!"

"Listen," Pete replied sharply, leaning closer to her. "I warned ya to stay away from the sheriff!"

"Don't you ever go near my brother again," Maegan said.

Pete Keller leaned back on his elbows against the bar counter, looking unfazed by her warning. "And don't you spend time with the sheriff," he paused, looking intently at her, "or I'll have to give your brother another message for you."

Before she could think it through, Maegan ripped out the pistol from her pocket and pressed it into Pete Keller's chest. From the corner of her eye, she could see she had the bartender's attention along with everyone else in the room.

"Promise me you'll leave Cody be. Swear it!"

Pete Keller's arms were slightly raised, his eyes not moving from Maegan's, which looked as convincing as any he'd ever seen.

"Swear it!" she said again, her tone firmer as she cocked the gun.

Pete glanced down at the gun pressing into his heart. "I swear it."

Maegan slowly stepped back, her pistol still aimed at him. "If you ever break that promise, you'll be sorry."

Those who had been distracted by her coming into the saloon were just as attentive watching her leave.

"I wouldn't want to get her ire up," one of the men near Pete joked after she had gone.

The man sitting at his table laughed. "You better keep your word, Pete!" he shouted. "I heard she can shoot the wings off a fly!"

"How's it feel havin' a woman pull a gun on ya?" another fellow yelled out to Pete. There was a round of laughter and more remarks at Pete Keller's expense.

Pete was fuming when he left the saloon. Mae McCoy

had made a fool of him, and he knew Garret Spencer was to blame. Had he not told him to do so, Pete would have never gone near Maegan or her brother. Pete was sick of Garret Spencer and, with unwavering determination, rode toward his house to tell him that he was done doing his bidding!

When he got there, he found Garret in the barn, resting on a stool while his brother Bobby mucked out the stables.

"Whatcha doin' here, Pete?" Garret asked him when he entered the barn. He couldn't miss the disgruntled look on his cousin's face.

"Came to let you know I ain't doin' your dirty work no more." Pete came out with it before he could change his mind. He could feel Bobby's eyes on him before they shifted to Garret. Pete knew, like him, Bobby was wondering what his brother would say to that.

"What's gotten into you, Pete? I ain't asked you to do nothin' for me," Garret said as he spat out a wad of tobacco on the ground and slowly came to his feet.

His response fired Pete up and quickened his steps toward Garret. "That's a lie. You're always telling me what to do, and I'm standin' up to you for once."

Garret stuffed his hands in his pockets and turned his bleary eyes to his cousin. Pete was shorter than him by three inches and scrawny compared to Garret's bulk. "Did something happen?" Garret wanted to know the reason for his cousin's sudden change of heart.

"I should have drawn the line when you told me to beat up on that McCoy kid."

"Did one of them call you out 'bout that?" Garret looked interested.

Pete knew Garret well enough to know the man was hoping for some fuel to add to his fire of hatred for the McCoys. He would have liked nothing better than for one of the McCoys to react so he could feel justified in some violent act of retaliation. Garret had a quick temper and a hunger for violence that had been too well fed during the war. While most men wanted to get back to their lives and forget the horrors of the Civil War, Garret missed the battle-field, which had given him a consistent outlet for his anger.

"The point is," Pete said, purposely leaving out Mae Mc-Coy's confrontation in the saloon, "if you want something done, you do it yourself from now on." He held his ground but could feel himself tensing up when Garret took a slow, deliberate step toward him, the look in the older man's eyes unreadable.

"I understand," Garret said in a tone that sounded pa-tronizing as he reached out and placed his hand on Pete's shoulder.

Pete relaxed a little but was still half-expecting Garret to take a swing at him.

"This doesn't mean we can't still be friends, does it?" Garret asked, a feigned expression of concern on his face. "I wouldn't want to find out that you were blabbering 'bout some of our past … adventures," he carefully chose the word. "I mean you'd just be throwin' dirt on yourself if you squeal on me or Bobby, anyway."

Pete glanced at Bobby, who looked like he was concerned about the same thing. "I ain't gonna talk," Pete assured him, knowing, among other things, he was referring to the time they'd poisoned Ben McCoy's well, thrown a rock through his window, and set Joshua McCoy's barn on fire. "What's done is done. I just don't wanna be a part of it no more."

Garret flickered a tight smile and then gave his cousin a firm pat on the back. "Alright, Pete. Just so long as you know what this means. If you aren't gonna do me any favors, it goes both ways."

Pete was fine with that. He'd as soon look out for himself than be mixed up with Garret and the foolishness he dragged him and Bobby into.

# *Chapter* Fifteen

"I still can't believe I let you talk me into this," Maegan said as she turned around so Alison could lace up her dress. Alison had chosen a dark red satin dress and already had it laid out on her bed when Maegan arrived. There were black gloves to match, which paired elegantly with the black lace on the hem and rounded neckline of the dress.

"I don't think I'll be able to fit through the door in this dress," Maegan worried as she tried to walk in the full skirt that swished and swayed around her.

Alison gave an encouraging smile. "You will, and it will look just stunning as you dance."

"That's the other thing that worries me," Maegan admitted. "I barely know a thing about dancing."

"Oh, I'll show you a few things," Alison promised before leading her to a chair in her room.

"I can't wait for you to see what I'm going to do with your hair," she said, smiling. "I'm going to pin the sides up and then gather a section so your curls hang in layers down your back!"

Momentarily, Alison told Maegan to turn around and look in the mirror for the final reveal. She had always thought Maegan to be pretty but was stunned at how beautiful she looked. "Quite the transformation from men's trousers and boots!" Alison practically squealed with delight.

For a full ten seconds, Maegan just stared at herself in shock. "How did you get my hair to do that?"

"Isn't it elegant? And just look at your figure! You've been hiding pure perfection under those baggy shirts and pants. Come on, it's getting late, and I can't wait for everyone to see how lovely you are!"

Maegan knew Alison was being generous with her compliments, but she couldn't deny that she had never felt so beautiful. "Now, if I can just walk in this dress without tripping and making a fool of myself," Maegan said.

The ride to town was cold, but Maegan didn't mind. They had blankets to keep them warm, and it was exciting to see the townsfolk funneling into the Millcreek Restaurant. It had been cleared out and transformed into a Christmas ballroom. Pine boughs were draped festively over the rails of the front porch of the restaurant. A wreath with red and gold ribbon hung over each of the windows of the large establishment, and tall, white candles flickered in all of the sills. The street lamps were burning brightly, providing light as the townspeople walked up the wide set of stairs leading up to the restaurant. Before she even reached the inside, Maegan could hear the melodic sound of a violin accompanying the dancers who had already begun waltzing.

The large room was warm and teeming with people; those who weren't dancing were talking and laughing along the perimeter of the room. Refreshment tables lined the far wall, and Maegan thought she had never seen such a jovial scene in all her life.

"Do you ladies want some punch?" Reverend Myles asked her and Maggie.

"Yes," Maggie replied, looping her arm in her husband's as she and Maegan walked across the room with him.

Near the tables, Sheriff Bridger stood talking to a fellow named Jack Dean. The man was in his early thirties and had lived in Millcreek all his life. "You're sure an improvement from the last sheriff we had," he told him. "Crooked and cunning are the best words I have to describe that four-flusher. You're from Jefferson City, right?"

"I lived just outside it, but I was a chief deputy in the city for a while before the marshal re-stationed me here in—"

"Who's that?" Jack Dean cut him off.

Bridger glanced in the direction Jack Dean gestured toward and saw he was referring to a woman who was walking across the room with Reverend Myles and his wife. The dark-haired woman was beautiful, to say the least … and familiar too.

"Excuse me, Sheriff," Jack Dean said, ending their conversation. "I just found myself a dancing partner."

The sheriff watched as he approached the girl and then led her onto the dance floor.

"Evening, Sheriff," Reverend Myles said to him a few minutes later after he and Maggie had made their way to where he stood.

"Enjoying the festivities?" Maggie asked.

"Yes, and yourselves?" Bridger returned with a kind smile.

"I'd enjoy it more if I didn't feel like a circus tent," Maggie said with a grin as she glanced down at her bulging stomach. The doctor told her she was on the smaller side, but having never been pregnant before, she felt huge.

"Well, you're a beautiful circus tent," Reverend Myles teased as he placed his arm around her.

They chatted for a few minutes, and then he said, "Do me a favor, Sheriff, if you can …" He knew Bridger and

Maegan had become friends. "Dance with Mae. I can tell she's nervous."

"Sure," Bridger said, a little hesitant since dancing wasn't one of his strongest suits. "Where is she?"

"She's been dancing with that young man who was talking with you," Maggie said.

Bridger's brows hiked in surprise. *That* woman was Mae McCoy? His eyes suddenly scanned the crowd of dancers until they rested on her. He could hardly believe it. He was so used to seeing her in trousers and a baggy shirt that he hadn't realized that the stunning woman was Mae.

"Not sure he'll have the chance," Maggie smiled slightly as she also glanced toward Maegan. "Looks like another man is claiming her for a dance."

"Just like I'm about to claim you," Reverend Myles said as he took his wife's hand and moved toward the dance floor. "See you later, Sheriff."

Bridger smiled as they moved away, thinking they were a good match. He took a few steps toward the punch table and set his drink down as his eyes searched for Maegan again.

"Good evening, Sheriff Bridger."

Bridger turned his attention to Emily Shaffer, a young woman he had seen in town and talked to on several occasions.

"Evenin', Miss Shaffer. Are you enjoying yourself?" He asked politely.

"I am. How about yourself?"

"A little out of my comfort zone," he admitted with a sheepish grin that she thought only made him look more handsome.

"Maybe the waltz will help put you at ease," she suggested with a coy smile.

"I can't promise I'm a good dancer, but I'll try my best." He offered his hand and then led her out to the dance floor.

Not far away, Maegan was dancing with Jack Dean for the second time. She listened to him talk about the ranch he worked at and about the recent cattle drive he had been on. She caught sight of Sheriff Bridger as he moved across the floor with a woman she'd seen at church and various times in town. She'd never met her but thought she seemed kind … and beautiful. It looked like the sheriff was enjoying her company as well.

"I just can't believe you're the same gal who won that shootin' contest. I didn't even recognize it was you right away since you was dressed like a girl." Jack cleared his throat and suddenly looked apologetic.

Maegan laughed, not at all offended. She remembered him from the fall picnic. "It's okay; I know what you mean."

"You sure shine up real nice, if you don't mind me saying."

"Thanks," she said, with a slight smile, finding his personality rather amusing.

They conversed easily while they danced, and then when the song had ended, Maegan tried to move off the dance floor, but another man approached her and asked her for the next dance. When that one was through, she quickly slipped to the side of the room for a rest before anyone else could get the chance to ask her. She smiled when she saw Claire Carter near her and fell into conversation with her for a few minutes. Across the room, Claire's husband, Will, was talking with the sheriff.

"I think I speak for the whole town when I say we're grateful you're here in Millcreek."

Sheriff Bridger knew Will Carter was highly respected and appreciated him saying it. "Jefferson City was getting too crowded for me, anyway. So, I was glad to be reassigned."

"My wife and I have been meaning to have you over to the ranch for dinner when you have time."

"I would like that; just let me know when," Bridger replied, remembering how he had told Maegan he wasn't very good at making friends. He knew it was something he needed to work on, and her encouragement in the matter had stuck with him.

They talked a few more minutes, Will noticing that the sheriff seemed a bit preoccupied. He followed the man's gaze and smiled to himself. "Are you gonna stare at Maegan McCoy all night or ask her to dance?"

Sheriff Bridger's eyes shot back at Will Carter, and he gave a guilty smile. "Am I that obvious?"

"'Fraid so."

"Well, in that case …" He excused himself and headed towards her. At the moment, he was feeling something considerably close to a magnet's pull where Maegan was concerned.

Standing by the wall, Maegan took out one of her hairpins and tried to readjust it in a way that would not jab her head. She just wasn't used to having her hair pinned up and could feel a headache coming on.

"Evenin', Mae."

Maegan turned slightly and met Sheriff Bridger's eyes. "Hello." She smiled warmly, her gloved fingers fiddling with the bracelet that Alison had let her borrow.

"I would have said hello sooner, but you've barely been off the dance floor. You must be exhausted. I think you've danced with half the men here."

"They danced; I just tried not to step on their feet," she admitted, biting her lip uncertainly.

He laughed softly. "You didn't seem like you were having any trouble."

"I think this huge skirt covers my mistakes well."

He wanted to tell her she was beautiful in it but suddenly felt tongue-tied.

She felt a little self-conscious as he stood there staring at her with his warm, blue eyes and wondered if he thought she looked nice.

"Would you care to?" he asked, extending his hand.

"Of course," she replied, hoping she wouldn't make a fool of herself by tripping on her dress or stepping on his feet.

"I'm afraid I'm not much of a dancer," Bridger apologized ahead of time.

Usually, his wide-brimmed hat shadowed his face, but tonight, without it, she thought him even more handsome. The usual stubble on his chiseled jawline was recently shaved, and for the first time, she noticed faint dimples on his cheeks when he smiled. Some of his dark hair fell over his forehead and accented his strong brow. "You seem like you know what you're doing," she said as they started dancing. "But then … I'm not the best judge."

He smiled … the slow, subtle smile that Maegan was becoming accustomed to.

"I have to admit, I didn't recognize you right away," Bridger told her.

"I didn't recognize myself right away when Alison was done with me," Maegan laughed softly. "I still can't believe I let her talk me into this."

"I'm glad you did," Bridger said. "You look beautiful."

In her entire adult life, Maegan had never had anyone say that to her before. She felt a blush creep into her cheeks and dropped her gaze slightly. "If I can be honest, I feel like Alison was that fairy godmother from Cinderella and that at the stroke of midnight, I'm going to be standing here in my trousers."

Bridger laughed at her description. "Then I guess we'll see what happens at midnight."

"I don't plan to stay that long to find out," she said with a smile, realizing she was chattering on in an effort to calm her racing heart at his nearness. She told herself not to stare too long into his eyes, afraid it might give away how much she was growing to like him. She glanced at his hand holding hers as they danced and wondered if he thought back to their time in the mine as often as she did.

While Maegan was wrestling with her thoughts, Bridger was juggling his own. He was trying to think of something to talk about so he wouldn't just be gawking at her the whole time, but he was struggling to think of anything except how exquisite she looked. He'd never been close enough to notice the sprinkle of freckles across her nose and cheeks and thought it only added to her appearance. Her nearness brought a peace and warmth that he'd never known before and, by the same token, made being alone more amplified.

"Have you heard from Austin?" he heard himself ask.

She was grateful for the diversion from her thoughts. "No, unfortunately. I feel bad for Alison. I told him to be careful where she was concerned."

Maegan's words confirmed Bridger's own suspicions that there was something going on between Austin and the reverend's sister. "Maybe he'll be back."

"I hope so."

"Me, too," Bridger said. "Your brother seemed like a good man to have around."

Maegan appreciated his words. "He and Sawyer are goin' after the James brothers again." She sighed. "I can't help but worry for them."

"Well, fortunately, they've got you praying for them, I'm sure."

Maegan smiled slightly at his words. She was praying every day and night. "Sheriff Bridger, do you think …"

"James."

"What?"

"My first name, it's James. In the mine, when you asked about Bridger being my last name, I realized I never told you what my first name was."

A soft smile touched her lips. "James Bridger," she tested it out, "It's a good name. I like it," she told him decidedly.

Bridger liked how it sounded when she said it. He didn't know why he had blurted it out, but he felt almost under a spell as he danced with her. He had never felt like this about anyone.

"Mae, can I ask you something?"

"Anything," Maegan said, feeling lost in his gaze, which seemed so attentive and inviting.

"Would you ever consider …"

Suddenly, the music changed, and Jack Dean was standing there asking for the next dance. Maegan and Bridger reluctantly stepped away from each other, Maegan looking at him apologetically. Sheriff Bridger smiled a "we'll talk later" kind of smile and politely stepped away for the other man to claim her.

Bridger wasn't sure what to do with himself after Maegan was taken away. Emily Shaffer wasn't dancing with anyone at present, but he hesitated to ask her since he got the impression that she wanted him to be more interested than he was. She was a nice girl, and pretty, too, but Bridger found his eyes unintentionally scanning the crowd again for Maegan.

A few minutes later, Emily Shaffer appeared at his side and struck up another conversation. He didn't want to be rude, and since she was rather obviously looking for a partner, he asked her for another dance. He hoped he was answering and nodding in all the right places, because his attention continued to wander to wherever Maegan was.

*****

$\mathcal{I}$t was getting overly warm, and Maegan felt the need for some fresh air. She moved along the border of the room and then stepped out onto the porch. A handful of others had the same idea and were gathered in various places, conversing and laughing. The cold night air was a welcome change to the temperature of the overcrowded room, and Maegan slipped into a corner of the porch, adjusting her skirt and resting against the rail. A small group of women had left a few minutes after her and were now moving down the steps, waiting for their carriage just below the porch where she stood. Maegan didn't take much notice of them until she caught her name in their conversation.

"Did you see Maegan McCoy this evening?" one of them said. "She made an absolute spectacle of herself, throwing herself at nearly every man in the room!"

"Maybe it was the first time she's ever worn a dress, and she didn't know how else to contain herself," one of them commented and laughed.

"She sure was turning heads, but I thought she looked ridiculously overdone."

"She even made an effort to attract Sheriff Bridger. She's aiming high, setting her sights on the best-looking man in town," another voice said.

"She's most likely better aiming her pistol than she is hitting a target like him," one of them laughed and was joined by the others.

"Well, Emily Shaffer's got her eye on the sheriff, and he seemed more than a little interested tonight. Why, they were dancing again when we walked out," the loudest of the three said.

Desperate to evade their gossip and hurtful words, Maegan

turned and maneuvered past a few people to get back inside. Once at the door, however, she paused, feeling strange about returning to the party. Did everyone think she was flaunting herself? Why, she hadn't sought out a single person to dance with, but rather, they had come to her. Would it have been better to refuse their invitations to dance? She felt confused and embarrassed, especially for enjoying her dance with Sheriff Bridger if he indeed had feelings for Emily Shaffer. Maybe what Maegan had thought was romantic interest on the sheriff's part was just friendliness.

Maegan suddenly moved down the stairs, and, in an effort to be unseen by those women, she turned to the left and walked down the street. She just needed a few minutes away from it all to gather herself together before she returned to the party. She hadn't grabbed her coat before stepping outside and now hugged herself against the cold December air. The music from the restaurant grew distant as she walked a little farther. Most folks were either in their homes or at the dance, so except for the light and noise coming from the saloon at the end of the street, Millcreek seemed asleep. She walked past a house that was separated from another by a narrow alley. As she stepped past the first house, making herself adjacent to the alley, movement caught her attention, and she saw the figures of two men.

Her heart thundered in her chest when one of the men violently stabbed the other man in the back. Unable to stifle her gasp, Maegan darted across the alley, hoping to remain unnoticed as she stepped in front of the next house. Trying not to panic, she waited, praying the man in the alley wouldn't come out to the street and see her. She knew she would have to pass the alley again to get back to the party, and her only hope was that he would be gone when she did so.

"I think the party's at the other end of this street, Miss."

Maegan's glance shot toward the voice, realizing the man had stepped around the corner of the house and was standing just a few feet away from her.

"I … I know. I was just heading there," she said, trying to keep her voice from trembling. His hat concealed his face, but as he stepped into the light of the streetlamp, she recognized Garret Spencer.

"Seems to me you were just comin' from that direction. I saw you pass by just a bit ago," he said.

"Yes, well … I'll be going back then." She was fiddling with her sleeve and forced her hands to her side as she stepped away from the house and tried to move past him.

"No need to rush off," his voice slurred slightly as he stepped to the right to block her. "Ain't you as fine as cream gravy," he said. His eyes that bluntly admired her suddenly grew round, and he grinned broadly. "Well, I'll be switched. That you, Mae McCoy?"

She lifted her chin a fraction, ignoring the amusement in his tone and eyes as she stepped around him.

"So, it is you." He reached out and took her by the arm. "How 'bout makin' friends with the enemy?"

"Don't touch me," she said between clenched teeth, trying to pull her arm free from his tightening grip.

She gasped when he jerked her closer, and the playfulness in his eyes suddenly turned to cold steel. "What did you see?"

"Nothing!" she said, a little cry escaping when he pulled her roughly into the alley. For a moment, she lost her breath when he pushed her against the wall. She squirmed as his hand pressed firmly over her mouth.

"Don't scream … don't say a word!" He pressed his face close to hers, and she could smell the liquor on his breath. "You say a word about what you saw tonight, and I'll make your life miserable! Do you hear me?"

Maegan nodded barely, his hold on her suppressing her movement. Slowly, he moved his hand from her mouth, and she released a shaky breath. "I won't say anything," she whispered.

"You better not, or that little brother of yours is going to suffer before I kill him!" He gave her a little thrust against the wall for emphasis. "Do we have an agreement?"

"Yes," she whispered. From the corner of her eye, she could see the dead body of the man he had stabbed lying just a few feet away, half-hidden in the shadows.

"What? I can't hear you!"

"Yes!" she answered louder.

"Good." He relaxed his hold a little but kept his hands on her arms. "Now, you're gonna help me."

Maegan wondered if she'd heard him right over the loudness of her heart pounding in her ears. "What?"

"Come on!" He yanked her to where the dead body lay. "Grab his arms and help me carry him!"

"I won't!" Maegan glanced toward the street, hoping someone would walk by and to whom she could cry out for help. She suddenly felt Garret's hands pressing hard into her arms.

"You do it, or I'll stick my knife into your brother's back next!"

To her repulsion, Maegan found herself complying. She held the man's arms while Garret held his legs. Together, they carried him to the end of the alley and then to another back street that intersected it. It was faintly illuminated by lights coming from the back windows of houses along that street.

"Drop him!" Garret whispered roughly. There was just enough light to see some bushes, and Maegan watched as Garret dragged his body behind them. He suddenly reached towards her, his one hand seizing her arm while his other went for the back of her neck. "Now, you get out of here, but you keep your mouth shut!" He jerked her closer to himself. "And you stay away from that sheriff!"

His intense hold on her emphasized his threat and, as he had intended, instilled a new level of fear in Maegan. He released her with a little shove, and Maegan thought her legs were going to give out as she stumbled away from him. Even in the dark, she could feel his eyes watching her as she ran down the back street and toward the alley.

"Don't forget to keep our secret!" he called to her, which only propelled her to move faster.

Maegan didn't look back. She just kept running, and by the time she had rounded the corner to go up the steps of the restaurant, she was feeling lightheaded and out of breath from the horrible incident. She let out a little cry of surprise when she accidentally crashed into someone. "I'm so sorry," she said before realizing who it was.

"Mae?"

She looked up into Sheriff Bridger's concerned eyes and stepped back, trying to catch her breath.

"What's wrong?" he asked, immediately seeing the frightened look on her flushed face. "And what happened to your dress?" In the streetlight, he could see the long tear that went from her shoulder to the middle of her arm, exposing her skin.

Self-consciously, she covered it with her other hand. "Oh, no, Alison's dress," she said, tears welling in her eyes.

"What happened?" Sheriff Bridger took a step past her to look toward the direction she'd come.

"I shouldn't have left the party," she said, wiping with irritation at a few tears that escaped. She suddenly felt so weak in the knees that she reached for the railing near the steps to steady herself.

"Mae, what's wrong?" Bridger asked again, his tender and concerned tone causing her to feel in stark contrast to how she'd felt just moments earlier.

"It's nothing," she lied, trying to think of something she could tell him. She felt his hands gently take her by the arms and turn her around, which forced her to look at him.

"Maegan, what happened?"

"I just had a little run-in with Garret Spencer," she said carefully, realizing she would have to divulge something. "He just frightened me, is all. You know how he can be," she tried to downplay her encounter with him. "He was just being a nuisance, but I got away."

"Got away?" Bridger didn't like what her words implied. "Did he hurt you?" The sheriff asked in a tone Maegan had never heard before.

"No. It's alright."

"It's not alright!" Sheriff Bridger instantly moved past her, walking quickly in the direction she'd come. He found Garret Spencer a few blocks away, leaning against a trough and draining the remains of a whiskey bottle into his mouth.

"Evenin', Sheriff," he said, fairly certain Maegan McCoy hadn't gone back on her word that quickly.

Sheriff Bridger walked right up to him and grabbed him by his collar. He paused for just a moment before punching the man across the jaw, sending him toppling to his knees. "That's for bothering Mae McCoy!"

Garret staggered to his feet, cursing and yelling at the sheriff. He swung at him and probably wouldn't have missed if he hadn't been so drunk.

Sheriff Bridger landed one more solid punch across the other side of his face. "And that's for ripping her dress! Don't touch her again!"

Maegan had watched from a distance and didn't know

what to say when the sheriff returned to her. "Let's get you back inside," he said, gently placing his hand at her back.

"I'd much rather go home," she told him with something akin to panic in her eyes at the thought of seeing anyone else at this point. "I wish I'd come separate from Reverend Myles and Maggie."

"I'll take you home," Bridger said gently but decidedly. He walked her back to the porch of the house, where she waited by the door while he collected her coat for her. He also found Reverend Myles and told him Maegan wasn't feeling well, so he was going to take her home.

"Eli won't mind if I borrow his buckboard. It'll just take a minute," he told Maegan when he rejoined her outside.

Maegan followed him across the street and waited while he hitched up his horse to the buckboard. "Cody's at the Myles'," Maegan said as he offered his hand so she could climb up onto the seat. "Maybe I should have just waited for Maggie and Reverend Myles."

"No, I can understand you not wanting to stay." He let out a heavy sigh and shook his head in frustration. "What a …" Sheriff Bridger stopped himself before he said a word he didn't want Maegan to hear. "… mudsill," he altered his preferred word for Garret Spencer. "I should have thrown him in jail for the night."

Maegan didn't know what to say. She just sat there quietly as the buckboard rumbled down the road. The combination of the hurt she'd felt from hearing the women's gossip and then the fear she'd known from Garret Spencer left her too upset to even find words. His threat of harming Cody was the worst part by far, aside from that poor man that now lay dead on a back street.

As they drove, Bridger also found himself struggling for words. "I'm sorry the night had to end like this," he finally thought to say.

"It's alright," she replied quietly, her mind swimming with the image of Garret stabbing the man in the back.

"It's really not," he said, feeling it was his duty to keep such things from happening. "I want you to tell me if Garret Spencer even looks at you the wrong way," he told her. "Just because you know how to shoot a gun, I wouldn't underestimate him, especially now that he knows what you look like in a dress."

Maegan felt the last part of his words in a way he hadn't intended. Did he think she had flaunted herself, too? She hugged her jacket tighter to herself and continued to stare out into the darkness as he drove. Had she made a fool of herself by playing dress-up with Alison's fine things? She dreaded having to tell Alison she had ripped her dress.

They picked up Cody and then headed to Uncle Ben's house. Throughout the drive, Bridger glanced at her in the darkness, wishing he could see her face to see if she was really alright. Once they arrived, he jumped down to help her out and found her struggling a little to find her footing underneath the layers of skirt she wasn't used to.

"Thank you for the ride home," she said as her feet hit the ground. She turned to follow Cody inside but felt the sheriff reach out for her hand.

"Mae?"

She was glad he couldn't see her face in the darkness, because she didn't think she could hide all the emotions rising inside of her at that moment.

"Are you really okay?"

"Yes," Maegan answered almost too quickly. "Good night."

After they'd gone inside, Bridger just stood there for a minute, feeling like he didn't want to leave. He saw a light come on in the house as a lamp was lit. Slowly, he climbed back into the buckboard and turned the horse around. With another glance toward the house, he headed back to town, wishing he could have said something that would have been more comforting to her.

# *Chapter* Sixteen

"What happened to you?" Robert asked his son when he saw him the next morning.

Garret Spencer stepped out of the small cabin he lived in and slammed the door behind him. It was on his parents' homestead, which allowed him to help with their farm but still have a level of privacy. He squinted against the bright sun that seemed intent on blinding him and staggered toward the well just a few yards away. He had gotten home late last night. After his run-in with the sheriff, Garret had returned to the saloon for a few more drinks.

"Looks like we ain't gonna get a fair deal from that new sheriff," he told his father.

Robert looked at his son with a questioning expression. "What are you jabbering 'bout?"

"He busted me up last night cuz I was talking to Mae McCoy, as if I'd be interested in the likes of her." Garret pulled up a bucket from the well and reached his hands into the ice-cold water. He splashed his face with it and felt the sobering effects immediately. "From what I could see, looked like she was using her charms to pull him to their side."

"Charms? Mae McCoy?" Robert asked doubtfully, thinking of the girl who dressed in trousers.

"She looked like a real sage hen last night, and like I said, he walloped me for just saying hello."

Robert shook his head. "Figures Ben would use his niece to get the sheriff on his side."

"Exactly." Garret winced as he touched his swollen cheek.

"Well, we'll watch our back, is all. I best tell Joe so he knows the sheriff's likely to be partial."

"And likely to be violent," added Garret as he wiggled his sore jaw. "I'll teach that sheriff a lesson. He'll learn he can't put his hands on me!"

"Don't be stirring up trouble," Robert warned his son, who he knew was hot-tempered. "I've never minded you boys sticking up for yourself and our family, but don't go startin' anything."

"Sure thing, Pa," Garret said as he leaned forward and dumped a bucket full of water over his head.

*****

It wasn't until Maegan was getting ready for church the next morning that she realized the bracelet Alison had let her borrow was missing. She assumed it must have come off when Garret Spencer had roughly pulled her into the alley, which was probably when her dress tore as well. She already felt bad about the tear in the dress, and she didn't want to have to tell Alison that she had lost her bracelet as well. After the service, Maegan told Cody to head home without her, and then she went to where she had encountered Garret Spencer the evening before.

It made her uneasy just to stand in the spot where she knew a man had been murdered, and she hated to think that she had aided Garret Spencer in carrying the dead man's body. She knelt on the ground to feel around the dirt for the bracelet, hoping not to see signs of blood. She couldn't stop wondering who the man was who now lay dead at the other end of the alley. It felt horrible and went against everything in her to keep the awful secret, but she knew she couldn't risk Cody's life.

"Mornin', Mae."

Maegan spun around as she came to her feet, surprised to hear the sheriff's voice.

"Sorry, I didn't mean to startle you," he apologized. "You lookin' for something?"

"Just the bracelet I lost last night," she said, hoping she didn't sound as flustered as she felt.

A scowl replaced the friendly look on Sheriff Bridger's face. "Did you lose it on account of Garret Spencer?" The anger he felt toward Garret Spencer for manhandling her surprised him a little. Of course, he would have felt the injustice keenly for any woman, but the idea of someone hurting Maegan McCoy was unthinkable. She was the kindest, most caring person he'd ever met.

"I'm afraid so," she admitted. "It was Alison's. I'll just buy her a new one."

"I should make Garret Spencer pay for it."

"I don't think that's a good idea," Maegan told him. "There's already enough animosity between his family and ours. I'd rather not stir up anything else."

"I can understand that," he said quietly. "It just doesn't seem right that he shouldn't pay for the harm he caused."

"He paid a little bit," she said with a slight smile. "I'd be surprised if his face isn't swollen for two weeks."

Bridger chuckled. "I guess I can find a little satisfaction in that."

"Thanks again for taking me home last night and for your help."

"Of course," he said, a mix of emotions coursing through

him. "Besides the way it ended, did you enjoy the party?" Bridger asked her.

"Yes," Maegan replied with a smile, her thoughts returning to the dance she had shared with the sheriff. As she met his gaze, she felt like he was remembering it, too.

"Are you … busy this week? I thought maybe we could get dinner again."

Maegan saw the hopeful look in his eyes and felt deep regret at what she knew she needed to say. His friendship was a treasure to her, and suppressing the feelings growing in her heart toward him was akin to being in pain. What Pete Keller had done to Cody on account of her being friends with the sheriff and then Garret's threat the previous night made a continued friendship with the sheriff impossible … at least for now.

"Or if you'd rather not do dinner," he added when he saw her hesitancy, "we could do something different. Maybe …"

"Sheriff Bridger …" Maegan stopped him more sharply than she had intended, her heart hurting to say the words, "I've appreciated your friendship, but right now, I think I just need to spend time focusing on Cody and all we need to do to keep up my uncle's farm."

Her response was so unexpected that it took Bridger several seconds to find a reply. He suddenly began questioning everything he thought had been a sign that she was as interested in him as he was in her.

Maegan hated that he seemed to be searching for words. "You've been very kind to Cody and I, but I just …"

"You don't have to explain." He interrupted her, flickering a mirthless smile. "I understand." He inwardly chided himself for entertaining the thought that she cared more deeply for him than she did. "I should be going," Bridger said and, tipping his hat briefly, began walking away. "See you around, Mae."

Maegan took a few steps toward him, wishing she could explain but knowing she would be jeopardizing Cody's safety if she did. It had been hard enough to know if reporting Pete's threats was the right thing to do, but now someone was dead, and the intensity of the threat had only heightened. She opened her mouth to speak, but no words surfaced, just a horrible feeling that she'd hurt someone she cared very much about.

*****

The following afternoon, Maegan headed toward Bell's Newspaper Press to talk to Alison. She found her at her desk when she entered.

"Hello, Mae!" Alison greeted her kindly. "What brings you here?"

"Well, I didn't get a chance to talk to you yesterday in church, and I came by to let you know why I haven't returned your dress yet. I'm trying to …"

"Oh, just keep the dress, Mae," Alison interrupted with a smile. "I honestly never wear that one anymore."

"It's too fine."

"Nonsense. I insist."

"It did undergo a tear," Maegan admitted as she tried to ignore the memory of Garret Spencer grabbing her.

"Well, if it's not something you can mend, you should take it to Mrs. Murry. Her dress shop's just on this street, and she could fix it easily." Alison noticed Maegan's expression. "Is there something else wrong?"

"It's the bracelet you lent me. I … I lost it."

"Oh, not to worry. It wasn't an expensive bracelet."

"I want to replace it," Maegan told her.

"Don't you dare," Alison laughed softly. "I promise I won't miss it."

"You were so kind to let me wear your things; at least let me replace the bracelet."

Alison saw the apologetic expression on her face. "If it makes you feel better, but only if you promise to keep the dress."

Maegan smiled at the compromise. "Alright. I guess I can agree to that." She hugged the other woman and then went back outside—her destination, the General Store, where she hoped to find Alison the perfect bracelet.

*****

"Only a few days until Christmas break!" Lilly said to Cody as they left school that same afternoon. It was cold outside, but they were bundled up in their coats. "You wanna head to the General Store and see what new toys Mr. Maison has in the window?" Lilly asked.

"Sure," Cody replied as he noticed Jeb just a few feet ahead of them on the road. The boy hadn't picked a fight or caused any trouble since getting stuck in the mine together.

"Hey Jeb, wait up!" Cody called over to him, causing the boy to stop in his tracks.

Jeb looked over his shoulder, surprised to hear his name.

"Whata ya want?" He asked as Cody and Lilly caught up to him.

"You wanna come with us? We're gonna head to the store and see what's new in Mr. Maison's window."

It wasn't the first time since the mine incident that Cody had been friendly, but Jeb was still surprised to be included, considering the way he treated Cody until recently. Cody inviting him to go along put a little smile on his face, but it also increased his guilt. After his pa had taken him home from the mine, he'd railed him out for playing in the mines. When Jeb saw his father starting to remove his belt for a whooping, he'd spurted out a lie that had spared him. "Don't whip me, Pa!" he'd said. "Cody McCoy tricked me into going into the mine and then tried to bring it down 'round my ears!"

The lie had spared him a sore bottom, but he'd felt guilt-ridden about blaming Cody, especially after the boy had risked his own life to help him when the tunnel had first caved in. It only added weight to another lie he'd told his pa weeks ago. Jeb had sneaked out and gone into a stall in the barn to smoke a cigar he'd found. He thought it was burnt out when he'd left it on the ground, but a short time after he had returned to the house, to his horror, he heard his pa screaming about the barn being on fire. When his pa had asked him if he knew how it started, Jeb had just blurted out that he'd seen Joshua McCoy set fire to it.

"You excited 'bout Christmas?" Lilly's question broke his reverie.

"I guess," Jeb said with a shrug, walking beside them. A few minutes later, they reached the store. Lilly was excitedly pointing out which toys she wanted.

"I don't know 'bout them toys, but I'd like that right there," Jeb said, pointing to a rifle.

"That's a Winchester." Cody admired it, thinking how much he'd like to own it as well.

"Jeb!"

Jeb Spencer whirled around to see his father standing behind him. "Whatcha doin' with this McCoy boy?"

"Nothin', Pa. Jest lookin' at some …"

"You git yourself to home!" Joe Spencer ordered as he gave his son a shove away from the window. "And you!" Joe stepped toward Cody, grabbing his arm firmly. "You stay away from my boy!"

"Leave him be!"

Joe Spencer glanced up to see Maegan McCoy stepping out of the General Store and quickly descending the stairs. Cody was surprised as well to see his sister, whom he hadn't realized was in the store.

"He tried to kill my boy!" Joe told her as he roughly let go of Cody's arm and took a step toward Maegan. "Jeb told me how Cody tricked him into going in that mine!"

"That's ridiculous!" Maegan retorted, her hands coming to her waist.

"Trapped him in the mine and then tried to bring it down on him!"

"You're wrong," Maegan told him, her eyes daring him to argue with her. She wasn't afraid of this man, whose coarse and drunken appearance spoke volumes. "If you asked Lilly and Cody what really happened, you might get a different story," Maegan said.

Joe shook his head, anger glowing in his eyes. "You callin' Jeb a liar?"

"I'm just saying he's not telling you the truth about what happened in the mine."

"You McCoys are all the same … always causin' trouble and just lookin' out for yourselves!"

"Uncle Joe," Maegan softened her tone and hoped to reason with him. "Cody would never try to intentionally hurt anyone, especially his cousin."

"Don't remind me that you're kin!" The man stepped closer to her, the veins in his neck bulging. "If it were up to me, I'd …"

"Everything alright over here?"

Joe Spencer turned his attention to Sheriff Bridger, who had noticed Joe losing his temper from across the street. Seeing that Maegan was on the receiving end of his anger, Bridger wasted no time heading toward them.

"Everything's fine, Sheriff!" Joe said, his gaze returning to Maegan. "You stay away from us, you hear!" he told her before moving away.

"You two alright?" Sheriff Bridger asked Maegan and Cody as Joe walked away.

Maegan nodded and released a sigh, her gaze following Joe Spencer. "I wish I could do something to change the way he feels about us."

"Some folks can't be changed," Bridger replied. "No matter how much you try." He couldn't help but speak from his own experience with his adoptive parents. He had tried everything he could think of to make them love him but eventually had to settle for their indifference. His thoughts kindled the memory of his conversation with Maegan the previous day. While his past had taught him to put his feelings on the back burner, it felt much harder to do where Maegan was concerned.

"I feel bad for Jeb having a pa like him." Cody's words broke into Bridger's thoughts.

"He's just hurting everyone around him because he's hurting," Maegan said, putting an arm around her little brother while thinking of her Uncle Ben and his wounded relationship with his son, Joshua. There was so much unforgiveness between the lot of them. "If they could just know the Lord," she said quietly, although more to herself than anyone else.

It wasn't the first time Bridger had heard Maegan speak about God with such confidence … as if He could make all the difference in any situation. Her faith gave Bridger the feeling that he was missing out on something.

He was still thinking about it minutes later when a man ran up to him as he returned to the jailhouse. "Sheriff!"

"What is it?" Bridger asked the anxious-looking fellow.

"A body's been found! You gotta come!"

# *Chapter* Seventeen

Even after his pa had shooed him away, Jeb had stayed in town. He hated that Cody would know he had told his pa a lie about the mine and that he had placed the blame on him. Jeb didn't make friends easily, and Cody's friendship recently meant a lot to him. Once his pa headed back to the saloon, Jeb hoped to find Cody and smooth things out. He didn't get the chance, however, because something else caught his attention. A small crowd of men, including the sheriff, was gathering down the street. Curious, Jeb followed. By the time he reached the gathering, he saw that two men were carrying another man who was obviously dead. He was laid in the back of a wagon, and a blanket was placed over him.

As the wagon was driven away, the men scattered, leaving Jeb alone on the back street. As he walked back to the main road, Jeb's foot met with an empty bottle, which he absently kicked around. As it rolled, an object in the dirt made it stop. Jeb bent down and picked up the object, which turned out to be a silver boot spur. Not thinking much of it, he dropped it into his pocket and continued kicking the bottle until he'd made his way to the main road.

*****

few days after the body was found and after making some inquiries at the saloon, Bridger rode over to Robert Spencer's homestead, since he knew Garret and Bobby Spencer lived in a cabin on Robert's property. After knocking on their door, he heard some movement from inside. Garret opened the door and looked even larger than usual as he all but filled the small doorframe. "Afternoon, Sheriff. Can I help you with something?"

"I'm here because Pete Keller's been murdered. I understand he's your cousin?"

"Yea, on my ma's side. I heard about his body being found. Durn shame."

Sheriff Bridger thought Garret's attempt to sound sorrowful seemed forced. "I have some witnesses at the saloon who say you were in a fight with Pete Keller Saturday night, which is most likely the night he was murdered. What were you two fightin' about?" Bridger asked.

Garret chuckled slightly as he rubbed his palm along his chin. "I end up in a fight with pretty much everyone, Sheriff. I really don't recall."

"One of the fellows at the saloon that night said it got pretty heated at one point. He said something about you losing your watch to your cousin in a poker game."

"Nah, that's bosh. I didn't lose my watch, but now that I think about it, I think our fight was on account of me catching Pete cheatin'."

"Folks I talked to said Pete was an honest player."

"Everyone's entitled to their own opinion."

Bridger studied his face, the man's bleary eyes not giving anything away other than the fact that he drank too much. "He was your cousin, but were you two close?"

Garret let out a sigh. "Just like brothers, we were."

"Keller was stabbed with a mid-size sheath knife," Sheriff Bridger proceeded, trying to see if more conversation would produce some kind of slip-up on Garret's part. "You own something like that?"

"I reckon most fellers own something like that." He shifted his weight as he leaned against the door frame and folded his arms across his chest. "You ain't pinnin' this on me, Sheriff. I didn't kill 'im."

"Saturday night, after you had the fight, where'd you go afterward?"

Garret's eyes squinted as if he was thinking hard. "I was drunk, so I can't rightly remember, but I ended up a few blocks away from the saloon. That's when I ran into Mae McCoy." A strange look crossed his face, almost as if he'd just thought of something. "Come to think of it … what was she doing so far from that Christmas party that night? As I recall, it weren't that long ago some fellows in the saloon overheard her threatenin' Pete. Pulled her gun on him too, what I heard."

"What are you saying, Garret?" Bridger asked with irritation. "That Mae snook away from the party to murder Pete Keller?" An amused expression crossed his face. "You really are pathetic."

Garret shrugged. "I'm just saying, Sheriff. You gotta look at all the suspects, and, shucks, everyone knows she ain't your average lady. 'Sides, why would I kill my own cousin?"

"I don't know, but I wouldn't put it past you."

"That hurts, Sheriff."

"Did you murder Pete Keller?" Sheriff Bridger asked him point-blank.

Garret's eyes narrowed slightly as he held the sheriff's gaze. "No. But, I reckon I wouldn't admit it if I did."

"Then I won't take up any more of your time," Sheriff Bridger said after a pause. He returned to his horse, having little confidence that the man was innocent.

"Hey, Sheriff …"

Bridger looked at him from his place on his saddle.

"I hope you find who done it."

Bridger knew justice was the last thing on Garret's mind. And how ridiculous to even bring Mae McCoy's name into it. For the first time since the Christmas dance, however, Bridger found himself wondering why she had left the party in the first place. He'd been so bothered that Garret had caused her trouble; he'd never even asked her why she had walked off. Bridger knew Maegan wouldn't pull her gun on anyone unless she had a good reason, and he couldn't trust Garret's account of anything. Either way, he knew Maegan had nothing to do with Pete Keller's murder.

*****

"Uncle Ben, you're back!" Cody shouted from the doorway one evening as he spotted his Uncle Ben driving into the yard.

Ben was climbing down from his wagon when Cody reached him. He thought the boy looked genuinely glad to see him, and it produced a twitch of a smile. He hadn't felt this good coming home in a long time … he hadn't had anyone glad to see him come home in a long time.

"Howdy, Cody," he said as the boy came closer.

"You sell all your pelts?" Cody asked.

"All but a few," he said.

"Uncle Ben! You're home! And just in time for supper." Maegan smiled from the doorway of the house as her brother and uncle approached.

"Place looks good," Ben complimented when he followed them into the house and saw how clean and orderly it was.

"You run into any trouble?" Cody asked him, excitement in his voice.

"Cody," Maegan reprimanded with a soft laugh, "It almost sounds like you're hoping he did."

"I have a few stories," Uncle Ben replied with a chuckle, and Maegan noted that he seemed a little different, or maybe he was just happy to be home.

*****

"Afternoon, Nick," Bridger said to the bartender, who was wiping up a recent spill on the counter. After his conversation with Garret, Bridger had decided to pay the bartender a visit to see if he could shed any light on the night Pete Keller was murdered.

"Afternoon, Sheriff," Nick replied. "Can I get you a drink?"

"No, thanks. I wanted to ask you something, though."

"Go on."

Bridger hadn't been in Millcreek all that long, but as far as he could tell, Nick had never lied to him and was more decent than most saloon owners he'd come across. "Fellows I talked to said Garret Spencer and Pete Keller had a fight in here Saturday night."

"Yep. It got so heated I had 'em both thrown out."

"Do you remember what it was about?"

"I couldn't tell you exactly, but something to the effect of Garret accusing Pete of cheatin'. Garret's known as being a sore loser, though, so chances are Pete just bested him."

"Did anyone else ever make any threats on Pete's life?" Bridger asked curiously.

"Not that I recall," Nick said, but then, a moment later, he grinned slightly. "Except one."

Sheriff Bridger's eyebrows hiked with interest as he waited for him to go on.

"That Mae McCoy. She was madder than a hornet when she came in here one day to confront Keller. From what I overheard, he gave her brother a walloping, and she weren't having it." He shook his head. "Can't say as I blame her, though." He chuckled. "I think she struck some fear into Keller when she pulled her gun on him, whether he'd admit it or not, but I wouldn't really consider her a threat," Nick added, but then he noticed the sheriff's expression. "Do you, Sheriff?"

Bridger wanted to ignore the knots that had formed in his stomach when Nick had mentioned Maegan's name. Nick's words confirmed that, surprisingly, what Garret had told him was true. "What exactly did she say? Do you remember?"

"Something about him being sorry if he ever harmed her brother again."

When Bridger left the saloon, he knew he needed to talk to Maegan. He felt certain she had nothing to do with Pete Keller's murder, but he still wanted to find out what exactly had provoked her to confront him.

*****

Ben McCoy went to answer a knock on his door and found the sheriff on the other side. "Afternoon, Sheriff," Ben said.

"I'm glad to see you made it back safe," Bridger replied, entering the house as Ben opened the door wider. The December air was cold, and he was grateful for the warmth of the cabin.

"How was your trip?" Bridger asked him.

"Successful," Ben replied, thinking of the furs he had sold. "What brings you out here?"

"I wondered if I might ask you a few questions."

"What about?"

"You know a fellow by the name of Pete Keller?"

"I reckon I do. He's been known to run with the Spencers, beings he's Garret and Bobby's cousin on their ma's side."

"You know him long?"

"Why, what's he done?"

"It's not what he's done; it's what's been done to him. Two days ago, he was found murdered in an alley in town."

Bridger saw Ben's face drop slightly. "Sorry to hear that," Ben said quietly, shaking his head.

"I'm new here, so I'm trying to talk to people who knew him. Is there anything you can tell me that would be helpful?"

Ben's expression was pensive. "He was a bit of a trouble-maker, but most of that was Garret's influence, I'm guessin'. I didn't know him well." He let out a heavy sigh. "I wish there was more I could say."

"Is Mae at home?" Bridger asked.

"She's 'round back."

Maegan was surprised to see the sheriff when she heard his greeting. She was pinning up a wet sheet that she had sprawled over the clothesline.

"Sure is cold to be hangin' laundry," Bridger said.

"It's got to be done," she smiled slightly. "Certainly not my favorite job in the winter, though. What brings you here?" she asked, giving him her full attention while stuffing her hands in her coat pockets to warm them.

"Something unfortunate, I'm afraid. There's been a murder in town."

Maegan felt a queasy sort of feeling wash over her. "Who?"

"Pete Keller. His body was found behind some bushes on a back street in town."

"Pete Keller? How was he killed?" Maegan was almost

afraid to ask, knowing it had to be the man Garret Spencer had murdered.

"Stabbed in the back."

The sheriff's words confirmed her fear. She couldn't believe Garret would murder his own cousin. The knowledge made her realize even more how dangerous Garret was. If he could murder someone close to him like Pete, then carrying out his threat to hurt Cody wouldn't even faze him.

"Did you know him at all?" Sheriff Bridger asked.

"A little," she replied honestly as she bent down to pick up an item of clothing from the laundry basket.

"I heard he gave you cause enough to pull a gun on him."

Maegan wasn't proud of it, but she nodded. "He gave Cody a black eye. I'm afraid when I saw Pete the following day, my temper got the best of me."

"You should have told me he hurt Cody," Bridger said, and Maegan saw his heart in his eyes. "I would have made sure it never happened again."

"I'm just used to takin' care of things myself," Maegan told him with a little shrug. "Especially where Cody's concerned."

Bridger could understand that. He just hoped her idea of taking care of things hadn't crossed the line. He mentally shook his head for even having such a thought. He knew Maegan McCoy couldn't hurt anyone. "The timeline of his murder seems to be the night of the Christmas dance. Since Keller's body was found not too far from where you ran into Garret, I wondered if you had seen anything suspicious?"

Maegan shook her head, turning to hang the last piece of wet laundry. "I'm sorry, I didn't," she said.

Bridger hesitated for a moment and then asked the last question in his mind. "Why did you leave the dance in the first place?"

The answer was a little embarrassing, and Maegan hesitated as she thought about how to get around it. "The room felt so warm, I went out for some fresh air."

"But you could have just stayed near the restaurant. Weren't you almost at the end of the street when you ran into Garret?"

Maegan nodded, turning to face him. "I overheard some ladies saying things about me, and I … I just needed a walk."

Bridger saw the insecurity in her eyes and understood. Although as beautiful as she had looked that night, he assumed anyone saying anything unkind was merely jealous. He thought she looked beautiful now, too, even in old trousers and a simple vest. "And that's when you ran into Garret?" he asked, trying to rein in his thoughts.

"Yes," Maegan replied.

Bridger let out a sigh. While Keller's body had been found a decent distance from where Bridger had confronted Garret that night, it still placed Garret close enough to the scene of the crime. Bridger knew he just needed evidence to prove it had been Garret, although the fact that Pete Keller was his cousin did impose a shred of doubt that Garret was guilty.

"I'm sorry I couldn't be of more help," Maegan said as she lifted the laundry basket from the ground and moved toward the door. She felt frustrated that she couldn't tell him the truth, but she had no other option. She had promised her mother to keep Cody safe, and no matter what, she was determined to keep that promise.

# *Chapter* Eighteen

"Would it be alright if I asked Lyn Hummel to join us for Christmas Eve dinner?" Alison asked her brother and sister-in-law a few days before Christmas.

"Why, that's a wonderful idea," Maggie said, her smile conveying how sincerely she meant it.

"You've really taken her under your wing, haven't you?" Reverend Myles said, a pleased expression on his face.

*Or she's taken me under hers*, Alison thought to herself. They had quite a few conversations that had left Alison wondering if the woman was more of a benefit to her or the other way around.

Lyn Hummel was obviously grateful to be with them on the eve of Christmas, her eyes tearing up with gratitude more than once. Both Maggie and Alison had wrapped a few gifts for her to open after supper, and she thanked them half a dozen times. She was just mentioning that it was getting late and that she should be getting home when Alison noticed Maggie from across the room.

"Maggie, are you alright?" she asked with concern when she saw Maggie holding onto the table and hunching over it.

Her question immediately grabbed the attention of everyone in the room. Reverend Myles moved to his wife and gently took her arm. "Should I go for the doctor?"

"It's too early for that." She suddenly gasped and clutched his hand. "Yes, maybe you better," she changed her mind. She saw the concerned expression on his face and smiled tenderly at him, knowing that losing his first wife made him more inclined to worry. "I'm going to be fine, Jacob," she assured him, although inwardly, she was trying to calm her own panic. She had never had a baby before, but something didn't feel right.

"I'll get you into bed," Alison said, already at Maggie's side, helping her toward her bedroom. Reverend Myles was halfway out the door, and Lyn had rallied the children to get them ready for bed.

"Your mama's gonna need some time by herself, but by morning, you'll have a new brother or sister," she told them.

"Can we just give her a hug goodnight?" Lilly asked, her voice trembling slightly. She'd been six when her Ma had died, and the thought of losing Maggie was unthinkable.

"Of course," Lyn replied kindly, gently gesturing for them to go to their mother.

After they had returned and gone to their room, Lyn joined Alison in Maggie's bedroom. Alison had helped her change into her nightgown and was propping a pillow behind her back and trying to make her comfortable. Maggie was breathing heavily, and her face was flushed as beads of sweat gathered on her forehead. Alison was surprised when Lyn came close and placed her hands on Maggie's protruding stomach.

"Your baby's breeched, hunnie."

Maggie's green eyes grew round as saucers. "What?" She groaned as a sharp contraction seemed to seize her entire body.

Lyn saw the fear in Maggie's eyes and reached a calming hand to her shoulder. "It's alright, hunnie; we'll get this baby turned around."

"But how?" Maggie asked, her anxious gaze unwavering from the woman's face. Alison came over with a cool, wet cloth and placed it on Maggie's forehead.

"Let's give it a little time, and maybe the baby will turn before the doctor gets here. Just take deep breaths and try to stay calm if you can."

Maggie nodded, but then a sharp contraction caused her to cry out in pain. "I hope he gets here soon!" she said breathlessly. Minutes passed, and then nearly an hour went by. Maggie cried out again as the contractions became closer and more intense. "Why is Jacob taking so long?" she moaned.

Lyn felt Maggie's stomach again, and Alison didn't miss the concern she saw in Lyn's eyes. "My husband was a doctor, and I helped him deliver more babies than I can count. If you'll trust me, I think we need to get this baby turned as soon as possible."

Maggie exchanged glances with Alison, whose expression of uncertainty mirrored her own. "Are you sure you know what to do?" Maggie asked, tears starting to flow down her cheeks. She was more scared than she'd ever been in her life. She had heard plenty of stories of women dying during childbirth, and what was worse, she had seen it happen firsthand to her own mother, giving birth to her second child, who, sadly, didn't survive either.

Lyn gave her a reassuring smile. "My dear, this is a natural part of life, and you were created to do it. Your baby just needs a little help to get in the right position."

Maggie nodded, not seeing any way around it and also feeling a determination to do whatever it took to bring this baby into the world. She could hear Alison praying softly beside her and felt a growing sense of peace that this woman knew what she was talking about.

"Boil some water and get me plenty of linens … and some more light," Lyn told Alison. "Don't you worry, Maggie," she said, turning her attention back to her. "This baby's going to be in your arms before you know it."

*****

When Reverend Myles returned home with the doctor, he could already hear the sound of a baby crying. Rushing into the room and to Maggie's bedside, he felt his heart almost stop at the sight of her, seemingly lifeless on the bed.

"She's just sleeping," Alison said when she saw her brother's panicked expression. She saw his entire countenance relax as he released a shaky breath. She gently reached out and placed a hand on his arm. "Do you want to hold your little girl?"

Seeing the baby for the first time, Jacob took her in his arms, her rosy cheeks and rosebud lips capturing his heart instantly. He stepped to the side as the doctor began examining Maggie, while Alison moved to help Lyn continue to clean up the bed sheets.

"Thank God Lyn was here," Alison said. "The baby was breached," she explained. "Things were happening so fast, and I hadn't the slightest notion what to do!"

Doctor Fletcher shook his head in amazement. "I was on a call several miles from town, and by the time Jacob found me and we got here … I might have been too late." He looked at Lyn. "You could have very well saved Maggie and this baby's life. The last time I checked, the baby wasn't in the right position, but Maggie still had a month to go, and I thought the baby would turn by then. There were no signs I could see of her going into labor early."

"I'm glad I could be here," Lyn said.

"I'm in your debt," Reverend Myles said to Lyn, gratitude in his eyes.

Maggie stirred and slowly opened her eyes. "Jacob!" she whispered, and then a huge smile lit her face when she saw the baby in his arms.

"She's beautiful, Maggie," he said as he carefully passed the baby to her.

"What are you going to name her?" Doctor Fletcher asked.

Maggie smiled as she looked down at her precious girl. She and Jacob had discussed names for months, but there was one they had both agreed on: "Marigold."

"I think that's perfect," Alison said, blinking away tears that were filling her eyes. It had been a long, nerve-racking couple of hours, but she'd never felt her heart so full as she did at that moment, watching her brother and sister-in-law smiling down on their little one. Alison turned and hugged Lyn as the women tried to slip out of the room. "You were wonderful!" she told her, placing a little kiss on her cheek. "I'm so thankful you were here and knew what to do."

Lyn smiled in that humble sort of way of hers. "I'm thankful it all worked out."

*****

The Christmas season was especially joyful that year, with Marigold's birth being a more exceptional gift than any of them could have asked for. The next few weeks were cherished ones as Lilly and Lucas marveled at their baby sister, and Maggie and Jacob grew more in love with Marigold each day. The newest Myles easily captured Alison's affection as well. The housework, cooking, and time with the children were also a welcome distraction from the ache that still remained in her heart. She knew she needed to let Austin go, but everything in her seemed to scream the opposite.

"Pray about what you're feeling," Maggie had told her

recently when the subject of Austin had come up. "The Lord's the best one to help you sort through what's in your head and heart."

While Alison had grown up attending church with her parents, the notion of praying to the Lord about her romantic feelings concerning Austin McCoy seemed rather whimsical. Surely, God wasn't paying *that* close attention to her life. Years ago, she had noticed a change in her brother when he had "met the Lord," as he put it. He often talked about how personal God was and how He wanted to be involved in the smallest details of their lives. While Alison had never argued with that idea, she had also never been in a position to need God in a personal way.

One afternoon in January, while Maggie and Jacob were with the baby and Lilly and Lucas played contentedly in their room, Alison grabbed her coat and slipped outside for a walk.

"Here I am, pining my heart away while he's probably out shootin' the breeze with some other woman!" she said out loud as she walked away from her brother's house. The January sky was gray and the air colder than it had been all winter. She buttoned up her coat and absently wished she had also remembered her hat and gloves. She told herself a quick walk was what she needed. That quick walk unintentionally ended up being closer to an hour. She followed the creek until it came to the orchard. During late summer, there would be apples on those trees, but today they were bare and only made to look alive because of the frigid wind that shook their branches.

Alison noticed that snow was beginning to fall. She could feel the cold ice flakes melting when they hit her cheeks. She ignored it, even when it began falling a little heavier, and pressed on as if her destination would be a place she could take her feelings to drop them off. How could she rip them out of her heart so they would stop haunting her?

She again remembered Maggie's suggestion to pray about what she was going through. Lyn Hummel had all but told her to do the same thing, as well. With a deep breath, Alison glanced around and found a seat on a large, fallen tree limb. Then, after a few minutes had passed, she bowed her head in her hands and began to pray.

*Humble yourselves, therefore, under God's mighty hand, that he may lift you up in due time; casting all your cares upon him, for he cares for you.* Alison heard the Bible verse in her heart, almost as if someone had just spoken it. She had heard that verse before in church, but now it was coming to her like a whisper … reminding her that the Lord was near enough and interested enough to help her.

"If that verse is true, Lord," Alison prayed out loud, "and if your eye is even on the sparrow, as they say, then I'm going to believe that you do care about something even like this. I don't know how to stop loving Austin, but if it was all a lie, and he's not who I thought he was, then please … please take away my feelings for him." She could feel tears stinging her eyes as she continued, and for quite some time, she sat there sharing her heart with the Lord. As peace settled in her, she realized it was the first time that she had ever felt God so near. She had heard her brother talk about God's presence many times, but until that moment, she had never experienced its realness for herself.

Alison suddenly felt prompted to ask God's forgiveness for believing He existed but never taking the time to know Him in a deep way or listen for his voice. She hadn't realized until that moment that she'd gone through the motions of attending church while ironically not giving much thought about God himself. She found it easy enough to pray for others, but concerning herself … why, she couldn't remember even including the Lord in her decisions. How could she have missed out on a friendship with the Lord all these years? How could she believe the Bible was God's word, but rarely read it for herself?

Sitting there alone, an uncanny lightness and joy pricked her heart, and for the first time since Austin had left, she felt like she wasn't carrying the ache of his betrayal alone. Something deep inside told her God had a plan and that she could trust Him for it. The realization came calmly yet definitely and radiated a new sense of hope. Slowly, Alison opened her eyes and, when she did, realized at least an inch of snow had gathered over her boots. Looking at the surrounding landscape, she saw it, too, was being blanketed in white. She smiled in awe at how beautiful it looked and marveled at the stillness and peace that hung thick in the air, fittingly reflecting the very emotions in her own heart.

A sudden chill made her blow into her hands to warm them, and she chided herself for not bringing her gloves along. Standing, she dusted off the snow that had gathered on her coat and began the walk home. A frosty breeze hit her face hard, sending swirling snow with such force that she had to turn her back to it for a moment. That's when she realized the snow was falling at an alarming rate and that it was so white, she could barely see more than two feet ahead of her at a time.

Telling herself not to panic, Alison trudged on. Surely, she hadn't gone that far from her brother's home. She looked for the creek and resolved she could just follow that back to keep her on track. After several minutes, she realized she couldn't find it. It should have been just to her right, but maybe she had gotten turned around somehow. She stopped to look around and took a few steps in another direction.

She began to walk faster as she told herself her brother's house was just over the next hill. But it wasn't.

Now trembling head to toe from the cold, Alison tried to see through the blizzard-like conditions, shielding her face with her hands when the wind blew against her. A few minutes later, as she was walking, she realized that she had stepped onto a section of the creek that had frozen just enough to be hidden under the snow. As the thin ice snapped, the freezing cold water rushed up to meet her. She let out a little cry as she fell to both knees in the water, catching herself with her hands but getting soaking wet.

Feeling numb from the wet and cold, she climbed out of the water and up the slight slope that led away from the creek, grabbing onto tree limbs and any available branches she could find to assist her in the climb.

"Please, God, please help me get back! Don't let me freeze out here," she prayed over and over. For another twenty minutes, she kept walking, the wind and snow rushing around her in such rough torrents that she sometimes had to stop and just kneel in the snow until it passed. The third time it happened, she feared she wouldn't be able to stand back up. Lifting her head and blinking against the snow rushing at her face, she saw what appeared to be light in the distance. Hoping it was coming from a cabin window, she pushed through the snow and thought she could smell smoke coming from a chimney. She kept praying to make it until, finally, she reached the doorstep of a cabin.

Weak from the cold and shivering from being soaked, she collapsed against the door. Huddled there, she began to knock as hard as she could. Not more than a few seconds later, the door opened, and she heard a familiar voice.

"Alison!"

Alison didn't even look up. She was so unbelievably cold

she could hardly think straight. She felt strong arms scooping her up, and then she felt a rush of warmth as Gideon Martin carried her into his house. He didn't put her down until he had reached a chair that sat near the fireplace and then, in a flash, grabbed a blanket and threw it over her shoulders. Kneeling in front of her, he unlaced her boots and took them off. Then he took her hands between his own and vigorously rubbed them until they didn't look so purple.

"Alison, you gotta get out of those wet clothes." He went into a nearby room and returned with some clothes and a robe. Gently, he took her by the arms and steered her toward his bedroom. "Go in there and change into these." He pressed the dry clothes into her hands. "We can dry out your things then."

Still shivering, Alison nodded and went into the room as he said. Concerned for her, Gideon remained outside the door, listening to make sure she was all right. It seemed to be taking a little too long.

"You okay, Alison?" he asked. There was no answer, so he hesitantly opened the door a crack, keeping his eyes down. "Are you okay?" he asked again.

"I … I can't stop shaking," she whispered. "I can't get the buttons …"

Gideon entered the room and saw she was trying to reach behind herself to unfasten the buttons on her dress, but she was trembling so hard she couldn't manage it. Quickly, he unfastened them, looking away as the dress began to slide off her shoulders. "Can you finish?" he asked as he undid the last button.

She nodded, and he moved out of the room but remained waiting at the door. A few minutes later, the door opened, and she stepped out, clutching the robe around her. He saw her bare feet and grabbed a pair of his socks for her to put on. Then he led her back to the chair by the fire and handed her a towel to dry her hair.

"Why can't I stop shaking?" she said, her lips quivering. "I can't seem to … to get warm."

Gideon grabbed another blanket and put it over her. "You'll get warm. Just give it a few more minutes."

"What were you doing out there?" he asked as he came to sit in front of her by the fire. He took one of her feet, which felt like a block of ice, and began to rub it with both hands.

"I was just walking, and the blizzard came up so … so suddenly." She glanced at him and gasped. "My brother will probably be out searching for me in this!"

Gideon sighed, knowing she was right. "There's nothing we can do about it right now. It's laid another inch just since you got here."

"Oh no! If something happens to him, I'll never forgive myself!"

"I'm sure he'll be fine, Alison."

Alison realized he was holding her hands again and gently rubbing them. She was finally starting to feel warmer. "Thanks, Gideon," she said quietly, her eyes meeting his. He smiled kindly. "No problem." He hesitated and then said, "You'll have to stay here for the night. It's too dangerous to go out in this."

Alison nodded. "I'm so sorry to show up like this."

"I'm just glad you didn't freeze to death out there."

"Me, too," Alison replied, praying inwardly that her brother would not be out looking for her.

*****

Alison sat up, a confused expression on her face as she looked around the small and unfamiliar bedroom. She looked down at the thick blankets that lay over her and suddenly remembered she was in Gideon Martin's bed. Realizing she was wearing his clothes, she glanced toward the door, feeling a rush of embarrassment. She spotted the robe he'd also given her and quickly wrapped it around herself as she climbed out of the bed. She smelled fresh coffee, eggs, and bacon and slowly opened the door. The sight of Gideon at the stove, his shirt untucked and his suspenders hanging down over his pants, wasn't something she was used to seeing on his usually tidy appearance. She cleared her throat before stepping into the room, and he turned. A little blush crept into his cheeks when he saw her in his robe. He hadn't paid much attention the day before since all he could think about was getting her warm.

"There's coffee ready if you want some."

Alison thanked him and moved toward the pot. He'd also put two mugs on the table, so she picked one up and poured herself a cup. As she took a sip, her gaze rested on the windowsill.

"Oh, my! Did it snow all night?" She went to the window and couldn't believe the snow that had piled up to the sill.

"Try opening the front door," he suggested.

Alison reached for the handle and opened it slightly, gasping when she saw the wall of snow halfway up the doorway. "There must be at least three feet out there!"

"At least. Probably more in some drifts."

Alison closed the door and turned back to the room, a look of concern on her face. "Maggie and Jacob must be so worried about me."

"I'll try and get out today. I might be able to make it on foot to your place, at least to let them know you're okay."

Alison nodded slowly, the gravity of the situation sinking in. "I can't believe I did something so foolish."

"Your dress is almost dry," he said as he nudged his head toward the chair that he'd hung it over.

"Thank you," she said as she took another sip of coffee. The idea of being snowed in with Gideon Martin wasn't something she would have ever imagined happening. But here he was, serving her bacon, eggs, and coffee while she sat at the table in his robe.

"How'd ya sleep?" he asked as he sat in the chair across from her.

"Good. I think being so cold made me more exhausted than usual."

"I have to admit, I was a little worried you might have had frostbite at first."

"Thank goodness it didn't come to that. Thanks for everything you did," she added. She suddenly remembered his assistance with the buttons on her dress and hoped he wasn't reading her mind.

A few minutes later, he stood from the table and went to look out the window. "I hate to say it, but the sky looks like it's about to give away more snow. I'm gonna try and dig out from the back door," he told her.

While he started trying to make a way out, Alison went into the bedroom and changed into her stockings and dress, which were now warm from being placed so close to the fire. She realized her hair had fallen out of whatever style she'd had it in the day before, which she couldn't even recall. She used her fingers to untangle it as best she could and then braided it. When she came out of the room, she found Gideon boiling a pot of snow he had collected from the mound at the back door.

"Gonna throw some hot water on all that snow," he told her.

Alison sent an uneasy look toward the window. What if she had to stay more than one night?

"I have snowshoes out in the barn," Gideon said. "Once

I get out the back, I'm gonna go feed the animals and see if I can make it to your brother's."

An hour later, Gideon returned from the barn and handed her a pail of milk from the opening he had created at the door. "It's too thick for you to get through," he told her. "I'll try and make it to your brother's and back before the next round of snow hits."

"Be careful," Alison said, hating that she was putting him in this position.

"I'll be back," he promised. He turned and stomped through the snow, his snowshoes leaving wide tracks.

Alison felt like a caged animal for the next few hours. To put her restless self to good use, she went through Gideon's cupboards, hoping to make something by the time he returned. She found some flour, which she used with the milk to make a broth, cut up and boiled some potatoes, and then sprinkled in leftover bacon from that morning. She ventured into his cellar and found corn among his canned goods, which she added along with a few spices. Turning the boiling pot down to a simmer, she waited and hoped it would turn out. The least she could do was have a hot meal ready when Gideon returned.

She anxiously went to the window and watched as more snow began to pour from the sky. What a mess she had caused. If only she had not let her feelings for Austin get the better of her. Now, she had put both Jacob and Gideon at risk. She paced and then picked up a book she found lying around. The place was already tidy, so she didn't have anything to clean to take her mind off her aimlessness. Finally, she heard someone at the back door. Jumping up from her chair, she went to the door and met Gideon just as he was pushing it open. He stumbled inside, shaking the snow off his scarf and boots.

Alison helped him remove his snow-covered coat, gloves, and hat and then hung them over a hook while he moved to the fire. "Did you make it?" she asked.

"Yep. And in the nick of time, too."

Alison sighed with relief. "Thank you, Gideon."

"They were right comforted to know you were safe. I told 'em I'd bring you back soon as the snow lets up."

"I have soup ready," she suddenly remembered as she saw him shivering by the fire. "That should help warm you up."

He thanked her and moved toward the table, still rubbing his hands together. He looked down at the bowl she set in front of him. "This is amazing."

"You haven't even tried it yet," she laughed softly. "Don't get your hopes up."

"I don't think there's a chance you could disappoint in any way."

Alison moved back to the stove, a little uncomfortable under his tender gaze and kind words. The house was quiet except for the sound of the wind howling outside and gently rattling the windows in their panes. The fire crackled in the fireplace, a nice stack of logs piled up beside it. An hour later, the snow was still coming down hard. Gideon stoked the fire, and Alison moved to the window.

"Do you like to play checkers?" he asked her.

She smiled softly, glad for something to do. "Sure. Lilly and I play all the time. I'm pretty good," she teased.

"Well, you haven't seen me play yet."

*****

The snow tapered off in the evening. By morning, the clouds had dispersed, and a bright sun was a promising sight. It took Alison and Gideon hours to clear the snow away from the front door and two more days until the snow was melted enough to even get a horse through it. Alison had wanted to try walking home, but it was just too deep.

"I'll go and saddle the horses," he told her in the afternoon that the snow was finally passable. She tidied up a few things and grabbed her coat to follow him. There was suddenly a knock on the door just as Gideon was about to go out.

"Why, Toby, I'm surprised you got through all that snow."

The older man, who looked every inch of a grizzled old-timer, chuckled. "Took some time, but I wanted to check on ya, make sure you weren't caught out in that blizzard."

Gideon thanked his neighbor, appreciating his concern. "It did come up unexpectedly," he said and noticed that his neighbor was glancing at something past him.

"Who's that in there with ya?"

Alison came closer to the door. "I'm afraid I was caught out in the storm when it started."

The older man scratched his whiskered cheek, and his eyes narrowed slightly. "Ain't you Reverend Myles' sister?"

Alison nodded, wondering why it sounded more like an accusation than a question.

"You mean you've been here for four days?"

"And I'm just about to take her home," Gideon informed him. He stepped outside past the man, Alison following behind him.

"Thanks for checking in, Toby," Gideon said over his shoulder.

Alison followed Gideon along the path he had made to the barn, noticing a high wall of snow on each side of the narrow walkway. She had to squint against the brightness of the white snow and the sun beaming overhead. As inconvenient as it had been, the wintry scene of snow-covered trees and fields stretching for miles was beautiful. Once inside the barn, she closed the doors behind them and watched as Gideon led a horse out of a stall. She thought Gideon seemed deep in thought about something and maybe a little frustrated.

"Are you okay?" she finally asked.

He threw a blanket over the horse's back, followed by a saddle, before answering. "Toby's a good neighbor, but he's also got a wobblin' jaw."

Alison knew that meant he was a talker, but she didn't comprehend the gravity of the situation until Gideon stopped what he was doing and looked at her directly. "Folks are gonna talk, just so you know."

"I'm sorry for putting you in this position, Gideon."

"I ain't sorry. I just wish ol' Toby Jackson hadn't come along and seen ya."

*******

"First, Lilly going missing, the baby coming early, and now this! I don't know if I can take any more scares!" Reverend Myles hugged his sister tight as he said the words and then turned to Gideon. "Thank you for taking such good care of her. Meant a lot knowing she was with you."

Gideon nodded. "I best be getting back before it gets any colder and the snow freezes." He stepped toward the door, thanked Maggie for the coffee she had given him while he was there, and then tipped his hat toward Alison. "See you later."

"Thanks, Gideon," she said, giving him a sincere smile of gratitude before he left.

"Oh, Alison! We were so worried that first night!" Maggie exclaimed. "Jacob was out searching for hours! Thank God you managed to find shelter."

"I thought I would freeze to death," she admitted and shivered just remembering how cold she had been.

"What did you do all that time?" Lilly asked.

Alison shrugged. "We played checkers a lot." She leaned down and hugged her niece. "But he wasn't nearly as good at it as you are."

"What were you doing out that far, anyway?" Maggie asked curiously.

"I took a walk toward the orchard. I don't know how I got so mixed up and ended up on his property."

"Well, the Lord had his eye on you, that's for sure," her brother said. "I haven't seen it snow like that since I've lived here. One thing is for certain, you couldn't have been in better hands."

"You're right about that," Alison said, thinking about her time alone with God before the storm had blown up. She knew her brother had been referring to Gideon Martin, but Alison knew her survival in the storm was the Lord's doing.

*****

"Alison didn't say much about spending nearly a whole week with Gideon," Maggie mentioned to her husband as they lay in bed that night. "I sure hope folks don't find out because the talk will be merciless."

"Nah. Gideon is a well-respected man."

"Well respected or not, four days alone in the house with a woman as beautiful as your sister … there's bound to be gossip."

Jacob hadn't thought of that, but now it began to worry him. "I hope it doesn't put Ali in a bad light."

"Well, we're the only ones who know, and I'm sure Gideon won't say anything."

"You're right. There's nothing to worry about."

*****

few days later at work, Jacob was feeling just the opposite after one of the men he worked with at the mill jokingly nudged him and said, "Bet you're going to make Gideon Martin marry your sister now."

Jacob's scowl told the other man he didn't find his words amusing. He overheard some of the men teasing Gideon as well when they thought Jacob wasn't around. Gideon didn't say much or just ignored them altogether.

Jacob wasn't the only one who heard murmurs. Alison came home from work one day, and Maggie could tell something was wrong. When she asked her, Alison just rolled her eyes. "That Toby Jackson, Gideon's neighbor, apparently told the whole town about me staying at Gideon's! It's ridiculous what they're saying!"

"I feared that might happen," Maggie said. "Give it a few weeks, and the rumors should die down with the leftover snow."

Alison hoped she was right. One day after work, she found Gideon standing just outside of the press as if waiting for her. "Hello," she greeted him.

He hadn't seen her since the blizzard, but he hadn't stopped thinking about her since the blizzard, either. "How have you been?" he asked.

"Good. And you?"

"Just fine," he replied. "You want a ride home?"

Alison noticed a few passing folks glancing at them and could imagine what they were whispering about. Not wanting the fear of gossip to dictate any of her decisions, she lifted her chin a fraction in a moment of self-standing. "I'd love a ride. Thanks, Gideon."

"Looks like folks are still talkin'," he said to her apologetically.

"Oh, let them talk!" Alison returned with irritation. "If people got nothing better to do than stick their noses in, their opinions aren't worth our time."

Her words filled Gideon with some confidence and even hope where she was concerned. He didn't realize how lonely his life was until he'd spent four days of it with Alison Myles. Having her around in the cabin made him recognize just how much he wanted a wife and how much he wanted Alison Myles to be that wife. He had been interested in her since Jacob introduced them, but then Austin McCoy arrived and seemingly captured her interest. Now, with Austin gone, Gideon hoped he had a better chance of kindling a relationship with Alison.

"You think you'll stay in Millcreek?" he asked a few minutes later.

"I think so."

"Nice place to settle down, I think."

"Yes. I've lived most my life near the city, and I think I prefer this quieter pace."

"Glad to hear it." He wanted to say more but decided to proceed carefully. He certainly didn't want to speak his feelings too soon and scare her off. He liked Alison a lot and knew she was a prize worth waiting for.

*****

"What's eatin' you up?"

Austin threw another log onto the fire. "Nothin'," he answered his brother's question.

After Austin left Millcreek in November and met up with Sawyer, they had scouted after the James brothers until snow and cold temperatures had forced them to return home, where they had been for the last few weeks.

Sawyer eyed Austin suspiciously from where he sat at the kitchen table, finishing his supper. He thought Austin had been acting differently since he'd returned from Millcreek.

"You just seem down in the mouth since you got back," Sawyer pressed him. "I guess it was hard to say goodbye to Mae and Cody."

"It was," he replied simply.

"Still don't know why she had to leave like that," Sawyer said.

"Don't you?" Austin said, a trace of irritation in his tone.

"I told her Cody didn't have to come with us no more," Sawyer defended himself.

"You told her, but we both know you didn't mean it."

"What's that supposed to mean?" Sawyer sat up a little straighter, a slight scowl on his face.

"Means what you said and what you meant are two different things." Austin didn't stand up to his brother often, and this was one of the rare occasions. "She did what she thought was best." He moved toward the door. "I gotta feed the stock."

Sawyer sat there for several minutes after Austin had left, trying his best to juggle the guilt that his brother had just dug up. Cody's near loss of his life had shaken him up more than anyone knew, and he had felt sorry for having insisted he come along. He wasn't one to make the same mistake twice, however. At least he told himself he'd never force Cody to go along again. The thing was, their line of work was dangerous, and it came with some close scrapes, but there was never one they didn't pull through. There was a resilience he'd grown to have, and consequently, he felt it was somewhat his duty to teach others to have that same buoyancy. Cody had a close call, but it would teach him a lot more than he would learn sitting at home reading with Mae.

Austin returned a few minutes later. "Saw this rolled up in your saddle bag," he said as he laid a reward poster on the table in front of Sawyer. It was a recent wanted poster for the James brothers with an even higher reward.

"I picked that up from town the other day," Sawyer told him.

"The snow's all but melted," Austin said as he picked up the poster again and stared at it. "Couple more weeks of winter, and we could head out again."

Sawyer perked up on these words, his eyes shooting over to Austin's. "You saying you'd come?"

"Why not. We might as well finish what we started."

A slight grin made its way across Sawyer's face. "I'm ready when you are."

# *Chapter* Nineteen

 aegan leaned against the fence of the small corral at Eli Greene's livery stable as she waited for him to finish repairing the stirrup irons on her saddle. She'd meant to get them fixed earlier that week, but with all the snow, the roads had just recently become passable again. A cold gust of wind tugged on her coat, and she buttoned the remaining top buttons and pulled her knit cap snug over her ears.

"Why, Mae McCoy. I've been hoping to run into you."

Maegan turned around at the voice and felt uneasy when she met Garret Spencer's bloodshot eyes that bulged against his oily skin. His greasy hair clung to his forehead from underneath his hat and seemed to match the overall slapdash appearance that he gave off.

"What do you want?" Her aloof tone matched her gaze.

"It's been over a month. Just wanted to make sure you was still keeping …" He leaned closer in and whispered, "… our little secret."

"You don't have any reason to think I haven't."

"The sheriff's been to my place a few times askin' questions," he said as he leaned against the fence beside her, studying her face and trying to intimidate her with his nearness.

"I haven't said anything," she said as she took a step away and looked toward the barn, hoping Eli Greene was almost finished.

"Good. You know," he said after a moment, "you're as much of a suspect as I am."

Maegan's eyes flitted to his. "What are you talking about?"

"I'm talking about how some fellas in the saloon say you threatened my cousin and held a gun to his chest."

Maegan suddenly realized why Sheriff Bridger had been asking so many questions. Did he really think that *she* could have murdered Pete Keller?

"I can see I've sparked some thoughts in that pretty head of yours," Garret chuckled.

"Stabbing someone in the back is your style, not mine," she retorted sharply. "Whether I turn you in or not, it's only a matter of time until evidence is found to prove your guilt," Maegan told him.

"There ain't no evidence," Garret replied with a cocky glint in his eyes. He pushed off the fence and leaned in close to her. "And we both know you ain't gonna say anything!" He practically spat the words as he gave her arm a little shove. "If you get any ideas about snitchin', just remember that even from behind bars, I've got friends who'll do just about anything I tell em' to."

Maegan hated that his words provoked fear in her and hated that she had been forced to be a part of his secret. Since witnessing Pete Keller's murder and having Cody's life threatened, she had wrestled with the thought of taking Cody and returning home. Winter was an unpredictable time for travel, but this most recent run-in with Garret convinced her it was the right thing to do.

Maegan knew it would come as a surprise to him, but she decided she would tell Cody of her plans to leave Millcreek just as soon as he returned from school that day. She regretted having to uproot him now when he was doing so well in school and had grown closer to their uncle, but she prayed he would trust her and not ask too many questions.

*****

When Cody walked through the front door, Maegan was surprised to see his teacher, Sylvia Cooper, behind him.

"I gave Cody a ride since I wanted to talk to you," Sylvia Cooper explained with a kind smile. Cody headed to the barn to start some chores, and Maegan offered Sylvia something to drink.

"Oh, no, thank you," she said. "This will just take a minute."

Maegan let out a sigh and gave the teacher an apologetic look. "What's he done?"

Sylvia laughed softly. "Absolutely nothing. Cody's a wonderful student."

Maegan was relieved. "I'm glad to hear it. He really is doing well?"

"Yes. And that has to do with why I'm here. You see, Cody is bright and a hard worker. He's ahead of everyone his age, so I can tell he's had an excellent teacher, which is why I wanted to ask you to consider something."

Maegan looked at her curiously, waiting for her to go on. She gestured for her to take one of the chairs at the table and then sat opposite her.

"As you can tell, I'm almost near my last trimester." Sylvia lovingly placed her hands on her round stomach. "By the end of March, this baby will be here, and I'm going to need someone to fill in for me for the rest of the school year. Would you consider doing that?"

Maegan's jaw dropped. "Are you serious?"

"Of course I am," she smiled. "You've done an excellent job

teaching Cody. He's easily my best student. I can imagine you would do just as well with other children. If you agreed, I thought you could sit in the class for a few weeks to see how we do things. Oh, and of course, you would be paid a salary. It's small but decent."

"I'm honored that you would even consider me, but I don't have proper training."

"Experience is often the best training, and Cody is proof that you've had that. Besides, it would only be for a few months. Just think about it, and let me know as soon as you can," Sylvia said. "I know it's a lot to ask," she added, "but I would so appreciate knowing the children are in good hands."

Maegan was touched by her kind words and wanted to help her. Cody had done so well under her instruction that Maegan felt like she owed it to Mrs. Cooper. Maegan could sense her resolve to leave with Cody beginning to falter. "I'll let you know soon," she promised. "Thank you for thinking of me."

When Cody returned from the barn a few minutes later, Maegan told him what Sylvia Cooper had said and waited for him to reassure her that it was a ridiculous idea.

"You'd be good at it." His answer surprised her.

His vote of confidence made her feel a little more inclined to the idea. "Really?"

"Sure. But you'd probably have to start dressing like Mrs. Cooper does, just so the kids think you're a real teacher."

Maegan felt a little panicked at the thought. It seemed that every time she put a dress on, something unfortunate happened. Could she actually fill in as a teacher? And what about Cody's safety? Maegan knew she couldn't go on forever keeping Garret's dastardly secret. Would staying in Millcreek until the end of school make a difference? For the next three days, Mrs. Cooper's request was all she thought about, and then, after much contemplation and prayer, Maegan went to give her an answer.

*****

A week later, Maegan felt a rush of nervousness as she stood in the General Store and picked out two different colored fabrics. She had agreed to fill in for Mrs. Cooper, which consequently led her to follow Cody's advice and get some dresses made.

Tom Maison was his usual friendly self as he asked her how much of the fabric she wanted.

"A dress worth's length of each," she replied before she could change her mind.

"Good choice," he said. "We just got these in a few weeks ago. My wife was eyeing up this gingham herself."

As she was leaving the store, Maegan collided with Sheriff Bridger.

"Sorry, Mae," he apologized. "I wasn't looking where I was going."

"It's alright," she flickered a smile as she bent down to pick up the parcels she'd dropped. He also leaned over to help, and their hands brushed as he handed one back to her. Maegan's eyes met his for a moment, and she quickly averted her gaze. "Thanks," she said as she situated the parcels in her arms and then started to move past him.

"I heard you're about to be Millcreek's new schoolteacher," Bridger blurted out, feeling like he didn't want her to go so soon.

"Oh," Maegan shrugged as she turned back to face him. She didn't know how the word had spread so fast. "It's just temporary for Mrs. Cooper while she has the baby."

"Temporary or not, it's still an important job."

"I'm really not very qualified," she admitted to him.

"Well, if Mrs. Cooper asked you, then she must think otherwise."

Maegan appreciated his encouragement. "I guess we'll see," she said, the uncertainty she felt still laced in her expression.

"How does Cody feel about it?" he asked her.

"Surprisingly, he doesn't seem to mind. He did tell me I would need to start dressing like a teacher, though," she added with a slight smile as she motioned to the packages in her arms.

"Folks might not recognize ya," he said and then wished he hadn't said that.

"Guess they'll have to get used to the new me, then," she replied. "I should get going. Have a good day, Sheriff Bridger."

Bridger mentally scolded himself for making such an insensitive comment since he knew she was insecure about wearing dresses. He had meant it as a compliment, but he got the sense she hadn't taken it that way. For a moment, he let himself watch her move down the street, not for the first time wondering if he had said or done anything to cause the sudden change in her toward him. He didn't have much experience in relationships, but he was smart enough to know when a woman was trying to let him down gently. Her words a few weeks ago had done something peculiar to his heart. She had made it clear that she wanted nothing more than friendship where he was concerned, and judging by the wall she had suddenly put up, he felt like maybe he'd even lost her friendship as well.

After leaving the store, Bridger returned to the jail, where he sat at his desk and for several minutes just stared at nothing in particular. A familiar band of loneliness tightened around his heart as memories from his past visited him.

*"We're all orphans until God adopts us as his children."* Maegan's words came back to him like they often did since their conversation in the mine.

Sighing, Bridger opened the drawer and pulled out the Bible that had gotten quite a bit of use in the last few months. Flipping it open, he picked up reading where he had left off, hoping to understand more about the God Maegan seemed to know so well.

*****

It was mid-March when all the snow finally melted, leaving the fields and streets muddy and arduous to travel. It was at this time that Maegan was driving herself and Cody to school one morning, her distracted thoughts causing her to hit nearly every mud puddle in their path.

"Geez!" Cody exclaimed as he leaned away from being splashed. "You'd think you've never driven a wagon before."

"I'm sorry," Maegan apologized. "I'm just so nervous about this."

Sylvia Cooper had gone into labor over the weekend, and on that Monday morning, with her nerves sky high, Maegan had put on one of the new dresses she had made. As anxious as she was, Maegan wanted to keep her word to Sylvia to fill in as Millcreek's teacher. Maegan had sat in the classes for a few weeks prior and had been feeling fairly certain that she could handle it. Now, however, as they approached the school, she was wishing she had never agreed to this.

Hours later, when it was time to dismiss everyone, Maegan was a little surprised at how smoothly the day had gone. She had expected at least one catastrophe, but it had only gone well. The entire week went that way, and by Friday,

Maegan was feeling much more comfortable. As she and Cody were leaving the schoolhouse, they noticed Jeb was waiting for them outside.

"Did you need something, Jeb?" Maegan asked him.

"I wanted to tell you I won't be coming back to school," he said quietly. He ran a hand through his hair and put his cap back on.

"Why?" Maegan asked.

"Cuz my pa found out you're teaching."

Maegan laid a gentle hand on his shoulder. "I'm sorry, Jeb. You could take your books with you, so you don't fall behind."

"Nah, that's ok. Pa said he wants me to help more on the farm, anyway."

"Summer will be here soon," Cody encouraged him.

Jeb shrugged, surprised that the thought of missing school bothered him. He'd become pretty good friends with Cody, too, and would miss seeing him almost every day.

Jeb walked away, and Maegan put her arm around Cody as they watched him go. "It's a shame I can't hang out with my own cousin," Cody remarked.

Maegan sighed, thinking of the tension between their families. "I know, Cody. Maybe that will change somehow." But even as she said the words, Garret Spencer's face came to her mind, and she knew it wasn't likely.

*****

"You find any new leads?" Austin asked Sawyer when he returned to their hotel room. They had been traveling for several weeks and made a stop in a small town called Spry to see what information, if any, they could pick up from the locals.

"A fellow named Jenkins said he was robbed at gunpoint

just outside Versailles the day before yesterday. The description of the men who held him up sound awfully close to Jesse and Frank."

"Versailles?" Austin said. "That's only a few hours from here."

"I know," Sawyer replied, clearly excited. "We'll leave at first light."

"You know," Austin said the following afternoon as they rode toward the town of Versailles, "Millcreek's only a two day's ride from here."

Sawyer knew what he was alluding to. "You suggesting we make a stop in Millcreek?"

"It would be nice to see Mae and Cody," Austin said, thinking of Alison as well. He hoped she wouldn't hate him for leaving like he had. Maybe if he could see her again, he could explain why he had left so suddenly. At the moment, it had felt like he had no other choice; after all, Reverend Myles had very plainly told him he had to go. In hindsight, however, Austin felt nothing but regret and heartache over not saying goodbye.

"I'd rather not take a chance of losing their trail," Sawyer told him.

"Wouldn't be a bad idea to let the sheriff in Millcreek know they're nearby. That way, he can be on guard in case they come through."

"Since when are we giving sheriffs the upper hand?" Sawyer asked with a touch of irritation. "We don't get the reward money if someone else gets to 'em first."

"I know, but I'd hate for them to cause any trouble in Millcreek."

"We'll decide later," Sawyer said.

Austin was used to him having the final say, so he didn't press the idea any further.

# *Chapter* Twenty

"Tom Maison gave me this advertisement for the paper," Harold Bell told Alison one Monday morning at work. He handed her a handwritten advertisement.

"I'll add it," she promised as she looked over the paper. He then handed her an envelope.

"What's this?" she asked.

"Just a little bonus."

"You don't have to do that," Alison protested.

"You've been reliable and certainly earned it." He hated to admit when he was wrong, but her column of fiction had single-handedly increased his sales. The way she left each edition dependent on the next was rather genius.

"I'm just thankful for the opportunity, Mr. Bell. Not everyone would hire a woman, especially one as young as myself."

"Yes, well, I'm not one for hindering progress, and I know times are changing."

Alison smiled to herself, knowing he was the sort who didn't relish change, but she was grateful he was slowly coming along. When she left that afternoon, she headed to the General Store to pick up some ink and a new tablet for writing. She was happy to see Maegan in the store and immediately approached her.

"How are you doing, teacher?" Alison asked teasingly.

Maegan turned around and smiled from where she stood at the counter. "It's only been a few weeks, but better than expected," she laughed softly.

"Lilly has told me numerous times that she enjoys having you as her teacher," Alison told her.

"That's encouraging," Maegan said.

"Lilly also tells me Cody's the smartest kid in school, so he must have had a good example," Alison complimented her. She noticed Maegan was wearing the dress that she and Austin had picked out for her, a memory that brought a wave of heartache.

"Oh, my goodness, Ali, I just read your latest edition! It was so good!" Maegan went on for a few minutes, eventually walking out of the store with Alison as they discussed it.

"I can't believe it!"

Alison turned around to see what Maegan had suddenly noticed behind her.

"It's Austin … and Sawyer!" Maegan exclaimed. She moved toward them, as they didn't seem to notice her yet. Carefully maneuvering around passing wagons and other men on horseback, Maegan waved and finally caught their eye. Austin spotted her first, and then Sawyer followed, both dismounting at the same time as they came beside her.

"Mae!" Austin said as he hugged her.

Maegan turned to Sawyer and saw the uncertainty mixed with guilt on his face. She stepped forward and threw her arms around him.

Sawyer breathed a sigh of relief. "Thought you'd still be mad at me," he admitted as he stepped back to look at her. He suddenly realized how different she looked. He wasn't sure if it was the dress or just the fact that he hadn't seen her in over half a year.

"What are you boys doing here?" Maegan asked with a little laugh of shock that they were actually there in Millcreek.

"We're just passing through," Sawyer told her.

"And thought we could spare time for a quick visit," Austin added, his eyes trailing just past Maegan to where Alison was.

Maegan suddenly remembered Alison and looked back to see if she had followed her. She was standing near, an emotionless look on her face. "I'm sorry, Alison," Maegan apologized. "This is my other brother, Sawyer." Then, turning to Sawyer, she introduced Alison.

"Very nice to meet you," Alison said with a sweet smile at Sawyer. She could feel Austin's eyes on her and forced herself not to look at him. "Maegan's told me so many good things," she added, her smile broadening.

"Surprised, but glad to hear it," Sawyer replied with a smile that reminded Alison of Austin.

"I'm sorry, but I have to get home," Alison said, gently touching Maegan's arm. "I'll see you later, Mae. And nice meeting you, Sawyer." She moved past them, walking quickly without even a glance back.

"Phew." Sawyer let out a low whistle, looking at Austin. "I've felt below-zero temperatures that weren't as cold as that shoulder she just gave you."

Ignoring him, Austin handed his horse's reins to Maegan and went after Alison. He dodged through the traffic, his gaze intent on the blonde hair and lavender dress of the woman several yards ahead of him.

"Ali, wait!"

Alison moved quicker when she heard his voice, hating the way her heart had almost stopped when she'd first seen him.

"Alison!"

Taking a deep breath, Alison finally stopped and then slowly turned around.

"I can tell you're mad at me," Austin said once he'd caught up to her. He searched her face, hoping to find even a trace of the Alison he'd left six months ago. She didn't say anything. She just looked at him with that icy glare.

"Okay, I can tell you're furious at me," he adjusted his words. "But I'm here now," he said when no other words would surface.

She cocked one eyebrow and tilted her head slightly. "I can see that."

He impulsively reached out to take her hand, but she saw it coming and took a step backward. "Ali, I know it wasn't right to leave like that. I should have said goodbye and …"

"Yes, you should have."

"Well, at least we can agree on that," he said. He paused, waiting to see if she would say anything, but she didn't. She actually looked away as if she were bored with the conversation. "What if I come by later tonight? We could talk?"

"I don't think tonight will work, actually," she said. "I'm sorry, I have to go."

Austin stood there watching her walk away, knowing she was heading toward the mill where her brother was probably waiting. The thought of Jacob Myles telling him to leave suddenly made his blood boil, especially seeing what it had done to his relationship with Alison. With one more glance in the direction she'd gone, Austin headed back to where Sawyer and Maegan were. He told himself this wasn't the end. He just had to talk to her. Once she heard him out, everything would be okay.

*****

"You're the spittin' image of your pa!" were Uncle Ben's words when he met Sawyer an hour later. Sawyer was glad to meet the man his father had told him so much about. As the oldest, he was privileged to have had the most time with their parents. It was a little hard to imagine this rough-looking old fellow as the young boy from his father's stories, but he sensed there was a kindred spirit in there somewhere behind his wild mustache and beard.

"Now I know what's been eatin' at you," Sawyer said to Austin later that night after supper. Maegan was washing the dishes, and Cody was drying them. Their uncle had turned in for the night, leaving the McCoy children alone. Sawyer set his cup of coffee on the table and leaned back in his chair. "I gotta hand it to ya, Austin. She's real pretty."

Austin scratched the stubble on his cheek. "She's boilin' mad at me, is what." He glanced over at Maegan. "You think I oughta go over to her place and try to talk to her tonight?"

Maegan looked uncertain. "Did she say anything when you caught up to her today?"

Austin shook his head and then let out a sigh. "Guess I really made a mess of things."

"Why don't you give her tonight to get used to you being back and try to talk to her tomorrow?"

Austin liked that idea and suddenly realized how tired he was. He and Sawyer headed back to town and got rooms at the hotel. With Jesse and Frank James possibly nearby, they wanted to be closer to town, although they hadn't divulged that bit of information to anyone. Austin had been looking forward to a good night's sleep in a soft bed after their travel, but two hours later, he was still wide awake, staring at the ceiling of his hotel room.

For years, the unpredictable life of adventure and travel had appealed to him, but since meeting Alison, he felt a very real longing for something different. He knew Sawyer would be the last to understand, so he hadn't said anything to him. Austin turned on his side and tried to turn off his mind. He ended up praying under his breath for wisdom. Finally, after what seemed like forever, he fell asleep.

*****

"You'll never guess who I saw in town," Reverend Myles said to his wife that evening as he lay in bed.

Maggie turned away from the crib on the other side of their room. "You'll never guess who I finally got to sleep," she joked, sending one last affectionate glance at her sleeping baby. Maggie slipped into her nightgown and crawled into bed beside him, eagerly pulling the covers up around them, as the April nights were still cold.

"Who did you see?" she asked, pulling a few pins out of her hair that she had missed.

"Austin McCoy."

Maggie gasped. "No wonder Alison was so quiet all evening. I had been wondering. Do you know if she talked to him?"

"I don't know. I just saw him and another man ride into town this afternoon."

"I hope they can resolve whatever was between them," she said.

"What's there to resolve?" Jacob asked. "He's not worth her time."

Maggie sighed. "One thing is for sure; I don't want him to hurt her again."

*****

Austin was up at the first light of dawn. After asking around, he found Sheriff Bridger at the Millcreek Restaurant, having coffee and a plate of hotcakes.

"Austin!" Bridger stood from his table as soon as he saw him approach. He gave the man a hearty slap on the back. "When did you get here?"

301

"Just yesterday," Austin told him, smiling as he took the seat across from him that Bridger gestured towards.

"What brings you back?" Bridger asked.

"My brother Sawyer and I are tracking the James brothers again."

"The rest of their gang was killed or captured after that robbery in Northfield, I heard."

"That's right," Austin replied, "but Jesse and Frank are still at large." He paused and then said, "Which is why I came to see you. There's been a few robberies near here that sound like their doin'. I just wanted to give you a heads-up."

"Appreciate the warning," Bridger said. "They're a dangerous lot. You sure about going after them?"

"I'm not too sure about anything right now, to be honest with you," Austin said as he folded his arms across his chest and glanced out the window. "Maybe if I help my brother get Jesse and Frank, I can move on to a new profession." He grinned, and although he said it lightheartedly, Bridger thought he looked serious. They talked for a few more minutes, and then Austin left. He had to go by the store first but then was determined to find Alison and make things right with her.

*****

Alison had never felt so at war with herself. She was disappointed that Austin had not come to see her last night, even though she had more or less told him not to, but yet, she didn't want to see him. She wasn't going to make it easy for him, just to ease his conscience, that was for sure. She was also frustrated that after months of trying to surrender her feelings for Austin and praying for a change of heart, here they were, hitting her full swing after seeing him for only minutes! She had thought that if she saw him again, she would be over feeling so strongly about him.

"Oh, Ali. I've started the wash and realized we're out of soap." Maggie looked at her sister-in-law apologetically. "Would you mind a quick trip to town?"

Alison was glad to have something to do and hitched up the buckboard within the next few minutes. After she arrived at the General Store and tied up the horse, she looked up toward the store entrance and locked eyes with Austin. He was just coming out, and a burlap sack of items he had just purchased was in his hands.

"Afternoon," he greeted with a polite tip of his hat.

His expression looked so apologetic; Alison felt some of her resolve begin to melt as he came down the steps toward her. Then, when he asked to speak with her, she heard herself agreeing. He led the way to the side of the store where they were out of the way of traffic and any nosy townsfolk.

"How have you been since … since I left?" he asked, a genuine interest in his eyes.

"Just fine. And yourself?" she answered, trying not to show an inkling of concern or let the warmth of his gaze change her mind about him.

"Alright."

He suddenly remembered that a few minutes earlier, he'd picked up last week's newspaper. Pulling it out of his pocket, he gestured toward the back page where he knew her column usually was. "Just read your latest. It was really good."

Something in his manner seemed suspicious to her. Alison folded her arms across her chest, thinking she would test him. "Oh really? Did you like that part about the train?"

Austin smiled. "Sure did. It was real excitin'!"

Alison grabbed the paper out of his hand, rolled it up, and promptly hit him with it. "There was no part about a train!" She put her hands angrily on her waist. "Is lying just second nature to you, Austin McCoy?"

"Of course not," he said, feeling a little off his game since she'd just caught him in a fib. "I was gonna read it; I just hadn't gotten to it yet."

"Then why did you say you had?"

"Just to have something to say, I guess."

She knew that was an honest answer. She dropped her gaze, feeling torn by what she used to feel and what she felt now. "Why did you leave without saying goodbye?" she asked quietly, slowly lifting her eyes to his.

"I didn't want to leave," he replied.

"Then why did you?"

"Didn't your brother tell you?"

Alison was shocked he would be so blunt, especially over an issue like this. "Yes. Yes, he did," she answered in a tone that felt as tight as her heart at that moment. It was true. She realized that up to that moment, she had been holding out with the hope that maybe her brother had made a mistake with what he had witnessed, that somehow it had all been a misunderstanding. But here Austin was, right in front of her, admitting it was true.

"Then you understand why I had to go. I'm sorry for leaving without saying goodbye, though."

Alison felt tears stinging the back of her eyes as she looked into his handsome face and owned the fact that she really had made a fool of herself. All she heard through his words was that his reason for leaving was because of being in love with someone else … that woman he'd been caught with. Alison supposed he still didn't have the courage or decency to tell her to her face that he had never been serious about her.

"I'd like to have that letter back that I wrote you," Alison said.

Austin's dark eyebrows rose a bit, and a look of surprise flashed across his green eyes. He'd kept that letter tucked safely in his breast pocket since she'd given it to him. Even now, he knew it was there under his vest. He'd yet to read it, but he liked having it with him just the same, knowing she had written it and that one day he'd find out what it said.

"And what if I don't want to give it back?" he asked.

"You don't have a right to what it says anymore. I only knew you for a month when I wrote it, and I was foolish to offer my heart so readily. I … I don't care about you that way anymore."

Austin's eyes narrowed slightly, and he impulsively took a little step toward her. "Now, you're the one who ain't telling the truth," he said quietly.

"Don't act like you know how I feel, because you don't!" she returned, angry tears pooling in her eyes. "Leave me alone, Austin McCoy!"

On that note, she moved around him and hurried into the store. Austin watched her go, more confused than ever. If she knew it was her brother who told him to leave, didn't she understand why he'd gone? Frustrated, he left town, wondering if there was anything he could do to make things right with Alison Myles.

# *Chapter* Twenty-One

Days later, Alison was trying to pay attention to her brother's sermon, but she couldn't keep her mind and her eyes from wandering to where Austin was sitting. After her brother concluded the sermon with prayer and everyone began to stand up, she made a conscious effort to leave as soon as possible, intent on avoiding Austin McCoy. As she headed toward the door, she kept from looking at him, even though she could feel his eyes on her.

"Alison."

She turned just before reaching the door and found Gideon approaching her. From the corner of her eye, she could see the McCoys also nearing the door, so she went out of her way to be more friendly than usual with Gideon, hoping Austin would notice.

"Oh, hello, Gideon," she gave him a sweet smile.

"Are you … busy today?" he asked, looking hopeful that she wasn't.

"No, not at all." She hesitated, sending Austin a side glance to see if he was in earshot, and then said, "Would you want to come to my brother's house for lunch?"

Gideon looked thrilled that she would ask and accepted the invitation without a moment's pause. "Maybe I'll just ride along with you then, if it's alright," she added.

"Of course!" he answered, leading the way out the door.

Alison followed him to his buggy, taking his hand as he reached down from the seat to help her. He took the reins and directed the horse out of the yard, subsequently passing the McCoy siblings on his way.

"Who's that?" Austin asked Maegan as they passed.

"That's Gideon Martin," Maegan replied.

"A friend of the family's or a friend of Alison's?" he asked next.

"Both."

"He doesn't look man enough to chop wood!"

Maegan shushed him and tried not to smile at his comment. "I think he's a kind and decent-looking man," she said in Gideon's defense.

"Can't see why she'd take up with that tin horn," Austin said.

"That tinhorn works with Reverend Myles at the mill."

"Of course he does," Austin replied with an annoyed shake of his head. Their buggy was almost out of sight, but he watched it just the same.

"C'mon," Maegan broke him out of his musings, and he realized he was the last one to climb up into the wagon. Long into their ride home, his thoughts still returned to Alison. If her indifference to him was on account of Gideon Martin, then Austin would find a way to change her mind real quick.

*****

Lunch seemed to be dragging on. Alison hid her boredom as best she could and tried to seem interested in whatever conversation was circulating. She was glad Lilly was asking Gideon questions and that he and Jacob were doing most of the talking, since she had regretted asking him for lunch the moment she climbed into his buggy. It pricked her conscience that she had merely used him to make Austin jealous, and now she was paying for her deceit by having to sit there and feign cheerfulness.

Alison was glad when Gideon said he had to be going, and she retreated to her room to work on her next installment for the paper.

"It's nice Alison invited Gideon over," Jacob later commented from behind his book as he sat at the table reading. "She's got a good head on her shoulders."

Maggie looked up from where she was rocking the baby. "You'd have to be blind to think Alison had feelings for Gideon."

Jacob lowered his book, a surprised look on his face. "What?"

Maggie laughed softly. "Jacob, couldn't you see how she was today? Her mind was a hundred miles away or at least one mile away to the McCoys' house."

Jacob's brows came together slightly. "Until recently, she hasn't seen him in months."

"Well, you know what they say about absence making the heart grow fonder."

Jacob didn't like that prospect. He glanced toward Alison's door. He hoped she didn't still have feelings for Austin McCoy.

*****

"We can't stay here much longer," Sawyer said to Austin that Sunday evening as they rode toward town after spending supper with their uncle, Mae, and Cody. Sawyer could tell his brother wasn't keen on leaving. "I know you wanted to work things out with that girl, but …"

"I can't leave until I do, Sawyer."

"Then I'm gonna go alone."

"Couldn't you wait another day or two?"

Sawyer let out a heavy sigh. "Alright. But just two at the most."

"I'll have things sorted out by then," Austin said quietly, more to himself than to Sawyer. He wasn't about to let another day pass without convincing Alison how much he cared about her.

*****

Alison was having a hard time keeping her thoughts on her work the next morning, but she forced herself to finish editing the stack of articles Mr. Bell had just given her. He had stepped out to run some errands, and she hoped to finish before he returned. When the bell rang over the door, Alison stood to greet whoever had arrived. She turned with a friendly smile.

"Can I help …" The words and the smile died on her lips when she saw Austin standing in the room.

"I'm looking for Harold Bell," Austin said, closing the door behind him.

"He's not here at the moment."

"Good, because I'm not really looking for him; I'm looking for you and wanted to catch you alone."

Her jaw dropped a little at his audacity.

"I really think we need to talk." He saw a flicker of something in her blue-green eyes that was encouraging, but then her expression changed. "I have work to do," she said.

"Can I come back on your lunch break?"

"I'm working through lunch," she lied to him.

He laughed outright and shook his head slightly. "You're somethin', Alison Myles. I'm trying to work things out, but you're making it …"

"There's nothing to work out, Austin."

"I told you I was sorry. Can't you forgive me?"

Alison ignored the way her heart softened when she looked into his eyes. She wanted more than anything to be with him, but how could she trust him again? How could she trust a man who told her he loved her one moment and then was found in the arms of another woman the next?

"I want my letter back," she surprised him by bringing it up again.

"No. You gave it to me, and it's mine."

She released a short and frustrated breath. "Doesn't it make any difference to you that I don't feel the same way as I did when I wrote that letter?"

"Your feelings couldn't have changed that much in a matter of months."

"Why not? Do you think you're that wonderful that I couldn't fall in love with someone else?"

She could tell her words had hit their mark, and her heart broke at the wounded look on his face. She just didn't want him to know how severely she had missed him if all along she had been one of many women in his life.

"I can tell I really hurt you, Ali, and I'm sorry." Austin suddenly felt regret like he'd never known it before. Maybe she wasn't just playing hard to get. Maybe she had moved on and was in love with someone else … maybe that fellow, Gideon Martin.

"Please go. I … I can't talk to you about this anymore." She turned and went back to her desk, feeling worse when she heard the door open and close. She glanced over her shoulder, wishing he were still there but wanting him gone at the same time. Her heart churned with the confusion of it all. *Lord, please take away my feelings for Austin,* she silently prayed. *I don't want to love a man like him.*

*****

 eeling at a loss for what to do next, Austin left their conversation with a heavy heart. He sauntered rather aimlessly down the street, eventually returning to the livery where he and Sawyer were keeping their horses during their stay in town. He figured he could ride out to his Uncle Ben's a while, since he and Sawyer were heading there later for dinner, anyway.

"You boys planning to stay in Millcreek for long?" Eli Greene asked Austin when he saw him approaching.

"Not sure," Austin answered honestly, leaning against one of the fence posts of the corral. "We'll probably be leaving soon. Why'd you ask?"

"I'm lookin' for some extra help here at the livery," he said as he leaned his tall frame against the corral gate. "Wanted to know if you were interested?"

Austin's face registered surprise. "I appreciate the offer. Can I get back to you on that?"

"Sure," Eli replied, an obliging smile under his dark mustache.

"Austin McCoy! Is that you?"

Austin turned to the voice and spotted Toby Jackson heading toward him from the direction of the saloon. The mountain man looked even more rugged since the rough winter had taken its course.

"I heard you was back," Toby said as a greeting.

"Yep."

"You have any luck catching them James boys?"

"Afraid not," Austin answered.

"Well, maybe you'll get luckier the next time."

"Maybe," Austin replied, not in the mood to talk.

"What you need is luck … like that fellow," Toby grinned

as he gestured toward a man passing in a wagon who Austin recognized as Gideon Martin. "Can't get any luckier than him!" Toby chuckled through his gappy teeth.

Austin looked at him curiously, not understanding what he was referring to.

"I've seen a lot of blizzards in my time, but none that blew in a pretty girl like the reverend's sister," he laughed. "I bet Reverend Myles was fit to be tied!"

"What are you talking about?" Austin asked.

"Didn't you hear 'bout it? Folks were talkin' for a while, are still talkin'." He grinned. "Quite the scandal. From what Gideon told me, Alison Myles got lost in the blizzard and just happened to end up at his place. They was snowed in near a week!"

Austin suddenly remembered Alison's words to him about not caring for him as she did before. He also recalled how attentive to Gideon she'd been at church on Sunday before they'd left together in his buckboard! Had she really fallen in love with Gideon? Austin realized Toby Jackson was still jabbering.

"Like I said, he's as lucky as they come! There's not a feller in town who wouldn't mind being snowed in with that woman for even one night, let alone …"

"I'll be thanking you to not talk like that or be spreading rumors about Alison Myles," Austin cut him off, not liking at all what the man was insinuating.

"Ain't rumors! I was the one who saw her at his house," the man chuckled. "Gideon and I are neighbors, and he looked none too thrilled for me to catch 'em together."

Austin wasn't going to stand around listening to such talk for another second. Without a word, he moved toward his horse and rode away from Toby's babbling. As much as he tried to dismiss them, however, the man's words continued to take a turn in his mind, and later that day, Austin asked Maegan about what he'd heard of Alison.

"The blizzard came up so suddenly," Maegan confirmed it was true. "Snow piled halfway up the door. It was days before we could get out as well."

"Have they been spending time together since I left?" Austin asked.

Maegan thought of a few instances where she'd seen them talking or him giving her a ride home, but nothing that indicated anything beyond friendship. She told Austin as much but could tell he was still bothered. "Folks gossip and exaggerate things. I wouldn't assume it's anything more than that," Maegan said.

"I'm surprised Reverend Myles didn't have a conniption, as protective of Alison as he is," Austin said, a hint of bitterness in his voice.

"What was he to do? He was just glad his sister didn't freeze to death and was with someone he trusted."

"I suppose."

"Don't let it bother you. Just ask Ali. I'm sure she'll explain everything."

Her words snapped him out of his unwelcome thoughts. "You're right. I don't know what got into me." He stood from the chair. "I think I'll ride over to her place tomorrow."

# Chapter Twenty-Two

Maggie finished brushing through her wet hair and braided it loosely. She had been exhausted lately, and when Jacob suggested he would take the baby and their other children over to the Carters to visit for a little while so she could take a hot bath and nap, she'd jumped at the idea. The quiet house and much-needed alone time were refreshing, to say the least.

Now, as she sat rocking on the chair in the main room, her eyes began to get heavy. She settled into a deep sleep, stirring only about an hour later when she heard someone knocking on the door. She came slowly to her feet and answered it.

"Hello, Austin," she smiled kindly. "Are you looking for Alison?"

"Yes, ma'am. Is she here?"

"She should be back any minute. Why don't you come in and wait for her?"

Austin removed his hat as he stepped inside and wiped his feet on the little rug by the door. "Thank you."

Maggie knew there had been quite a bit of tension between Alison and Austin. As much as she didn't approve of the young man's actions, she hoped they could resolve it so Alison could move on. "Why don't you sit down, and I'll get you some coffee," she offered.

"Congratulations on your newest addition," he said. "Maegan tells me she's adorable."

"Thank you," she smiled at him. "She certainly is."

They talked for a few minutes, and then the door opened. Jacob entered, holding Marigold in his arms with his other children in tow.

"Austin!" Lilly and Lucas exclaimed simultaneously. They ran over to hug him.

Reverend Myles's reaction to seeing him there was not as enthusiastic. He met the man's gaze with civility and nothing more. "How are you, Austin?" Reverend Myles heard himself ask.

"Just fine. And you?"

"I'm well, thanks. I understand you and your brother Sawyer are here for a visit."

Austin hadn't forgotten their last conversation and could feel the reverend's distrust for him as thick as ever. "I don't want to intrude on your time any longer." Austin avoided the question and made a move toward the door.

"Nonsense," Maggie said. "You've waited this long. I'm sure it will only be a few more minutes."

"Sure! And you can play with us until Aunt Ali gets here," Lilly said with a big smile, assuming that was who he was waiting for. "Come on, I want to show you the kittens our barn cat just had!"

"Please do," Maggie said with a smile at Lilly, "And try to persuade Austin to take as many as he wants!"

*****

Alison shifted in her seat, trying to think of something else to talk about. Gideon had come by unexpectedly and asked if she would take a ride with him because he wanted to talk to her. She noted, however, that he'd barely said more than a few words, and she had been doing most of the talking to save them from an awkward silence.

"So, what is it you wanted to talk to me about?" Alison finally asked, unable to take the uncomfortable silence another moment.

"Oh, I ... ugh ..." He pulled back gently on the reins to slow the horses and then led them a little way off the road to a glen of newly blossoming dogwood trees. "Do you mind if we stop for a moment?"

"Not at all," she said. She took his offered hand when he came around to help her down, lifting her dress slightly to avoid getting it caught in the wheel. She followed him a few steps when he abruptly stopped and turned to face her.

"I don't know how to say this, but ..." He paused and then suddenly removed his hat, holding it between his hands as he looked into her eyes. "Alison, I'm real fond of you, and if you're in agreement, I'd like us to think about a future together."

Alison looked into his hopeful eyes and felt like the worst person imaginable. They had become better friends during her stay in his cabin, but nothing romantic had transpired between them. She couldn't remember a time she'd given him even an inkling that she was interested in him as more than a friend but then realized her inviting him to lunch on Sunday may have sent the wrong message. Knowing she was about to disappoint him left her searching for words.

"You don't have to answer now," he said when she didn't respond right away. "You can have time to think about it."

"Gideon, I ... I don't need time to think about it," she said quietly, her expression already telling him what he didn't want to hear. "You've been a good friend to me, and I do care about you, but not in ... that way. I'm sorry."

"But you saw how well we did together those four days during that blizzard." He took a small step toward her, wanting desperately to take her hands. "I can't seem to forget that week."

"We do get along, Gideon … but it's because we're friends. That's … how I'd like it to stay."

"Is it because Austin McCoy came back?" Gideon saw the answer in her eyes before she lowered her gaze and sighed. "Are you in love with him?" he asked.

"I don't know," Alison answered quietly, honestly. She looked up at him. "But even if Austin hadn't come back, I … I just want to remain friends, Gideon." She could tell he was disappointed, and the ride home was quieter and more uncomfortable than it had been earlier.

When he pulled into the yard, she climbed down quickly to prevent him from having to help her. Being the gentleman that he was, however, he still came around to her.

Wishing to smooth things over, Alison reached up to touch his arm when he started to move away. "Please don't be upset," she said softly. "You're a good man, Gideon, and you're going to find someone who will make you really happy."

He paused and, for the first time, didn't restrain himself from going with his feelings. He gently reached over and tucked a loose wisp of hair behind her ear. "You would make me really happy."

Alison slowly stepped away. "I'm so sorry," she said before turning and heading toward the house.

*****

With Lilly's persuading, Austin had held each of the six kittens, which he learned from Lilly was the barn cat's second litter. He'd guessed as much with as many cats that he'd seen around the property. As they left the barn, the children ran to the back door where their mother was calling them to come in, but upon hearing a wagon, Austin rounded the house toward the front yard.

The sight of what appeared to be a rather tender exchange between Alison and Gideon Martin halted him in his steps. The man climbed into his wagon when Alison walked toward the house, but she stopped when she spotted him.

"Austin," she said with surprise. "What are you doing here?"

"I, ugh, came to tell you something, but …" his gaze moved past her to Gideon, whose wagon was starting to move out of the yard. "I didn't realize you wouldn't be here."

Alison glanced over her shoulder for a moment, following his gaze. "I'm here now," she said quietly. "What did you want to tell me?" she asked, feeling like she didn't want him to leave. How could she be so angry with him and so in love with him all at once?

"I should just go," he said, suddenly feeling like the wind of determination had been knocked out of him. He moved toward his horse, still secured to a tree in the front yard.

"Yes, you're good at that," she couldn't resist saying but then regretted her words when he turned around and looked at her.

"I thought about you every day I was gone," he told her.

There was something in his eyes that made her want to apologize for her words, but then she remembered what her brother had relayed to her. The image in her mind of him with another woman once again made anger crash through her.

"Me and how many other women?" Alison asked, folding her arms across her chest and lifting her chin slightly.

"What?"

He looked genuinely confused, but she was feeling too hurt to try to understand why. "I'm not going to lie. I did care for you, Austin. But that's all changed now."

"I can see that. But I have to say, I didn't take you to be fickle with your feelings, Ali."

"Me fickle?" Her eyes widened, and her mouth dropped. "You have a lot of nerve to say that!"

"Well, there's obviously something going on between you and Gideon Martin." He untethered his horse's reins and led him toward the road. "How long did it take for you to move on after I left?"

"We're just friends."

Austin's expression was one of doubt. "I heard you spent nearly a week alone together."

Hearing the insinuation in his voice, a spark of fire lit her eyes. "Are you questioning my propriety, Austin McCoy?"

"Kind of hard not to, under the circumstances and after seeing you two at church the other day and just now. You look pretty comfortable 'round each other."

"What?"

"I've got eyes on my face, Ali."

"What you saw today was him asking to court me, and I was ..."

"Ha! So, there is something going on between you two, then!" he interrupted with a shake of his head. "Admit it," Austin pressed her, crossing his arms and looking at her reprovingly.

"Don't make me feel like I'm the one who's done something wrong, Austin, when you are clearly the one who ruined our relationship!" Alison turned on those words and stormed toward the front door of the house.

"Ali, wait!"

She stopped and slowly turned around. "What?"

"I know I messed up, but can you look me in the eyes and honestly tell me you don't care for me at all?"

Alison told herself it was better to stay angry with him so that she wouldn't risk losing her heart to him a second time. But the warmth she saw in his penetrating eyes unwittingly softened her heart. She couldn't say anything.

Her hesitancy was all the encouragement he needed. "Just because I left without saying goodbye doesn't mean I wasn't serious about you."

"How can you say that?" Her voice caught a little. "How can you say you cared for me, all the while being involved with someone else?"

"What in the Sam Hill are you talking about, Ali?"

She held his gaze, which looked as innocent as anything she'd ever seen. "I'm talking about the woman my brother saw you with! What else?" She watched a play of emotions on his face, from confusion to understanding and then relief. He slapped his hat against his leg and strode toward her.

"Of all the ridiculous bosh I've ever heard! No wonder you're boilin' mad at me!" He looked at her as understanding rushed through him, and then he impulsively hugged her tight.

"Let go of me!" she said, pushing at his chest and stepping away from his embrace.

"I'm sorry, Ali," he said, laughing. "I'm just so relieved, I had to."

"Relieved?"

"I thought you didn't care for me anymore, but you're only mad cuz, well, because I was foolish enough to not talk to you before I left, but really because you thought I was involved with another woman! And that's plain horse feathers!"

"But my brother saw you …"

"What your brother saw was some drunk saloon girl throwing herself at me before I pried her loose and pushed her away."

Alison's hand flew to her heart, and she stared at him, completely speechless.

"I was only at the saloon that night to talk to a fellow regarding the James gang. When I stepped outside, she was there. Your brother must have been riding by at just that moment.

"I left so suddenly because your brother told me to!" Austin went on to explain. "He was fired up, and I wouldn't cross your brother because what would you think of me, then? He didn't say anything about seeing me with that woman, but looking back at the timing, that must have been why he was so adamant that I leave."

"You mean, there really was nothing going on between you and someone else?"

"No! You're the only woman I've ever even kissed, for Pete's sake!"

Her eyes narrowed slightly, studying him to see if he was telling the truth.

"Alright!" he suddenly blurted. "That ain't completely true." He tried to maintain a straight face as he confessed. "When I was ten, I kissed Lucy Hendrick behind her pa's barn. But he whupped me so hard, I ain't ever touched a woman until you. And that's the truth!"

Alison bit her bottom lip to try to stop the smile that he seemed to easily bring out of her. She felt such a rush of joy that it made her want to throw her arms around him, but the months of trying to close her heart to him told her to proceed with caution. "I want to believe you," she said quietly.

"Then do."

"It's not that easy. I spent months trying to forget you.

But if what you say is true, then my brother made a huge mistake." She glanced toward the house and then let out a frustrated sigh. "I can't believe he told you to leave!"

"Well, in his defense, I can see how it must have looked, so I can understand why he felt he had to step in. Guess I would have done the same if it had been Mae."

"It's good of you to not be angry with him," Alison said.

"I didn't say I'm not angry with him," Austin told her. "But I'm trying to be forgiving since he's your brother."

There was a moment's pause. Alison felt so torn. She wanted to pick up where they had left off, but part of her was afraid he wasn't being completely honest. How could she be sure what he said was the truth? If he really loved her, how could he just leave without saying he'd be back? He could have written to her, at the very least! Had he always intended to return? Before she could give her heart again, she needed to know he wasn't going to pick up and leave at any moment.

"I need some time," she finally spoke. "I just want to be careful."

He nodded, fully understanding. "Take all the time you need, but I want you to know you won't ever have to doubt me or how I feel about you, Ali, not ever again."

*****

As he headed back to his uncle's, Austin was feeling more than a little hopeful about his relationship with Alison. He knew he needed to earn her trust back, and he was determined to prove himself. The first thing he knew he needed to do wasn't going to be easy, and he decided to do it before his nerve faltered.

Austin found Sawyer in the barn and wasted no time saying what needed to be said. "I can't go with you." The words came out in such a decisive tone that it surprised even himself. Until now, Austin had let Sawyer make the decisions and had always found it easiest to just follow along.

"What do you mean?" Sawyer said. The pitchfork he'd been spreading straw with suddenly came to a standstill in his hands.

Austin let out a sigh and shook his head slowly. "I'm feeling pretty strong that I need to stay here in Millcreek."

"To work things out with Alison?"

Austin nodded. "Things are a little better between us, but I sure can't leave now."

Sawyer was quiet for a moment and then turned to face him. "Thought we were gonna finish what we started."

"I'm sorry, Sawyer." Austin knew his brother was disappointed, but there was no other way.

Sawyer looked back at him for a moment before turning back to the stall to finish spreading the straw. "You're your own man, Austin. Do what seems right to you."

Austin knew that was the extent of blessing and approval he was going to get from Sawyer, but it was enough. Deep in his heart, Austin knew even if Sawyer had put up a fight about him staying behind, it still wouldn't have deterred him. He didn't know what his future held, but he did know he was in love with Alison Myles and didn't want to make the same mistake twice.

*****

Alison was glad to find her brother alone when she returned to the house. She could hear Maggie's voice along with her niece and nephew's and knew they were just in the next room.

"When you told Austin to leave, why didn't you tell him what you had seen outside the saloon?"

Jacob looked up from the newspaper he'd been reading at the table. "What do you mean?"

Alison walked toward him. "I mean, if you would have told him that you saw him with another woman, he could have explained the misunderstanding. You made a mistake, Jacob!"

She hadn't raised her voice in any way, but Jacob could hear the intensity in it. He sat up a little straighter. "And what would have been his defense? I know what I saw."

"She threw herself at him, and he was working on pulling away."

"That's what he told you?"

"You don't believe it?" she asked.

"Whether I believe it or not doesn't matter. Even if it wasn't what it appeared, do you want to be with a man who spends most his time in a saloon?"

"He doesn't! And he was only there to meet with someone because they had information about the outlaws he was looking for."

Jacob released a heavy sigh. "Because he's a bounty hunter … does that make it better?" He shook his head. "I've known men like him, Ali, and the main thing they care about is themselves."

Alison let out a short, frustrated breath. Her brother's opinion meant so much to her, and she wanted his blessing and approval where Austin was concerned. "I'm not planning to rush into anything too soon where Austin's concerned, but I still think it was wrong for you to interfere!"

"I'm sorry," Jacob said. "I thought I was doing the right thing." He still thought he had done the right thing. No matter what excuse Austin used, Jacob had his doubts.

"From here out, I'm askin' you to give Austin McCoy a fair chance."

Jacob saw how much it meant to his sister and agreed. He would just have to pray and trust the Lord that she would come to the right conclusions on her own.

# *Chapter* Twenty-Three

"Eli Greene's gonna give me a job at the livery," Austin told Maegan a few days later after she and Cody had arrived home from school.

"That's wonderful," Maegan said, her heart still brimming with joy that Austin had decided to stay in Millcreek for a while. It hurt to see Sawyer ride off alone, but she knew God had a plan for all of her brothers, and right now, it seemed right that Austin had stayed. Maegan also knew Alison would be pleased and hoped they could finally work things out.

"That's not all. He told me he has a small house for rent not far from here. Thought maybe you, Cody, and I could look into it."

"Uncle Ben will miss us," Maegan said with a sad smile. "But it's probably a good idea if you're staying for a while. That loft isn't big enough for you and Cody." She didn't think now was the time to tell him that she was planning to leave with Cody as soon as school was over. Besides, either with or without them, she knew Austin would want his own place.

Ben didn't realize just how attached he'd become to his brother's kids until Maegan told him they would be leaving. The fact that they were only a mile away eased the situation, though.

"We thought we could still come by once a week for supper, and you're welcome at our place any time," Maegan assured him on the day they left.

"Don't feel sorry for me," Uncle Ben said, a little scowl on his face. "I'll be just fine. But … I will miss having you all around," he added.

The house that Eli Greene rented to them was about the same size as their uncle's and was well-kept. Aside from a few minor repairs, the house was already furnished and had strong walls and a solid roof. Austin and Cody took one room while Maegan took the other. The small barn in the back would house their horses and eventually a cow, as Austin was planning to buy one from Will Carter that week.

One afternoon, Austin headed toward the General Store with a list Maegan had given him. As he was leaving, he spotted Alison as she was making her way into the store.

"Nice coincidence running into you like this," he said, tipping his hat.

Alison hadn't noticed him until he was practically beside her, and she looked surprised to see him. She hadn't seen him since a few days ago when they'd talked. "I heard Sawyer left Millcreek."

"Yep. Honestly, for me, huntin' down outlaws is losing its luster."

"Is that so?" she asked, determined to remain cautious where Austin McCoy was concerned.

"Yep. Got a job at the livery and just rented out a house."

"So, you really are planning to stay," she said, unable to keep a measure of hope from her tone.

"Until I wear out my welcome," he replied.

Alison remembered he'd also said that the first time she'd met him. "Well, I guess we'll see how long that takes," she said with a brief smile before continuing into the store.

When she returned outside a few minutes later, she was surprised to see him still at the bottom of the steps. "Are you waiting for someone?" she asked, glancing behind him to see if maybe Maegan or Cody were around.

"Yep. You."

Alison tilted her head slightly and looked at him with a questioning expression.

"Thought maybe I could give you a ride home since your brother's house is on the way."

"My brother's house is out of your way," she laughed softly. "Besides that, I can get a ride home with him in a few minutes when he's through at the mill."

Austin glanced up at the sky. "Looks like rain. Just thought it might be a good idea to get you home before you get caught in it."

"That's very thoughtful," she replied.

He noticed the writing tablet in her hands and assumed that was what she had been going to the store to buy. "You wouldn't want to risk getting that wet," he said.

"I certainly wouldn't. Maybe I should take you up on your offer."

Austin grinned and then offered his hand to help her climb up onto the wagon seat.

*****

"I'm really sorry, Ali," Austin apologized for the third time. He stood up from where he was kneeling on the ground, trying to fix the busted spoke on the wagon. Halfway to her brother's house, he had been forced to pull over because the wheel was giving them so much trouble. "I had no idea the wheel was about to bust."

Alison smiled understandingly. "It's alright. You couldn't have known." She came closer and leaned over to look at the wheel Austin had just been trying to repair. "It's starting to rain. I think we should give up trying to fix it. I can walk the rest of the way home if you want to take the wagon back to town."

"I'll walk with you home and then come back," he said, glancing up at the sky, which was darkening fast. "You've never ridden bareback, so I think I'll just tie the horses up to that tree and come back for them later."

"Will they be okay in the rain?" Alison asked, a little worried as the drizzle became a little heavier.

"Sure. It won't be all that long." He led the horses off the main road and then under some trees that would provide somewhat of a shelter for them. "C'mon, we better hurry." He took her hand and was about to lead her back to the road when a loud crash of thunder preceded a sudden downpour of rain.

"Now what?" Alison said with a little shiver against the chilly spring rain.

Austin scanned the surroundings for somewhere to take shelter. He glimpsed what looked like some sort of shack half-hidden behind some pine trees. "This way!" he said, taking off his hat and dropping it on her head. The rain beat down on them as they ran, mud splashing up from underneath them.

"Where are we going?" Alison called over the roar of the rain.

"There's some kind of building just over there," Austin told her, leading the way. As they got closer, he realized it was an abandoned building that had probably been used as a barn at some point. The door creaked on its rusty hinges as he pushed it open, and the rain pellets falling on the tin roof made a loud clatter as if nails were being dropped from the sky.

"It's not ideal, but at least we'll be dry," Austin said. He started to wring out his shirt as best he could, and Alison did the same with her long skirt.

"Guess you would have been better off waiting for your brother," Austin said with an apologetic sigh. "Storm shouldn't last too long, though," he said. Another crack of thunder seemed to rattle the walls and roof, causing Alison to jump slightly at the sound.

"Guess we could sit a spell," Austin suggested when he noticed some clean straw in the corner. Resting their backs against the wall, they settled on the straw beside each other. For a moment, they just sat there, quietly listening as the rain and wind beat against the building.

"Will you miss Sawyer?" Alison suddenly asked some minutes later.

"Yeah, but he understood why I had to stay."

"Had to?" she echoed quietly.

"*Wanted* to," he adjusted his words. He turned his head to smile softly at her. She smiled back but then lowered her gaze.

"You know, I really did think about you every day."

"I thought about you, too," Alison whispered, hoping the voice inside telling her she could trust him was real.

"Guess you spent the last few months thinkin' the worst of me, though."

"The worst part was thinking you didn't really care as much as I did ... and still do," she added softly.

Austin had been aware of her hand just inches away from his and now closed the remaining distance. He lifted it and gently kissed the back of it. "I know promises are often made and broken, but one thing I can promise for sure is that I'll never leave like that again. I love you, Alison."

At that moment, sitting in that dusty, old shack, nothing

seemed to matter except that they were together. And at that moment, those months of heartache and uncertainty became a distant memory. Austin was here, he loved her, and he always had. As that realization grew in her heart, Alison squirmed a little closer to him to place a soft kiss on his cheek before she rested her head on his shoulder.

"Is this you being careful?" Austin said quietly through his smile.

"I did say something like that the other day, didn't I?" Feeling his hand holding hers, she smiled contentedly. "I don't want this rain to ever stop," she added softly.

"I was thinkin' the same thing," Austin replied.

To both of their disappointment, the rain did stop about twenty minutes later. Austin came to his feet and helped her up, then he went over and opened the door.

"We best try and make it now while there's a lull," he said. He reached for her hand and helped her around a rather large puddle that had gathered by the door.

"Oh, my goodness! I must have three feet of mud on me," Alison laughed a few minutes later, lifting her skirts as the mud leading from the building became thicker.

"Here," Austin said, scooping her up so fast she didn't have time to protest.

"You can't carry me all the way!" she told him. "Besides, the damage is already done."

"You look pretty good in my hat," he said, ignoring her.

"I feel pretty good in it," she teased him. "I think it did keep my hair dry for the most part."

They caught sight of a wagon approaching just as they neared the road. Austin kept walking with her in his arms until the wagon was close enough for him to make out the driver. Slowly, he let Alison down to her feet.

"Is she okay?" Reverend Myles asked with concern. Seeing

his sister being carried alarmed him that she had maybe injured herself. As soon as he'd gotten home and found she wasn't there, he waited a few minutes for the rain to let up and then went out to look for her.

"I'm fine," she smiled up at him. "Just wet. Austin was giving me a ride home, and we got caught in the rain," she explained.

"I see that," he replied with less enthusiasm than she seemed to have.

"My, ugh, wagon busted just down the road there," Austin glanced over his shoulder toward the trees.

"Will you be able to get it back to town?" Reverend Myles asked thoughtfully, although his main concern was putting distance between his sister and Austin.

"Yep," Austin replied, already starting to move toward where his horses were waiting.

Alison took her brother's extended hand to climb up into the seat beside him and then remembered she was still wearing Austin's hat. "Austin! Your hat!"

"Keep it!" he called over his shoulder. "I'll get it later!"

A few minutes into their ride home, Reverend Myles glanced at his sister. "So, you're giving him a second chance, I gather."

"Yes," Alison sighed softly and turned to look at her brother. "It's not often you're wrong, Jacob, but this time you are."

It was Jacob's turn to sigh. "I hope you're right, Ali. I really do hope I've been wrong about him."

*****

Alison caught Austin's glance and smiled at him from across the church during the service that Sunday. He sat with his sister and Cody on the opposite side of the room, but he readily met her eyes each time she looked for him. Alison spotted Gideon just a few rows behind the McCoys and chided herself for not being more careful to avoid giving him false hope.

"We'll be out in the wagon," Maggie told her husband after the service. He was still talking to several people, and she could tell their kids were getting antsy. Once outside, she saw that Alison was chatting with a few women, and Maggie instinctively looked for Austin. After a moment, she noticed him coming out of the church, his coat draped over his arm. His other siblings were in the yard in a wagon and seemed to be waiting for him.

Inside the church, Reverend Myles was gathering his notes and Bible and putting them in his satchel. As he was walking to the door, he reached into his pocket, expecting to feel his pocket watch. When it wasn't there, he remembered he'd set it on the podium at the beginning of the service. He went back to the podium, but it wasn't there, nor was it in his satchel.

Puzzled, he headed outside to meet his wife and kids. "Sorry I took so long," he apologized. "I couldn't find my pocket watch."

"Are you sure you didn't leave it at the house?" Maggie asked as he climbed into the wagon seat beside her.

"No. I'm certain I had it with me this morning."

"Hmm. I'm sure it will turn up."

As they were finishing lunch, Alison stood up to answer a knock on the door. She was surprised to see Gideon on the other side. "Afternoon," he greeted. "Is your brother home?"

Alison stepped to the side and showed him in.

"I'm sorry to interrupt when you're eating," he apologized when he saw them at the table. "I tried to wait until after the lunch hour."

"No problem at all," Reverend Myles assured him as he wiped his mouth and came to his feet. "What can we help you with?"

"I wanted to talk to you. Privately," he added. "It'll just take a minute."

"Certainly." Reverend Myles excused himself and followed Gideon outside.

"I wonder what that's about," Maggie thought aloud, her eyes glancing curiously toward the window.

"I think I can guess," Alison said with a soft sigh. She hoped Gideon didn't think that he could convince Jacob to change her mind.

"What is it?" Maggie asked her husband when he returned a few minutes later, a pensive expression on his face.

"I'll tell you later," he said, rejoining them at the table and making Maggie and Alison even more curious as to what Gideon had come to see him about.

*****

Later that Sunday, Maegan answered the knock on the door to find Sheriff Bridger on the other side. She noticed immediately by his serious expression that something was wrong. She also noticed Reverend Myles was with him. "Can I help you, Sheriff?"

"Is Austin here?" Bridger asked.

"Out in the barn," Maegan replied. "Is something wrong?" Sheriff Bridger didn't answer right away, which only made her more concerned.

"I'd like to talk to your brother first."

Maegan couldn't keep herself from following him as he and the reverend headed toward the barn. They found both Austin and Cody in the barn, almost finished mucking out the stables.

"Howdy, Sheriff," Austin greeted brightly. "Reverend Myles," he acknowledged him politely.

"Unfortunately, I'm here because a claim's been made against you, Austin," Bridger came right to the point. "I hate to do it, but I'm going to have to ask you to hand me your coat."

"What?" Austin gave a confused grin. "What's this about?" He didn't like the sense he was getting from Reverend Myles' stern expression.

"Just hand me your coat, if you don't mind."

With a chuckle, Austin shrugged out of it. "Alright," he said, handing it to him. "What's this about?"

Sheriff Bridger laid it over his arm and reached into the inside pocket. It was only seconds before he pulled out an expensive gold pocket watch.

"That's it," Reverend Myles said quietly as the sheriff handed it to him.

"Woah, woah, woah! I haven't the slightest clue how that ended up in there," Austin said. "Honest!"

Sheriff Bridger released a heavy sigh. "I sure hate to do this, Austin, but I'm gonna have to ask you to come with me."

"Wait!" Maegan said, coming to stand beside her brother. Her eyes flashed from him to the sheriff. "Austin's no thief."

"Then how do you explain my watch ending up in his coat pocket?" Reverend Myles asked, not unkindly. He honestly wished there was another explanation.

"My brother's no thief!" Cody echoed his sister.

"I don't know how that got in there, Reverend. Honest to God, I don't," Austin said.

"Best just come with me," Sheriff Bridger said, his voice apologetic but firm.

Austin put his coat back on when the sheriff handed it to him and willingly followed him outside the barn. "I'll go with you, Sheriff. But I didn't steal that watch. I didn't do this," Austin said over his shoulder to Maegan and Cody.

Maegan watched helplessly as her brother was led away. She saw Cody was angry and placed a calming hand on his shoulder. "They'll get it sorted out, Cody. Don't worry." She was confident that Sheriff Bridger would get to the bottom of it, and when he did, they would all find out what she already knew: Austin was innocent.

# Chapter Twenty-Four

"I really hate doing this," Sheriff Bridger said as he turned the key in the lock of the cell door.

"I know you're just doing your job," Austin said, taking a few steps back and sitting on the makeshift bed.

"They'll be jail time and a fine to pay, unless you can prove you didn't do it," Bridger said.

"I don't know how to prove I didn't do it. All I know is that I didn't."

Bridger sighed, crossing his arms and studying Austin. He believed him, but finding the pocket watch on his person was going to be tough to get around. "Did anyone bump into you after you left church?"

Austin shook his head. "No one. I went straight home after church." He let out a sigh. "This will really seal the deal."

"What?"

"Of Reverend Myles not liking me."

"There's got to be an explanation."

"It had to have been someone at church. Maybe the reverend himself," Austin joked.

"Nah, he would never do that. He seemed pretty upset to come to me about it. Who else isn't too keen on you?" Bridger asked.

Austin shrugged. "Just the Spencers, from what I know."

Bridger's eyes widened. "Could one of them have taken it and slipped it into your coat pocket somehow?"

Austin straightened a bit. "Maybe, but how? None of them were in church except Aunt Becky, and she wouldn't do a thing like that."

"Was Jeb there?" Bridger asked, suddenly warming to the idea. "Reverend Myles said he last saw it on his podium. Maybe Jeb sneaked over, grabbed it, and then managed to get it in your coat pocket without you noticing."

"Nah," Austin dismissed the idea. "He and Cody are friends now."

"Unless … unless he was told to plant it by his pa or uncle to stir up trouble for you," Bridger suggested.

"I don't know," Austin let out a sigh. "Guess it could have happened like that."

"I'll talk to Cody," Bridger said. "He might have seen something."

Just as Bridger was about to leave, Maegan and Cody arrived at the jail.

"That dirty rat!" Cody exclaimed when the sheriff asked him about Jeb.

"Now, Cody, there's no proof that Jeb has anything to do with this. I'm only asking if you saw him hanging around the podium."

"We became friends," Cody said, but then an angry look shadowed his face. "But he did stay in the church with his ma after I left. Maybe he was waiting to do something like this all along."

"Don't jump to conclusions," Maegan said gently.

"Your sister's right," Bridger said. "No point tossin' blame until we know for sure. I'm just trying to find someone with a motive."

"Austin." Maegan suddenly thought of something. "You went back into the church because you forgot your coat, remember?"

"That's right!" Austin replied. "We were about to leave, but I remembered I'd left it hanging in the entrance of the church!"

"So, someone could have easily slipped the watch in your coat while it hung in there," Bridger explained.

Austin breathed a sigh of relief. "That has to be what happened."

"But who would do a thing like that?" Maegan asked, her expression pensive.

Even though he knew he was innocent, Austin inwardly cringed when he thought of Alison hearing about this, just when she was starting to trust him again!

As they left the jailhouse, Sheriff Bridger followed them out. Maegan turned to him, a pleading look in her eyes. "I know you're just doing your job, and I know Austin can be a little unruly and unpredictable, but he's no thief."

Bridger met her gaze. "I'm a pretty good judge of character, and I do believe you."

She smiled softly, beyond grateful for his understanding. "It means so much that you believe he's innocent. If there's anything I can help with, please let me know."

"I'll get to the bottom of this. Don't worry, Mae."

She felt his hand reach out and gently touch her arm, and for just a moment, she forgot all about Austin and the stolen watch.

*****

Alison was beside herself with confusion after learning why Gideon had come to talk to her brother. He said he had seen Austin take her brother's watch from the podium.

She couldn't believe Austin was capable of something so dastardly! She thought of their recent moment the other day and now wondered if, once again, she had given her heart too quickly.

That Monday morning, she was having a terrible time keeping her mind on her duties. She had gone to the window at least three times just to stare across the street at the jailhouse where she knew he was. She wanted to see Austin so badly, but she was afraid of what it would mean if he ended up being guilty. If he had done this and then lied to her about his innocence, how could she ever trust him again? Her heart told her he wasn't guilty, but there was still a shred of uncertainty.

She went back to her desk and pulled out a piece of paper, along with a pencil. Maybe she could get her thoughts out best if she wrote Austin a letter. Several minutes later, she was feeling a little better. Now, just to get the letter to him.

She went to the window again and then smiled at her good luck! Cody McCoy was making his way down the street, probably on his way to see Austin! She opened the door and stepped out. "Cody!" she called with a wave.

The boy stopped and glanced across the street, looking past the buggies and wagons toward the voice. He spotted Alison Myles crossing the street to catch up to him. "Would you do me a favor?" she asked.

"Sure," Cody replied.

"Can you give this to Austin?"

Cody looked down at the letter that she'd placed in his hands. "But, wouldn't you rather just give it to him?"

"I've got to get back to work. I'd really appreciate it if you could."

Cody stared at the letter and then looked up at her as if he wanted to tell her something. She thanked him and then turned to go.

"Ali."

Alison turned around at Cody's voice, noticing the turmoil in his expression. "What is it?"

"It's Austin. He … he can't read."

"What?" The surprise was as clear on her face as the sky was blue.

"He might know a few words, but he won't be able to read this unless I read it for him, and … I figure it's probably personal."

"Oh." She took the letter back. "I had no idea." Her mind raced to the times she had asked him about her newspaper column, and then she almost gasped aloud when she remembered the love letter she had written to him. Why, he had never been able to read it! That explained why she had also never received any letters from him.

"Don't let him know I was the one who told you," Cody told her. "He'll want to box my ears."

"No, I won't. Thanks, Cody." She headed back to the press and waited until she knew Cody had visited and gone. Then, mustering her courage, she went across the street and into the jailhouse. Sheriff Bridger wasn't there, and Austin was leaning against the wall when she entered.

"Oh, Austin," she said quietly as she moved toward the cell.

"I didn't do it" was the first thing out of his mouth.

"My brother said his pocket watch ended up in your coat."

"It ended up there, but I didn't put it there."

She wanted to believe him, but reluctance pricked her heart. "My brother never trusted you from the beginning, and this looks …"

"I know how it looks, Ali, but you gotta believe me. I would never do something like that, 'specially not to your brother, of all people. Why, doing this would only make him hate me more."

"He doesn't hate you," she said quietly.

"Well, whatever he feels for me sure seems similar." He began to pace the small cell.

"Do you have any idea why someone would try to frame you?"

"No. Unless one of the Spencers put Jeb up to do it."

"He was in church on Sunday," Alison said. "I saw him talking with Lilly and Cody."

"More important than the reason someone would frame me is the importance of you believing I'm innocent." His expression looked defeated. "I know that's a lot to ask right now."

"I could believe you if I knew you had never lied to me before," Alison said, thinking of all the times he had pretended to have read her newspaper column. It was a small thing, but did it mean he had lied about other things, too?

"I haven't lied to you, Ali, not once." The letter that was still tucked inside his vest pocket suddenly prodded his conscience. "Except for one thing."

Alison felt like she was holding her breath while she waited for him to go on. She took another step toward him and reached up to rest her hands on the cell bars. "Except for what?" she asked when he seemed to be hesitating. She watched as he reached inside his vest and pulled out her letter.

"I ain't ever read this. I can't read, Ali."

That was the *one thing* he had been talking about? At that moment, she realized his admitting that to her in an effort to come clean of any deception proved his innocence to her in every respect.

"Oh, Austin. I believe you … about everything!"

He was suddenly near her, the bars alone separating them. He reached out and held the bars as well, his hands gradually sliding down to rest over hers. He could see tears pooling in her eyes and wished he could put his arms around her.

"I'm sorry I ever doubted you," she said.

"I'm sorry I ever gave you a reason to. I've said it before, and I'll say it again. I should have never left Millcreek the way I did."

"Well, you're here now."

"In a jail cell," he chuckled, shaking his head.

Alison laughed softly through her tears. "Not for long. The truth is bound to come to the light."

*****

"I've been looking for you."

Jeb Spencer straightened from his hunched-over position mucking out the stable. He was surprised to see Cody standing in his barn. "What are you doing here?" Jeb asked.

"Came to talk to you about Reverend Myles' pocket watch ending up in Austin's coat pocket."

"What? I don't know nothing 'bout no pocket watch."

Cody took a step closer toward him. "Are you sure? 'Cuz my brother ain't a thief, and someone framed him."

Jeb's hold on the pitchfork tightened. "What are you tryin' to say?"

"Just that your family's the only folks that would want to cause my brother harm, and I wouldn't be surprised if your pa or uncle put you up to a thing like that."

"I thought we were friends now, Cody. You really think I'd pull a stunt like that?"

Cody's lips pressed together, almost as if he was trying to keep from saying something.

"You do, don't you?" Jeb read his expression.

"You told your pa I tried to bring the mine down on ya," Cody called him out.

343

"He was about to whip me, and it just came out!"

"So, you threw dirt on me to save your own skin?" Cody pressed the issue.

"I plan to tell my pa the truth … eventually."

"Eventually ain't good enough, Jeb. And if you lied about that, you could be lying about the watch."

"I didn't touch Reverend Myles' watch! I never even saw it!"

Cody studied him for a good five seconds and then turned away. "I hope that's true."

"So much for being friends!" Jeb called after him. He released a heavy sigh when he heard the barn door close. His conscience had been heavy about not telling his pa the truth about the mine incident and for blaming Joshua McCoy for the barn fire, but no one understood how frightening his pa could be. Jeb told himself Cody would have done the same thing if he were in his shoes.

*****

Reverend Myles went to visit Austin later that same day, appreciating the privacy of meeting with him alone. Austin came to his feet when he saw him. "Afternoon, Reverend."

"Contrary to what you might think, I don't take any pleasure in seeing you behind those bars."

"I didn't take your pocket watch," Austin told him again.

"You're either a very good liar, or you're innocent, as you say. You do understand that the latter is difficult to believe."

"It wouldn't be if you knew me better," Austin replied.

"I give everyone a fair chance, Austin, but since you came to Millcreek, you've seemed to end up in one scrape after another. Your character has been in question only because of your actions, starting with multiple fights and then that saloon girl …"

"That was not what you thought it was."

"Alison told me it was a misunderstanding, but had you not been there at that late hour in the first place …" he let the sentence hang.

"What is it you've come to talk to me about?" Austin asked, not bothering to explain he had only been at the saloon late that night to find information about the James brothers.

"It's the same thing I told you before," Reverend Myles said. "I want you out of Millcreek."

Austin was surprised at the man's persistence. "What if I told you I wanted to make it my home and leave my life as a bounty hunter?"

It was Jacob Myles' turn to be surprised. "You'd give that up to be with Alison?"

"That and anything else she asked me to."

For a moment, Reverend Myles saw something in the man's eyes that could only be described as sincere, and in that moment, he believed that Austin might truly love Alison. The bars that stood between them suddenly brought him back to reality. This man had been fooling around with another woman while professing to love Alison, and this man had stolen from him in broad daylight, inside a church, no less. Actions spoke louder than words, and Jacob could not ignore that.

"I'll drop the charges, and you wouldn't even have to pay a fine if …" Reverend Myles felt a jab of guilt but pressed on. "… if you leave Millcreek, and this time, don't come back."

"I can't do that," Austin replied without any hesitancy. "I left her once, and I'm not going to do that again."

"I wasn't sure what you'd say to that."

"That's because you don't know me, and you don't know how much I care about your sister."

"If you really cared, you would let her fall in love with someone else. Someone who will keep her safe."

"We've already been down this road, and I'm not leaving."

"Then I'll have to let the sheriff wire the judge, and he can take it from here."

"Alright by me. Even though I'm innocent, no punishment is as bad as leaving Alison."

Again, Reverend Myles saw in his face someone who appeared genuine. He'd chosen the fine and whatever sentence he got over leaving Alison. That said something about him.

"Why not just confess? Your conscience would be clear, and I'm sure Alison would forgive you."

"Because I ain't got nothing to confess. I didn't take your watch."

Reverend Myles stepped back and released a sigh. Maybe he was telling the truth, but in case he wasn't, Reverend Myles had wanted to try to get a confession out of him.

Austin watched him leave and then gave the bars a kick of frustration once he'd gone. When he found out who framed him, he was going to give him a piece of his mind and maybe a good thrashing, too.

# *Chapter* Twenty-Five

"*I* visited Austin today," Alison said as she dragged her fork through her baked potato, not hungry in the slightest. She was sitting at the table with her brother and his family, too distraught to eat the delicious dinner she and Maggie had prepared.

Maggie sat across from her with an empathetic look in her eyes. "Does he have any idea who might want to frame him?" she asked.

"The Spencers don't like his family, so there's a thought that maybe Jeb Spencer was put up to it, but he told Cody he didn't do it, and there's no proof he did."

Jacob Myles listened to them, remembering his conversation with Austin earlier that day. "A judge will probably be out by the end of the week."

Alison's eyes shot up from her plate to her brother. "Couldn't you just drop the charges?"

"I wish I could, Ali, but when a man steals … or appears to have stolen," he added quickly for her benefit, "there has to be consequences. There really is no other explanation for how my pocket watch ended up in his coat pocket."

"Couldn't there be a chance Gideon mistook what he saw?" Alison asked. "We're taking his word over Austin's."

"I trust Gideon," Jacob told her. "He wouldn't make a claim like that if it wasn't true."

"Pa …"

Jacob turned his attention to his daughter sitting beside him. "What is it, Lilly?"

"I … I should have said something before, I guess, but I didn't think it mattered."

"What?" he said.

Lilly realized she now had everyone's eyes on her. "After service on that Sunday, you lost your watch, I saw it on the podium, and I picked it up to give it to you because I thought you might go home without it."

"Lilly! Why didn't you say something sooner?" Maggie asked.

"I didn't want you or Pa to think I was the one who lost it," she replied in her defense. "I was holding it when Gideon came up from behind me and told me I should put it back."

"And did you?" Jacob asked.

"Well, kind of."

"What do you mean, Lilly? And you better give me a straight answer," Jacob said, turning in his chair to fully face her.

"Gideon said he'd put it back for me, so I gave it to him."

Maggie gasped at nearly the same moment as Alison. "You mean you saw Gideon put the watch back on the podium?" Alison asked.

Lilly shook her head. "I went outside after that, but he said he would."

"Lilly, why didn't you tell us this sooner?" Jacob asked.

"I didn't want you to think I'd lost it since I'd been the last one to touch it," she admitted remorsefully.

"But you weren't the last one to touch it, were you?" Alison said, her eyes finding her brother's. "Gideon Martin was the last one to touch it."

Maggie's eyes locked with her husband's, seeming to ask the question all of them were thinking and not voicing.

"I think it's pretty obvious what happened," Alison said, suddenly coming to her feet. "I'm going to go have a little chat with Gideon Martin!"

Reverend Myles stood as well, trying to wrap his mind around what seemed too implausible to be the truth. "Let me go first and speak with him. I think it would be best if I talked to him alone."

*****

$\mathcal{I}$t felt like an exceedingly long ride to town from Gideon Martin's house that evening. Reverend Myles spent half of it in disbelief over his own lack of discernment of character and the other half repenting for it. He dismounted his horse, slowly tied it to the hitching post, and then, for a full minute, just stared at the jailhouse. What he had to do needed to be done, but with every step he took, his heart seemed to get heavier.

"Evenin', Reverend," Sheriff Bridger greeted him from behind his desk when the door opened and Jacob Myles entered. Austin was lying on the bed, his fingers laced behind his head.

"I came by because I've just learned something." He saw Austin sit up at his words, and the sheriff shifted in his chair. "What about?"

"Turns out Austin is innocent, just as he claimed."

On those words, Austin came to his feet and moved close to the bars, his hands resting on them.

"You have evidence?" Sheriff Bridger asked.

"A confession from the thief himself." He saw he had both men's full attention. "Gideon Martin took the watch, and he put it in Austin's coat pocket to frame him."

"What!" Austin was as shocked as the reverend had been.

"Did he say why he did it?" Bridger wanted to know.

Reverend Myles sighed, his eyes meeting Austin's. "Seems he was hoping it would sway Alison's interest away from you."

Austin shook his head, his lips pursing tightly together in anger. "Of all the low-down things to do!"

"It was wrong," Reverend Myles agreed. "And he knows that."

"Well, I would hope he does!" Austin said.

"He also knows that any hopes of achieving his goal will be dashed as soon as Alison finds out, and that his good standing in this community will be lost."

"He should have thought of that before he did such a pig-headed thing," Austin said. "But …" he cleared his throat. "… I guess I can't blame the guy for trying."

Sheriff Bridger unlocked the cell door, and Austin walked out, a sigh of relief leaving his lungs. "Never wanna be on the other side of these bars again."

Sheriff Bridger smiled at him, glad his own intuition of Austin's innocence had been correct. "You're free to go." He turned his attention back to Reverend Myles. "Guess I need to arrest the right thief."

"That's what I was hoping to talk to you both about. I have an idea that will exonerate Austin while also avoiding exposing Gideon's very unwise and impulsive act. I know he was very much in the wrong," Reverend Myles added, "but I also think he's learned his lesson and should be spared the embarrassment of the town's censure."

"Austin wasn't given that same courtesy," Sheriff Bridger reminded him.

"To which I can only offer my heartfelt apology, Austin. I was very wrong about you, and I'm sorry."

Austin saw the man had extended his hand in a show

of making amends. He reached out and shook it. "Weren't your fault that I was framed, Reverend."

"I appreciate your forgiveness, especially after some of the things I said to you."

"What's this plan of yours?" Austin asked.

"My daughter Lilly had taken the watch off the podium before Gideon took it. I thought we could chalk up the whole incident as a misunderstanding."

"You're willing to tell a lie, Reverend?" A small grin tugged on Austin's lips.

"In this instance, I'd like to look at it as showing mercy. I feel it's for the greater good. Such an act was very out of character for Gideon, and he's already eaten up with guilt as it is."

"I'll go along with it under two conditions," Sheriff Bridger said, his gaze sweeping past the reverend to Austin. "If Austin here agrees to it, and if Gideon makes it up to Austin somehow."

Reverend Myles fully agreed and looked toward Austin, uncertain of what the man would say.

Austin folded his arms and looked like he was deliberating. Finally, he said, "What's that verse you quoted the other day, Reverend? 'To the merciful, God shows himself to be merciful'? Guess I won't pass up a chance to give what I'll inevitably need."

Reverend Myles looked at him as if really seeing him for the first time. "It's magnanimous of you to do this for me … and for Gideon, especially under the circumstances."

Austin shrugged. "I'm just grateful Alison knows I was telling the truth."

"I have my rig outside. I'll give you a ride home," Reverend Myles offered.

"I'd appreciate that," Austin accepted, feeling like the man was holding out an olive branch and hoping it was the start of Reverend Myles having a much different opinion of him.

*****

"You seem awfully happy today," Lyn Hummel commented to Alison as she sat beside her and Reverend Myles in the wagon. On their way home from town a week later, they had seen her walking the street and invited her to come have supper with them that evening.

"Tonight, you'll get to meet the reason for my happy mood," Alison told her with a smile. Austin was coming for supper, too, and Alison was looking forward to Lyn meeting him.

Austin arrived shortly after they reached home, and the evening was quite a change from the first time Austin had come for supper. When they were done eating, Lyn moved to the rocking chair in the room and proceeded to answer questions from Lilly, who had found out that, at one time, Lyn had traveled with a circus. Austin and Alison conversed at the table with Maggie and Jacob, the conversation flowing easily. When the hour grew late, Austin offered to take Lyn back to town. As Lilly jumped to her feet to help Lyn out of the rocker, the old woman suddenly gasped. "Where did you get that?" she asked Lilly.

"My necklace?" Lilly asked as she touched it.

"Yes!" Lyn replied, her eyes large and obviously interested.

Alison walked over to them to see what had caused such a spark from Lyn. "It's very unique," Alison commented as she looked at it, too.

"Where did you get it?" Lyn asked again, and Alison thought she looked white as a ghost.

"My friend Cody gave it to me," Lilly said with a shrug, not understanding its apparent importance. It had been a Christmas present from Cody and definitely her favorite.

"He likes to whittle all kinds of things," Austin interjected, not knowing that Cody hadn't made that necklace.

Lyn lifted her eyes to Alison. "My son … he used to whittle crosses like that. I have one myself," she said.

Alison smiled kindly at her. "I'm sure he was very good at it." She shared a glance with Austin, whose expression told her he, too, felt sympathy for the woman.

Lyn shook her head as if Alison didn't understand. "It looks exactly like this one!"

Alison could see that the sight of the familiar-looking cross was really causing a stir in her, so she gently laid a hand on her shoulder. "Austin's going to take you home, ok?"

The woman nodded, but as she followed Austin to the door, she kept glancing over her shoulder to look at the necklace on Lilly's neck.

"Breaks my heart that she still thinks her son is alive," Maggie said quietly after Lyn and Austin had left.

"I'm surprised she's still in Millcreek," Reverend Myles said. "When she first arrived, she told me she never stayed in one place more than a few weeks."

"I thank the Lord she's been here as long as she has." Maggie looked down at the baby asleep in her arms. "We have her to thank for Marigold's safe delivery into this world."

"I'm glad she's still here, too," Alison said with a little sigh. "She shouldn't be traveling alone in her condition."

"I'm sure you're glad Austin is here, too," Reverend Myles said. "I was really wrong about that young man." Just that night, watching Austin interact with the others had given him a better glimpse into the man's personality and character.

"Well, I'm glad to hear he's starting to improve on you," Alison said.

"I am sorry for my hasty judgment of Austin," Jacob apologized to his sister, not for the first time since Austin had been proven innocent.

"I know your heart was in the right place," Alison reassured him of her forgiveness.

"Even though I was wrong about Austin, I would still not rush into anything too soon," Reverend Myles encouraged. "There's nothing wrong with a little patience in these matters. I would have done well to listen to my own advice instead of trying to match you with Gideon so hastily."

The mention of Gideon Martin brought a combination of anger and compunction. She regretted she had not been more guarded where he was concerned, but she was furious that he would frame Austin! She could tell Gideon was avoiding her whenever he saw her in town, and he hadn't been to church since the watch incident. She knew she needed to speak with him and decided she wouldn't put it off another day.

*****

Taking a deep breath, Alison lifted her hand to Gideon Martin's front door and knocked. The sight of the doorframe reminded her of the last time she had been outside it. The warm spring day was quite a contrast to the blizzard that had brought her there months ago.

When the door opened, Gideon's eyes clearly registered surprise and then something akin to dread at seeing her. He had already gone to see Austin and apologized for his dishonesty. The man's ready forgiveness had only made him feel worse, and he was eager to put the ordeal behind him.

"Can I talk to you?" Alison asked.

He nodded and opened the door wider for her to enter. Alison glanced around the room, the memories of her time there suddenly sweeping over her.

"Listen, Alison, I ... I know I messed up, and I ..."

"How could you do something like that, Gideon? It was a terrible lie and a horrible thing to do to Austin!"

"I know," Gideon said, rubbing the back of his neck and lowering his gaze. "I'm ashamed of what I did, and I'm sorry."

"But … why would you do something like that?"

"Isn't it obvious?" Gideon said.

"It's obvious you don't like Austin, but he's never done anything to you."

"Except ruin my chances with you," Gideon said flat out. "I know it was an impulsive and foolish thing to do, but I guess I was … desperate. I just thought if he looked guilty of something like that, you wouldn't be as interested in him."

"You would have me believe a lie?"

Her words cut him to the heart. "It was wrong. I'm really sorry. The idea came to me on the spot, and I was foolish to go along with it."

Alison saw the sincerity in his eyes and felt her anger toward him subside. "You've been a good friend to me, Gideon, but even if Austin wasn't in the picture, we would still be just friends."

"I see that now. Austin was good to not give me what I deserved … which only makes me feel worse … but at least my stupidity won't be aired to the whole town."

Alison gave him a weak smile. "You're a good man, Gideon, and one day, the right girl will come along."

He wasn't as confident as she was and still keenly felt the disappointment of her not wanting to be more than friends. "Thanks," he muttered. It was all he could think of saying. Alison left not long after that, and not for the first time, he chided himself. Framing Austin had made her think less of him, and now he had to live with that, besides losing his hope of her being his wife. In the back of his mind, he hoped she was right, that another girl would come along … and soon.

# *Chapter* Twenty-Six

One afternoon, on her lunch break, Alison spotted Lyn Hummel sitting on the front steps of the General Store.

"Afternoon, Lyn," Alison greeted kindly.

"Why, Alison! So nice to see you, dear," she said in her usual high-pitched, amiable tone. "How's that baby?"

"Getting chubbier by the day," Alison smiled and then looked at her questioningly. "What are you doing sitting here?"

"Waitin' for the stage, dear. He could arrive on it, you know."

Alison had forgotten that Lyn Hummel always waited for the stage on days it was due. Unfortunately, today wasn't one of those days. "Mrs. Hummel," she said softly, squatting down to be eye level with the woman. "Today's Thursday. I don't think the stage will be arriving today."

"Thursday?" The woman's thinning, gray eyebrows rose. "Oh my, I've got my days mixed up somehow." She shook her head, laughing softly at herself, and then reached for the rail to stand.

Alison took her arm and helped her to her feet. "It's a lovely day," Alison said, lifting her face slightly to the warm sun overhead. "Is there anywhere you want to go?" Alison asked.

"What I really need is to go home."

"I'll take you there now."

"No, I mean home … in St. Louis."

Alison looked at her face, noting the woman's weary expression. Alison was surprised to hear her admit it, knowing the woman had been gone for so long. "Do you have family there or friends who could help take care of you? I could help you make the arrangements to get there."

"I can't go back without William." Her eyes fell, as did her whole countenance.

"Mrs. Hummel, are you sure you shouldn't just accept that William might be …"

"Don't say it!"

Alison instantly saw strength return to the woman. She pushed her shoulders back a bit and lifted her chin. "I swore I'd not return home until he was found. If he's not here, he could be in the next town. I just have to keep looking. I stayed in this town longer than I have anywhere … I just had a feeling, you know?"

Alison nodded, hoping to make the woman feel understood. She gently put her arm around Lyn's shoulders and hugged her. "I know what you mean."

As she returned to work, Alison couldn't help but wish there was something more she could do for her. An idea suddenly came to her, and she tapped on Harold Bell's office door as soon as she returned to work.

"Mr. Bell, can I talk to you about something?"

Harold Bell looked up from his desk at Alison standing in the doorway of his office. He took off his spectacles and rubbed the bridge of his nose. "What's on your mind?"

Alison entered his office, glad she had his attention. "Remember that time Lyn Hummel came in here asking to put an article of some sort in the paper about looking for her son?"

"Yes, I remember."

"Well, I was wondering if I could write something up. I know it's not likely that he's alive or living around here, but just the gesture would help bring her some comfort, I think."

"You might be too soft-hearted for your own good, Miss Myles."

"It probably won't do any good, but it wouldn't do any harm, either. Please, Mr. Bell?" She waited while he deliberated, and then he sighed and gave a sort of shrug. "If you really want to, and if there's space for it, go ahead."

"Oh, thank you!" She said, "I'll keep it concise." Smiling to herself, she went to her desk, hoping the gesture would at least be an encouragement to the woman.

*****

A little over a week later, Cody knocked on Billy Turner's door and waited.

"I got everything you asked for," Cody said after Billy opened the door. Cody followed him inside and went to unload the items on the table. "Sugar, tea, coffee, tobacco …" Cody listed the items as he pulled them out of a burlap sack, "… and a newspaper."

Billy Turner handed him some coins. "Thanks, Cody," was all he said. Once Cody had left, Billy slouched into a chair and picked up the newspaper. Thanks to Cody, he had access to it more regularly and looked forward to reading it. Just as he was about to fold it up to read the rest later, something caught his eye. There, as clear as day and as piercing as a knife, was the name he hadn't seen in years: *William T. Hummel.* He read and reread the listing half a dozen times. Someone was looking for William T. Hummel … someone right there in Millcreek.

Over thirteen years before, William T. Hummel had woken up in a St. Louis hospital with burn wounds so severe he did not recognize himself anymore. The idea of returning home to his family, of them seeing him so deformed, was unthinkable. He would rather be dead than for them to see him, and that's what he had chosen. In his mind and heart, William T. Hummel had died in the war, leaving Billy Turner in his place. A life of solitude had suited him well, far from curious glances and painful questions.

A few years following the war, after wandering from town to town trying to remain in the shadows, Billy stumbled upon the property he now lived on. He had been passing through Millcreek, and a brief, late-night stop in the saloon had landed him in a conversation with Joe Spencer. The man was in a hard way and had been desperate to sell a piece of land he owned to pay off debt. They'd agreed on a price, and Billy had bought it from him some five years ago.

Now, as Billy paced his cabin, he felt something akin to panic surging through him. Seeing his full name in the paper, he knew he had to leave Millcreek and fast. Whoever was looking for him was close … too close. He decided at that moment that the next week, when Cody came by, he would give him an advertisement to put in the paper for him. He would be selling his land at a price that would ensure a swift sale.

*****

"Esau had a long-standing grudge with his brother, Jacob, and vowed to kill him," Reverend Myles said to his congregation after he had read from Genesis that Sunday morning. "Jacob was used to winning through cunning and deceit and had caused a lot of animosity with his brother by tricking him out of his inheritance and taking it for himself.

While Jacob didn't go about it the right way, he saw the value of a lasting inheritance over temporary pleasure.

"Years later, Jacob finds out that Esau, along with 400 men, were coming to kill him. Fearing for his life and in an effort to seek forgiveness, Jacob cried out to God for mercy and sent Esau lavish gifts. Jacob feared the worst and divided his family and herds so that, in case one group fell victim to Esau's men, the other group might escape. With the prospect of facing the attack, Jacob humbled himself and cried out to the Lord for his help. He was visited by God, and the Bible tells us he wrestled God all night long and prevailed. The gifts that Jacob sent to his brother pleased Esau, and the two brothers reconciled in the end.

"But it was what happened behind the scenes that really altered things," Reverend Myles made sure to point out. "Jacob *prayed* and wrestled with God, determined to receive a blessing, to receive the answer to his prayer that his brother would relent from doing harm to him. In all of his mistakes and failures, he knew that God was merciful and that, if God was on his side, he would be saved."

Reverend Myles closed his Bible and paused. "So often we try to make things happen in our own strength, and sometimes our efforts are even coming from the right motives. But, apart from God's blessing, and if we do not first win the battle through prayer, ultimately our efforts will avail to nothing."

Maegan listened intently as Reverend Myles spoke. The story resonated with her, and she couldn't stop thinking about it even after the service. Finally, unable to shake the feeling that she was supposed to share it with her Uncle Ben, she rode out to see him. When he answered her knock on the door, he seemed genuinely glad to see her. Maegan was pleased to see he'd kept up with the house and yard since she and Cody had left.

"I hope it's not a bad time," Maegan said. "There was just something I wanted to share with you."

Ben took a seat at the table after she had. "Go on."

"I have an idea," she began. "Actually, Reverend Myles' sermon is what made me think of it. Today, he told a story from the Bible about two brothers. The younger of the two, Jacob, had cheated his brother Esau, and Esau held a grudge toward him for years. There was trouble between them, and at one point, Jacob found out that Esau was sending 400 men to kill him and his family." She saw interest grow in her uncle's expression.

"Jacob was very afraid and cried out to God to save him and his family. In the meantime, Jacob also sent lavish gifts to his brother. Because God regarded Jacob's prayer, the generous gifts actually changed Esau's heart, and he relented from the harm he was going to cause."

Ben was silent for a moment as he gathered what she was saying. Then he shook his head slightly, a doubtful look in his eyes. "And you think if I send Joe a present, he'll forgive me for killing his boy … and Eliza?" Ben released a heavy sigh. "Don't seem likely."

"I don't know Uncle Ben. I can't get that story out of my head. I think …" she bit her bottom lip uncertainly, not wanting to sound presumptuous, "… I think the Lord is impressing it on my heart so that you would do it. Maybe it would help along something that God's already working behind the scenes." She watched as he scratched his whiskered cheek and looked off toward the window as if contemplating what she was saying.

"Won't you at least consider it? Pray about it?" Maegan asked.

"I ain't prayed for over a decade," Ben told her. "That's well long enough for God to forget I'm alive."

"He hasn't forgotten," Maegan told him with such tenderness and conviction in her voice that it almost made him want to believe it.

"I wouldn't even have anything Joe wants," Ben said.

"I'm sure there's something," Maegan pressed. "Just think about it, alright?"

"Alright," Ben agreed after a moment, although he was still doubtful.

Maegan paused at the door before leaving, "I also wanted to invite you for supper tomorrow night."

Ben nodded. "I'll be there, thanks."

*****

"The place looks good," Uncle Ben said the following evening when he arrived for supper. Maegan gave him a welcome smile and gestured toward the table for him to sit.

"Hi, Uncle Ben!" Cody greeted, coming out of his room and going to give his uncle a hug. "You can sit next to me," he said as they walked toward the table.

"Why are there so many plates on the table?" Ben asked.

"Well, I may have invited a few others," Maegan told him.

"A few others?" He turned around to look at her, his eyebrows furrowed. "What others?"

"Just Joshua and Aunt Becky and Jeb. Don't worry," she added when she saw the uncertain look on his face. "Uncle Joe is out of town for a few days, so he won't even know."

Ben released a sigh and shook his head as if he disapproved, but he didn't say anything else against the idea.

Momentarily, Austin arrived home, and soon, the others arrived as well. It made Maegan's heart full to see her aunt's smile as she embraced her brother. "It's good to see you, Ben," she said, her voice thick with emotion.

"It's good to see you too, Becky," Ben replied, and Maegan could tell he meant it.

"How about this! Larson's daughter bringing us together after all these years," Becky said with a look of gratitude in Maegan's direction. Her gaze swung to Austin, and while she had spoken to him briefly at church before, she was still amazed at his resemblance to his father. "You certainly look like your pa, Austin."

"It's a shame you missed Sawyer," Ben spoke up. "He's the spittin' image of Larson, too."

"You're all a fine bunch," Becky said proudly as she glanced across the table at her late brother's children.

For the next hour, Maegan enjoyed listening to her aunt and uncle talk about old times when they were kids growing up with her father. It sounded like they had all been close. Jeb and Cody eventually wandered outside while the adults continued to converse. With the watch incident behind them, they could pick up being friends again. Maegan noticed that Joshua seemed more friendly and talkative than she'd ever seen him, and he and Austin conversed easily.

Maegan could overhear Austin mentioning to Joshua how impressed he'd been with Will Carter's land and that one day, he'd like a piece of land like that himself.

"There's a homestead near my place that's just gone up for sale," Joshua was telling him. "One of the best properties 'round here."

Apparently, Ben heard him as well because he turned his eyes in their direction. "That property ain't for sale," he interjected.

Joshua drew a calming breath. The last thing he wanted was to get into it with his father. "Mr. Turner is selling it, Pa. I saw a listing in the paper."

"Not to a McCoy, he ain't," Ben said, his words sounding like a warning.

Maegan felt a sudden rise of tension between Ben and

Joshua, and even Becky looked uncomfortable. "Why can't Mr. Turner sell it to a McCoy?" Maegan had to come out and ask.

No one answered right away, but then Becky explained. "Before the war, Joe helped my son, Thomas, buy that piece of land they're talking about. Thomas had even started building a cabin before he had to enlist. After … after he died, the land went to my husband, but he drank and gambled everything we had, and eventually, we had to sell Thomas' land to get back on our feet. We sold it to a man named Billy Turner about five years ago. He had just come to the area and was eager to buy something far from town. I think my brother's worried that Joe would not take kindly to anyone from the McCoy family living where Thomas would have been … and since he's also buried on that land."

Ben gently laid his hand on his sister's as it rested on the table. "I'm so sorry, Becky."

"None of this fightin' will bring Thomas back," she said, tears in her eyes but strength in her voice. "Joe's got to see that by now! If only there was some way to … to change him."

"It ain't likely anything will change Uncle Joe," Joshua spoke up.

On Joshua's words, Maegan glanced at her uncle and saw a contemplative look on his face. She hoped and prayed that he was giving more thought to what she had talked to him about the previous day.

*****

*M*aegan looked fondly at all the thank-you cards the children had brought to her that last day of school, along with bouquets of wildflowers. She felt a wave of sadness wash over her that her job of teaching them was over. Not just because she had become fond of the children but because it meant she would be leaving Millcreek. She hadn't told anyone about her plan to go home, but now that she was done helping Mrs. Cooper, she could get Cody far from Garret Spencer. Once she and Cody reached Lexington, she would post a letter to the sheriff explaining everything and disclosing Garret Spencer as the murderer he was. That would put a safe distance between Cody and any schemes Garret would try to work from behind bars. She hoped that she and Cody could return once Garret was no longer a threat.

Trying to think through how she was going to convince Cody to leave Millcreek, Maegan wiped the blackboard for the last time and finished tidying up the room. After the room looked cleaned up and fit for church service on Sunday, Maegan headed outside. She spotted a lunch pail someone had forgotten in the yard and went to pick it up. Moving across the yard caused her to notice something else. One of the shutters was lopsided on its hinges.

Knowing where a box of tools was kept, Maegan returned inside and retrieved what she knew she would need. Then, once back at the window, she set to work. She pulled over a ladder that was resting against the side of the building and positioned it under the window. Lifting her skirt, she climbed up until she was parallel to the window.

"Need some help?"

It was twenty minutes later, and Maegan had nearly completed the task. She glanced over her shoulder as Sheriff Bridger walked into the yard, stopping just beside the ladder.

"I'm just about finished," she said, looking down at him.

He held the ladder as she climbed down. "You know, you can ask for help once in a while."

Once on the ground, Maegan dusted her hands off. "It looked like an easy enough fix."

He looked at her for just a moment, thinking how pretty she looked in a dress the shade of her eyes and her dark curls, half pulled up and half down her back.

"Last day, right?" he asked her, hoping his admiration of her wasn't obvious.

"Yes."

"Will you miss it?"

"I will," she said with a sad smile. "How … have you been?" she asked him, knowing it had been quite some time since they had talked. She had done a good job avoiding him all winter and early spring.

"Alright. I'm sure you're glad to have Austin back," he changed the subject, not wanting to focus on himself. In truth, he had been struggling for months with the way she had put a wall up between them.

"I am, and so is Cody."

"Seems like he's here to stay this time."

"I think he found a reason to stay." Maegan smiled, thinking of Alison. She began to walk across the yard toward the road that led to town, since she would have to go to the livery to get her horse. Sheriff Bridger fell into step beside her.

There was a moment of silence between them before Bridger came out and asked what he had been thinking for months. "Mae, did I do something to offend you? Months ago?"

Maegan stopped walking so she could face him. How could she explain without divulging the full truth?

"I did do something, didn't I?" he asked when he saw the uneasy look in her eyes, as if she was searching for the right words to explain.

Impulsively, Maegan took a step toward him and reached out to touch his arm. "Nothing could be further from the truth." She wanted more than anything to reassure him.

"Then why do I get the feeling you've been working hard to avoid me?"

Here it was. The perfect opening to tell him the truth. Garret's threats could all be a bluff. Once he was behind bars, Cody might be safe. All she had to do was tell Sheriff Bridger what really happened that night. She looked up into his eyes and realized it had been foolish to keep the truth from him.

"There is something I need to tell you." Her voice caught on the words, and she closed her eyes for a moment against the thought that telling the sheriff would put Cody's life in danger.

"What is it, Mae?" Bridger asked, taking her arm gently when he saw she was near to tears.

"That night of the Christmas dance, when I came back and was upset …"

Bridger could feel his apprehension rising as he waited for her to go on. He knew there had been more to that night than she had divulged.

"… it wasn't just a run-in with Garret Spencer. Before he saw me, I …"

"Sheriff Bridger!"

The sound of Austin's voice grabbed Bridger's and Maegan's attention, and they quickly turned to see Austin calling and running toward them from the direction of the livery.

"What is it?" Bridger asked, noting the urgency in Austin's demeanor.

"It's Joe Spencer. He's in some sort of a rage. He came to the livery going off on me and then went into the saloon. I saw some men runnin' out who said he was in a fit, drawing his gun on everyone. I don't have my gun on me, or I'd have …"

"No, I'm glad you found me," Bridger said. Just then, they

heard several shots being fired from the saloon. Bridger hated to leave Maegan in that vulnerable moment, but he had no choice. He broke into a run, following Austin toward the saloon.

*****

"I didn't hurt no one!" Joe Spencer hollered.

Bridger locked the jail cell and tossed the ring of keys on his desk. "I warned you this would happen the last time you went off," Bridger said. Twenty minutes ago, he and Austin had burst into the saloon and, working together, managed to hold Joe down and take his gun. Handcuffing him, Bridger had then walked him down to the jailhouse and deservedly into a cell.

"I ain't gonna stand idle while someone tells lies about my family!" Joe hollered as he gripped the cell bars and pressed his face close to them.

"You went too far, Joe!" Sheriff Bridger said. "Someone could have been killed!"

"My brother's nephew was killed … and you still haven't found the murderer!"

"Don't change the subject, Joe! Take responsibility for yourself for once."

"That feller in the saloon accused Garret of killin' his own cousin!" Joe argued his point. "I ain't lettin' no one throw dirt on my kin!" He thumped the bars with his fists. "How long you gonna keep me in here?" Joe bellowed. "Sheriff!"

But Bridger was already heading out the door. He saw Austin was waiting outside. "He needs to cool off," Bridger told him.

Austin let out a sigh as he shook his head. "He's lucky he didn't kill anyone."

"Very lucky. He's gonna think twice before doing that

again. Thanks for your help," Bridger said, thinking how Austin had aided him in subduing Joe.

Austin didn't even think anything of it. "How long you gonna hold him?" he asked.

"I figure a day for every shot he fired."

Austin grinned, thinking the punishment fit the crime.

The remainder of the day, Joe's mention of Pete Keller's murderer still being on the loose took a turn in Bridger's thoughts, eventually provoking him to return to the place where Keller's dead body had been discovered. The day he had been found, Bridger had walked the surrounding streets and alleys, looking intently for clues. While nothing had surfaced then or any of the other times he'd searched for a lead, Bridger found himself there now, slowly walking from one end to the other.

After a few minutes, he approached the bushes that had hidden Keller's body for a short time. Kneeling, Bridger scanned the ground like he had before, but this time, he noticed something half-buried in the dirt. Picking it up, he dusted it off and saw it was a pearl bracelet.

The memory flashed of Maegan wearing that same bracelet during the Christmas dance, and then the day after, he had found her searching for it in the alley … the same alley that led to the back street where Pete Keller had been found.

Confused at the discovery, he just stared at the piece of jewelry in his hand, wondering at its connection to Maegan. He suddenly recalled their conversation just a few hours ago. She had been on the verge of telling him something about that night. It was getting late, so he decided the next morning, he'd ride out to her place and finish their conversation.

*****

"Garret, I need to talk to you," Robert said as he entered his son's cabin, closing the door behind him and going to stand at his table. Garret was in the middle of a poker game with his brother and didn't even look up. "What is it, Pa?"

"Did you kill Pete?"

Garret's eyes jumped up to his father. "Whatcha talkin' 'bout, Pa? You drunk?"

Robert slammed his fist on the table, immediately gaining the attention of both of his sons. "You tell me straight, boy!"

"Where'd you get a fool-headed notion like that?" Garret asked.

"Your Uncle Joe's in jail for going off on a feller who accused you of the murder. Feller said he saw you and Pete arguing in an alley just before he died."

"Shucks, Pa, I ain't killed nobody."

"You better not have," Robert said as he slowly straightened and took a step back. "Pete was kin, and your ma's sister is terrible grieved. You best not have blood on your hands!"

The chair made a loud scraping noise as Garret came to his feet. "You're accusing me of killin' my own cousin, Pa?" he shouted.

Robert held his son's livid gaze. "I'm just makin' sure that temper of yours didn't override your good sense … if you have any left!" Robert glanced around the unkempt room. "Look at this place! You gotta earn your keep 'round here."

"I finished fixing that fence in the south pasture this morning," Garret replied as he reached for a nearly empty bottle of whiskey on the table.

"A job that should have taken you a few hours took you weeks! You're lazy, Garret, and you're drunk near all the time!" Robert reached over and yanked the bottle out of his son's hand. "I need your help on this farm. That was part of the agreement for you still livin' here. Bobby can't do everything."

"Sure, Pa," Garret said, looping his thumbs under his overalls. "I'll do my share."

Robert met his eldest son's gaze, thinking the rebellious look in his eyes didn't match his words. "I can overlook a lot, but the only thing I can't abide is disloyalty to your family. You remember that, and don't bring any shame on us."

A smile twitched across Garret's mouth, lifting the corners of his blotchy, unkempt mustache. "Sure, Pa. I'll remember."

There was a knock on the door, and Robert moved to answer it. His nephew, Jeb, stood on the other side.

"I heard my pa's in jail. That true?" Jeb asked.

Robert nodded. "He was just defending Garret and our family name. He did right to do that."

Jeb's eyes switched from his uncle to his cousin, Garret, whose smirk was as irritating as usual. "Did my pa hurt anyone?"

"If he did, they deserved it," Garret said, brushing past him as he stepped outside. Garret didn't feel guilty, but the thought of his pa finding out he'd killed Pete Keller did make him uneasy. He knew he needed to get the attention off himself and pin this murder on someone else. As he walked toward the barn, an idea came to him.

Robert's attention went from Garret to Jeb, and he placed a hand on the boy's shoulder. "Your pa didn't do wrong, Jeb. There ain't nothin' so right as defending your family and fightin' for them." If the war had taught Robert anything, it was that.

Jeb nodded slightly and then turned to leave. As he walked across the yard, Jeb was thinking about what his uncle had said, but his thoughts were interrupted as he passed the barn and heard Garret's voice.

"Hey! Get over here," Garret called to him.

Reluctantly, Jeb approached him. "What do you want?"

"Just wanted to say I'm sorry about your pa being in jail on my account."

"Was he right in defendin' you?" Jeb wanted to know. "You innocent?"

Anger pumped through Garret's veins. "Of course, I'm innocent! You think I'd kill my own cousin?" Garret sighed and shook his head. "Fires me up to think your pa's behind bars when Mae McCoy should be there instead."

"What?"

Garret knew he'd hooked Jeb's interest. "I don't want you to get involved," he said, feigning a look of concern.

"Why should Mae be behind bars?" Jeb asked.

"If I tell you, you can't let anyone know you heard it from me."

"Tell me what?"

"That Mae McCoy was the one who killed Pete."

"What?"

"You heard me!"

"That ain't true," Jeb defended her. He knew her enough to know she wasn't capable of that.

"How do you know it ain't true!" he replied, giving the boy a little shove.

"Because she wouldn't do a thing like that, and she had no reason to! Give me one reason Mae would kill Pete," Jeb tested him.

"You're friends with her brother, Cody, right?"

Jeb nodded slightly, wondering what lies Garret would tell next.

"Well, Mae's real protective of him, and Pete beat Cody up. There's witnesses who saw her pull her gun and practically threaten to kill him, and then a friend of mine saw her lure him into an alley and stab him in the back." Garret shook his head and summoned up an expression of grief. "Tears me up to think of poor Pete dying like that."

Jeb couldn't believe what he was hearing. "Who saw her? Why doesn't he go to the sheriff if he saw her do it?"

"Same reason I won't, because Mae McCoy's got that sheriff eatin' out of her hand! He's covering up for her cuz he's sweet on her, that's why!"

Garret slumped onto a stool and propped his feet up on a bale of hay. Crossing his ankles, he leaned back against the wall. "The sheriff's trying to pin this on me, but I wouldn't do a thing like that."

Jeb's eyes had been drawn to Garret's boots, and he realized the right one was missing a spur! Jeb immediately remembered the spur he had found in the alley that day Pete's body had been found. Jeb had heard rumors that Garret might have been Pete Keller's murderer, and although Garret was a troublemaker, Jeb didn't want to believe he was capable of murdering kin.

Garret looked at Jeb's pensive expression and thought his words were hitting their mark. "You believe me, don't you, Jeb?"

His silence made Garret put his feet down and lean forward, a hard glare in his eye. "Well? You believe me, right?"

Jeb nodded. "Sure, Garret, whatever you say."

When he left, Jeb rode home and ran into his bedroom. Opening a trunk in his room, he reached inside a smaller box where he kept things and pulled out the spur he had found those months ago. Staring at it in his hands, he knew deep down Garret had taken Pete's life. It made him sick to think of the kind of person Garret was. At that moment, a determination to see justice done rose up in him. Jeb knew that loyalty to the family was deeply rooted in the Spencer blood, but he also knew the way his pa, uncle, and older cousins acted was wrong. Robert had said there was nothing wrong with defending your family and fighting for them. Jeb knew there was truth in those words, but he also knew he couldn't let Garret get away with murder.

Weeks ago, Jeb had been angry when Cody accused him of stealing the reverend's watch, but it also made him realize that his dishonesty about that mine had given Cody reason to doubt his integrity. He hated that feeling and resolved then and there to come clean. Jeb's ma was constantly reminding him to listen to his conscience and to do the right thing. It seemed choosing right and wrong had been a struggle most of his young life, but today, he knew what he would choose.

Jeb rode toward town, and when he entered the jail and approached the cell, he thought his pa was asleep, but then the man sat up and stepped toward the bars. Sheriff Bridger was sitting at his desk.

"Hello, Jeb," Bridger said.

"Sheriff." Jeb nodded toward him before his gaze swung back to his father.

"I'll give you two a few minutes," Bridger said, stepping outside onto the porch of the jailhouse.

Jeb swallowed the lump in his throat. It wasn't the first time that his pa had been thrown in jail, but it was what Jeb was preparing to tell him that made him nervous.

"Whatcha doin' here, boy?" Joe asked his son.

"I have something to tell you, Pa." Jeb said the words before he could talk himself out of it.

"That sheriff shouldn't have thrown me in here!" Joe said in his defense. He didn't like his son seeing him behind bars.

"What happened?" Jeb asked.

"Some feller accused Garret of killing Pete. What was I supposed to do? Stand by and let him drag our family's name through the mud?"

His words reminded Jeb of why he was there. "I got something to tell you, Pa," he repeated.

Joe was a decent-looking man, but years of drinking and neglecting his health had altered his appearance. A scowl seemed to be his constant expression, and even now, Jeb felt afraid as he looked into his pa's eyes.

"I lied to you, Pa. Not once, but twice." There, it was out! Jeb felt a mixture of relief and fear all at once.

"You lied to me?"

Jeb cleared his throat, which suddenly felt dry and dusty. "I told you I saw Joshua set fire to our barn, but it wasn't Joshua; it was me." He saw he had his father's attention and went on. "I found a cigar and smoked it in the barn, and it started the fire."

Jeb took a firm breath. "I also told you Cody McCoy tried to trap me in the mine. That was a lie, too. It was Cody who saved me from the mine." Jeb paused and then explained further. "I was the one who led him and Lilly deeper in, and then when it started caving in, Cody risked his neck to save me."

Jeb felt like he could scarcely breathe as he waited for his pa to say something. The silence in the air felt as hard as the iron bars between them. And then Joe turned and went back to the makeshift bed to sit down.

"I'm sorry, Pa," Jeb said. He had expected his father to holler and swear, so his quiet, almost indifferent response to his confession was surprising. He knew once his pa was free, he'd probably get the whooping of his life, but to him, a clear conscience was worth it.

"There's something else," Jeb said, taking a deep breath. "Something you ain't gonna like to hear."

Joe stood back on his feet and approached the bars, his eyes intently on his son. "Well? Out with it, boy!"

Jeb instinctively glanced around the room, even though he knew no one was there. "I know who murdered Pete."

"What?"

Jeb reached into his pocket and showed his father the spur. "The day Pete's body turned up, I found this spur near his body."

"So?"

"It's Garret's spur, Pa. He had to have done it."

Joe looked on edge as he began to pace the cell. "You tell anyone else?"

"No. Garret's trying to pin this on Mae McCoy, but she ain't a murderer."

Joe took off his hat and ran a shaky hand through his overgrown mass of hair. He suddenly turned back to Jeb. "Don't tell anyone else what you told me, hear?"

"Pa … we can't let Garret get away with this! Pete was family!"

"Shh! I know!" He released a heavy sigh. "I just need some time to think how to tell Robert."

Jeb nodded. "Alright, Pa. I won't say anything."

For a moment, Joe's gaze rested on his son, feeling a surge of pride amidst the turmoil of hearing such news. Jeb's honesty and integrity stirred something in Joe that had been dormant for a long time. "Go on, get outta here," he said quietly, watching as his son left the jailhouse and left him alone with a torrent of thoughts and unearthed emotions.

*****

Ben McCoy was finding it difficult to forget the conversation he'd had with Maegan, that story from the Bible occupying much of his thoughts. There wasn't any gift that he could give that would change the past, but could it in some way change his relationship with Joe? Joe was a stubborn man, but Ben also knew the depths of foolishness that pain could send a person into. Alone in his house, Ben went to the mantle and took the Bible that had been untouched for years.

Slowly, he sat down and opened it, feeling like he was holding his breath as the pages rustled open. He saw some passages that were underlined and pages that had handwritten notes on them. The sight of his own markings gripped his heart. It had been so long. Heaving a shaky sigh, he read for a while until tears flooded his eyes and forced him to stop reading. Bowing his head in his hands, only a few words surfaced, but in his heart, he knew he'd taken a big step.

The next day, he rode out to Billy Turner's and knocked on the door. It opened a moment later, Billy looking at him curiously.

"Can I help you?"

"I heard you were selling your property," Ben said. "I'd like to buy it."

Billy opened his door wider and invited him inside. After settling on the price, Ben returned the following day with the money, and Billy assured him he'd be gone by the end of the week.

Ben's next stop was his sister's house. When no one answered his knock on the door, he opened it slowly while glancing around apprehensively, hoping Joe wouldn't come out of somewhere to jump him. Had he known Joe was in jail, Ben would have gone there.

"Anyone home?" Ben called out.

After a moment of waiting, he pulled an envelope out of his pocket and propped it up on the mantle so it would be seen. Exiting the house, he mounted his horse and rode home.

# *Chapter* Twenty-Seven

"Now that school's over, what would you think of spending the summer back home … with Sawyer?"

"What?" Cody looked up from his plate of scrambled eggs, surprise in his blue eyes. "You mean leave Millcreek?" It was the day after school had ended, and Maegan had just sprung the question.

"Um-hm. Just for a few months."

Had she asked him half a year ago, he might have said yes, but not anymore. This felt like home now. It was strange to think of returning to their farm, especially now that Austin was here in Millcreek with them. "Honestly, I think I'd rather stay here," Cody said.

"Cody, you didn't like it or understand when we first came here, remember?"

He nodded, recalling just how upset he had been at her for making him leave his brothers.

"But it all worked out, and now I'm asking you to trust me one more time."

"But Austin's here!"

"It would only be for a few months."

"But why? You at least gotta tell me why!" Cody had come to his feet now, his expression demanding answers.

"I can't tell you right now, Cody, but once we're a distance from Millcreek, I promise I will."

Cody saw something in her eyes that caused the fight in him to yield slightly. "What did Austin say?"

"I haven't told him yet," Maegan said.

Cody released an irritated sigh. "I don't like it, Mae."

"You'll understand soon if you'll just trust me."

Cody was obviously unhappy about the prospect of leaving Millcreek as he walked out of the house, just as Sheriff Bridger was riding into the yard.

"I won't keep you long," Bridger told Maegan as she allowed him inside. "I just wanted to show you something I found."

Maegan looked at him curiously as he reached into his vest pocket and held something out to her. "Is this the bracelet you lost?"

Maegan gasped softly. "Yes! Where did you find it?" She reached out and gingerly took it from his hand.

"Near where Pete Keller's body was found."

Maegan looked up slowly, meeting his eyes. She felt like her cheeks were suddenly on fire and hoped he couldn't tell.

"How do you think it ended up there?"

Yesterday, she had been on the verge of telling him … or at least trying to tell him, but the more she had thought about it, the more she decided that leaving town was the safest course for Cody.

"I … I don't know," she finally replied, hating to lie to him.

"Mae, I know there's something you're not telling me. Yesterday, you were about to say something about the night of the Christmas dance."

Maegan could feel her heart pounding in her chest. "It was nothing."

"There's only two people I know of who were relatively

close to the place Pete Keller's body ended up that night. Garret Spencer … and you."

Maegan could hear the confusion in his tone and forced herself not to look up into his eyes, as they would surely persuade her to tell everything. She looked down at the bracelet in her hand. "I wish I could explain how the bracelet came to be there, but … I just can't."

"You can't, or you won't?" he asked, his tone still gentle but with a firmer edge. Bridger knew now more than ever that she was hiding something, and it bothered him more than anything ever had. "I wish you could trust me enough to tell me what you're hiding," Bridger suddenly said, not willing to let the matter go.

"I can't tell you now," Maegan said, "but I promise to soon."

Her cryptic words made Bridger even more confused and curious. He stood there, having difficulty separating his personal feelings for her from his sense of responsibility as Millcreek's sheriff.

"I guess I'll have to be content with that," Bridger said, although his eyes told her he wanted more. He tipped his hat slightly and left without another word.

When Maegan heard the door close, she released a shaky breath and sat down for a moment. She couldn't keep up this lie any longer. The sooner she could leave with Cody, the better.

That evening, after Cody had gone to bed, Maegan told Austin about leaving Millcreek.

"I don't like it," he said immediately. "Something don't feel right about you leaving. Sawyer might not even be at the farm," Austin told her.

"Cody doesn't want to leave, but he would be much more willing to go if he felt like you were behind me," Maegan said.

"Then give me a good reason to be behind you," Austin said.

"I miss the farm and want to make sure everything there is in order," Maegan said, knowing it wasn't the truth. She wouldn't mind seeing home again, but nothing in her wanted to leave Millcreek aside from the reason of protecting Cody.

Austin sighed. "I should just go with you two."

"No. You finally worked things out with Alison, and you have a job now. Cody and I will be fine."

"When would you leave?" Austin asked.

"Soon as I can."

Austin paced the cabin floor, still not warming to the idea. "You've never given me cause to doubt you before, so I'll support your decision, but I still don't like it."

"Thanks, Austin. Trust me, it's for the best."

*****

Maegan knew that saying goodbye to Uncle Ben would be difficult for both her and Cody, but before she made that stop, Maegan headed toward her cousin's house. As she rode into Joshua's yard, she noticed another horse tied up outside, and she could hear voices coming from the backyard. One she recognized as Joshua, and the other sounded familiar. When she came around the corner, she saw it was Garret Spencer. He seemed in a spit-fire mood about something, his voice angry as he and Joshua went back and forth.

"I knew it was for sale, but I'm not the one who bought it," Joshua was saying.

"What about your cousin, Austin?" Garret said. "Did he buy it?"

At that moment, they both noticed Maegan. "I'm sorry to interrupt," she said. "Everything ok?" she asked, thinking about the pistol in her trouser pocket as her gaze shot toward Garret.

"Yep. Garret here was just about to leave. Weren't you, Garret?"

Garret scowled at Joshua before turning to walk past Maegan. Once he'd gone, Maegan took a few steps closer to Joshua. "What was that all about?"

"He came to tell me Billy Turner sold his land and wanted to know if I'd bought it. It was news to me that it was sold already." He scooped up some logs he had just chopped. "I wish someone in our family would have bought it. Thought it would make a great homestead for Austin if he's thinking about settling here permanently."

"Maybe something else will turn up," Maegan said optimistically, and then a sad smile touched her lips. "Cody and I are leaving Millcreek. We're heading back to our farm for a few months."

"What? Why?"

Maegan appreciated the look of disappointment in his eyes. "Besides wanting to see Sawyer, we've been gone near a year, and I need to make sure the farm is alright."

"You'll come back though, won't you? Especially now that Austin's plannin' to stay?"

"I hope so," Maegan replied sincerely. "I'm glad you and Uncle Ben are getting along. Keep at it," she encouraged kindly before rising on tiptoe to hug him.

"Mae?" Joshua said as she was starting to walk away.

Maegan turned back toward him. "Yes?"

"Do you still pray there'll be peace between Uncle Joe and my pa?"

Maegan smiled softly, her heart in her eyes as she looked at her cousin. "I do, every day."

As skeptical as he was about prayer, knowing she hadn't forgotten was a comfort.

As Maegan rode away from Joshua's, she wished she had brought her hat to shield her face from the warm June sun. She decided to take a shortcut through the forest, where the trees would offer some shade. Some minutes later, she thought she heard another horse and glanced behind her. The green foliage was thick, making it difficult to see. She rode on, dismounting for just a minute when she came alongside a creek. It was peaceful there, the water rushing over rocks and the wind nestling in one tree branch after the other.

Maegan let her horse drink while she crouched down on a rock and brought some of the cool water to her mouth. That's when she knew she heard the distinct sound of another horse. Straightening, she looked up to see Garret Spencer just a short distance away. His horse was farther behind him, and she realized he must have been edging closer on foot.

"Are you following me?" Maegan asked sharply as she came to her feet.

"I heard what you told Joshua."

Maegan pretended like she didn't know what he was talking about, wondering if he really had been eavesdropping.

"Why are you suddenly in a hurry to get out of Millcreek?" he asked.

"I'm not," she lied, moving toward her horse that had wandered a few feet away.

"I think you are," he said, moving quickly to catch up to her. "I think you snitched, and now you're high-tailing it out of here because you're scared. Hey! I'm talkin' to you!" he hollered as he grabbed her arm before she could reach her horse and whirled her around to face him.

"Don't turn your back on me, Mae McCoy!"

"Don't touch me!" she said through clenched teeth, pulling her arm free from his hold.

"You know, you're the only thing standing between me and the prospect of jail."

"I told you I wasn't going to tell, and I haven't," she replied, trying to discreetly slip her hand into her pocket. She didn't like the look in his eyes and wanted to have her pistol within reach. She made another attempt to move to her horse, but again, he grabbed her arm.

"I'm sick of worrying 'bout you rattling your mouth," he said through gritted teeth, and then he suddenly jerked her close toward him.

Maegan let out a little cry and squirmed under his hold. He had her by her left arm, but she'd managed to reach for her pistol. Whipping it out, she pressed it against his chest.

"Let me go, or I'll shoot you!" she warned.

Garret smiled, and the amused glint in his eyes told her he didn't take her seriously. "I'm the killer, remember? You ain't gonna pull that trigger."

"Let go of me and back up!" she ordered him.

Chuckling, Garret slowly released his hold on her and stepped backward. He held up his hands in mock surrender, his eyes taunting her.

Maegan edged away slowly, keeping her eye on him. As she reached her horse and tried to put her foot in the stirrup, Garret suddenly lunged at her, knocking her to the ground. Horrified by the evil intent in his eyes, Maegan scurried backward in the dirt, trying to fight him off as he reached for her throat. Just as his hands came around her neck to strangle her, she gripped her gun firmer and pulled the trigger.

The gunshot pierced the air, seemingly louder than any shot she'd ever heard before. At close range, the bullet was lodged in Garret's shoulder. His body collapsed onto hers, and she rolled out from underneath him, his blood smearing across her shirt. He was moaning as she got to her feet, and she stared in horror at him lying there, a dark circle of blood soaking his white shirt. Maegan was breathing heavily and sank down to her knees. She quickly untied the bandanna from around his neck and pressed it into the wound. Then she untucked her shirt and tore it across the bottom to get a long strip. She wrapped it diagonally around his shoulder and back and tied it firmly over the bandanna to keep it in place.

"I'll get the doctor!" she told him, already scurrying toward her horse.

"Don't leave me!" he groaned. "I'm gonna bleed to death! Don't leave me!"

"I'll be back with the doctor! Lay still!" Maegan rode off at high speed, jumping logs and darting between trees in the forest until she reached the main road. Then, she urged the horse into an even faster pace, riding into town at record speed. She jumped down before the horse had even come to a stop and frantically ran to burst open the doctor's door.

"Doc Fletcher!" she yelled, walking into his clinic and searching the doorways that led to other rooms. "Doc!"

There was no answer! He wasn't there! She ran back outside, her eyes darting in every direction in search of him. "Do you know where Doc Fletcher is?" she asked a man who was nearby. He shook his head, so she ran to a woman who had just come out of the bank. "Have you seen the doctor?"

"Saw him ride out 'bout an hour ago," the woman said, looking at her curiously.

"Which direction?"

"Looked to be heading out of town toward Pond Point. I think he was planning on doing some fishing."

"Thank you!" Maegan said, instantly back on her horse and heading out of town within seconds.

*****

"He's just through these woods," Maegan shouted over her shoulder to the doctor about thirty minutes later. She'd met him on the road as she was on her way to find him and told him what had happened. He was in a buggy but kept a good pace with her as she galloped ahead. Once they neared the wooded area where she had left Garret, the doctor followed her on foot.

"Just this way," she said.

Doc Fletcher side-stepped thorn bushes and brush and tried to keep up. A moment later, Maegan turned around, exasperated. "He was right here!" she said, seeing the trail of blood. "He must have managed to get home."

"I'll head that way now," the doctor said.

He returned to where they'd come from, Maegan close behind. As she watched his buggy ride off toward Robert Spencer's, she felt for a few minutes like she couldn't even move. What a disaster. If Garret died, the Spencers would hate the McCoys even more! She chided herself for pulling the trigger, but it truly had been self-defense, and it had happened so quickly that she barely had time to think.

"Please, God," she prayed aloud. "Don't let Garret Spencer die. Please keep him alive!"

*****

When Robert Spencer saw Garret riding into the yard half-conscious and dripping with blood, he sprang into action and, with Bobby's help, carried Garret to his bed.

"What happened, boy?" Robert asked Garret.

Garret moaned against the pain. "It was … it was Mae McCoy," he grunted. "She tried to kill me after I told her I knew she'd … killed Pete."

On Garret's words, rage pumped through Robert's veins. He held firm to his son's hand. "Shh, rest now, son." Robert had sent Bobby to get the doctor, but he returned only moments later as Doc Fletcher was already riding into the yard.

"Is he gonna be okay?" Robert asked anxiously from behind the doctor as he began cutting Garret's shirt away to get to the bullet.

"Doc!" Robert said with alarm when it seemed Garret had breathed his last. Doctor Fletcher felt for his pulse, but Robert was already running out of the house, anger mounting in him as he called for Bobby to follow him.

# Chapter Twenty-Eight

"You're back," Becky said when the front door opened and her husband walked into their home.

Joe avoided eye contact with his wife as he closed the door behind him and moved across the room to the sink. "As you can see."

Becky released a weary sigh, hoping half a week in jail had taught her husband to control his temper. She doubted it, though.

"This came for you … while you were gone."

Joe dried his hands on a towel and turned to take the envelope his wife held toward him. "What is it?"

"Just open it," Becky said, wanting him to see it for himself. She watched as her husband opened the envelope and pulled out its contents. The play of emotions on his face wasn't something she had seen in a long time. Wordlessly, he sat down, reading through everything again.

Suddenly, Jeb burst through the door. "Pa!"

"What's wrong?" Joe sprang to his feet.

"It's Uncle Robert and Bobby! They're in a rage and heading to Cody's!"

"What!"

"I don't know what all happened, but Garret's been shot!"

"Stay here," Joe told his son as he hurried out the door.

"Be careful, Joe!" Becky called after him, praying desperately for protection over all those she loved.

*****

When Maegan returned home, she spotted Austin outside chopping wood. He smiled and called a greeting, but then, on second glance, he set down the ax and went to her.

"Mae! What happened?" Aside from the distressed look on her face, her hair was disheveled and her shirt untucked and sporting an obvious tear, not to mention a smear of blood!

Immediately, tears started flooding her cheeks. She lifted her hands to her face and cried.

This wasn't like his sister at all. Austin could barely remember ever seeing her cry. "Mae, what's wrong? Are you hurt?" he asked, gently taking her arms.

"I've really done it now," she said in between tears. "If Garret dies, the Spencers will go crazy!"

"What? What are you saying?"

"I shot Garret, Austin. And it looked really bad."

"Was it an accident?"

"No."

"So, self-defense, then?" he asked, the muscles in his jaw jumping. He knew she wouldn't shoot for any other reason than that. "What did he do to you? If your shot doesn't kill him, maybe I will!"

"I wasn't harmed," she assured him. "Please. We can't make this feud any worse!"

As if on cue, a loud gunshot rang out. Maegan screamed, and Austin whirled around, reaching for his own gun when he saw a rider approaching with his weapon aimed toward them. "Get in the house!" Austin yelled to Maegan.

Having been in the house when he heard the shot, Cody

had opened the front door only to see Maegan and Austin running toward him.

"Get down!" Maegan called to Cody as she reached the doorway and pushed him back inside.

Austin backed up toward the doorway, firing a shot toward the rider that was aimed to scare him but not hit him. Once inside, he slammed the door. "Get down and under something!" he yelled to Cody and Maegan.

"What's going on?" Cody asked, glancing toward the window with panic in his eyes.

"It looks like Robert Spencer!" Austin said as he ducked down under the window.

Maegan screamed when a shot broke through the glass of one of the front windows, shattering it to the floor.

"The way Robert's acting, Garret must be dead!" Austin said.

"Please don't say that!" Maegan whimpered from where she crouched down beside the kitchen table. "Don't kill him."

"I'm just trying to scare him," Austin said, ducking as another shot zipped into the cabin. "There's another one of them now," he added.

Maegan crawled toward the window, pulling out her own gun, which was still in her pocket from earlier. She dared a glance out the window and saw the two men were positioned, one behind a tree and the other behind the shed. "It's probably Bobby," she said.

"Or Joe," Austin said.

"Cody! Go into the bedroom and hide behind something!" Maegan told him.

"I wanna stay and fight!" Cody argued.

"Cody!" Austin hollered. "Do it!"

Realizing they needed more bullets, Maegan crawled over to the fireplace and retrieved them, along with the rifle that hung over the mantle.

"Go and find shelter yourself," Austin told her. "I can hold these two off."

Just then, a shot tore through the wall, ripping through Austin's arm. He winced against the pain but managed to fire a shot back at them.

"We've got to stop this somehow!" Maegan said over another round of shots fired at them. "Ugh, Austin, you're bleeding so much!"

"I'm fine!" he said. "Now get back!"

"This is serious, Austin," Maegan said, near tears.

"They only got so many bullets. I can hold 'em off."

Maegan scrambled to drag some furniture over to make more of a barricade, and she also grabbed a dishcloth and wrapped it around Austin's arm.

"I'm fine," he insisted.

She moved to the other window and ducked down after taking a shot toward the tree. It must have been fifteen minutes that they fired back and forth. She and Austin were aiming close but purposely missing, while Bobby and Robert Spencer appeared to be shooting to kill. Maegan sent an anxious glance to the room Cody was hiding in, praying to God he would be safe.

"Cody! Cody, are you alright?" Maegan called out to him a few minutes later. There was no answer, so she called him again. Frantic, she ran toward the bedroom, ducking down as a shot fired through the bedroom window. Cody wasn't under the bed or anywhere in the room.

"Austin! He's not in there!" Maegan said as she returned to the main room. She suddenly caught sight of the back door, which was slightly ajar. She ducked down as she moved toward it, but just as she reached it, something that felt like a knife struck her back. The overwhelming pain dropped her to her knees. When she tried to move, it felt like a bolt of lightning through her whole body. Clutching the back of a chair to try to get to her feet, she sank back down against the pain. A strange, high-pitched noise filled her head as she crawled toward the door. Where was Cody?

"I think they're out of bullets!" Austin said. Then, he realized the gunfire had stopped because another rider had ridden up. It was Joe Spencer! "We've got more trouble!" Austin called over his shoulder. "Where's the …" Austin's words died on his lips when he realized Maegan was lying on the ground toward the back of the room, just a few feet from the back door.

"Oh, my God! Maegan!" He ran to her, gasping at the large pool of blood under her back. Kneeling, he lifted her head onto his lap. "Maegan!"

She seemed so lifeless lying there. He felt her pulse. It was weak. A rage suddenly rose in him that he never thought he could possess. He grabbed the rifle and burst through the door, firing in both directions where he knew the Spencers were hiding.

"Enough!" he hollered before firing another shot into the air. "No more of this!" Austin said, throwing the rifle onto the ground and raising his hands. "I've got to go for the doctor!"

Austin noticed Sheriff Bridger had just ridden into the yard. He jumped off his horse and ran toward Austin. Bridger immediately spotted the blood-stained sleeve on Austin's shirt.

"One of you fools go for the doctor!" Bridger hollered toward the Spencers, having heard what Austin said.

"It ain't for me," Austin told him. "It's for Mae."

On those words, Bridger whipped out his caliber and aimed it at Joe. "Get the doctor, now!" Bridger told him. He then tore into the house. Seeing Maegan lying motionless on the floor, he went to her and scooped her up in his arms.

Austin was right behind him. "Joe went for the doc," Austin said. "I'm gonna ride out, too, in case he can't find him."

"Good idea," Bridger said as he moved toward the bedroom. He saw some of the furniture had been turned into a makeshift barricade, but there was a bed along the nearest wall that he laid her in. Quickly, he returned to the kitchen, grabbed a bucket of water, and opened various cabinets, searching for supplies. With what he found, Bridger rushed back to the bedroom. Carefully rolling Maegan to her side, he ripped the back of her shirt, alarmed at the damage done to her back. Glancing at the front of her, he saw blood on the front of her shirt, but it wasn't from exit wounds, telling him the bullets were still lodged in her back.

He cleaned the wounded areas, and when he pressed cloth into the gaping holes of the wounds, he realized one of the bullets in her back was close to the surface. "You're not going to die," he said, overcome by the thought of losing her. "You're not going to die, Mae!"

Bridger took a deep breath. He'd seen a bullet removed once before and knew he'd have to try. There was no telling when the doctor would get there. Praying under his breath, he pressed his finger into the shallower wound and was relieved to feel the bullet almost immediately. He pulled it out and then cleaned the wound again before wrapping scraps of cloth around her back to stop the bleeding. The other gunshot wound looked much worse, indicating the bullet was nowhere near the surface.

To Bridger's great relief, he heard footsteps, and Doc Fletcher was suddenly in the room.

"How bad is it?" the doctor asked as he immediately stepped in and examined her back.

"I got the one bullet out, but I think the other is lodged deep."

Doctor Fletcher turned to his bag and pulled out a long probe. He knelt by the bed so he would be more on level with Maegan's back and proceeded to reach the probe into the wound, tapping around to find the bullet. After he slid it out, he pulled a cloth out of his bag and threaded it through the eye of the probe, wrapping it around to form a wider end. He pressed it into the wound, turning it back and forth.

"Hand me those," he pointed to the forceps lying on his bag. Bridger handed them to him and watched as the doctor pressed them into the hole and, just a moment later, removed them, with the bullet clasped firmly between the forceps.

"Thank God," Bridger said, relief flooding through him.

"She's not in the clear yet," Doc Fletcher said as he cleaned the area and began making a bandage. "Infection could set in, and she's lost a lot of blood." He reached for her wrist. "Her pulse is very weak." He straightened up and took a step away from the bed. "I heard Austin's wounded, too. Where's he at?"

"He went in search of you."

"Joe was the one who found me. I was at Robert's house, digging a bullet out of that fool son of his."

"Garret?"

The doctor nodded. "From what Maegan told me earlier, she'd had no other choice but to shoot him."

Bridger's eyes darted toward the doctor. "What?"

"That's what she said. It happened just a while ago, and I reckon Robert and Bobby thought he wasn't going to pull through and charged over here in a rage."

They both heard the door and turned toward the sound of footsteps in the house. Austin appeared in the doorway, his face a mixture of relief at seeing the doctor and concern at seeing Maegan. "Is she okay?" Austin was almost afraid to ask as he moved toward the bed and knelt by his sister.

"She lost a lot of blood. I've seen situations like this go both ways." Doctor Fletcher paused but then said, "It would be best to prepare yourself for whatever the outcome."

Austin's eyes suddenly burned with tears as he gently took her hand. "She's gonna pull through, Doc. You watch and see."

"I'd like to look at your arm," the doctor said.

"It's nothin'," Austin replied, his attention still intent on Maegan.

"Go on," Bridger encouraged Austin. "I'll stay right here until you get back."

Austin stood slowly and followed the doctor out to the kitchen.

Bridger pulled over a chair and sat it beside Maegan's bed. His heart heavy, he reached for her hand, which seemed so small and frail resting in his, and then he began to pray like he knew Maegan would.

# *Chapter* Twenty-Nine

During the fighting, Cody had slipped out the back door and made a beeline for the barn. After mounting his horse, he took a back route to town so he wouldn't have to go through the front yard to the main road. He'd never ridden that fast in his life, and when he arrived at the jailhouse, he'd nearly fallen to the ground on his dismount. After telling Sheriff Bridger what was happening, Cody went to his Uncle Ben's house. Joshua happened to be there, and together, the three of them headed toward the fighting. By the time they arrived, however, the doctor was just finishing bandaging up Austin. Cody ran in and, seeing Austin, asked where Maegan was.

"She's hurt pretty bad," Austin cautioned him. He knew Cody would take it hard and watched the boy move quickly into the bedroom. As Cody came in, Bridger left to join Austin.

"You feelin' better?" he asked Austin, who was sitting at the kitchen table with his arm wrapped up.

"We oughta go kill every last one of 'em!" Joshua said angrily from where he and his father stood near Austin.

"Joe's the one who stopped the shooting," Doctor Fletcher shocked them by saying.

"How do you know that?" Ben asked, his expression pensive.

"He's the one that came to get me, and he told me what happened," the doctor replied.

Austin remembered Joe riding into their yard. At first, he thought Joe was coming to join Robert and Bobby, but the gunfire stopped once he got there. Austin filled them in about what Maegan had told him happened with Garret. "After Mae shot him, Robert and Bobby thought Garret wasn't going to live, so they came to take us out, I guess."

"If he didn't live, it would have served him right," Joshua said.

"He's going to live," Doc Fletcher said. "Which, unfortunately, is more than I can say with certainty for Maegan." He looked at Austin. "I'll stay the night just in case things worsen."

Hearing the soberness in his voice, Bridger felt his chest tighten. "If it's all the same to you, I'm going to stay the night, too," he said to Austin. "I don't think the Spencers will come back, but I'm not willing to take a chance."

Austin nodded, glad to have the extra protection there. His arm was giving him a lot of pain, although he would never let on. Hours later, the two men sat at the table. Cody was in the room with Maegan, unwilling to leave her side.

"I wonder why Joe stopped the shooting," Austin said, staring into the cup of coffee in his hands.

"I was wondering the same thing. Seems more like him to join in. He's usually the ringleader," Bridger said.

"I thought they ran out of bullets," Austin told him. "Good thing Joe didn't join 'em. Things could have ended a lot worse. I didn't even know Cody had left to get help."

"He's a brave boy." As Bridger said the words, he saw a look of remorse cross Austin's face.

"All she wanted was to protect him. She'd give her life for that boy … or for any of us. If she doesn't pull through, I don't know what I'll do."

Bridger could hear Austin's love for his sister in his voice. "She's going to be alright," Bridger said with more confidence than he felt.

"When I think she's lying there on account of Garret Spencer, well, it takes everything in me not to go and beat him within an inch of his life."

"That makes two of us," Bridger said as he glanced toward the bedroom. He knew he cared about Maegan, but in those hours when he thought of her not making it, he realized he couldn't bear the thought of losing her.

"I'm gonna check on her," Austin said as he stood and took a lamp off the kitchen table. He walked quietly into the room, setting the lamp on a side table before sitting on the chair by her bed. Cody had moved a cot into the room to be near her and now lay sleeping on it.

Austin touched the back of his hand to Maegan's forehead and was alarmed by how hot she was.

"I'm gonna go wake the doctor. She's burning with fever," Austin said to Bridger when he returned to the main room and headed toward the loft where Doctor Fletcher was sleeping.

Bridger paced the floor while the doctor and Austin returned to Maegan. Under his breath, he prayed. "Lord, I don't know if it's right to pray this way, but if you ever cared about me or what happens in my life, then I ask you to let Mae live. I'm not one for breaking promises, and I swear to you, I'll give you my whole life and do whatever you want if you'll just let her live."

*****

Alison gasped when she and her brother pulled up to the McCoys' cabin the following day and saw the windowpanes that were shattered, as well as the bullet holes in the walls. When she came through the door, it was to find the sheriff, Austin, and Cody finishing breakfast.

"We came as soon as we heard," she said, walking towards Austin. Reverend Myles entered just a minute behind her, removing his hat and asking how Maegan was.

"You can go back and see her if you want, Reverend. Lord knows she could use all the prayin' she can get," Austin said.

"Are you okay?" Alison asked when she saw Austin's bandaged arm.

"Ain't nothing compared to Mae." He hugged her with his good arm.

"I want to see her," Alison said as she followed her brother into the room. She knelt by the bed and gently took Maegan's hand as she listened to her brother praying, adding her own prayer when he had finished.

"She hasn't come to yet," Austin said quietly from the doorway of the bedroom.

"She's so warm," Alison remarked quietly as she gently placed her hand on Maegan's head. She could imagine how upset Cody and Austin must be. How anyone could harm Mae McCoy was beyond comprehension. She was constantly doing for others with little thought to herself. Alison dabbed at a tear that escaped and quietly left the room.

"I've got to get back to town," the doctor said. "But send for me if there's any change for the worse."

Austin nodded. "We'll keep a close eye on her."

Bridger also knew he needed to leave but felt the pull on his heart to stay. "Will you let me know as well if there's any change?" he asked Austin.

"Of course," Austin promised. He extended his hand and clasped Bridger's. "Thank you."

Bridger nodded, thinking he was grateful for the friendship he'd found in the McCoy family.

*****

The following day, Ben headed to his door when he heard knocking. He thought it might be Austin or Cody with news about Maegan. When he opened it, he was surprised to see Joe Spencer on the other side.

"Morning," Joe said, standing there almost motionless as if at a loss for what to say next. "Can I talk to you?" he finally asked.

Wordlessly, Ben opened the door. He moved to the table and took a seat, assuming Joe would do the same. "What did you come here for?" Ben asked after the man had sat down.

Joe took a deep breath and released it. It came out shaky, and Ben noticed the man's hands were trembling as he removed his hat. "I got that letter you left at the house … and the deed."

Ben's lips came together as his eyebrows furrowed slightly, waiting for him to go on.

"At first, I wanted to rip it up. Just the idea of you being able to buy something I can't afford got my hackles up. Then I realized it was the idea of you *giving* me something I can't afford that made me angry, especially something I used to own and lost."

Ben shifted slightly in his chair. "No one but you should own that property, Joe."

Joe felt like he was holding his breath as he looked at Ben, not knowing what to do with the rush of new emotions stirring inside him. "I've wanted to kill you for a long time," he finally breathed the words. "Or better yet, make you suffer while you're still livin'. I wanted you to feel the pain I've felt every morning and night since Thomas died. I've been consumed with it, so much so that I've been making everyone around me suffer. I only knew my own grief; it was like I couldn't see anyone else's, or the grief I was causing. I don't know why, but …" he paused, lifting his eyes to meet Ben's. "… when I saw you meant to give me Thomas' land, something shifted in me. It's the only way I can describe it. I can't even explain it to myself, but it was like a domino effect. Does any of this make sense?"

Ben nodded slightly. "It does." He sighed. "Joe, I'll say it again because I want you to hear it this time. I didn't know it was Thomas, and if I could take it back, I would put myself at the other end of that barrel."

Joe saw for the first time what looked like a reflection of himself in Ben's face. Years of regret and anguish were all too familiar. "I believe you now, Ben. I believe you."

*I forgive you*, was what Ben heard in those words, and for a moment, he felt like the wind was knocked out of him, or maybe it was a feeling of it being restored to him. "Thank you, Joe. And thank you for what you did yesterday, intervening like you did."

A shadow of guilt crossed the man's face. "I'm glad no one was killed. I've fed Robert's hurt too … over losing Eliza, and he's passed it down to his sons." Joe exhaled another shaky breath. "My son Jeb told me he lied about Joshua starting that fire in our barn and about Cody trapping him in the mine." Joe shook his head. "I blamed the McCoys for both of those things, but I see now I just wanted fuel for my anger. Robert's gotta come to terms with his own grievances, but he knows I ain't got mine no more."

Ben was shocked further by the other man's words. In a million years, he hadn't expected this. Was Joe Spencer really sitting at his table having this conversation with him? "Your sister … my wife … was the best thing that ever happened to me," Ben said quietly. "I never meant for any of this to happen."

Joe saw the turmoil that lived in the man's eyes even years after the accident. "Weren't your fault, Ben. We all know it was an accident. It just felt easier to be angry than to deal with the pain."

Ben was having a hard time keeping his own emotions in check and could feel hot tears stinging his eyes. He wiped quickly at them and then came to his feet. "If there's any-thing else I can do, Joe, just let me know."

"You've already done more than you know. It's been a long time coming, but I think I'm ready to set things right." On those words, he came to his feet and put his hat back on. "I'll be seeing you, Ben."

Ben followed him to the door and then stood in his doorway, watching his former enemy ride away. He was still in a state of astonishment when his son came by to ask about Maegan. Joshua was as stunned as his father to hear of Joe's visit.

"What made him change so sudden, Pa?" Joshua asked.

"Maegan's idea worked," Ben replied quietly, as if in a daze, "and … God working behind the scenes."

Joshua hadn't heard his father speak of God for a long time. It reminded his own heart of what Maegan had said to him months ago. "I reckon praying *is* worth its time," Joshua said.

Ben's eyes found his son's. "I reckon it is."

*****

Bridger walked up to the McCoy's house and knocked on the door, feeling like he was holding his breath. Cody answered it and let him in.

"Any change?" Bridger asked. It was only the next day, but he couldn't stay away.

"Not yet," Cody answered quietly. "I've been reading to her, hoping she'll wake up and scold me for something," he said with a watery grin that tugged on Bridger's heart.

"You'll have your chance for plenty more scoldings," he tried to assure him with a small smile at the boy. "Where's Austin?"

"Out at the barn. You want me to get him?"

"No, it's okay. I'll see him then. I'm gonna go sit a spell by your sister, if it's alright."

Cody nodded, and the sheriff moved past him to the bedroom.

Bridger laid his hand against her skin and thought she still felt hot. He quietly sat in the chair and just watched her sleeping. Closing his eyes, he prayed under his breath.

"I won't tell …"

Bridger's eyes opened to the sound of Maegan mumbling something. Her head was moving back and forth on the pillow, and she groaned. "Don't hurt Cody … I won't tell …"

"Maegan?" Bridger whispered her name. He had hoped she was waking up, but as she continued to groan and mutter words, he realized she was talking in her sleep. Bridger smoothed back some curls that had fallen over her face, wishing he could ease the distress she was in.

And then, some minutes later, as he sat there watching her, she slowly opened her eyes. "Why does everything hurt?" she whispered.

Bridger released a sigh of relief that she had awakened and leaned a little closer. "You were shot, remember?" He watched as her eyes suddenly filled with concern.

"Is Cody okay?" she whispered breathlessly.

"He's just fine. But you've been hurt pretty bad, so you

need to just focus on getting better. Here, can you drink something?"

Bridger reached for a glass of water sitting nearby and helped her to drink it. As he lowered her head back on the pillow, Maegan closed her eyes again but then reopened them slowly. "James," she whispered his name for the first time, her eyes finding his. "Can you stay?"

"Of course," he said, feeling his heart swell with emotion. He took her hand in his, remembering when she'd done the same for him in the mine. Gently, he kissed the back of it and then sat there praying, knowing he wouldn't leave her side for the world.

*****

"Things are mending nicely," Doctor Fletcher said a few days later as he stepped out of Maegan's room. "I think she's over the worst."

Austin and Cody relaxed, obviously relieved to hear his report.

"She still needs a lot of rest, and I'll be back in a day or two."

After the doctor left, Cody turned to his brother. "What would we have done if Mae had …" Cody could hardly bring himself to say it.

The look on his brother's face reminded Austin how much the boy had depended on their sister. She'd been the only mother figure he'd known since he was three.

"We're gonna take real good care of her," Austin said with an encouraging smile. "And I'll make sure nothing like that ever happens to her again."

There was a knock on the door. "Howdy, Uncle Ben," Austin greeted the man as he opened the door wider to let him in.

"I came to see Mae. How is she?" Ben had stopped by one other time, but she had been sleeping then.

"Doc says she's gonna pull through," Austin was glad to tell him.

The man looked visibly relieved. "Can I see her?"

"Of course."

Ben moved to the room where Maegan was and tapped lightly on the door as he pushed it open.

"Uncle Ben," she smiled when he entered, trying to sit up a little. The pain of her wounds shot through her, though, and she had to let her head rest back against her pillow.

Ben removed his hat and walked over to the chair at her bedside. He was glad to see there was more color in her face since the last time he'd been to visit. "Just wanted to come by and see how you were doing," he told her.

"I'm gonna be fine, from what they tell me," she said.

"That's good. That's real good," he said, the wrinkles at the corners of his eyes growing deeper when a heartfelt smile lifted the corners of his mouth. "I know you need your rest, and I won't stay long, but I just had to tell you something."

He shook his head, still in disbelief. "I don't know how you knew it would work, but … that idea you had, the one from the Bible about Esau and Jacob … I tried it, and somehow it changed things."

Maegan's eyes widened slightly. "What do you mean?"

"I bought back Thomas' land, and then I gave it to Joe."

"Oh, Uncle Ben. That's wonderful!"

"Joe came to see me, and well, it seems this fightin' is gonna be a thing of the past." He looked up, tears in his eyes. "All because of you."

"It wasn't just me. It was the Lord … using Reverend Myles and then me … and then you. You were the one who decided peace and forgiveness are more valuable than anything else."

"I haven't given much heed to God for a long time," he quietly admitted. "But this makes me want to … know him again."

Maegan smiled as tears escaped her eyes and rolled down her cheeks. "I'm so glad, Uncle Ben."

He pulled out a handkerchief and dabbed her eyes before wiping his own. "You get well, Mae McCoy." He leaned over and placed a kiss on her forehead. "Your ma and pa did a real good job with you kids."

Maegan wiped at more tears as she watched her uncle leave the room, his words bringing an overwhelming joy to her heart. She let out a contented sigh and turned her head toward the window. Summer was here, and it seemed to be bringing with it better times for the McCoys and the Spencers. She suddenly remembered the secret she was still keeping, and her heart sank a little.

"You're looking much better."

Maegan's attention swung to the doorway where Sheriff Bridger was now entering. He smiled at her as he walked over.

"You really had me worried," he told her, the tenderness in his eyes reminding her of the way he'd looked at her when they danced.

"It all happened so fast," she said, her mind spinning a little at the memory of it all. "What happened to Garret?" she suddenly thought to ask.

"He's recovering from the gunshot wound you appropriately gave him, and his brother and pa are going to pay a price for opening fire on you and your brothers like that."

"My Uncle Ben says the feuding's going to stop. He and Uncle Joe worked things out."

"Well, I'm glad to hear it," Bridger said. He'd sat in the chair beside her bed and was fighting the urge to reach out and take her hand again. Now that she was fully awake, he didn't know if the gesture would be welcome or not.

"Thank you for everything," Maegan said, her eyes meeting his. "Austin told me you took out the first bullet yourself."

"I wasn't about to let you die," he told her, swallowing down a sudden rise of emotion. She had no idea how much he loved her. Knowing she didn't feel the same way about him was painful, but for now, he was content to just be near her.

Just then, Cody entered the room, balancing a tray of food in his hands. "Alison just brought dinner over," Cody told her.

Bridger moved away to give Cody space. "I'll see you later," he said to Maegan.

Maegan nodded slightly, watching as he left the room before swinging her attention back to Cody. "Thanks for taking such good care of me," she said to him with a kind smile. He carefully situated another pillow behind her to make her more comfortable.

"I figure you've done it enough times for me. It's about time somebody takes care of you."

Maegan laughed softly at his words, touched by the love he was showing her. It reminded her of why she was keeping her secret about Garret in the first place. It may have been wrong not to tell, but she had a promise to keep where Cody was concerned, and nothing would get in the way of that.

# Chapter Thirty

When Bridger returned to town, he was surprised to see Joe Spencer waiting for him outside the jailhouse. "I think this is the first time I've seen you sober," Bridger said as he stopped in front of him. He looked cleaned up, and there was a different air about him.

"I've come to tell you something, Sheriff. I know who killed Pete Keller."

Bridger's eyebrow hiked up at his words. "You got evidence?"

"Unfortunately, it implicates a relative, but yeah, I got evidence." Joe had ridden over to Robert's and told him the awful truth and then came straight to town. He knew he needed to tell the sheriff before he talked himself out of it. Until this point, right or wrong made little difference when loyalty to his family was involved, but an uncanny stirring in his heart to make things right had suddenly become a priority. Jeb had trusted him enough to tell the truth, and now Joe wanted to honor that trust. It felt like the first step of many in making amends for all the pain he had caused his family.

*****

Robert stormed out of his house and up the slight hill behind it that led to the cabin his sons stayed in. Raising his fist, he forcefully pounded on it. When there was no answer, he pushed it open and stepped inside. "Bobby?" he called, knowing Garret was probably still in bed nursing his injured shoulder.

Robert pushed back a curtain that hung in a doorway separating Garret's room from the main room of the house. One glance at the empty bed and Robert headed toward the outhouse. Finding that empty, he headed to the barn. He spotted Bobby climbing down the loft ladder.

"Bobby! Where's your brother?"

Bobby's feet hit the ground, and he turned to face his pa. "Sleepin'."

"No, he ain't. I was just at the house."

Bobby shrugged. "You try the outhouse?"

Robert's eyes narrowed as he stepped closer to his son. "When did you see him last?"

"Last night. But I've been up since sunrise, and I could hear him snorin' when I left to do the chores."

Robert released a sigh. "Then he can't be far."

"What's goin' on, Pa?" Bobby asked.

"Your brother's a liar and worse."

"What do you mean?"

"Your Uncle Joe just came by the house to tell me something Jeb told him."

Simultaneously, they turned toward the open barn door as Sheriff Bridger came walking in. "Just the two fellas I came to see," he said.

"It ain't what it looked like, Sheriff," Robert started.

"You mean those bullets flying at the McCoys weren't from your guns?" Bridger replied.

"I thought Mae McCoy had killed Garret! I was angry!"

"So, you took the law into your own hands? You almost killed her!"

"I shouldn't have gone after them like that, but I …"

"No! You shouldn't have, and lucky for you no one ended up dead! There's jail time and a steep fine waitin' for both of you fools!"

"Fair enough, Sheriff."

Bridger was shocked at the man's surrendered reply. He took a few steps closer, his eyes glancing past the loft and stalls. "Where's Garret?" he asked, feeling like Robert was only yielding to get rid of him.

"I don't know," Robert answered honestly. "I was just lookin' for him myself."

"Did you know he killed Pete Keller?" Sheriff Bridger asked.

"What!" Bobby's voice was incredulous. "That's a lie!"

"It ain't a lie!" Robert surprised Bobby by saying. His voice was as definite as any time Bobby had ever heard it.

"But Pete was our cousin," Bobby argued.

"And Garret is a fool," Robert replied bitterly. He turned his attention back to the sheriff. "I didn't know until just now when my brother told me."

"If either of you are hiding Garret, you best …"

"I don't want to see his face ever again," Robert interrupted him, the decisive glint in his eyes mixed with anger. "He had a nasty wound," Robert added. "I can't imagine he could have gotten far."

Bridger knew he wouldn't be able to rest until he had Garret in custody. He searched the property and then headed toward the McCoys to make sure they were safe. He wasn't about to take any chances with Garret being on the loose.

*****

As soon as Sheriff Bridger left, Bobby went to find his brother. He knew him well enough to know he'd be hiding out in the old shanty they'd discovered years ago in the woods.

"Sheriff's lookin' for you," Bobby said as he pushed open the squeaky door and stepped into the dim, dusty room. Garret was lying on one of the only pieces of furniture in the room, a cot that didn't look big enough or stable enough to hold his weight. Bobby went to stand above him. "Is it true what he said? You killed Pete?"

Slowly, Garret pushed himself to a sitting position, wincing against the pain in his shoulder. "What if it is?" he mumbled. He carefully swung his feet over the cot and, for a moment, just stared at the ground as if mustering the strength to stand up.

"Why?" Bobby demanded. "Pete didn't deserve that!"

Garret looked up with irritation. "He was the one who told me he didn't wanna be friends no more … said he was done with helpin' us. You heard him!"

"Done with doin' your dirty work, you mean," Bobby replied angrily.

Garret came to his feet. "Listen! I don't need to hear it from you!"

Bobby shook his head in disbelief as he began to pace the tiny room. He kicked a chair that was on its side and in his way. "How could you do somethin' like that!" he hollered. "Pete was kin!"

Garret had moved to one of the two windows in the shanty. "Which way did the sheriff head?" When Bobby didn't answer, Garret turned from the window. "I said, where'd he head?" he repeated himself louder.

"Pa's done with you, and so am I," Bobby said evenly. He shook his head in disgust as he looked at his older brother. "Ma would be right ashamed of you," he said before he moved to the door.

The mention of their ma, who had been dead for over twenty years, sparked something almost akin to guilt in Garret. Desperate for his brother not to desert him, he attempted to block the door, but Bobby shoved him to the side. It was easy since Garret's usual strength had been weakened by his injury. "Don't ever get in my way again!" Bobby told him.

"Bobby!" Garret called after him, following him outside. "Bobby! Don't do this!" A deep feeling of loss coursed through him, and then, just as quickly, it was replaced with rage. After Bobby had left, Garret found himself overcome with the knowledge that he had no one left. And then Maegan McCoy's face flashed through his mind. She had ratted him out! She had to have been the one to tell the sheriff.

Furious and ignoring the pain in his shoulder, Garret charged toward his horse. There was nothing left for him to do but leave Millcreek, but before he did, he was going to make Maegan McCoy pay for what she did.

*****

When Bridger reached the McCoys, he was relieved to find everything in order. Austin was surprised to see him back so soon and even more surprised at the sheriff's next words.

"I came back to let you know Garret Spencer is missing, and I believe him more dangerous than ever. Looks like he's the one who killed Pete Keller."

While the murder had taken place when he wasn't in Millcreek, Austin had heard about it. "His own cousin," Austin said, shaking his head in disbelief that Garret would stoop that low.

"I thought you should know how dangerous Garret is in case he comes 'round here. I'm heading out now to track him down."

"Wish I could go with you," Austin said, frustration in his voice. He glanced at his arm, which was in a sling.

"You're better off staying here." Bridger paused a moment, glancing around. "Where's Cody?"

"Out in the barn last time I checked." Austin saw something in Bridger's eyes that alarmed him. "Do you think Cody's in danger for some reason?"

"I don't know. I don't put anything past Garret. It would make me feel better if you went and checked on him. I'm just gonna talk to Mae quick."

On his words, Austin headed outside, and Bridger went into the room with Maegan.

"You're back," she said with surprise when she saw him. She watched as he sat in the chair near her bed and thought he looked distressed. "What is it?" she asked.

"I didn't want to bring this up until you were in better condition, but Joe Spencer came to see me and has evidence that it was Garret who murdered Pete Keller." Bridger paused and then said, "I need to know what you're hiding, Mae."

"I wanted to be honest with you," Maegan began, feeling like now that he already knew about Garret Spencer, she could tell the rest. "That night of the Christmas dance ... I saw Garret Spencer kill Pete Keller."

Her words confirmed the evidence Jeb Spencer had given his pa, and the gravity of it all began to sink in. All this time, she had known. "Mae, why didn't you say something?"

"I wanted to." Tears poured down her cheeks as she looked at him. "Garret threatened to kill Cody if I told anyone ... especially you."

"So, Garret knew you'd seen him."

"Not only that, but he forced me to help him carry Pete's body to where it was later found."

Bridger released a sigh, realizing why she had been so distraught that night. "And that's why your bracelet ended up there," he reasoned aloud.

Maegan nodded. "I'm sorry I didn't just tell you right away. I thought I was doing the best thing for Cody."

"You really think it's completely up to you to protect him, don't you?"

"It is," Maegan answered simply.

"Mae, if what I've been reading in the Bible is true, God has more control over that than anyone. Even if you do everything in your power to protect him, ultimately, Cody's life belongs to God."

Maegan wordlessly looked at the sheriff, taking in his words. It was as if a haze had cleared from her eyes. "You're right," she finally whispered. Somehow, she had forgotten that and been carrying the burden of looking out for him herself. Maegan suddenly realized that in her determination to keep her promise to her mother and see Cody safe, she had made a terrible mistake by not going to the sheriff right away about the murder. In fact, she had probably endangered Cody's life even more by keeping the secret.

"I hate that you were forced to keep that secret. I understand why you did," he quickly assured her. "But you should have told me. I could have helped you," he added quietly.

"They had me scared from way back," she admitted. "Before the murder, Pete threatened to hurt Cody unless I avoided you," Maegan explained.

"And that's why Pete beat Cody that day, because you didn't listen?" Bridger asked.

Maegan nodded. "It happened right after that Friday we went out. Then, after I was a witness to the murder, Garret only heightened the threat. I didn't know the man he murdered was Pete Keller until you came to my uncle's that one day asking questions. I knew if Garret could kill his own cousin, then he could easily hurt Cody." She found his eyes again. "That's why I had to stay away from you."

Her words resonated in his heart as he realized that's why she had ended their friendship so suddenly. "I'm so relieved."

"What?" Maegan asked, but then Austin came running into the house, and Bridger didn't get a chance to answer.

"Sheriff!"

Both Maegan and Bridger's attention shot toward the door when they heard Austin's voice.

Maegan was left alone to wonder when Bridger jumped out of his chair and quickly went out of the room to meet Austin.

"He's not there!" Austin said, breathing heavily, "and there's signs of a struggle!"

Bridger moved toward the door, and Austin followed. "I'm coming with you!" Austin said. "I swear if he hurts Cody, I'll kill him!"

Bridger had almost reached his horse but turned around suddenly. "No! What you're going to do is stay here and make sure Mae is safe!"

Austin knew the sheriff was right. Someone had to stay back and protect Maegan in case Garret came back.

*****

After sneaking onto the McCoy property and finding Cody in the barn, Garret had gagged him and tied his hands before tossing him up on his horse. If he was going to be charged with murder, what was one more? When Garret reached the gorge, he dismounted and roughly pulled Cody off the horse. Cody struggled against him, but even with Garret's injury, Cody's strength was no match for him.

"C'mon!" Garret ordered, pulling Cody along. "Get up!" he barked when Cody tripped over a mound of rocks. Garret grabbed him by the shirt and yanked him back to his feet. The action caused him to grimace in pain and reminded him of the bullet wound that still throbbed at his shoulder. Pausing, Garret took a quick swig of the whiskey from his flask, helping to numb the pain a little.

"I'm a man of my word!" he hollered. "I told your sister I'd kill you if she snitched!" He shoved Cody down toward the slope of the gorge. "Keep walkin'!"

Cody could hear his heart pounding in his ears, and his lungs felt like they were burning in his chest as he struggled to breathe around the bandanna tied tightly over his mouth. When he neared the edge, Cody backed up into a tree, trying desperately to free his wrists.

"You see this!"

Cody felt like he was choking on his own fear when Garret grabbed him by the shirt and pushed him down, holding a sheath knife close to his face. "This is what killed Pete, and now you're about to get it!"

Feeling the dirt and forest floor against his bound hands, Cody tried his best to scramble backward. His eyes grew round as saucers when Garret raised his knife. And then a loud gunshot followed. It didn't make sense. Cody watched as Garret simultaneously dropped the knife and fell to his knees. Cody rolled out of the way as the man fell forward onto his stomach, his face landing in the dirt.

Getting to his feet, Cody suddenly realized where the gunshot had come from. There, just behind some trees, stood Billy Turner. Relief flooded through Cody's body as the man moved toward him. Even with one hand, Billy made fast work of untying the gag around Cody's mouth and loosening the knots that bound his wrists.

"You alright?" Billy asked, his eyes anxiously searching the boy for any signs of blood.

Cody nodded as he slid the rope off his hands the rest of the way. "Thanks to you!" he said, gratitude beaming from his eyes.

Billy knelt in the dirt beside Garret and felt for a pulse. "Who is this?" he asked with alarm.

"Garret Spencer."

Billy had never met Garret, but the name was familiar since he'd bought his property from a Spencer. "Why was he trying to kill you?"

Just then, Sheriff Bridger appeared at the top of the ridge. Having found tracks leading from the barn, he'd followed them and been able to track Garret's path. "Cody!" he called, eagerly jumping from his horse.

Billy and Cody both turned at the sound of his voice. "I'm alright," Cody told him, his eyes then going to where Garret lay dead. "Billy saved my life," Cody said quietly.

Sheriff Bridger looked at the man. "Words can't even begin to thank you."

"I'm glad I was here," Billy replied earnestly. He was surprised when Cody took a step toward him and hugged him tight. "Thanks, Mr. Turner."

# *Chapter* Thirty-One

"Alison, can I go with you?" Lilly asked. It was the next afternoon, and Alison was preparing to take lunch to the McCoys.

Alison smiled at her niece. "Of course you can." She knew Lilly was eager to see Cody after they had all heard of his near-death experience with Garret Spencer. As they rode side by side in the buggy Alison drove, she glanced toward the younger girl and noticed the necklace she wore.

"Cody gave that to you, didn't he?"

Lilly nodded, reaching up to touch it. "For Christmas," she said with a little smile.

Alison remembered Lyn Hummel's reaction to seeing Lilly's necklace. The memory lingered even after they had arrived at the McCoys. As she was cleaning up after the meal, Alison noticed Cody was whittling at the table, Lilly watching from beside him.

"That necklace you made for Lilly is beautiful," Alison complimented him.

"I didn't make it," Cody told her, not looking up from what he was doing. "Billy Turner did, and he gave it to me when I first met him."

His words slammed through Alison. She set down the

dish towel in her hands and walked over to him. "What? The same Billy Turner who found you all in the mine … and came to your rescue yesterday?"

Cody nodded, looking up at her. "He stays away from folks, but he's a real nice guy."

"Billy …" she said his name. "That's short for William, isn't it?" she thought aloud. "Oh my!" Alison gasped as her hand came to her throat. "I can't believe it!"

Austin came from Maegan's room carrying a tray she'd had her lunch on. "What's wrong?" he asked. "What's going on?"

"I've got to get to Lyn Hummel!" Alison exclaimed. "Right now!"

"Is something wrong?" Austin asked with concern.

"No! Something's right!" Alison turned toward Cody. "Do you know where he lives?"

Cody nodded and proceeded to explain where his house was.

"Stay here, Lilly," Alison said. "I have to go find Lyn!"

"I'll go with you," Austin said, barely able to keep up with Alison as she flew out the door.

*****

"Mrs. Hummel! Lyn!" Alison knocked on the woman's door before opening it and glancing inside. When she didn't find her there, Alison went to Mrs. Lyddie's boarding house. She was relieved to find Lyn had been in Lyddie's parlor having lunch with her.

"Mrs. Hummel, you have to come with me!" Alison told her.

"What? Why?"

"I think I found your son!"

"Is he …" Lyn's hand came to her heart as if she were afraid to voice the word.

"No," Alison read her mind. "He's not dead; he's alive."

"I'm scared to believe it's true," Lyn said, but she let Alison take her hand and lead her outside.

"I pray to God I'm not wrong, but I think I've found him. What name does his middle initial stand for?" Alison asked.

"Turner. William Turner Hummel."

Alison's eyes met Austin's before returning to Lyn's. "It's got to be him! He goes by Billy Turner, and … you should prepare yourself. He may look very different to you than the last time you saw him."

"That must be why he's never come home." Lyn's voice caught with emotion, and she cried softly. Alison put her arm around the older woman and for the rest of the ride prayed that the reunion between mother and son would be what they both needed.

*****

When they pulled into Billy Turner's yard, Alison immediately noticed his wagon was loaded with furniture and supplies that were tied down, a large tarp covering it as if he was planning on a long journey ahead. Alison jumped down and knocked on the front door while, for the moment, Austin and Lyn Hummel waited in the wagon. When Billy Turner answered the door, Alison could tell he was surprised to see her.

"Hello, Mr. Turner," she said. "I know this may come out awkwardly, but is your full name William … William T. Hummel?"

He just looked at her, the skin, where his eyebrows once were, furrowed in confusion. "Why do you ask?"

"Your mother has been looking for you … for a very long time."

He shook his head and began to shut the door, but Alison put out her hand to stop it from closing. "Please, Mr. Turner; she's desperate to find you."

For the first time, Billy looked past her and saw the others. The familiarity of the woman climbing out of the wagon caused a wave of faintness to almost overtake him. "I … I can't," he said, feeling panicked as she drew closer. "Tell her to go!" he whispered roughly.

"Mr. Turner … Billy," Alison said gently, "I know this must feel incredibly painful, but no matter what happened or happens … your mother loves you. Please let her end her search for you … she's too old to keep going."

As she finished speaking, Austin and Lyn neared. Alison stepped out of the way so Lyn could see her son.

"William?" Lyn stepped right through the doorway and laid her hand on his arm. "It's you … it really is you! Oh, my boy!"

Crying, she fell against him, her sobs growing louder when she felt his arm go around her. "Why?" she said in between sobs. "Why didn't you come home? Why!"

"Isn't it obvious?" he whispered through his own tears. Towering over her, Billy leaned forward slightly so his head could rest on the top of hers. The warmth of his mother's embrace, her nearness, and sensing her undaunted love for him … it was almost too much to take in. For years, he'd been running and hiding from people and from anyone who could remind him of what his life used to be like. It had seemed unbearably painful to return to his childhood home looking the way he did, but he'd never considered the pain that would grow in his heart from staying away.

"I'm sorry … I'm sorry, Ma," his words came out broken and trembling.

"I've found you," Lyn said, looking up at him. "My precious boy." Gently, she lifted her hands to cradle his cheeks. "You're taller than I remember," she laughed softly.

Billy smiled slightly at her words. "It's been a long time, hasn't it?" He shook his head in disbelief. "How did you even find me?"

"The hand of God, I think," Lyn said, and then, looking toward Alison, she added, "and with the help of this dear girl."

Alison took a few steps toward the doorway, her own heart overflowing with joy. She noticed the house looked cleaned out, aside from some items still on the kitchen table. It looked like they had just caught him in the process of packing. "I think we caught you just in time," Alison said.

"I was planning to head out tomorrow morning," Billy told her, amazed at the timing of his mother finding him. "You can leave my mother here. I'll see to her." He let out a shaky breath, still trying to take it all in.

Alison moved to hug Lyn Hummel. "You were right all along, Lyn. You were right!"

Lyn smiled affectionately at her, squeezing her hand. "Thank you, Alison, for not giving up on me."

As they rode away, Austin and Alison were quiet for several minutes and then Alison heard Austin sniff … more than once. "Are you crying?" she asked him.

"No," he sniffed again, using the bottom of his palm to wipe quickly at his eyes. He gave a little laugh. "Guess I'm gettin' soft."

Alison laughed as she looped her arm in his, blinking back her own tears that had been falling off and on since Lyn had seen her son. "I don't know how anyone could not cry after witnessing that."

"You did good, Ali," Austin said proudly, putting his arm around her and pulling her close. "You did real good."

*****

"Here, sit down," Billy said to his mother once they were alone in his house. He pulled out a chair at the table for her.

"I still can't believe it's you!" Lyn said, her eyes still teary. "You should have come home, William."

Billy sat in the chair near hers. There was so much she couldn't understand. The horrors he'd seen, the trauma he'd experienced. The pain of wanting to go home but feeling like it would never be the same again … and the loneliness. He looked into her eyes and realized the loneliness was something she could relate to. "You sure are stubborn to look for me all these years."

"What else was I supposed to do?"

"Move on with your life. Accept the fact that I'm dead."

"But you're not dead!"

"I might as well be. Look at me! What kind of life can I have?"

"You've done pretty well so far," she encouraged.

He released a heavy sigh. "When I saw that article in the paper, I sold this place and was fixin' to leave."

She shook her head in disbelief. "And to think, I might have never found you had Alison not come after me." She paused and then said, "Where were you planning to go?"

Billy shrugged and leaned back in his chair. "I don't know. I just panicked when I saw my name in the paper. I wanted to stay hidden," he added quietly.

"As long as you have air in your lungs, you got a responsibility to live!"

Billy sighed, knowing she couldn't understand. "Will you head back to St. Louis now … now that your search is over?"

"Not without you, I'm not."

"No, Ma. I can't go back there."

"Because you're afraid."

He didn't want to hear that. "I'm not foolish enough to think I'm gonna return home and pick up where I left off … as if *anything* could be the same."

"I can't promise you it won't be painful … at first, but how is living on your own, hiding from the world, making your life any less painful?"

"It's not," Billy admitted.

"I haven't been home for years myself. If we go back, you don't have to see anyone you don't want to. We could go back together … face whatever difficulty there is … together."

A hint of a smile touched Billy's mouth. Being back with his mother made him realize how much he loved her and had missed her. She had aged considerably since he'd last seen her, in part because of the taxing hours of travel … on his account. He knew his mother wouldn't be with him forever, and he did owe her for years of heartache. The resistance in his heart to embrace anything from his past suddenly felt like it was giving way. "Alright, Ma," he said, his voice quiet but resolved. "I'll go home with you."

*****

"Are you sure you're up to this?" Austin asked Maegan two weeks later as he led her outside and to a bench near the corner of the house.

"I feel like I've been in that room and in that bed for an eternity!" Maegan told him. "I just need some fresh air," she said. He offered his arm as she went to sit down.

After a moment, she laughed softly, looking up at him. "You don't have to stand there watching over me, you know."

Austin grinned, not realizing he had been doing just that. "Just making sure you're okay."

"I'm fine, and I know you have to get to work."

"Will you be alright, then?"

"Of course, and Cody's around if I need anything."

"Don't overdo it!" Maegan called after him, thinking he probably shouldn't be returning to work yet with his injury, but he assured her he felt fine.

Maegan watched as he rode off, waving when he glanced over his shoulder before disappearing around the bend.

She thought he had come back when she heard another rider coming, but soon realized it was Sheriff Bridger. Once in the yard, he dismounted and walked toward her, a smile on his face at the sight of her.

"I didn't expect to find you up and about," he said, thinking she looked remarkably well since he'd last seen her.

"Austin almost didn't let me out, but I needed a break from that room," she told him.

Bridger sat beside her on the bench, feeling a surge of gratitude that she was alive. For a moment, he just stared at her.

"What?" she asked, feeling his eyes on her. She self-consciously pushed a stray curl behind her ear.

He shook his head slightly and smiled. "Nothing. I'm just glad you're alright."

"Even though I'll never wish death on anyone, I'm glad I no longer have to worry about Garret Spencer." She let out a sigh. "You were right."

He looked at her curiously. "What do you mean?"

"When you said it wasn't all on me to protect Cody. You reminded me that Cody's life belongs to God, and even if I do everything in my power to protect him, ultimately, God's in control. I don't know how I lost sight of that," she added quietly. "That fact that the Lord had Billy Turner there to save Cody proves it's not all up to me."

"As I recall, the Lord had Billy Turner there to save us, too. I think that's more evidence of his faithfulness."

A slow smile touched Maegan's lips. "It sounds like you're getting to know Him."

"I made Him a promise," Bridger admitted with a small shrug. Even though, in a moment of desperation for Maegan's life, he had made a bargain with the Lord, he was beginning to realize keeping his end of the deal wasn't a duty but instead a growing desire of his heart.

"I've been meaning to ask you something," Bridger changed the subject as he remembered his reason for coming to see her. "But I'm asking for your opinion as a woman and not just Austin's sister."

Maegan laughed softly, "So, you want me to give impartial advice about Austin?"

"Yes. I spoke with him the other day while he was working at the livery, and he seems pretty serious about settling here … and about Alison Myles."

"Yes, I'm happy for them both," Maegan said. "I know things were uncertain for a while."

"I'm glad they seem to be working it out, which is what brings me to my question. How would a woman feel about marrying a lawman?"

Maegan looked at him curiously. "What?"

"I mean, would it change a woman's decision to marry someone if he happened to be a sheriff … or, in this case, a deputy? You see, I'm thinking about asking Austin to be my deputy, but I don't want it to hinder anything between him and Alison."

"It's very good of you to think so considerately about Alison's feelings in the matter."

"I'm pretty inexperienced in this area," he admitted, "… that is, knowing how women think."

"I'm pretty sure all men are," she smiled subtly.

"Which is why I'm coming to you," he said. "If I offered the job to Austin and he took it, do you think that would discourage Alison from accepting a marriage proposal? I don't want to do anything that would change things for them."

"Well, if it did, then she didn't love him enough to begin with."

Bridger was surprised to hear her say that. "So, are you saying a person's occupation, one even as dangerous as mine, wouldn't matter if the two people involved truly loved each other?"

"Well, it's not that it wouldn't matter," Maegan clarified. "It's just that it wouldn't be reason enough for them not to marry … at least in Austin and Ali's case."

"And what about in your case?"

Maegan suddenly realized Sheriff Bridger was looking at her with those gorgeous blue eyes, waiting for her answer. "In my case?"

"Yeah, would you marry a man who was a sheriff?"

"Well, it would depend on who the sheriff was … and how quick his draw is," she added with a hint of a smile on her lips. "If I'm going through the trouble of marrying him, I wouldn't want to be a widow any time soon after."

Bridger grinned, noting the glimmer in her eyes. "Let's say if the man in question was very quick with his draw."

"Then his job wouldn't make a difference to me."

"I'm glad to hear you say that."

Maegan wondered if she was imagining the warmth in his gaze. "I don't think it will make a difference with Alison either," she said. "It can't hurt to talk to Austin about it and leave it up to him and Alison. I'm sure if she objects, he'd turn it down."

"That sounds like sound advice."

She smiled at him. "Glad I could help." And then, glancing up at the azure sky and smelling the scent of honeysuckles on the wind, she said, "Would you want to walk a little?"

"Are you up to it?"

"Yes," Maegan assured him, already coming to her feet. They walked for several minutes along the road, and then Bridger suddenly stopped and turned to face her.

"Mae, I don't know how to tell you this, so maybe I'll just come out and say it." He removed his hat and nervously ran a hand through his wavy hair. "I don't want to be presumptuous, but months ago, when you said you didn't have time for our friendship … was that only because …"

"Yes," Maegan answered, knowing exactly what he was going to say. "Nothing pained me more than to have to lie to you about that. Staying away from you was the last thing I wanted."

"This is going to sound blunt, but I think I've loved you since you saved me from that rattlesnake."

Maegan felt like laughing and crying all at once. Did Sheriff Bridger just tell her he loved her?

"Could you … do you think you could care for me?" he asked.

Maegan saw the uncertainty in his eyes and wanted more than anything to dispel it. "Oh, you don't have to wonder about that," she said, instinctively taking a step closer to him.

"You mean …" He didn't know how to finish the sentence, but he didn't have to. The smile on Maegan's face and the love shining in her eyes answered any doubts he had. For a second, it almost knocked him off his feet to think that Maegan loved him. He realized at that moment how badly he had been hoping for it. As natural as breathing, he felt himself reaching out for her hands.

"I didn't know what I was missing until you came along, Mae McCoy, but now I know my life would be empty without you in it."

Maegan felt her heart swirl when he gently pulled her in for a kiss, and then when he lifted his head, she slipped her arms around his neck and kissed him again.

"Sorry, Sheriff," she laughed softly. "I've wanted to do that for a while."

"It's James to you," he corrected with a smile. "And don't apologize. You can kiss me like that anytime you want!"

*****

"Mae and Sheriff Bridger?"

Alison laughed at the shock on Austin's face and in his voice when he said it. "Why do you sound so surprised?" she asked. It was the following day, and Alison and Austin were heading for a picnic after church.

"I just had no idea. He's never let on, and neither did she."

"Not everyone is as bold as you are, Austin McCoy," Alison reminded him with a cheeky smile, but she loved that he had always been so open about his feelings for her.

"I did wonder today when he sat with her at church," Austin admitted, and then he shook his head and grinned. "It's great how this all worked out. Mae's going to marry Sheriff Bridger, and I'm gonna marry you."

"Not so fast."

Alison's words caused him to glance at her from his place beside her in the wagon. "What do you mean?"

"You haven't even asked me yet," she tried to sound put out and folded her arms across her chest.

"Maybe that's the reason I asked you to a picnic," Austin said. Since Alison's father wasn't around, Austin had already spoken with Reverend Myles and got the man's blessing.

He knew he would have asked Alison regardless, but he still felt better knowing her brother was in agreement.

Alison looped her arm around his. "Then hurry up so we can get to that part."

Austin chuckled. "I just want to get to the part after I ask ya."

"You mean the part when I say, 'yes'?" Alison smiled.

"No, the part where I kiss you after you say, 'yes.'"

Alison laughed as she leaned in closer, planting a quick kiss on his cheek. "You're pretty sure of yourself, aren't you?"

"I'm only sure of one thing, Ali, and it's that I want to spend the rest of my life with you."

Alison felt a wave of warmth and joy fill her heart at his words, and she laid her head against his shoulder. "Good, because I want to spend the rest of my life with you, too."

*****

"What do you think about the sheriff being engaged to your sister?" Lilly asked Cody a few days later as they stepped outside after supper. Maegan and Austin had invited Sheriff Bridger and Alison over for supper, as well as Reverend Myles and his family.

"I'm fine with it," Cody said. It was an honest answer, although he did have a moment's uncertainty after Maegan had told him she was going to marry the sheriff. He liked Sheriff Bridger a lot, but the idea of him living with him and Maegan was something to get used to. Maegan was more like a mother figure to him, so did that make the sheriff something of a father? It had felt confusing until Maegan had taken the time to sort it through with him.

"You probably won't call him Sheriff Bridger anymore."

"Maegan said his name is James, so I guess I'll call him that," Cody told her.

"You know what else," Lilly said next as she reached up to swing on a tree limb that hung overhead. They had wandered to a large tree in the front yard. "I think Austin is going to marry my Aunt Ali." She suddenly jumped down to her feet and looked at Cody. "If my aunt is marrying your brother, what does that make us?"

Cody shrugged. "Kind of related in an unrelated way, I guess," he laughed slightly.

"Then we'll probably see each other even more than we already do," she said as she reached up again for a limb and tried to climb the tree.

Seeing that she was struggling, Cody laced his hands for her to step on and helped give her a boost onto the branch.

"You wanna know something else?" Lilly asked next as she finished climbing and settled between two limbs.

"What?" Cody asked, looking up at her.

"I'm gonna marry you when we're older."

Cody rolled his eyes and smiled at her. "I doubt it."

"Why do you say that?" Lilly asked, a little scowl on her face.

"First of all, you're a lot younger than me and …"

"Only three years younger!"

"… and second, I plan to do a lot of traveling once I'm old enough."

"You mean, you don't plan to live in Millcreek when you're older?"

Cody shrugged again. "Probably not. I want to travel and see things!"

"Well, maybe I can come with you," Lilly suggested.

"You couldn't keep up," Cody teased her.

"Yes, I could!"

"You can't even keep up in a race over to the barn," he prompted her, smiling when she jumped down from the tree almost instantly. He let her win the race and told her she was getting faster.

Lilly smiled with pride. "I told you I can keep up."

A moment later, they heard Maegan's voice calling them in for dessert, so they headed back toward the house. As they sat around the table with the grown-ups, Austin stood to get everyone's attention.

"Before you all leave, Ali and I just wanted you to know that we're engaged."

There was a mixture of smiles and congratulations exchanged, even though the announcement didn't come as a surprise to any of them.

Maegan caught Bridger's glance and felt her heart swell with affection. They, too, were going to be married, and it overwhelmed her to think of how the Lord's faithfulness had brought her to this point. She had come to Millcreek to honor her father's wishes and to keep a promise made to her mother, but now she realized all along that God had been orchestrating a plan. While promises were often made and more often broken, Maegan knew without a doubt God's promise to never leave her was one he would always keep.

9 781957 497556